New York Times Bestselling Author Harry Turtledove

Winner of the Hugo, Sidewise, and John Esthen Cook Awards
Nebula Award Nominee
"Nobody plays the what-if game of alternative history better than
Harry Turtledove."   —*Publishers Weekly*

National Bestselling Author S. M. Stirling

Sidewise Award Nominee
"S. M. Stirling is writing some of the best straight-ahead science
fiction the genre has ever seen."   —*Amazing*

Mary Gentle

Winner of the Sidewise and BSFA Awards
"Mary Gentle is a writer of violence: Her style is muscular and
thrusting; her conclusions tend to be dangerous; and her stories
are never comfortable."   —*The Encyclopedia of Fantasy*

New York Times Bestselling Author Walter Jon Williams

Winner of the Nebula and Sidewise Awards
Hugo and World Fantasy Award Nominee
"[Walter Jon] Williams exhibits cunning, dexterity, and
tenaciousness."   —*Asimov's Science Fiction Magazine*

WORLDS THAT WEREN'T

HARRY TURTLEDOVE

S. M. STIRLING

MARY GENTLE

WALTER JON WILLIAMS

 A ROC BOOK

ROC
Published by New American Library, a division of
Penguin Group (USA) Inc., 375 Hudson Street,
New York, New York 10014, U.S.A.
Penguin Books Ltd, 80 Strand,
London WC2R 0RL, England
Penguin Books Australia Ltd, 250 Camberwell Road,
Camberwell, Victoria 3124, Australia
Penguin Books Canada Ltd, 10 Alcorn Avenue,
Toronto, Ontario, Canada M4V 3B2
Penguin Books (N.Z.) Ltd, Cnr Rosedale and Airborne Roads,
Albany, Auckland 1310, New Zealand

Penguin Books Ltd, Registered Offices:
80 Strand, London WC2R 0RL, England

Published by Roc, an imprint of New American Library, a division of Penguin Group (USA) Inc.
Previously published in a Roc hardcover edition.

First Trade Paperback Printing, September 2003
10 9 8 7 6 5 4 3 2 1

R⌀C REGISTERED TRADEMARK—MARCA REGISTRADA

Roc Trade Paperback ISBN: 0-451-52898-0

The Library of Congress has cataloged the hardcover edition of this title as follows:

Worlds that weren't / Harry Turtledove . . . [et al.].
    p. cm.
    Contents: The daimon / Harry Turtledove—Shikari in Galveston / S.M. Stirling—The
logistics of Carthage / Mary Gentle—The last ride of German Freddie / Walter Jon Williams.
    1. Science fiction, American.   I. Turtledove, Harry.

PS648.S3 W67 2002
813'.0876608—dc21   2002017936

Printed in the United States of America

The Daimon

HARRY TURTLEDOVE

SIMON the shoemaker's shop stood close to the southwestern corner of the Athenian agora, near the boundary stone marking the edge of the market square and across a narrow dirt lane from the Tholos, the round building where the executive committee of the Boulê met. Inside the shop, Simon pounded iron hobnails into the sole of a sandal. His son worked with an awl, shaping bone eyelets through which rawhide laces would go. Two grandsons cut leather for more shoes.

Outside, in the shade of an olive tree, a man in his mid-fifties strode back and forth, arguing with a knot of younger men and youths. He was engagingly ugly: bald, heavy-browed, snub-nosed, with a gray beard that should have been more neatly trimmed. "And so you see, my friends," he was saying, "my daimon has told me that this choice does indeed come from the gods, and that something great may spring from it. Thus, though I love you and honor you, I shall obey the spirit inside me rather than you."

"But, Sokrates, you have already given Athens all she could want of you," exclaimed Kritias, far and away the most prominent of the men gathered there and, next to Sokrates, the eldest. "You fought at Potidaia and Delion and Amphipolis. But the last of those battles was seven years ago. You are neither so young nor so strong as you used to be. You need not go to Sicily. Stay here in the polis. Your wisdom is worth more to the city than your spear ever could be."

The others dipped their heads in agreement. A youth whose first beard was just beginning to darken his cheeks said, "He speaks for all of us, Sokrates. We need you here more than the expedition ever could."

"How can one man speak for another, Xenophon?" Sokrates asked. Then he held up a hand. "Let that be a question for another time. The question for now is, why should I be any less willing to fight for my polis than, say, *he* is?"

He pointed to a hoplite tramping past in front of Simon's shop. The infantryman wore his crested bronze helm pushed back on his head, so the cheekpieces and noseguard did not hide his face. He rested the shaft of his long thrusting spear on his shoulder; a short-sword swung from his hip. Behind him, a slave carried his corselet and greaves and round, bronze-faced shield.

Kritias abandoned the philosophic calm he usually kept up in Sokrates' company. "To the crows with Alkibiades!" he burst out. "He didn't ask you to sail with him to Sicily for the sake of your strong right arm. He just wants you for the sake of your conversation, the same way as he'll probably bring along a hetaira to keep his bed warm. You're going for the sake of *his* cursed vanity: no other reason."

"No." Sokrates tossed his head. "I am going because it is important that I go. So my daimon tells me. I have listened to it all my life, and it has never led me astray."

"We're not going to change his mind now," one of the young men whispered to another. "When he gets that look in his eye, he's stubborn as a donkey."

Sokrates glanced toward the herm in front of Simon's shop: a stone pillar with a crude carving of Hermes' face at the top and the god's genitals halfway down. "Guard me well, patron of travelers," he murmured.

"Be careful you don't get your nose or your prong knocked off, Sokrates, the way a lot of the herms did last year," somebody said.

"Yes, and people say Alkibiades was hip-deep in that sacrilege, too," Kritias added. A considerable silence followed. Kritias was hardly the one to speak of sacrilege. He was at least as scornful of the gods as Alkibiades; he'd once claimed priests had invented them to keep ordinary people in line.

But, instead of rising to that, Sokrates only said, "Have we not seen, O best one, that we should not accept what is said without first attempting to learn how much truth it holds?" Kritias went red, then turned away in anger. If Sokrates noticed, he gave no sign.

I am the golden one.

Alkibiades looked at the triremes and transports in Athens' harbor, Peiraieus. All sixty triremes and forty transport ships about to sail for Sicily were as magnificent as their captains could make them. The eyes painted at their bows seemed to look eagerly toward the west. The ships were long and low and sleek, lean almost as eels. Some skippers had polished the three-finned, bronze-faced rams at their bows so they were a gleaming, coppery red rather than the usual green that almost matched the sea. Paint and even gilding ornamented curved stemposts and sternposts with fanlike ends.

Hoplites boarded the transports, which were triremes with the fittings for their two lower banks of oars removed to make more room for the foot soldiers. Now and then, before going up the gangplanks and into the ships, the men would pause to embrace kinsmen or youths who were dear to them or even hetairai or wives who, veiled against the public eye, had ventured forth for this farewell.

A hundred ships. More than five thousand hoplites. More than twelve thousand rowers. Mine. Every bit of it mine, Alkibiades thought.

He stood at the stern of his own ship, the *Thraseia*. Even thinking of the name made him smile. What else would he call his ship but *Boldness*? If any one trait distinguished him, that was it.

Every so often, a soldier on the way to a transport would wave to him. He always smiled and waved back. Admiration was as essential to him as the air he breathed. *And I deserve every bit I get, too.*

He was thirty-five, the picture of what a man—or perhaps a god—should look like. He'd been the most beautiful boy in Athens, the one all the men wanted. He threw back his head and laughed, remembering the pranks he'd played on some of the rich fools who wanted to be his lover. A lot of boys lost their looks when they came into manhood. *Not me*, he thought complacently. He remained every bit as splendid, if in a different way—still the target of every man's eye . . . and every woman's.

A hoplite trudged by, helmet on his head: a sturdy, wide-shouldered fellow with a gray beard. He carried his own armor and weapons, and didn't seem to be bringing a slave along to attend to him while on campaign. Even though Sokrates had pushed back the helm, as a man did when not wearing it into battle, it made Alkibiades need an extra heartbeat or two to recognize him.

"Hail, O best one!" Alkibiades called.

Sokrates stopped and dipped his head in polite acknowledgment. "Hail."

"Where are you bound?"

"Why, to Sicily: so the Assembly voted, and so we shall go."

Alkibiades snorted. Sokrates could be most annoying when he was most literal, as the younger man had found out studying with him. "No, my dear. That's not what I meant. Where are you bound *now*?"

"To a transport. How else shall I go to Sicily? I cannot swim so far, and I doubt a dolphin would bear me up, as one did for Arion long ago."

"How else shall you go?" Alkibiades said grandly. "Why, here aboard the *Thraseia* with me, of course. I've had the decking cut away to make the ship lighter and faster—and to give more breeze below it. And I've slung a hammock down there, and I can easily sling another for you, my dear. No need to bed down on hard planking."

Sokrates stood there and started to think. When he did that, nothing and no one could reach him till he finished. The fleet might sail without him, and he would never notice. He'd thought through a day and a night up at Potidaia years before, not moving or speaking. Here, though, only a couple of minutes went by before he came out of his trance. "Which other hoplites will go aboard your trireme?" he asked.

"Why, no others—only rowers and marines and officers," Alkibiades answered with a laugh. "We can, if you like, sleep under one blanket, as we did up in the north." He batted his eyes with an alluring smile.

Most Athenians would have sailed with him forever after an offer like that. Sokrates might not even have heard it. "And how many hoplites will be aboard the other triremes of the fleet?" he inquired.

"None I know of," Alkibiades said.

"Then does it not seem to you, O marvelous one, that the proper place for rowers and marines is aboard the triremes, while the proper place for hoplites is aboard the transports?" Having solved the problem to his own satisfaction, Sokrates walked on toward the transports. Alkibiades stared after him. After a moment, he shook his head and laughed again.

Once the Athenians sneaked a few soldiers into Katane by breaking down a poorly built gate, the handful of men in it who supported Syracuse panicked and fled south toward the city they favored. That amused Alkibiades, for he hadn't got enough men into the Sicilian polis to seize it in the face of a determined resistance. *Boldness*, he thought again. *Always boldness*. With the pro-Syracusans gone, Katane promptly opened its gates to the Athenian expeditionary force.

The polis lay about two thirds of the way down from Messane at the northern corner of Sicily to Syracuse. Mount Aetna dominated the northwestern horizon, a great cone shouldering its way up into the sky. Even with spring well along, snow still clung to the upper slopes of the volcano. Here and there, smoke issued from vents in the flanks and at the top. Every so often, lava would gush from them. When it flowed in the wrong direction, it destroyed the Katanians' fields and olive groves and vineyards. If it flowed in exactly the wrong direction, it would destroy their town.

Alkibiades felt like the volcano himself after another fight with Nikias. The Athenians had sent Nikias along with the expedition to serve as an anchor for Alkibiades. He knew it, knew it and hated it. He didn't particularly hate Nikias himself; he just found him laughable, to say nothing of irrelevant. Nikias was twenty years older than he, and those twenty years might just as well have been a thousand.

Nikias dithered and worried and fretted. Alkibiades thrust home. Nikias gave reverence to the gods with obsessive piety, and did nothing without checking the omens first. Alkibiades laughed at the gods when he didn't ignore them. Nikias had opposed this expedition to Sicily. It had been Alkibiades' idea.

"We were lucky ever to take this place," Nikias had grumbled. He kept fooling with his beard, as if he had lice. For all Alkibiades knew, he did.

"Yes, my dear," Alkibiades had said with such patience as he could muster. "Luck favors us. We should—we had better—take advantage of it. Ask Lamakhos. He'll tell you the same." Lamakhos was the other leading officer in the force. Alkibiades didn't despise him. He wasn't worth despising. He was just . . . dull.

"I don't care what Lamakhos thinks," Nikias had said testily. "I think we ought to thank the gods we've come this far safely. We ought to thank them, and then go home."

"And make Athens the laughingstock of Hellas?" *And make* me *the laughingstock of Hellas?* "Not likely!"

"We cannot do what we came to Sicily to do," Nikias had insisted.

"You were the one who told the Assembly we needed such a great force. Now we have it, and you still aren't happy with it?"

"I never dreamt they would be mad enough actually to send so much."

Alkibiades hadn't hit him then. He might have, but he'd been interrupted. A commotion outside made both men hurry out of Alkibiades' tent. "What is it?" Alkibiades called to a man running his way. "Is the Syracusan fleet coming up to fight us?" It had stayed in the harbor when an Athenian reconnaissance squadron sailed south a couple of weeks before. Maybe the Syracusans hoped to catch the Athenian triremes beached and burn or wreck them. If they did, they would get a nasty surprise.

But the Athenian tossed his head. "It's not the polluted Syracusans," he answered. "It's the *Salaminia*. She's just come into the harbor here."

"The *Salaminia*?" Alkibiades and Nikias spoke together, and in identical astonishment. The *Salaminia* was Athens' official state trireme, and wouldn't venture far from home except on most important business. Sure enough, peering toward the harbor, Alkibiades could see her crew dragging her out of the sea and up onto the yellow sand of the beach. "What's she doing here?" he asked.

Nikias eyed him with an expression compounded of equal parts loathing and gloating. "I'll bet I know," the older man said. "I'll bet they found someone who told the citizens of Athens the real story, the true story, of how the herms all through the polis were profaned."

"I had nothing to do with that," Alkibiades said. He'd said the same thing ever since the mutilations happened. "And besides," he added, "just about as many of the citizens of Athens are here in Sicily as are back at the polis."

"You can't evade like that," Nikias said. "You remind me of your dear teacher Sokrates, using bad logic to beat down good."

Alkibiades stared at him as if he'd found him squashed on the sole of his sandal. "What you say about Sokrates would be a lie even if you'd thought of it yourself. But it comes from Aristophanes' *Clouds*, and you croak it out like a raven trained to speak but without the wit to understand its words."

Nikias' cheeks flamed red as hot iron beaten on the anvil. Alkibiades would have liked to beat him. Instead, he contemptuously turned his back. But that pointed his gaze toward the *Salaminia* again. Athenians down there on the shore were pointing up to the high ground on which he stood. A pair of men whose gold wreaths declared they were on official business made their way toward him.

He hurried to meet them. That was always his style. He wanted to make things happen, not have them happen to him. Nikias followed. "Hail, friends!" Alkibiades called, tasting the lie. "Are you looking for me? I am here."

"Alkibiades son of Kleinias?" one of the newcomers asked formally.

"You know who I am, Herakleides," Alkibiades said. "What do you want?"

"I think, son of Kleinias, that you know what I want," Herakleides replied. "You are ordered by the people of Athens to return to the polis to defend yourself against serious charges that have been raised against you."

More and more hoplites and rowers gathered around Alkibiades and the men newly come from Athens. This was an armed camp, not a peaceful city; many of them carried spears or wore swords on their hips. Alkibiades smiled to see them, for he knew they were well inclined toward him. In a loud voice, he asked, "Am I under arrest?"

Herakleides and his wreathed comrade licked their lips. The mere word made soldiers growl and heft their spears; several of them drew their swords. Gathering himself, Herakleides answered, "No, you are not under arrest. But you are summoned to defend yourself, as I said. How can a man with such charges hanging over his head hope to hold an important position of public trust?"

"Yes—how indeed?" Nikias murmured.

Again, Alkibiades gave him a look full of withering scorn. Then he forgot about him. Herakleides and his friend were more important at the moment. So were the soldiers and sailors—much more important. With a smile and a mocking bow, Alkibiades said, "How can any man hope to hold an important position of public trust when a lying fool can trump up such charges and hang them over his head?"

"That's the truth," a hoplite growled, right in Herakleides' ear. He was a big, burly fellow with a thick black beard—a man built like a wrestler or a pankratiast. Alkibiades wouldn't have wanted a man like that growling in his ear and clenching a spearshaft till his knuckles whitened.

By the involuntary step back Herakleides took, he didn't care for it, either. His voice quavered as he said, "You deny the charges, then?"

"Of course I do," Alkibiades answered. Out of the corner of his eye, he noticed Sokrates pushing through the crowd toward the front. A lot of men were pushing forward, but somehow Sokrates, despite his years, made more progress than most. Maybe the avid curiosity on his face helped propel him forward. Or maybe not; he almost always seemed that curious. But Sokrates would have to wait now, too. Alkibiades went on, "I say they're nothing but a pack of lies put forward by scavenger dogs who, unable to do anything great themselves, want to pull down those who can."

Snarls of agreement rose from the soldiers and sailors. Herakleides licked his lips again. He must have known recalling Alkibiades wouldn't be easy before the *Salaminia* sailed. Had he known it would be *this* hard? Alkibiades had his doubts. With something like a sigh, Herakleides said, "At the motion of Thettalos son of Kimon, it has seemed good to the people of Athens to summon you home. Will you obey the democratic will of the Assembly, or will you not?"

Alkibiades grimaced. He had no use for the democracy of Athens, and had never bothered hiding that. As a result, the demagogues who loved to hear themselves talk in the Assembly hated him. He said, "I have no hope of getting a fair hearing in Athens. My enemies have poisoned the people of the polis against me."

Herakleides frowned portentously. "Would you refuse the Assembly's summons?"

"I don't know what I'll do right now." Alkibiades clenched his fists. What he wanted to do was pound the smugness out of the plump, prosperous fool in front of him. But no. It would not do. Here, though, even he, normally so quick and decisive, had trouble figuring out what *would* do. "Let me have time to think, O marvelous one," he said, and watched Herakleides redden at the sarcasm. "I will give you my answer tomorrow."

"Do you want to be declared a rebel against the people of Athens?" Herakleides' frown got deeper and darker.

"No, but I don't care to go home and be ordered to guzzle hemlock no matter what I say or do, either," Alkibiades answered. "Were it your life, Herakleides, such as that is, would you not want time to plan out what to do?"

That *such as that is* made the man just come from Athens redden again. But soldiers and sailors jostled forward, getting louder by the minute in support of their general. Herakleides yielded with such grace as he could: "Let it be as you say, most noble one." He turned the title of respect into one of reproach. "I will hear your answer tomorrow. For now . . . hail." He turned and walked back toward the *Salaminia*. The sun glinted dazzlingly off his gold wreath.

Sokrates stood in line to get his evening rations. Talk of Alkibiades and the herms and the profanation of the sacred mysteries was on everyone's lips. Some men thought he'd done what he was accused of doing. Others insisted the charges against him were invented to discredit him.

"Wait," Sokrates told a man who'd been talking about unholy deeds and how the gods despised them. "Say that again, Euthyphron, if you please. I don't follow your thought, which is surely much too wise for a simple fellow like me."

"I'd be glad to, Sokrates," the other hoplite said, and he did.

"I'm sorry, best one. I really must be dense," Sokrates said when he'd finished. "I still do not quite see. Do you say deeds are unholy because the gods hate them, or do you say the gods hate them because they are unholy?"

"I certainly do," Euthyphron answered.

"No, wait. I see what Sokrates means," another soldier broke in. "You can't have that both ways. It's one or the other. Which do you say it is?"

Euthyphron tried to have it both ways. Sokrates' questions wouldn't let him. Some of the other Athenians jeered at him. Others showed more sympathy for him, even in his confusion, than they did for Sokrates. "Do you have to be a gadfly *all* the time?" a hoplite asked him after Euthyphron, very red in the face, bolted out of the line without getting his supper.

"I can only be what I am," Sokrates answered. "Am I wrong for trying to find the truth in everything I do?"

The other man shrugged. "I don't know whether you're right or wrong. What I do know is, you're cursed *annoying*."

When Sokrates blinked his big round eyes in surprise, he looked uncommonly like a frog. "Why should the search for truth be annoying? Would you not think preventing that search to be a greater annoyance for mankind?"

But the hoplite threw up his hands. "Oh, no, you don't. I won't play. You're not going to twist me up in knots, the way you did with poor Euthyphron."

"Euthyphron's thinking was not straight before I ever said a word to him. All I did was show him his inconsistencies. Now maybe he will try to root them out."

The other soldier tossed his head. But he still refused to argue. Sighing, Sokrates snaked forward with the rest of the line. A bored-looking cook handed him a small loaf of dark bread, a chunk of cheese, and an onion. The man filled his cup with watered wine and poured olive oil for the bread into a little cruet he held out.

"I thank you," Sokrates said. The cook looked surprised. Soldiers and sailors were likelier to grumble about the fare than thank him for it.

Men clustered in little knots of friends to eat and to go on hashing over the coming of the *Salaminia* and what it was liable to mean. Sokrates had no usual group to join. Part of the reason there was that he was at least twenty years older than most of the other Athenians who'd traveled west to Sicily. But his age was only part of the reason, and he knew it. He sighed. He didn't *want* to make people uncomfortable. He didn't want to, but he'd never been able to avoid it.

He walked back to his tent to eat his supper. When he was done, he went outside and stared up at Mount Aetna. Why, he wondered, did it stay cold enough for snow to linger on the mountain's upper slopes even on this sweltering midsummer evening?

He was no closer to finding the answer when someone called his name. He got the idea this wasn't the first time the man had called. Sure enough, when he turned, there stood Alkibiades with a sardonic grin on his face. "Hail, O wisest of all," the younger man said. "Good to see you with us again."

"If I am wisest—which I doubt, no matter what the gods may say—it is because I know how ignorant I am, where other men are ignorant even of that," Sokrates replied.

Alkibiades' grin grew impudent. "Other men don't know how ignorant you are?" he suggested slyly. Sokrates laughed. But Alkibiades' grin slipped. "Ignorant or not, will you walk with me?"

"If you like," Sokrates said. "You know I never could resist your beauty." He imitated the little lisp for which Alkibiades was famous, and sighed like a lover gazing upon his beloved.

"Oh, go howl!" Alkibiades said. "Even when we slept under the same blanket, we only slept. You did your best to ruin my reputation."

"I cannot ruin your reputation." Sokrates' voice grew sharp. "Only you can do that."

Alkibiades made a face at him. "Come along, best one, if you'd be so kind." They walked away from the Athenian encampment on a winding dirt track that led up towards Aetna. Alkibiades wore a chiton with purple edging and shoes with golden clasps. Sokrates' tunic was threadbare and raggedy; he went barefoot the way he usually did, as if he were a sailor.

The sight of the most and least elegant men in the Athenian expedition walking along together would have been plenty to draw eyes even if the *Salaminia* hadn't just come to Katane. As things were, they had to tramp along for several stadia before shaking off the last of the curious. Sokrates ignored the men who followed hoping to eavesdrop. Alkibiades glowered at them till they finally gave up.

"Vultures," he muttered. "Now I know how Prometheus must have felt." He put a hand over his liver.

"Is that what you wanted to talk about?" Sokrates asked.

"You know what I want to talk about. You were there when those idiots in gold wreaths summoned me back to Athens," Alkibiades answered. Sokrates looked over at him, his face showing nothing but gentle interest. Alkibiades snorted. "And don't pretend you don't, either, if you please. I haven't the time for it."

"I am only the most ignorant of men—" Sokrates began. Alkibiades cursed him, as vilely as he knew how. Sokrates gave back a mild smile in return. That made Alkibiades curse harder yet. Sokrates went on as if he hadn't spoken: "So you *will* have to tell me what it is you want, I fear."

"All right. All *right*." Alkibiades kicked at a pebble. It spun into the brush by the track. "I'll play your polluted game. What am I supposed to do about the *Salaminia* and the summons?"

"Why, that which is best, of course."

"Thank you so much, O most noble one," Alkibiades snarled. He kicked another pebble, a bigger one this time. "*Oimoi!* That hurt!" He hopped a couple of times before hurrying to catch up with Sokrates, who'd never slowed.

Sokrates eyed him with honest perplexity. "What else *can* a man who knows what the good is do but that which is best?"

"What *is* the good here?" Alkibiades demanded.

"Why ask me, when I am so ignorant?" Sokrates replied. Alkibiades started to kick yet another pebble, thought better of it, and cursed again instead. Sokrates waited till he'd finished, then inquired, "What do *you* think the good is here?"

"Games," Alkibiades muttered. He breathed heavily, mastering himself. Then he laughed, and seemed to take himself by surprise. "I'll pretend I'm an ephebe again, eighteen years old and curious as a puppy. By the gods, I wish I were. The good here is that which is best for me and that which is best for Athens."

He paused, waiting to see what Sokrates would say to that. Sokrates, as was his way, asked another question: "And what will happen if you return to Athens on the *Salaminia*?"

"My enemies there will murder me under form of law," Alkibiades answered. After another couple of strides, he seemed to remember he was supposed to think of Athens, too. "And Nikias will find some way to botch this expedition. For one thing, he's a fool. For another, he doesn't want to be here in the first place. He doesn't think we can win. With *him* in command, he's likely right."

"Is this best for you and best for Athens, then?" Sokrates asked.

Alkibiades gave him a mocking bow. "It would seem not, O best one," he answered, as if he were chopping logic in front of Simon the shoemaker's.

"All right, then. What other possibilities exist?" Sokrates asked.

"I could make as if to go back to Athens, then escape somewhere and live my own life," Alkibiades said. "That's what I'm thinking of doing now, to tell you the truth."

"I see," Sokrates said. "And is this best for you?"

A wild wolf would have envied Alkibiades' smile. "I think so. It would give me the chance to avenge myself on all my enemies. And I would, too. Oh, wouldn't I just?"

"I believe you," Sokrates said, and he did. Alkibiades was a great many things, but no one had ever reckoned him less than able. "Now, what of Athens if you do this?"

"As for the expedition, the same as in the first case. As for the polis, to the crows with it," Alkibiades said savagely. "It is my enemy, and I its."

"And is this that which is best for Athens, which you said you sought?" Sokrates asked. Yes, Alkibiades would make a formidable enemy.

"A man should do his friends good and his enemies harm," he said now. "If the city made me flee her, she would be my enemy, not my friend. Up till now, I have done her as much good as I could. I would do the same in respect to harm."

A wall lizard stared at Sokrates from a boulder sticking up out of the scrubby brush by the side of the track. He took one step closer to it. It scrambled off the boulder and away. For a moment, he could hear it skittering through dry weeds. Then it must have found a hole, for silence returned. He wondered how it knew to run when something that might be danger approached. But that riddle would have to wait for another time. He gave his attention back to Alkibiades, who was watching him with an expression of wry amusement, and asked, "If you go back with the *Salaminia* to Athens, then, you say, you will suffer?"

"That is what I say, yes." Alkibiades dipped his head in agreement.

"And if you do not accompany the *Salaminia* all the way back to Athens, you say that the polis will be the one to suffer?"

"Certainly. I say that also," Alkibiades replied with a wry chuckle. "See how much I sound like any of the other poor fools you question?"

Sokrates waved away the gibe. "Do you say that either of these things is best for you and best for Athens?"

Now Alkibiades tossed his head. "It would seem not, O best one. But what else can I do? The Assembly is back at the city. It voted what it voted. I don't see how I could change its mind unless. . . ." His voice trailed away. He suddenly laughed out loud, laughed out loud and sprang forward to kiss Sokrates on the mouth. "Thank you, my dear! You have given me the answer."

"Nonsense!" Sokrates pushed him away hard enough to make him stumble back a couple of paces; those stonecutter's shoulders still held a good deal of strength. "I only ask questions. If you found an answer, it came from inside you."

"Your questions shone light on it."

"But it was there all along, or I could not have illuminated it. And as for the kiss, if you lured me out into this barren land to seduce me, I am afraid you will find yourself disappointed despite your beauty."

"Ah, Sokrates, if you hadn't put in that last I think you would have broken my heart forever." Alkibiades made as if to kiss the older man again. Sokrates made as if to pick up a rock and clout him with it. Laughing, they turned and walked back toward the Athenians' encampment.

* * *

Herakleides threw up shocked hands. "This is illegal!" he exclaimed.

Nikias wagged a finger in Alkibiades' face. "This is unprecedented!" he cried. By the way he said it, that was worse than anything merely illegal could ever be.

Alkibiades bowed to each of them in turn. "Ordering me home when I wasn't in Athens to defend myself is illegal," he said. "Recalling a commander in the middle of such an important campaign is unprecedented. We have plenty of Athenians here. Let's see what *they* think about it."

He looked across the square in Katane. He'd spoken here to the Assembly of the locals not long before, while Athenian soldiers filtered into the polis and brought it under their control. Now Athenian hoplites and rowers and marines filled the square. They made an Assembly of their own. It probably was illegal. It certainly was unprecedented. Alkibiades didn't care. It just as certainly was his only chance.

He took a couple of steps forward, right to the edge of the speakers' platform. Sokrates was out there somewhere. Alkibiades couldn't pick him out, though. He shrugged. He was on his own anyhow. Sokrates might have given him some of the tools he used, but *he* had to use them. He was fighting for *his* life.

"Here me, men of Athens! Here me, *people* of Athens!" he said. The soldiers and sailors leaned forward, intent on his ever word. The people of Athens had sent them forth to Sicily. The idea that they might *be* the people of Athens as well as its representatives here in the west was new to them. They had to believe it. Alkibiades had to make them believe it. If they didn't, he was doomed.

"Back in the polis, the Assembly there"—he wouldn't call that *the people of Athens*—"has ordered me home so they can condemn me and kill me without most of my friends—without *you*—there to protect me. They say I desecrated the herms in the city. They say I profaned the sacred mysteries of Eleusis. One of their so-called witnesses claims I broke the herms by moonlight, when everyone knows it was done in the last days of the month, when there was no moonlight. These are the sorts of people my enemies produce against me."

He never said he hadn't mutilated the herms. He never said he hadn't burlesqued the mysteries. He said the witnesses his opponents produced lied—and they did.

He went on, "Even if I went back to Athens, my enemies' witnesses would say one thing, my few friends and I another. No matter how the jury finally voted, no one would ever be sure of the truth. And so I say to you, men of Athens, *people* of Athens, let us not rely on lies and jurymen who can be swayed by lies. Let us rest my fate on the laps of the gods."

Nikias started. Alkibiades almost laughed out loud. *Didn't expect that, did you, you omen-mongering fool?*

Aloud, he continued, "If we triumph here in Sicily under my command, will that not prove I have done no wrong in the eyes of heaven? If we triumph—as triumph we can, as triumph we *shall*—then I shall return to Athens with you, and let these stupid charges against me be forgotten forevermore. But if we fail here . . . If we fail here, I swear to you I shall not leave Sicily alive, but will be the offering to repay the gods for whatever sins they reckon me to have committed. That is my offer, to you and to the gods. Time will show what they say of it. But what say you, men of Athens? What say you, *people* of Athens?"

He waited for the decision of the Assembly he'd convened. He didn't have to wait long. Cries of, "Yes!" rang out, and, "We accept!" and, "Alkibiades!" A few men tossed their heads and yelled things like, "No!" and, "Let the decision of the Assembly in Athens stand!" But they were only a few, overwhelmed and outshouted by Alkibiades' backers.

Turning to Herakleides and Nikias, Alkibiades bowed once more. They'd thought they would be able to address the Athenian soldiers and sailors after he finished. But the decision was already made. Herakleides looked stunned, Nikias dyspeptic.

With another bow, Alkibiades said to Herakleides, "You will take my answer and the true choice of the people of Athens back to the polis?"

The other man needed two or three tries before he managed to stammer out, "Y-Yes."

"Good." Alkibiades smiled. "Tell the polis also, I hope to be back there myself before too long."

Sokrates settled his helmet on his head. The bronze and the glued-in padded lining would, with luck, keep some Syracusan from smashing in his skull. The walls of Syracuse loomed ahead. The Athenians were building their own wall around the city, to cut it off from the countryside and starve it into submission. Now the Syracusans had started a counterwall, thrust out from the fortifications of the polis. If it blocked the one the Athenians were building, Syracuse might stand. If the hoplites Alkibiades led could stop that counterwall . . . A man didn't need to be a general to see what would happen then.

Sweat streamed down Sokrates' face. Summer in Sicily was hotter than it ever got back home in Attica. He had a skin full of watered wine, and squirted some into his mouth. Swallowing felt good. A little of the wine splashed his face. That felt good, too.

"*Pheu!*" said another hoplite close by. "Only thing left of me'll be my shadow by the time we're done here."

Sokrates smiled. "I like that." He tilted back his helmet so he could drag a hairy forearm across his sweaty forehead, then let the helm fall down into place again. He tapped the nodding crimson-dyed horsehair plume with a forefinger. "This makes me seem fiercer than I am. But since all hoplites wear crested helms, and all therefore seem fiercer than they are, is it not true that the intended effect of the crest is wasted?"

Laughing, the other hoplite said, "You come up with some of the strangest things, Sokrates, Furies take me if you don't."

"How can the search for truth be strange?" Sokrates asked. "Do you say the truth is somehow alien to mankind, and that he has no knowledge of it from birth?"

Instead of answering, the other Athenian pointed to one of the rough little forts in which the Syracusans working on their counterwall sheltered. "Look! They're coming out." So they were, laborers in short chitons or loincloths, with armored hoplites to protect them while they piled stone on stone. "Doesn't look like they've got very many guards out today, does it?"

"Certainly not," Sokrates answered. "The next question to be asked is, why have they sent forth so few?"

Horns blared in the Athenian camp. "I don't think our captain cares why," the other hoplite said, pulling down his helmet so the cheekpieces and nasal protected his face. "Whatever the reason is, he's going to make them sorry for being so stupid."

"But do you not agree that *why* is always the most important question?" Sokrates asked. Instead of answering, the other hoplite turned to take his place in line. The horns cried out again. Sokrates picked up his shield and his spear and also joined the building phalanx. In the face of battle, all questions had to wait. Sometimes the fighting answered them without words.

The Athenian captain pointed toward the Syracusans a couple of stadia away. "They've goofed, boys. Let's make 'em pay. We'll beat their hoplites, run their workers off or else kill 'em, and we'll tear down some of that wall they're trying to build. We can do it. It'll be easy. Give the war cry good and loud so they know we're coming. That'll scare the shit out of 'em, just like on the comic stage."

"How about the comic stage?" the hoplite next to Sokrates asked. "You were up there, in Aristophanes' *Clouds*."

"I wasn't there in person, though the mask the actor wore looked so much like me, I stood up in the audience to show the resemblance," Sokrates answered. "And it's the Syracusans we want to do the shitting, not ourselves."

"Forward!" the captain shouted, and pointed at the Syracusans with his spear.

Sokrates shouted, *"Eleleu! Eleleu!"* with the rest of the Athenians as they advanced on their foes. It wasn't a wild charge at top speed. A phalanx, even a small one like this, would fall to pieces and lose much of its force in such a charge. What made the formation strong was each soldier protecting his neighbor's right as well as his own left with his shield, and two or three serried ranks of spearheads projecting out beyond the front line of hoplites. No soldiers in the world could match Hellenic hoplites. The Great Kings of Persia knew as much, and hired Hellenes by the thousands as mercenaries.

The Athenians might have made short work of Persians or other barbarians. The Syracusans, though, were just as much Hellenes as they were. Though outnumbered, the soldiers guarding the men building the counterwall shouted back and forth in their drawling Doric dialect and then also formed a phalanx—only four or five rows deep, for they were short of men—and hurried to block the Athenians' descent on the laborers. They too cried, *"Eleleu!"*

As a man will do on the battlefield, Sokrates tried to spot the soldier he would likely have to fight. He knew that was a foolish exercise. He marched in the third row of the Athenians, and the enemy he picked might go down or shift position before they met. But, with the universal human longing to find patterns whether they really existed or not, he did it anyway.

"Eleleu! Elel—" *Crash!* Both sides' war cries were lost in what sounded like a disaster in a madman's smithy as the two front lines collided. Spearpoints clattered off bronze corselets and bronze-faced shields. Those shields smacked together, men from each side trying to force their foes to danger. Some spearpoints struck flesh instead of bronze. Shrieks and curses rang through the metallic clangor.

Where the man on whom Sokrates had fixed went, he never knew. He thrust underhanded at another Syracusan, a young fellow with reddish streaks in his black beard. The spearpoint bit into the enemy's thigh, below the bronze-studded leather strips he wore over his kilt and above the top of his greave. Blood spurted, red as the feathers of a spotted woodpecker's crest. The Syracusan's mouth opened enormously wide in a great wail of anguish. He toppled, doing his best to pull his shield over himself so he wouldn't be trampled.

Relying on weight of numbers, the Athenians bulled their way forward, forcing their foes to give ground and spearing them down one after another. Most of the laborers the Syracusans had protected ran back toward the fort from which they'd come. Some, though, hovered on the outskirts of the battle and flung stones at the Athenians. One banged off Sokrates' shield.

And if it had hit me in the face? he wondered. The answer to that was obvious enough, though not one even a lover of wisdom cared to contemplate.

A Syracusan thrust a spear at Sokrates. He turned it aside with his shield, then quickly stepped forward, using the shield as a battering ram. The enemy soldier gave ground. He was younger than Sokrates—what hoplite wasn't?—but on the scrawny side. Broad-shouldered and thick through the chest and belly, Sokrates made the most of his weight. The Syracusan tripped over a stone and went down, arms flailing, with a cry of despair. The Athenian behind Sokrates drove a spear into the fallen man's throat. His blood splashed Sokrates' greaves.

Athenians went down, too, in almost equal numbers, but they still had the advantage. Before long, their foes wouldn't be able to hold their line together. Once the Syracusans fled, all running as individuals instead of fighting together in a single unit, they would fall like barley before the scythe.

But then, only moments before that would surely happen, horns blared from the walls of Syracuse. A gate opened. Out poured more Syracusans, rank upon rank of them, the sun gleaming ruddy from their bronzen armor and reflecting in silvery sparkles off countless iron spearheads. *"Eleleu!"* they roared, and thundered down on the Athenians like a landslide.

"A trap!" groaned a hoplite near Sokrates. "They used those few fellows as bait to lure us in, and now they're going to bugger us."

"They have to have twice the men we do," another man agreed.

"Then we shall have to fight twice as hard," Sokrates said. "For is it not true that a man who shows he is anything but easy meat will often come out of danger safe, where one who breaks and runs is surely lost? I have seen both victory and defeat, and so it seems to me."

The more worried he was himself, the more he wanted to keep his comrades steady. The Syracusans out here by the counterwall had hung together well, waiting for their rescuers. Now the Athenians had to do the same. Sokrates looked around. He saw no rescuers. He shrugged inside his corselet. If the Syracusans wanted him, they would have to drag him down.

"Eleleu!" they cried. *"Eleleu!"*

Screaming like men gone mad, Athenian officers swung their men to face the new onslaught. Nothing was more hopeless, more defenseless, than a phalanx struck in the flank. This way, at least, they would make the enemy earn whatever he got. "Come on, boys!" a captain shouted. "They're only Syracusans. We can beat them."

Sokrates wanted to ask him how he knew. No chance for that. The two phalanxes smashed together. Now it was the Athenians who were outnumbered. They fought to keep from being driven back, and to keep the Syracusans from breaking through or sliding around their front. As men in the first few ranks went down, others shoved forward to take their places.

He found himself facing a Syracusan whose spear had broken. The enemy hoplite had thrown away the shaft and drawn his sword—a good enough emergency weapon, but only an emergency weapon when facing a man with a pike. Sokrates could reach him, but he had no chance to reach Sokrates.

He had no chance, that is, till he hacked at Sokrates' spearshaft just below the head and watched the iron point fly free and thump down on the ground. *"Papai!"* Sokrates exclaimed in dismay. The Syracusan let out a triumphant whoop. A sword might not be much against a spear, but against a spearshaft. . . .

A sword proved not so much. In the front line, Sokrates had more room to wield what was left of his weapon than he would have farther back. He swung the beheaded shaft as if it were a club. It thudded against the Syracusan's shield. The next blow would have caved in his skull, helm or no helm, if he hadn't brought the shield up in a hurry. And the third stroke smacked into the side of his knee—he hadn't got the shield down again fast enough. No greave could protect him against a blow like that. Down he went, clutching his leg. In a scene straight from the *Iliad*, the hoplite behind him sprang forward to ward him with shield and armored body till comrades farther back could drag him out of the fight.

Sokrates used the moment's respite to throw down the ruined spear and snatch up one that somebody else had dropped. He dipped his head to the Syracusan across from him. "Bravely done, my friend."

"Same to you, old man," the other soldier answered. "A lot of hoplites would have cut and run when they lost their pikes." He gathered himself. "Brave or not, though, Athenian, I'll kill you if I can." Fast as a striking snake, his spearhead darted for Sokrates' face.

Ducking away from the thrust, Sokrates answered with one of his own. The Syracusan turned it on his shield. They both stepped forward to struggle shield to shield. The Syracusan kept up a steady stream of curses. Panting, winded, Sokrates needed all his breath to fight.

He drew back a couple of paces, not because the enemy hoplite was getting the better of him but because the rest of the Athenians had had to retreat. "Should have stayed, old man," the Syracusan jeered. "I'd have had you then, or my pals would if I didn't."

"If you want me, come and fight me," Sokrates said. "You won't kill me with words." *I might fall dead over of my own accord, though.* He couldn't remember the last time he'd been so worn. Maybe—probably—he'd never been so worn before. *Maybe my friends back in Athens were right, and I should have stayed in the city. War is a young man's sport. Am I young?* He laughed. The Syracusan hoplite who'd been trying to kill him knew the answer to that.

"What's funny, old man?" the Syracusan demanded.

"What's funny, young man? That you are what I wish I were," Sokrates replied.

In the shadowed space between his nasal and cheekpieces, the other man's eyes widened slightly. "You talk like a sophist."

"So my enemies have always— Ha!" Sokrates fended off a sudden spearthrust with his shield. "Thought you'd take me unawares, did you?"

"I am your enemy. I—" Now the Syracusan was the one who broke off. He turned his head this way and that to look about. With his helmet on, a hoplite couldn't move only his eyes. Sokrates looked, too, with quick, wary flicks of the head. He saw nothing. For a moment, he also heard nothing. Then his ears—*an old man's ears, sure enough,* he thought—caught the trumpet notes the Syracusan hoplite must have heard a few heartbeats sooner.

Sokrates looked around again. This time, when he looked . . . he saw. Over the crest of a nearby hill came men on horseback, peltasts—light-armed foot soldiers—and a solid column of hoplites. No possible way to doubt which side they belonged to, either. At the head of the column rode Alkibiades, his bright hair shining in the sun, a chiton all of purple—an outrageous, and outrageously expensive, garment—marking him out from every other man.

Shouting out their war cry, the Athenian newcomers roared down on the Syracusans. "We are undone!" one of the Syracusan hoplites cried. They broke ranks and ran back toward their polis. Some of them threw away spears and even shields to flee the faster.

Other Syracusans—perhaps a quarter of their number—tried to go on against the Athenian phalanx they'd been fighting. One of those was the hoplite who'd tussled so long against Sokrates. "Yield," Sokrates urged. "Yield to me, and I will see to it that you suffer no evil."

"I serve my polis no less than you serve yours, Athenian," the man answered, and hurled himself at Sokrates once more. Now, though, with the Syracusan line melting away like rotting ice, he fought not Sokrates alone but three or four Athenians. He fought bravely, but he didn't last long.

"Forward!" an Athenian officer cried. "Forward, and they break. *Eleleu!*"

Forward the Athenians went. Hoplites in a body had a chance, often a good chance, against peltasts and horsemen, even if they moved more slowly than their foes. Peltasts could only use their bows and slings and fling javelins from a distance. Likewise, cavalry had trouble closing because the riders would pop off over their horses' tails if they drove home a charge with the lance. But the panicked, running Syracusans, also hard-pressed by the Athenian hoplites, went down like trees under carpenters' axes.

Alkibiades at their head, the Athenian horsemen got in amongst the Syracusans. They speared some and felled others with slashes from their long cavalrymen's swords. The peltasts tormented the foe with arrows and leaden sling bullets and javelins. And, now roaring, *"Eleleu!"* like men seized by Furies, the Athenian hoplites rolled over the slower and more stubborn Syracusans.

The whole enemy host might have fallen there in front of their polis. But the defenders on the walls saw what was happening to them. The gate from which the Syracusan phalanx had marched forth flew open again. The Syracusans ran for their salvation. The Athenians ran after them—and with them.

Like a lot of veterans, Sokrates saw what that might mean. No matter how winded, no matter how parched, he was, he shouted, "As fast as we can now, men of Athens! If we get into Syracuse among them, the city is ours!" He made his stubby legs twinkle over the ground.

Up ahead, Alkibiades heard his voice. He waved and made his horse rear, clinging to the animal with his knees and with one hand clutching its mane. Then he too pointed toward that open gate. The horse came down onto all fours. It galloped forward, bounding past the Syracusans on foot. Other riders saw what was toward and followed.

The first Syracusan hoplites were already inside the polis. In stormed the horsemen. They turned on the gate crew, killing some and scattering others. Some of the Syracusan hoplites tried to haul the gates closed. The cavalrymen fought them, delayed them. Athenian peltasts rushed up to the horsemen's aid. Madness reigned around the gate.

What is madness, Sokrates thought, *save the absence of order?* Still in good order, the Athenian phalanx hammered its way through the chaos—through the chaos, through the gate, and into Syracuse. The Syracusan women and children and old men wailed in horror. The Athenian hoplites roared in triumph.

Sokrates roared with the rest: "Syracuse is ours!"

Women wept. Wounded men moaned. The stinks of smoke and blood and spilled guts filled the air. A drunk Athenian peltast danced the kordax, howling out filthy words to go with the filthy dance. His pecker flipped up to smack against his stomach at every prancing step. It was all bread and fine fish and wine—especially wine—to Alkibiades. He stood in front of—appropriately enough—the temple of Athena, watching chained Syracusan captives shamble past.

Nikias came up to him, looking slightly—no, more than slightly—dazed. Alkibiades gave his fellow general his prettiest bow. "Hail," he said, and then, as if Nikias couldn't see it for himself, "We have Syracuse."

"Er—yes." Nikias might see it, but he seemed hardly able to credit it. "We do."

"Do you believe, then, that the gods have shown I'm innocent of sacrilege?" Alkibiades asked. He wasn't sure he believed that himself; some of the things Sokrates and Kritias had said about the gods made him have even more questions than he would have had otherwise. But it was important that prominent, conservative Nikias should believe it.

And the older man dipped his head. "Why, yes, son of Kleinias, I do. I must. I don't see how any man could doubt it, considering what has happened here in Sicily."

I have to make sure he never talks to Sokrates, Alkibiades thought. *He'd find out exactly how a man could doubt it.* Sokrates was a great one for making anybody doubt anything. But there wasn't much risk that he and Nikias would put their heads together. Sokrates would talk with anyone. Nikias, on the other hand, was a born snob. With another bow, carefully controlled so it didn't seem mocking, Alkibiades asked, "What did you expect to happen on this campaign?"

Nikias' eyes got big and round. "I feared . . . disaster," he said hoarsely. "I feared our men failing when they tried to wall off Syracuse. I feared our fleet trapped and beaten by the Syracusans. I feared our brave soldiers worsted and worked to death in the mines. I had . . . dreams." His voice wobbled.

Grinning, Alkibiades clapped him on the shoulder. "And they were all moonshine, weren't they? These amateurs made a mistake, and we made them pay for it. We'll put the people *we* want into power here—you can always find men who will do what you want—and then, before the sailing season ends, we'll go back and see what we can do about giving the Spartans a clout in the teeth."

At that, Nikias' eyes got bigger and rounder than ever. But he said, "We shall have to be careful here. The men we establish may turn against us, or others may rise up and overthrow them."

He was right. Naïveté and superstition sometimes made him a fool; never stupidity. Alkibiades said, "True enough, O best one. Still, once we're done here, Syracuse will be years getting her strength back, even if she does turn against us. And that's what we came west for, isn't it? To weaken her, I mean. We've done it."

"We have," Nikias agreed wonderingly. "With the help of the gods, we have."

Alkibiades' grin got wider. "Then let's enjoy it, shall we? If we don't enjoy ourselves while we're here on earth, when are we going to do it?"

Nikias sent him a severe frown, the frown a pedagogue might have sent a boy who, on the way to school, paused to stare at the naked women in a brothel. "Is *that* why you staged a *komos* last night?"

"I didn't stage the drinking bout. It just happened," Alkibiades answered. After a night of revelry like that, his head should have ached as if a smith's hammer were falling on it. It should have, but it didn't. Victory made a better anodyne than poppy juice. He went on, "But if you think I didn't enjoy it, you're wrong. And if you think I didn't deserve it, you're wrong about that, too. If I can't celebrate after taking Syracuse when nobody thought I could"—he didn't say the other general had thought that, though he knew Nikias had—"when *am* I entitled to, by the dog of Egypt?"

Nikias muttered at the oath, which Alkibiades had picked up from Sokrates. But he had no answer. Alkibiades hadn't thought he would.

The Peloponnesos is shaped like a hand, narrow wrist by Corinth in the northeast, thumb and three short, stubby fingers of land pointing south (the little island of Kythera lies off the easternmost finger like a detached nail). Sparta sits in the palm, not far from the base of the middle finger. Having rowed through the night, the Athenian fleet beached itself between the little towns of Abia and Pherai, in the indentation between the middle and westernmost fingers, just as dawn was breaking.

Alkibiades ran from one ship to another like a man possessed. "Move! Move! Move!" he shouted as the hoplites and peltasts and the small force of cavalry emerged from the transports. "No time to wait! No time to waste! Sparta's only a day's march ahead of us. If we strike hard enough and fast enough, we get there before the Spartans can pull enough men together to stop us. They've been ravaging Attica for years. Now it's our turn on their home ground."

To the east, the Taygetos Mountains sawbacked the horizon. But the pass that led to Sparta was visible even from the beach. Alkibiades vaulted onto his horse's back, disdaining a leg up. Like any horseman, he wished there were some better way to mount and to stay on a beast's back. But there wasn't, or nobody had ever found one, and so, like any horseman, he made the best of things.

"Come on!" he called, trotting out ahead of the hoplites. "All of us against not all of them! How can we help but whip 'em?"

They hadn't gone far before they came across a farmer looking up at the not yet ripe olives on his trees. He wasn't a Spartan, of course; he was a Messenian, a helot—next thing to a slave. His eyes bugged out of his head. He took off running, and he might have beaten the man who'd won the sprint at the last games at Olympia.

"Pity we can't cut down their olive groves, the way they've done to ours in Attica," Alkibiades said to Nikias, who rode not far away.

"No time for that," Nikias answered.

Alkibiades dipped his head. "We'll do what we can with fire," he said. But olives were tough. The trees soon recovered from burning alone; really harming them required long, hard axework.

The ground rose beneath the Athenians' feet. Sweat rivered off the hoplites marching in armor. Alkibiades had made every man carry a jug full of heavily watered wine. Every so often, one of them would pause to swig. Most of the streambeds were dry at this season of the year, and would be till the rain came in winter. When the army found one with a trickle of water in it, men fell out to drink.

"They say the Persian host drank steams dry on the way to Hellas," Alkibiades remarked. "Now we can do the same."

"I do not care to be like the Persians in any way," Nikias said stiffly.

"Oh, I don't know," Alkibiades said. "I wouldn't mind having the Great King's wealth. No, I wouldn't mind that a bit. By the dog, I'd use it better than he has."

Except for the track that led up toward the pass, the country around the Athenians got wilder and wilder. Oaks and brush gave way to dark, frowning pines. A bear lumbered across the track in front of Alkibiades. His horse snorted and tried to rear. He fought it down.

"Good hunting in these woods," Nikias said. "Bear, as you saw. Wild boar, too, and goat and deer."

If I'd gone back towards Athens and then fled as I first planned to do, I suppose I would have ended up in Sparta, Alkibiades thought. *I would have wanted to harm Athens all I could for casting me out, and Sparta would have been the place to do it. I might have hunted through these mountains myself if I hadn't hashed things out with Sokrates. The world would have been a different place.*

He laughed. *I'm still hunting through these mountains. Not bear or boar, though. Not goat or deer. I'm hunting Spartans—better game still.*

No forts blocked the crown of the pass. The Spartans weren't in the habit of defending themselves with forts. They used men instead. *This time, by Zeus, some men are going to use them.* Laughing, Alkibiades called, "All downhill from now on, boys." The Athenians raised a cheer.

A hoplite near Sokrates pointed ahead. "That's *it?*" he said in disbelief. "*That's* the place we've been fighting all these years? That miserable dump? It looks like a bunch of villages, and not rich ones, either."

"You can't always tell by looking," Sokrates said. "If Sparta were to become a ruin, no one would believe how powerful the Spartans really are. They don't go in for fancy temples or walls. This looks more like a collection of villages, as you say, not a proper polis. If Athens were to be deserted, visitors to the ruins would reckon us twice as strong as we really are. And yet, have the Spartans shown they can stand against us for the mastery of Hellas, or have they not?"

"They have," the other hoplite replied. "Up till now."

Now, everything in the valley of the Eurotas that would burn burned: olive groves, fields, houses, the barracks where the full Spartan citizens ate, the relative handful of shops that supported the Spartans and the *perioikoi*—those who lived among them, the second-class citizens on whose labor the Spartans proper depended. A great cloud of smoke rose into the heavens. Sokrates remembered seeing the smudges on the horizon that meant the Spartans were burning the cropland of Attica. Those had been as nothing next to this.

Down through the smoke spiraled the carrion birds—vultures and ravens and hooded crows and even jackdaws. They had not known a feast like this for long and long and long. Most of the dead were those who lived here. The folk of Sparta had tried to attack the Athenians whenever and wherever they could. Not just the men had come at them, but also the Spartan women, the women who were used to exercising naked like men and to throwing the javelin.

No, they'd shown no lack of courage. But the Athenians had stayed in a single compact body, and the Spartans, taken by surprise, had attacked them by ones and twos, by tens and twenties. The only way to beat a phalanx in the open field was with another phalanx. With most of their full citizens, their hoplites, not close enough to their home polis, the Spartans didn't, couldn't, assemble one. And they paid. Oh, how they paid.

Through the roar of the flames, an officer shouted, "We take back no prisoners. None, do you hear me? Nothing to slow us down on the march back to the fleet. If you want these Spartan women to bear half-Athenian children, do it here, do it now!"

The other hoplite said, "A woman like that, you drag her into the dirt, she's liable to try and stab you while you're on top."

"I'm too old to find rape much of a sport," Sokrates replied.

An officer called, "Come on, lend a hand on the ropes, you two! We've got to pull down this barracks hall before we set it afire!"

Sokrates and the other Athenian set down their shields and spears and went to haul on the ropes. The Athenians had guards standing close by, so Sokrates didn't worry about losing his weapons. He pulled with all his might. The corner post crashed down. Half the barracks collapsed. The Athenians cheered. A man with a torch held it to a beam till the flames took hold. When they did, another cheer rose to the heavens with the smoke.

Wearily, Sokrates strode back to pick up his equipment. A little Spartan boy—he couldn't have been more than ten—darted in like a fox to try to grab the shield and spear first. The boy had just bent to snatch them up when a peltast's javelin caught him in the small of the back. He shrieked and fell, writhing in torment. Laughing, the peltast pulled out the throwing spear. "He'll take a while to die," he said.

"That is an evil end," Sokrates said. "Let there be as much pain as war must have, but only so much." He knelt, drew his sword, and cut the boy's throat. The end came soon after that.

An old woman—older than Sokrates, too old for any of the Athenians to bother—said, "Thank you for the mercy to my grandson."

Her Doric drawl and some missing front teeth made her hard to understand, but the Athenian managed. "I did not do it for him," he replied. "I did it for myself, for the sake of what I thought to be right."

Her scrawny shoulders went up and down in a shrug. "You did it. That is what matters. He has peace now." After a moment, she added, "You know I would kill you if I could?"

He dipped his head. "Oh, yes. So the old women of Athens say of the Spartans who despoiled them of a loved one. The symmetry does not surprise me."

"Symmetry. Gylippos is dead, and you speak of symmetry." She spat at his feet. "That for your symmetry." She turned her back and walked away. Sokrates found no answer for her.

Even before the sun rose red and bloody over the smoke-filled valley of the Eurotas, Alkibiades booted the Athenian trumpeters out of sleep. "Get up, you wide-arsed catamites," he called genially. "Blare the men awake. We don't want to overstay our welcome in beautiful, charming Sparta, now do we?"

Hoplites groaned as they staggered to their feet. Spatters of fighting had gone on all through the night. If the army lingered, the fighting today wouldn't be spatters. It would be a storm, a flood, a sea. *And so*, Alkibiades thought, *we don't linger.*

Some of the men grumbled. "We haven't done enough here. Too many buildings still standing," was what Alkibiades heard most often.

He said, "The lion yawned. We reached into his mouth and gave his tongue a good yank. Do you want to hang on to it till he bites down?"

A lot of them did. They'd lost farmhouses. They'd seen olive groves that had stood for centuries hacked down and burned. They hungered for as much revenge as they could take. But they obeyed him. They followed him. He'd led them here. Without him, they never would have come. When he told them it was time to go, they were willing to believe him.

They didn't have much to eat—bread they'd brought, bread and porridge they'd stolen, whatever sheep and pigs they'd killed. That alone would have kept them from staying very long. They didn't worry about such things. Alkibiades had to.

Away they marched, back down the trail of destruction they'd left on the way to Sparta, back up toward the pass through the Taygetos Mountains. Even if nobody had pointed the way, the Spartans would have had no trouble pursuing. That didn't matter. The Spartans could chase as hard as they pleased, but they wouldn't catch up.

As he had on the way to Sparta, Nikias rode beside Alkibiades on the way back to the ships. He reminded Alkibiades of a man who'd spent too much time talking with Sokrates (though he hadn't really spent any), or of one who'd been stunned by taking hold of an electric ray. "Son of Kleinias, I never thought any man could do what you have done," he said in amazement. "Never."

"A man who believes he will fail is surely right," Alkibiades replied. "A man who believes he can do great things may yet fail, but if he succeeds. . . . Ah, if he succeeds! He who does not dare does not win. Say what you will of me, but *I dare*."

Nikias stared, shook his head—a gesture of bewilderment, not disagreement—and guided his horse off to one side. Alkibiades threw back his head and laughed. Nikias flinched as if a javelin had hissed past his head.

Halfway up the eastern slope of the mountains, where the woods came down close to the track on either side, a knot of Spartans and *perioikoi*, some armored, some in their shirts, made a stand. "They want to stall us, keep us here till pursuit can reach us," Alkibiades called. "Thermopylai was a long time ago, though. And holding the pass didn't work for these fellows then, either."

He flung his hoplites at the enemy, keeping them busy. The peltasts, meanwhile, slipped among the trees till they came out on the track behind the embattled Spartans. After that, it wasn't a fight any more. It was a slaughter.

"They were brave," Nikias said, looking at the huddled corpses, at the torn cloaks dyed red so they would not show blood.

"They were stupid," Alkibiades said. "They couldn't stop us. Since they couldn't, what was the point of trying?" Nikias opened his mouth once or twice. Now he looked like nothing so much as a tunny freshly pulled from the sea. Dismissing him from his mind, Alkibiades urged his horse forward with pressure from his knees against its barrel and a flick of the reins. He raised his voice to a shout once more: "Come on, men! Almost halfway back to the ships!"

At the height of the pass through the mountains, he looked west toward the bay where the Athenian fleet waited. He couldn't see the ships, of course, not from about a hundred stadia away, but he looked anyhow. If anything had gone wrong with them, he would end up looking just as stupid as those Spartans who'd tried to slow down the Athenian phalanx.

He lost a few men on the journey down to the seashore. One or two had their hearts give out, and fell over dead. Others, unable to bear the pace, fell out by the side of the road to rest. "We wait for nobody," Alkibiades said, over and over. "Waiting for anyone endangers everyone." Maybe some soldiers didn't believe him. Maybe they were too exhausted to care. They would later, but that would be too late.

Where was Sokrates? Alkibiades peered anxiously at the marching Athenians. The dear old boy could have been father to most of the hoplites in the force. Had he been able to stand the pace? All at once, Alkibiades burst out laughing once more. There he was, not only keeping up but volubly arguing with the younger soldier to his right. Say what you would about his ideas—and Alkibiades, despite listening to him for years, still wasn't sure about those—but the man himself was solid.

As the Athenians descended the western slopes of the Taygetos Mountains, they pointed, calling, "*Thalatta! Thalatta!*"—The sea! The sea!—and, "*Nêes! Nêes!*"—The ships! The ships! Sure enough, the transports and the triremes protecting them still waited there. Alkibiades allowed himself the luxury of a sigh of relief.

Then sand flew up under his horse's hooves. He'd reached the beach from which he and the Athenians had set out early the morning before. "We did our part," he called to the waiting sailors. "How was it here?"

"The Spartans' triremes stuck their noses in to see what we had," a man answered. "When they saw, they turned around and skedad-dled."

"Did they?" Alkibiades had hoped they would. The sailor dipped his head. Alkibiades said, "Well, best one, now we shall do the same."

"And then what?" the fellow asked.

"And then what?" Alkibiades echoed. "Why, then we head back to our polis, and we find out just who 'the people of Athens' really are." The sailor grinned. So did Alkibiades.

Down in the hold of his transport, Sokrates could see very little. That being so, he spent as little time as he could down there, and as much as he could up on the narrow strip of decking that ran from bow to stern. "For is it not unreasonable, and clean against nature," he said to a sailor who grumbled about his being up there, "for a man to travel far, and see not a bit of where he has gone?"

"I don't care about unreasonable or reasonable," the sailor said, which made Sokrates flinch. "If you get in our way, we'll chuck you down where you belong."

"I shall be very careful," Sokrates promised.

And so he was . . . for a while. The fleet had come back into the Saronic Gulf, bound for Athens and home. There was the island of Aigina—Athens' old rival—to the left, famous Salamis closer to the port of Peiraieus, with the high headland of Cape Sounion, the southeastern corner of Attica, off to the right. The sun sparkled from myriads of little waves. Seabirds dove for fish and then robbed one another, for all the world as if they were men.

Sokrates squatted on the decking and asked a rower, "How is your work here, compared to what you would be doing in a trireme?"

"Oh, it's a harder pull," the fellow answered, grunting as he stroked with the six-cubit oar. "We've only got the one deck of row-ers, and the ship's heavier than a trireme would be. Still and all, though, this has its points, too. If you're a thalamite or a zeugite in a trireme—anything but a thranite, up on the top bank of oars—the wide-arsed rogue in front of you is always farting in your face."

"Yes, I've heard Aristophanes speak of this in comedies," Sokrates said.

"Don't have to worry about that here, by Zeus," the rower said. His buttocks slid across his leather cushion as he stroked again.

Up at the bow of the transport, an officer pointed north, toward Peiraieus. "Look! A galley's coming out to meet us."

"Only one, though," a man close by him said. "I wondered if they'd bring out a fleet against us."

"They'd be sorry if they tried," the officer said. "We've got the best ships and best crews right here. They couldn't hope to match us."

"Oh, they could hope," the other man said, "but you're right— they'd be sorry." Now he pointed toward the approaching trireme. "It's the *Salaminia*."

"Haven't seen her since Sicily," the officer said sourly. "I wonder if they've heard the news about everything we did. We'll find out."

The triremes traveled ahead of the transports to protect them, but the ship carrying Sokrates was only a couple of plethra behind the warships: close enough to let him hear shouts across the water. There in the middle of the line of triremes sailed Alkibiades' flagship. The commander of the expeditionary force was easy for the men of the *Salaminia* to spot. His bright hair flashed in the sun, and he wore that purple tunic that had to be just this side of hubris. The ceremonial galley steered toward the *Thraseia*.

"Hail!" Alkibiades called to the *Salaminia* as she drew near.

"Alkibiades son of Kleinias?" someone on the other galley replied.

"Is that you again, Herakleides, who don't know who I am?" Alkibiades answered. Sokrates couldn't make out the other man's reply. Whatever it was, Alkibiades laughed and went on, "Go on back to the harbor and tell those stay-at-home fools the gods have given their judgment. We conquered Syracuse, and a government loyal to Athens rules there now. And on the way home we burned Sparta down around the haughty Spartans' ears."

By the sudden buzz—almost a roar—from the crew of the *Salaminia*, that news *hadn't* reached Athens yet. Even so, the spokesman aboard the ceremonial galley, whether Herakleides or another man, went on, "Alkibiades son of Kleinias, it seems good to the people of Athens"—the ancient formula for an Assembly decree— "for your men not to enter the city in arms, but to lay down their weapons as they disembark from their ships at Peiraieus. And it further seems good to the people of Athens that you yourself should enter the city alone before they go in, to explain to the said people of Athens your reasons for flouting their previous summons."

A rumble of anger went up from all the ships in the fleet close enough for the crews to make out the spokesman's words. "Hear that, boys?" Alkibiades shouted in a great voice. "I won the war for them, and they want to tell me to drink hemlock. *You* won the war for them, and they want to take your spears and your corselets away from you. Are we going to let 'em get away with it?"

"*Nooooo!*" The great roar came from the whole fleet, or as much of it as Alkibiades' voice could reach. Most of the rowers and the officers—and many of the hoplites, who, being belowdecks, couldn't hear so well—aboard Sokrates' transport joined in it.

"You hear that?" Alkibiades called to the *Salaminia* as aftershocks of outrage kept erupting from the wings of the fleet. "There's your answer. You can take it back to the demagogues who lie when they call themselves the people of Athens. But you'd better hurry if you do, because we're bringing it ourselves."

Being the polis' state trireme, the *Salaminia* naturally had a crack crew. Her starboard rowers pulled normally, while those on the port side backed oars. The galley spun in the water, turning almost in her own length. She also enjoyed the luxury of a dry hull, having laid up in a shipshed most of the time. That made her lighter and swifter than the ships of Alkibiades' fleet, which were waterlogged and heavy from hard service. She raced back toward Peiraieus.

The triremes that had gone to Sicily followed. So did the transports, though a little more sedately. A naked sailor nudged Sokrates. "What do you think, old-timer? We going to have to fight our way in?"

"I have opinions on a great many things," Sokrates replied. "Some of them, I hope, are true opinions. Here, however, I shall not venture any opinion. The unfolding of events will yield the answer."

"You don't know either, eh?" The sailor shrugged. "Well, we'll find out pretty cursed quick."

"I thought I just said that," Sokrates said plaintively. But the other man wasn't listening to him any more.

* * *

No triremes came forth from Peiraieus to challenge the fleet's entry. Indeed, Athens' harbor seemed all but deserted; most of the sailors and longshoremen and quayside loungers had fled. A herald bearing the staff of his office stood on a quay and shouted in a great voice, "Let all know that any who proceed in arms from this place shall be judged traitors against the city and people of Athens!"

"We *are* the city and people of Athens!" Alkibiades shouted back, and the whole fleet roared agreement. "We have done great things! We will do more!" Again, soldiers and sailors bellowed to back him up.

That sailor came back to Sokrates. "Aren't you going to arm?" he asked. "That's what the orders are."

"I shall do that which seems right," Sokrates answered, which sent the other man off scratching his head.

Sokrates went below. Down in the hold, hoplites were struggling into their armor, poking one another with elbows and knees, and cursing as they were elbowed in turn. He pushed his way through the arming foot soldiers to his own leather duffel. "Come on!" someone said to him, voice cracking with excitement. "Hurry up! High time we cleaned out that whole nest of polluted catamites!"

"Is it?" Sokrates said. "Are they? How do you know?"

The hoplite stared at him. He saw that he might as well have been speaking Persian. The soldier fixed his scabbard on his belt. He reached around his body with his right hand to make sure he could draw his sword in a hurry if he had to.

Up on deck, the oarmaster shouted, *"Oöp!"* and the rowers rested at their oars. Somebody said, "No one's here to make us fast to the pier. Furies take 'em! We'll do it ourselves." The ship swayed slightly as a sailor sprang ashore. Other sailors flung him lines. They thumped on the quays. He tied the transport to the side of the pier.

A moment later, the gangplank thudded into place. Up on deck, an officer shouted, "All hoplites out! Go down the quay and form up on dry land!" With a cheer, the soldiers—almost all of them now ready for battle—did as they were told, crowding toward the transport's stern to reach the gangplank. Duffel over his shoulder, Sokrates returned to Athenian soil, too.

This wasn't the first transport to disembark its men. On the shore, red-caped officers were bellowing, "Form a phalanx! We've got work to do yet, and we'll do it, by Zeus!" As the battle formation took shape, Sokrates started north towards Athens all by himself.

"Here, you!" a captain yelled. "Where do you think you're going?"

He stopped for a moment. "Home," he answered calmly.

"What? What are you talking about? We've got fighting to do yet," the man said.

Sokrates tossed his head. "No. When Athenian fights Athenian, who can say which side has the just cause, which the unjust? Not wishing to do the unjust or to suffer it, I shall go home. Good day." With a polite dip of the head, he started walking again.

Pounding sandals said the captain was coming after him. The man grabbed his arm. "You can't do that!"

"Oh, but I can. I will." Sokrates shook him off. The captain grabbed him again—and then, quite suddenly, found himself sitting in the dust. Sokrates kept walking.

"You'll be sorry!" the other man shouted after him, slowly getting to his feet. "Wait till Alkibiades finds out about this!"

"No one can make me sorry for doing what is right," Sokrates said. At his own pace, following his own will, he tramped along toward the city.

He was going along between the Long Walls, still at his own pace, when hoofbeats and the rhythmic thud of thousands of marching feet came from behind him. He got off the path, but kept going. Alkibiades trotted by on horseback in his purple chiton. Catching Sokrates' eye, he grinned and waved. Sokrates dipped his head again.

Alkibiades and the rest of the horsemen rode on. Behind them came the hoplites and peltasts. Behind *them* came a great throng of rowers, unarmored and armed with belt knives and whatever else they could scrounge. They moved at a fine martial tempo, and left ambling Sokrates behind. He kept walking nonetheless.

"Tyrant!" the men on the walls of Athens shouted at Alkibiades. "Impious, sacrilegious defiler of the mysteries! Herm-smasher!"

"I put my fate in the hands of the gods," Alkibiades told them, speaking for the benefit of his own soldiers as well as those who hadn't gone to Sicily. "I prayed that they destroy me if I were guilty of the charges against me, or let me live and let me triumph if I was innocent. I lived. I triumphed. The gods know the right. Do you, men of Athens?" He raised his voice: "Nikias!"

"Yes? What is it?" Nikias sounded apprehensive. Had he been in the city, he would surely have tried to hold it against Alkibiades. But he was out here, and so he could be used.

"You were there. You can tell the men of Athens whether I speak the truth. Did I not call on the gods? Did they not reward me with victory, as I asked them to do to show my innocence?"

A lie here would make Alkibiades' life much more difficult. Nikias had to know that. Alkibiades would have been tempted— more than tempted—to lie. But Nikias was a painfully honest man as well as a painfully pious one. Though he looked as if he'd just taken a big bite of bad fish, he dipped his head. "Yes, son of Kleinias. It is as you say."

His voice was barely audible to Alkibiades, let alone to the soldiers on the walls of the city. Alkibiades pointed their way, saying, "Tell the men of Athens the truth."

Nikias looked more revolted yet. Even so, he did as Alkibiades asked. *Everybody does as I ask,* Alkibiades thought complacently. Having spoken to the defenders of the city, Nikias turned back to Alkibiades. In a low, furious voice, he said, "I'll thank you to leave me out of your schemes from now on."

"What schemes, O best one?" Alkibiades asked, his eyes going wide with injured innocence. "All I asked you to do was tell the truth to the men there."

"You did it so you could seize the city," Nikias said.

"No." Alkibiades tossed his head, though the true answer was of course yes. But he went on, "Even if no one opens a gate to me, I'll hold the advantage soon enough. We draw our grain from Byzantion and beyond. I hold Peiraieus, so nothing can come in by sea. Before too long, if it comes to that, Athens will get hungry—and then she'll get hungrier. But I don't think we need to worry about that."

"Why not?" Nikias demanded. "The whole polis stands in arms against you."

"Oh, rubbish," Alkibiades said genially. "I've got at least half the polis here on the outside of the city with me. And if you think everyone in there is against me, you'd better think again. You could do worse than talk with Sokrates about the whole and its parts." As he'd expected, that provoked Nikias again. Alkibiades hid his smile and looked around. "Where *is* Sokrates, anyway?"

A hoplite standing close by answered, "He went into the city, most noble one."

"*Into* the city?" Alkibiades and Nikias said together, in identical surprise. Recovering first, Alkibiades asked, "By the dog of Egypt, how did he manage that?"

The hoplite pointed to a small postern gate. "He told the soldiers on guard there that he didn't intend to fight anybody, that he thought it was wrong for Athenians to fight Athenians"—as most men of Athens would have, he took a certain cheeky pleasure in reporting that to Alkibiades—"and that he wanted to come in and see his wife."

"To see Xanthippe? I wouldn't have thought he'd been away from home *that* long," Alkibiades said; Sokrates was married to a shrew. "But the gate guards let him in?"

"Yes, sir. I think one of them knew him," the hoplite replied.

Nikias clucked like a hen. "You see, Alkibiades? Even your pet sophist wants no part of civil war."

"He's not my pet. He's no more anyone's pet than a fox running on the hills," Alkibiades said. "And he would say he's no sophist, either. He's never taken even an obolos for teaching, you know."

Nikias went right on clucking. Alkibiades stopped listening to him. He eyed the postern gate. That Sokrates had got into Athens only proved his own point. Not all the soldiers defending the city were loyal to the men who'd tried to execute him under form of law. A little discreet talk, preferably in the nighttime when fewer outside ears might hear, and who could say what would happen next?

Alkibiades thought he could. He looked forward to finding out whether he was right.

Quietly, ever so quietly, a postern gate swung open. At Alkibiades' whispered urging the night before, the guards who held it had anointed with olive oil the posts that secured it to the stone lintel above and the stone set into the ground below. A squeak now would be ... *very embarrassing*, Alkibiades thought as he hurried toward the gate at the head of a column of hoplites.

"You shouldn't go first," one of them whispered to him. "If it's a trap, they'll nail you straightaway."

"If it's a trap, they'll nail me anyhow," he answered easily. "But if I thought it were a trap, I wouldn't be doing this, would I?"

"Who knows?" the hoplite said. "You might just figure you could talk them around once you got inside."

He laughed at that. "You're right. I might. But I don't. Come on. It's the same with a city as it is with a woman—once you're inside, you've won." The soldiers laughed, too. But Alkibiades hadn't been joking, or not very much.

He carried no spear. His left hand gripped his shield, marked with his own emblem. His right tightened on the hilt of his sword as he went through the gate, through the wall itself, and into Athens. It was indeed a penetration of sorts. *Bend forward, my polis. Here I am, taking you unawares.*

If he wasn't taking the city unawares, if his foes did have a trap waiting for him, they would spring it as soon as he came through. This would be the only moment when they knew exactly where he was. But everything inside seemed dark and quiet and sleepy. Except for his own followers, the only men who moved and talked were the guards who'd opened the gate.

In flowed his soldiers, a couple of hundred of them. He sent bands out to the right and left, to seize other gates and let in more men back from Sicily. How long would it be before the defenders realized the city was secure no more? Shouts and the sounds of fighting from another gate said the moment was here.

"Come on," Alkibiades told the rest of the men with him. "We seize the agora, we seize the Akropolis, and the city's ours."

They hurried on through darkness as near absolute as made no difference. Night was a time for sleeping. Here and there, a lamp would glow faintly behind a closed shutter. Once, Alkibiades passed the sounds of flutes and raucous, drunken singing: someone was holding a symposion, civil strife or no civil strife. The streets wandered, twisted, doubled back on themselves, dead-ended. No one not an Athenian born could have hoped to find his way.

More lights showed when Alkibiades and his comrades got to the agora. Torches flared around the Tholos. At least seventeen members of the Boulê were always on duty there. Alkibiades pointed toward the building. "We'll take it," he said. "That will leave them running around headless. Let's go, my dears. Forward!"

"*Eleleu!*" the hoplites roared. A handful of guards stood outside the building. When so many men thundered down upon them, they dropped their spears and threw up their hands. A couple of them fell to their knees to beg for mercy.

"Spare them," Alkibiades said. "We shed as little blood as we can."

A voice came from inside the Tholos: "What's that racket out there?"

Alkibiades had never been able to resist a dramatic gesture. Here, he didn't even try. Marching into the building, he displayed the Eros with a thunderbolt on his shield that had helped make him famous—or, to some people, notorious. "Good evening, O best ones," he said politely.

The councilors sprang to their feet. It was even better than he'd hoped. There with them were Androkles and Thettalos son of Kimon, two of his chief enemies—Thettalos had introduced the motion against him in the Assembly. "Alkibiades!" Androkles exclaimed in dismay. He could have sounded no more horrified if he'd seen Medusa standing before him—the last thing he would have seen before gazing upon her turned him to stone. No one else in the Tholos seemed any more delighted.

Bowing, Alkibiades answered, "Very much at your service, my dear. I will have you know that my whole army is in the city now. Those who are wise will comport themselves accordingly. Those who are not so wise will resist, for a little while—and pay the price for resisting."

He bowed again, and smiled his sweetest smile. If his enemies chose to, they could still put up a fight for Athens, and perhaps even win. He wanted them to believe they had no chance, no hope. If they did believe it, their belief would help turn it true.

"Surely you are a kakodaimon, spawned from some pit of

Tartaros!" Thettalos burst out. "We should have dealt with you before you sailed for Sicily."

"You had your chance," Alkibiades answered. "When the question of who mutilated the herms first came up, I asked for a speedy trial. I wanted my name cleared before the fleet sailed. You were the ones who delayed."

"We needed to find witnesses who would talk," Thettalos said.

"You needed to invent witnesses who would lie, you mean," Alkibiades answered.

"They aren't lying. They speak the truth," Thettalos said stubbornly.

"I tell you, they lie." Alkibiades cocked his head to one side. Yes, that was the sound of hoplites moving through the city, shields now and then clanking on greaves and corselets. And that was the sound of his name in the hoplites' mouths. He'd told the truth here after all. By all appearances, his soldiers *did* hold Athens. He turned back to the men in the Tholos. "And I tell you this is your last chance to surrender and spare your lives. If you wait till my main force gets here, that will be too late. What do you say, gentlemen of Athens?" He used the title with savage irony.

They said what he'd thought they would: "We yield." It was a glum, grumbling chorus, but a chorus nonetheless.

"Take them away," Alkibiades told the soldiers with him. "We'll put some honest people in the Tholos instead." Laughing and grinning, the hoplites led the men of the Boulê out into the night. Alkibiades stayed behind. He set down his shield and flung his arms wide in delight. *At last!* he thought. *By all the gods—if gods there be—at last! Athens is mine!*

As if nothing had changed in the polis, Simon the shoemaker drove hobnails into the sole of a sandal. As if nothing had changed, a small crowd of youths and young men gathered under the shade of the olive tree outside his shop. And, as if nothing had changed, Sokrates still argued with them about whatever came to mind.

He showed no inclination to talk about what had happened while he was away. After a while, a boy named Aristokles, who couldn't have been above twelve, piped up: "Do you think your daimon was right, Sokrates, in urging you to go to the west?"

However young he was, he had a power and clarity to his thought that appealed to Sokrates. He'd phrased his question with a man's directness, too. Sokrates wished he could answer so directly. After some hesitation—unusual for him—he said, "We won a victory in Sicily, which can only be good for the polis. And we won a victory in Sparta, where no foreign foe has ever won before. The Kings of Sparta are treating with Alkibiades for peace even while we speak here. That too can only be good for the polis."

He sought truth like a lover pursuing his beloved. He always had. He always would. Here today, though, he wouldn't have been disappointed to have his reply taken as full agreement, which it was not. And Aristokles saw as much, saying, "And yet you still have doubts. Why?"

"I know why," Kritias said. "On account of Alkibiades, that's why."

Sokrates knew why Kritias spoke as he did—he was sick-jealous of Alkibiades. The other man had done things in Athens Kritias hadn't matched and couldn't hope to match. Ambition had always blazed in Kritias, perhaps to do good for his polis, certainly to do well for himself. Now he saw himself outdone, outdone by too much to make it even a contest. All he could do was fume.

Which did not mean he was altogether wrong. Alkibiades worried Sokrates, and had for years. He was brilliant, clever, handsome, dashing, charming—and, in him, all those traits led to vice as readily as to virtue. Sokrates had done everything he could to turn Alkibiades in the direction he should go. But another could do only so much; in the end, a man had to do for himself, too.

Aristokles' eyes flicked from Sokrates to Kritias (they had a family connection, Sokrates recalled) and back again. "Is he right?" the boy asked. "Do you fear Alkibiades?"

"I fear *for* Alkibiades," Sokrates answered. "Is it not reasonable that a man who has gained an uncommon amount of power should also have an uncommon amount of attention aimed at him to see what he does with it?"

"Surely he has done nothing wrong yet," Aristokles said.

"Yet," Kritias murmured.

The boy ignored that, which most men would have found hard to do. He said, "Why should we aim uncommon attention at a man who has done nothing wrong, unless we seek to learn his virtues and imitate them?"

Kritias said, "When we speak of Alkibiades, at least as many would seek to learn his vices and imitate *them*."

"Yes, many might do that," Aristokles said. "But is it right that they should?"

"Who cares whether it is right? It is *true*," Kritias said.

"Wait." Sokrates held up a hand, then waved out toward the agora. "Hail, Kritias. I wish no more of your company today, nor that of any man who asks, 'Who cares whether it is right?' For what could be more important than that? How can a man who knows what is right choose what is wrong?"

"Why ask me?" Kritias retorted. "Better you should inquire of Alkibiades."

That held enough truth to sting, but Sokrates was too angry to care. He waved again, more vehemently than before. "Get out. You are not welcome here until you mend your tongue, or, better, your spirit."

"Oh, I'll go," Kritias said. "But you blame me when you ought to blame yourself, for you taught Alkibiades the virtue he so blithely ignores." He stalked off.

Again, that arrow hadn't missed its target. Pretending not to feel the wound, Sokrates turned back to the other men standing under the olive tree. "Well, my friends, where were we?"

They did not break up till nearly sunset. Then Aristokles came over to Sokrates and said, "Since my kinsman will not apologize for himself, please let me do it in his place."

"You are gracious," Sokrates said with a smile. Aristokles was worth smiling at: he was a good-looking boy, and would make a striking youth in two or three years, although broad shoulders and a squat build left him short of perfection. However pleasant he was to see, though, Sokrates went on, "How can any man act in such a way on another's behalf?"

With a sigh, Aristokles answered, "In truth, I cannot. But I wish I could."

That made Sokrates' smile get wider. "A noble wish. You are one who seeks the good, I see. That is not common in one so young. Truth to tell, it is not common at any age, but less so in the very young, who have not reflected on these things."

"I can see in my mind the images—the *forms*, if you like—of perfect good, of perfect truth, of perfect beauty," Aristokles said. "In the world, though, they are always flawed. How do we, how can we, approach them?"

"Let us walk." Sokrates set a hand on the boy's shoulder, not in physical longing but in a painful hope he had almost abandoned. Had he at last met someone whose thoughts might march with his? Even so young, the eagle displayed its claws.

They talked far into the night.

King Agis was a short, muscular man with a scar on the upper lip he shaved in the usual Spartan fashion. His face wore what looked like a permanent scowl. He had to fight to hold the expression, because he plainly kept wanting to turn and gape at everything he saw in Athens. However much he wanted to, though, he didn't, which placed him a cut above the usual run of country bumpkins seeing the big city for the first time.

"Hail," Alkibiades said smoothly, holding out his hands. "Welcome to Athens. Let us have peace, if we can."

Agis' right hand was ridged with callus, hard as a rower's. He'd toughened it with swordhilt and spearshaft, though, and not with the oar. "Hail," he replied. "Yes, let us have peace. Boys who were at their mothers' breasts when we began this fight are old enough to wear armor now. And what have we got for it? Only our homeland ravaged. Enough, I say. Let us have peace." The word seemed all the more emphatic in his flat Doric drawl.

He said nothing about the way the Spartans had devastated Attica for years. Alkibiades hadn't expected him to. A man didn't feel it when he stepped on someone else's toes, only when his own got hurt.

Confirming that, Agis went on, "I thought no man could do what you did to my polis. Since you did . . ." He grimaced. "Yes, let us have peace."

"My terms are not hard," Alkibiades said. "Here in Hellas, let all be as it was before the war began. In Sicily . . . Well, we won in Sicily. We will not give back what we won. If you had done the same, neither would you."

Grimly, Agis dipped his head in agreement. He said, "I can rely on you to get the people of Athens to accept these terms?"

"You can rely on me to get these terms accepted in this polis," Alkibiades answered. How much the people of Athens would have to do with that, he didn't know. His own position was . . . irregular. He was not a magistrate. He had been a general, yes, but the campaign for which he'd commanded was over. And yet, he was unquestionably the most powerful man in the city. Soldiers leaped to do his bidding. He didn't want the name of tyrant—tyrants attracted tyrannicides as honey drew flies—but he had everything except that name.

"I would treat with no one else," Agis said. "You beat us. You shamed us. You should have been a Spartan yourself. You should breed sons on our women, that we might add your bloodline to our stock." He might have been talking of horses.

"You are gracious, but I have women enough here," Alkibiades said. Inside, he laughed. Would Agis offer his own wife next? What was her name? Timaia, that was it. If King Agis did, it would insure that Alkibiades' descendants ruled Sparta. He liked the idea.

But Agis did no such thing. Instead, he said, "If we are to have no more war, son of Kleinias, how shall we live at peace? For both of us aim to rule all of Hellas."

"Yes." Alkibiades rubbed his chin. Agis might be dour, but he was no fool. The Athenian went on, "Hear me. While we fought, who ruled Hellas? My polis? No. Yours? No again. Anyone's? Not at all. The only ruler Hellas had was war. Whereas if we both pull together, like two horses in harness pulling a chariot, who knows where we might go?"

Agis stood stock-still for some little while, considering that. At last, he said, "I can think of a place where we might go if we pull in harness," and spoke one word more.

Now Alkibiades laughed out loud. He leaned forward and kissed Agis on the cheek, as if the King of Sparta were a pretty boy. "Do you know, my dear," he said, "we are not so very different after all."

Kritias strode through the agora in a perfect transport of fury. He might have been a whirlwind trying to blow down everything around him. He made not the slightest effort to restrain himself or keep his voice down. When he drew near the Tholos—in fact, even before he drew very near the Tholos—his words were plainly audible under the olive tree in front of Simon's cobbler's shop. They were not only audible, they were loud enough to make the discussion already under way beneath that olive tree falter.

"Us, yoked together with the Spartans?" Kritias raged. "You might as well yoke a dolphin and a wolf! They will surely turn on us and rend us first chance they get!"

"What do you think of that, Sokrates?" a young man asked.

Before Sokrates could answer, someone else said, "Kritias is just jealous he didn't think of it himself. If he had, he'd be screaming every bit as loud that it's the best thing that could possibly happen to Athens."

"Quiet," another man said in a quick, low voice. "That's Kritias' kinsman over there by Sokrates." He jerked a thumb at Aristokles.

"So?" said the man who'd spoken before. "I don't care if that's Kritias' mother over there by Sokrates. It's still true."

Sokrates looked across the agora at the rampaging Kritias. His former pupil came to a stop by the statues of Harmodios and Aristogeiton near the center of the market square. There under the images of the young men said to have liberated Athens from her last tyranny, his fist pumping furiously, he harangued a growing crowd.

With a sigh, Sokrates said, "How is a man who cannot control himself to see clearly what the good is and what it is not?" Slowly and deliberately, he turned his back on Kritias. "Since he is not *quite* so noisy as he was, shall we resume our own discussion? Is knowledge innate and merely evoked by teachers, or do teachers impart new knowledge to those who study under them?"

"You have certainly shown me many things I never knew before, Sokrates," a man named Apollodoros said.

"Ah, but did I show them to you for the first time, or did I merely bring them to light?" Sokrates replied. "That is what we need to. . . ."

He stopped, for the others weren't listening to him any more. That irked him; he had an elegant demonstration planned, one that would use a slave boy of Simon's to show that knowledge already existed and merely wanted bringing forth. But no one was paying any attention to him. Instead, his followers stared out into the agora, toward the statues of Harmodios and Aristogeiton and toward Kritias.

Part of Sokrates didn't want to look, not when he'd already turned away. But he was no less curious than any other Hellene: was, indeed, perhaps more curious about more different things than any other Hellene. And so, muttering curses under his breath like the stonecutter he had been for so long, he looked back into the market square himself.

Three men, he saw, had come up out of the crowd and surrounded Kritias. "They wouldn't dare," somebody—Sokrates thought it was Apollodoros, but he wasn't sure—said just as Kritias shoved one of the men away from him. Things happened very quickly after that. All three men—they wore only tunics and went barefoot, as sailors usually did—drew knives. The sun sparkled off the blades' sharp edges. They stabbed Kritias, again and again. His bubbling shriek and the cries of horror from the crowd filled the agora. As he fell, the murderers loped off. A few men started to chase them, but one of them turned back to threaten the pursuers with his now-bloody weapon. They drew back. The three men made good their escape.

With a low wail, Aristokles dashed out toward his fallen relative. Sokrates hurried after the boy to keep anything from happening to him. Several of the other men who frequented the shade in front of Simon's shop trailed along behind them.

"Make way!" Aristokles shouted, his voice full of command even though it had yet to break. "Make way, there! I am Kritias' kinsman!"

People *did* step aside for him. Sokrates followed in his wake, but realized before he got very close to Kritias that Aristokles could do nothing for him now. He lay on his back in a still-spreading pool of his own blood. He'd been stabbed in the chest, the belly, and the throat—probably from behind, as well, but Sokrates couldn't see that. His eyes were wide and staring and unblinking. His chest neither rose nor fell.

Aristokles knelt beside him, careless of the blood. "Who did this?" he asked, and then answered his own question: "Alkibiades." No one contradicted him. He reached out and closed Kritias' eyes. "My kinsman was, perhaps, not the best of men, but he did not deserve—this. He shall be avenged." Unbroken voice or not, he sounded every bit a man.

The Assembly never met to ratify Alkibiades' peace with Sparta. His argument—to the degree that he bothered making an argument—was that the peace was so self-evidently good, it needed no formal approval. That subverted the Athenian constitution, but few people complained out loud. Kritias' murder made another sort of argument, one prudent men could not ignore. So did the untimely demise of a young relative of his who might have thought his youth granted his outspokenness immunity.

Over the years, the Athenians had called Sokrates a great many things. Few, though, had ever called him lacking in courage. A couple of weeks after Kritias died—and only a couple of days after Aristokles was laid to rest—Sokrates walked out across the agora from the safe, comfortable shade of the olive tree in front of Simon the shoemaker's toward the statues of Harmodios and Aristogeiton in the heart of the market square. Several of his followers came along with him.

Apollodoros tugged at his chiton. "You don't have to do this," he said in a choked voice, as if about to burst into tears.

"No?" Sokrates looked around. "Men need to hear the truth. Men need to speak the truth. Do you see anyone else doing those things?" He kept walking.

"But what will happen to you?" Apollodoros wailed.

"What will happen to Athens?" Sokrates answered.

He took his place where Kritias must have stood. Blood still stained the base of Aristogeiton's statue. Blocky and foursquare, Sokrates stood and waited. The men and youths who listened to him formed the beginnings of an audience—and the Athenians recognized the attitude of a man about to make a speech. By ones and twos, they wandered over to hear what he had to say.

"Men of Athens, I have always tried to do the good, so far as I could see what that was," he began. "For I believe the good is most important to man: more important than ease, more important than wealth, more important even than peace. Our grandfathers could have had peace with Persia by giving the Great King's envoys earth and water. Yet they saw that was not good, and they fought to stay free.

"Now we have peace with Sparta. Is it good? Alkibiades says it is. Someone asked that question once before, and now that man is dead, as is his young kinsman who dared be outraged at an unjust death. We all know who arranged these things. I tell no secrets. And I tell no secrets when I say these murders were not good."

"You were the one who taught Alkibiades!" someone called.

"I tried to teach him the good and the true, or rather to show him what was already in his mind, as it is in all our minds," Sokrates replied. "Yet I must have failed, for what man, knowing the good, would willingly do evil? And the murder of Kritias, and especially that of young Aristokles, was evil. How can anyone doubt that?"

"What do we do about it, then?" asked someone in the crowd—not one of Sokrates' followers.

"We are Athenians," he replied. "If we are not a light for Hellas to follow, who is? We rule ourselves, and have for a century, since we cast out the last tyrants, the sons of Peisistratos." He set his hand on the statue of Aristogeiton, reminding the men who listened why that statue stood here. "The sons of Peisistratos were the last tyrants before Alkibiades, I should say. We Athenians beat the Persians. We have beaten the Spartans. We—"

"Alkibiades beat the Spartans!" somebody else yelled.

"I was there, my good fellow. Were you?" Sokrates asked. Sudden silence answered him. Into it, he went on, "Yes, Alkibiades led us. But we Athenians triumphed. Peisistratos was a fine general, too, or so they say. Yet he was also a tyrant. Will any man deny that? Alkibiades the man has good qualities. We all know as much. Alkibiades the tyrant . . . What qualities can a tyrant have, save those *of* a tyrant?"

"Do you say we should cast him out?" a man called.

"I say we should do what is good, what is right. We are men. We know what that is," Sokrates said. "We have known what the good is since before birth. If you need me to remind you of it, I will do that. It is why I stand here before you now."

"Alkibiades won't like it," another man predicted in a doleful voice.

Sokrates shrugged broad shoulders. "I have not liked many of the things he has done. If he does not care for my deeds, I doubt I shall lose any sleep over that."

Bang! Bang! Bang! The pounding on the door woke Sokrates and Xanthippe at the same time. It was black as pitch inside their bedroom. "Stupid drunk," Xanthippe grumbled when the racket went on and on. She pushed at her husband. "Go out there and tell the fool he's trying to get into the wrong house."

"I don't think he is," Sokrates answered as he got out of bed.

"What are you talking about?" Xanthippe demanded.

"Something I said in the market square. I seem to have been wrong," Sokrates said. "Here I am, losing sleep after all."

"You waste too much time in the agora." Xanthippe shoved him again as the pounding got louder. "Now go give that drunk a piece of your mind."

"Whoever is out there, I do not think he is drunk." But Sokrates pulled his chiton on over his head. He went out through the crowded little courtyard where Xanthippe grew herbs and up to the front door. As he unbarred it, the pounding stopped. He opened the door. Half a dozen large, burly men stood outside. Three carried torches. They all carried cudgels. "Hail, friends," Sokrates said mildly. "What do you want that cannot keep till morning?"

"Sokrates son of Sophroniskos?" one of the bruisers demanded.

"That's Sokrates, all right," another one said, even as Sokrates dipped his head.

"Got to be sure," the first man said, and then, to Sokrates, "Come along with us."

"And if I don't?" he asked.

They all raised their bludgeons. "You will—one way or the other," the leader said. "Your choice. Which is it?"

"What does the idiot want, Sokrates?" Xanthippe shrilled from the back of the house.

"Me," he said, and went with the men into the night.

Alkibiades yawned. Even to him, an experienced roisterer, staying up into the middle of the night felt strange and unnatural. Once the sun went down, most people went to bed and waited for morning. Most of the time, even roisterers did. The clay lamps that cast a faint, flickering yellow light over this bare little courtyard and filled it with the smell of burning olive oil were a far cry from Helios' bright, warm, cheerful rays.

A bat fluttered down, snatched a moth out of the air near a lamp, and disappeared again. "Hate those things," muttered one of the men in the courtyard with Alkibiades. "They can't be natural."

"People have said the same thing about me," Alkibiades answered lightly. "I will say, though, that I'm prettier than a bat." He preened. He might have had reason to be, but he *was* vain about his looks.

His henchmen chuckled. The door to the house opened. "Here they are," said the man who didn't like bats. "About time, too."

In came Sokrates, in the midst of half a dozen ruffians. "Hail," Alkibiades said. "I wish you hadn't forced me to this."

Sokrates cocked his head to one side and studied him. He showed only curiosity, not fear, though he had to know what lay ahead for him. "How can one man force another to do anything?" he asked. "How, especially, can one man force another to do that which he knows not to be good?"

"This is good—for me," Alkibiades answered. "You have been making a nuisance of yourself in the agora."

"A nuisance?" Sokrates tossed his head. "I am sorry, but whoever told you these things is misinformed. I have spoken the truth and asked questions that might help others decide what is true."

Voice dry, Alkibiades said, "That constitutes being a nuisance, my dear. If you criticize me, what else are you but a nuisance?"

"A truth-teller, as I said before," Sokrates replied. "You must know this. We have discussed it often enough." He sighed. "I think my daimon was wrong to bid me accompany you to Sicily. I have never known it to be wrong before, but how can you so lightly put aside what has been shown to be true?"

"True, you showed me the gods cannot be as Homer and Hesiod imagined them," Alkibiades said. "But you have drawn the wrong lesson from that. You say we should live as if the gods were there watching us, even though they are not."

"And so we should, for our own sake," Sokrates said.

"But if the gods are not, O best one, why not grab with both hands?" Alkibiades asked. "This being all I have, I intend to make the most of it. And if anyone should stand in the way . . ." He shrugged. "Too bad."

The henchman who didn't like bats said, "Enough of this chatter. Give him the drug. It's late. I want to go home."

Alkibiades held up a small black-glazed jar with three horizontal incised grooves showing the red clay beneath the glaze. "Hemlock," he told Sokrates. "It's fairly quick and fairly easy—and a lot less messy than what Kritias got."

"Generous of you," Sokrates remarked. He stepped forward and reached out to take the jar. Alkibiades' henchmen let him advance. Why not? If he'd swallow the poison without any fuss, so much the better.

But, when he got within a couple of paces of Alkibiades, he shouted out, *"Eleleu!"* and flung himself at the younger man. The jar of hemlock smashed on the hard dirt of the courtyard. Alkibiades knew at once he was fighting for his life. Sokrates gave away twenty years, but his stocky, broad-shouldered frame seemed nothing but rock-hard muscle.

He and Alkibiades rolled in the dirt, punching and cursing and gouging and kneeing and kicking each other. This was the pankration, the all-in fight of the Olympic and Panathenaic Games, without even the handful of rules the Games enforced. Alkibiades tucked his head down into his chest. The thumb that would have extracted one of his eyes scraped across his forehead instead.

Back when he was a youth, he'd sunk his teeth into a foe who'd got a good wrestling hold on him. "You bite like a woman!" the other boy had cried.

"No, like a lion!" he answered.

He'd bitten then because he couldn't stand to lose. He bit now to keep Sokrates from getting a meaty forearm under his chin and strangling him. Sokrates roared. His hot, salty blood filled Alkibiades' mouth. Alkibiades dug an elbow into his belly, but it might have been made from the marble that had gone into the Parthenon.

Shouting, Alkibiades' henchmen ran up and started clubbing Sokrates. The only trouble was, they hit Alkibiades nearly as often. Then, suddenly, Sokrates groaned and went limp. Alkibiades scrambled away from him. The hilt of a knife stood in the older man's back. The point, surely, had reached his heart.

Sokrates' eyes still held reason as he stared up at Alkibiades. He tried to say something, but only blood poured from his mouth. The hand he'd raised fell back. A stench filled the courtyard; his bowels had let go in death.

"*Pheu!*" Alkibiades said, just starting to feel his aches and bruises. "He almost did for me there."

"Who would've thought the old blabbermouth could fight like that?" one of his followers marveled, surprise and respect in his voice.

"He was a blabbermouth, sure enough." Alkibiades bent down and closed the staring eyes. Gently, as a lover might, he kissed Sokrates on the cheek and on the tip of the snub nose. "He was a blabbermouth, yes, but oh, by the gods! he was a man."

Alkibiades and King Agis of Sparta stood side by side on the speakers' platform in the Pnyx, the fan-shaped open area west of the agora where the Athenian Assembly convened. Since Alkibiades had taken the rule of Athens into his own hands, this wasn't really a meeting of the Assembly. But, along with the theater of Dionysos, the Pnyx still made a convenient place to gather the citizens so he—and Agis—could speak to them.

Along with the milling, chattering Athenians, several hundred Spartans who had come up from the Peloponnesos with Agis occupied a corner of the Pnyx. They stood out not only for their red cloaks and shaven upper lips: they stayed in place without movement or talk. Next to the voluble locals, they might almost have been statues.

Nor were they the only Hellenes from other poleis here today. Thebes had sent a delegation to Athens. So had Corinth. So had the Thessalians, from the towns in the north of Hellas proper. And so had the half-wild Macedonians. Their envoys kept staring every which way, especially back toward the Akropolis. Nodding toward them, Alkibiades murmured to Agis, "They haven't got anything like this up in their backwoods country."

"We have nothing like this, either," Agis said. "I doubt whether so much luxury is a good thing."

"It hasn't spoiled us or made us soft," Alkibiades replied. *As you have reason to know.* He didn't say that. It hung in the air nonetheless.

"Yes," Agis said laconically.

What Alkibiades did say was, "We've spent enough time—too much time—fighting among ourselves. If Athens and Sparta agree, if the rest of Hellas—and even Macedonia—follows . . ."

"Yes," Agis said again. This time, he added, "That is why I have come. This job is worth doing, and Sparta cannot do it alone. Neither can Athens."

Getting a bit of your own back? Alkibiades wondered. It wasn't as if Agis were wrong. Alkibiades gestured to a herald who stood on the platform with him and the Spartan. The man stepped up and called in a great voice, "People of Hellas, hear the words of Alkibiades, leader of Hellas, and of Agis, King of Sparta."

Leader sounded ever so much better than *tyrant*, even if they amounted to the same thing. Alkibiades took a step forward. He loved having thousands of pairs of eyes on him, where Agis seemed uncomfortable under that scrutiny. Agis, of course, was King because of his bloodline. Alkibiades had had to earn all the attention he'd got. He'd had to, and he'd done it.

Now he said, "People of Hellas, you see before you Athenian and Spartan, with neither one quarreling over who should lead us Hellenes in *his* direction." *Of course we're not quarreling,* he thought. *I've won.* He wondered how well Agis understood that. Such worries, though, would have to wait for another time. He went on, "For too long, Hellenes have fought other Hellenes. And while we fought among ourselves, while we spent our own treasure and our own blood, who benefited? Who smiled? Who, by the gods, laughed?"

A few of the men in the audience—the more clever, more alert ones—stirred, catching his drift. The rest stood there, waiting for him to explain. *Sokrates would have understood.* The gouge on Alkibiades' forehead was only a pink scar now. *Sokrates would have said I'm pointing the Athenians in a new direction so they don't look* my *way. He would have been right, too. But now he's dead, and not too many miss him. He wasn't a nuisance only to me.*

Such musing swallowed no more than a couple of heartbeats. Aloud, Alkibiades continued, "In our grandfathers' day, the Great Kings of Persia tried to conquer Hellas with soldiers, and found they could not. We have men in Athens still alive who fought at Marathon and Salamis and Plataia."

A handful of those ancient veterans stood in the crowd, white-bearded and bent and leaning on sticks like the last part of the answer to the riddle of the Sphinx. Some of them cupped a hand behind an ear to follow him better. What they'd seen in their long lives!

"Since then, though, Hellenes have battled other Hellenes and forgotten the common foe," Alkibiades said. "Indeed, with all his gold Great King Dareios II has sought to buy mastery of Hellas, and has come closer to gaining it than Kyros and Xerxes did with their great swarms of men. For enmities among us suit Persia well. She gains from our disunion what she could not with spears and arrows.

"A lifetime ago, Great King Xerxes took Athens and burnt it. We have made it a finer polis, a grander polis, since, but our ashes are yet unavenged. Only when we Hellenes have burnt Persepolis to the ground can we say we are, at last, even with the Persians."

Some fellow from Halikarnassos had written a great long book about the struggles between Hellenes and Persians. The burning of Athens was the least of it; he'd traced the conflict back even before the days of the Trojan War. What was his name? Alkibiades couldn't recall. It didn't matter. People knew Athens had gone up in flames. The rest? Long ago and far away.

Almost everyone in the Pnyx saw where he was going now. A low, excited murmur ran through the crowd. He continued, "We've shown one thing, and shown it plainly. *Only Hellenes can beat other Hellenes.* The Great King knows as much. That's why he hires mercenaries from Hellas. But if all our poleis pull together, if all our poleis send hoplites and rowers and ships against Persia, not even those traitors can hope to hold us back.

"Persia and the wealth of Persia will be ours. We will have new lands to rule, new lands to settle. We won't have to expose unwanted infants any more. They will have places where they can live. The Great King's treasury will fall into *our* hands. Now we starve for silver. Once we beat the Persians, we'll have our fill of gold."

No more low, excited murmur. Now the people in the Pnyx burst into cheers. Alkibiades watched the Spartans. They were shouting as loud as the Athenians. The idea of a war against Persia made them forget their usual reserve. The Thebans cheered, too, as did the men from the towns of Thessaly. During Xerxes' invasion, they'd given the Persians earth and water in token of submission.

And the Macedonians cheered more enthusiastically still, pounding one another and their neighbors on the back. Seeing that made Alkibiades smile. For one thing, the Macedonians had also yielded to the Persians. For another, he had no intention of using them to any great degree in his campaign against Persia. Their King, Perdikkas son of Alexandros, was a hill bandit who squabbled with other hill bandits nearby. Macedonia had always been like that. It always would be. Expecting it to amount to anything was a waste of time, a waste of hope.

Alkibiades stepped back and waved King Agis forward. The Spartan said, "Alkibiades has spoken well. We owe our forefathers revenge against Persia. We can win it. We should win it. We *will* win it. So long as we stand together, no one can stop us. Let us go on, then, on to victory!"

He stepped back. More cheers rang out. In his plain way, he had spoken well. An Athenian would have been laughed off the platform for such a bare-bones speech, but standards were different for the Spartans. *Poor fellows*, Alkibiades thought. *They can't help being dull.*

He eyed Agis. Just how dull *was* the Spartan King? *So long as we stand together, no one can stop us.* That was true. Alkibiades was sure of it. But how long *would* the Hellenes stand together? Long enough to beat Great King Dareios? Fighting a common foe would help.

How long *after* beating the Persians would the Hellenes stand together? *Till we start quarreling over who will rule the lands we've won.* Alkibiades eyed Agis again. Did he see that, too, or did he think they would go on sharing? He might. Spartans could be slow on the uptake.

I am alone at the top of Athens now, Alkibiades thought. *Soon I will be alone at the top of the civilized world, from Sicily all the way to India. This must be what Sokrates' daimon saw. This must be why it sent him to Sicily with me, to smooth my way to standing here at the pinnacle. Sure enough, it knew what it was doing, whether he thought so or not.* Alkibiades smiled at Agis. Agis, fool that he was, smiled back.

The Real History Behind "The Daimon"

In the real world, Sokrates did not accompany the Athenians' expedition to Sicily in 415 B.C.E. As told in the story, Alkibiades' political foes in Athens did arrange his recall. In real history, he left the expedition but fled on the way to Athens. He eventually wound up in Sparta, the Athenians' bitter foe in the Peloponnesian War, and advised the Spartans to aid Syracuse and to continue the war against Athens. (He also, incidentally, fathered a bastard on King Agis' wife, whose bed Agis was avoiding due to religious scruples.)

The Athenian expedition, despite substantial reinforcements in 413 B.C.E., was a disastrous failure. It did not take Syracuse, and few of the approximately 50,000 hoplites and sailors sent west ever saw Athens again. Nikias, who headed the force after Alkibiades' recall, was executed by the Syracusans. Alkibiades returned to the Athenian side, then abandoned Athens' cause after further political strife and was murdered in 404 B.C.E. In that same year, the Spartans decisively defeated the Athenians and, at a crushing cost, won the Peloponnesian War.

In the aftermath of the war, Sokrates' pupil Kritias became the head of the Thirty Tyrants, and was killed during the civil war leading to the restoration of Athenian democracy in 403 B.C.E. Sokrates himself, convicted on a charge of bringing new gods to Athens, drank hemlock in 399 B.C.E., refusing to flee, though many might have wished he would have gone into exile instead. His pupil Aristokles—far more often known as Platon because of his broad shoulders—survived for more than half a century; it is through the writings of Platon, Xenophon, and Aristophanes that we know Sokrates, who himself left nothing in writing.

In real history, the assault on Persia waited until the reign of Alexander the Great (336–323 B.C.E.), and occurred under Macedonian domination, not that of the Hellenic poleis.

Harry Turtledove was born in Los Angeles in 1949. After flunking out of Caltech, he earned a Ph.D. in Byzantine history from UCLA. He has taught ancient and medieval history at UCLA, Cal State Fullerton, and Cal State L.A., and has published a translation of a ninth-century Byzantine chronicle and several scholarly articles. He is, however, primarily a full-time science fiction and fantasy writer; much of his work involves either alternate histories or historically based fantasy.

Among his science fiction are the alternate history novel *The Guns of the South*; the *Worldwar* series (an alternate history involving alien invasion during World War II); *How Few Remain*, a Nebula finalist; and *Ruled Britannia*, set largely in the theatres of Shakespeare's London in a world where the Spanish Armada was successful.

His alternate history novella, "Down in the Bottomlands," won the 1994 Hugo Award in its category. An alternate history novelette, "Must and Shall," was a 1996 Hugo and 1997 Nebula finalist. The science-fiction novella "Forty, Counting Down" was a 2000 Hugo finalist, and is under option for film production.

He is married to fellow novelist Laura Frankos Turtledove. They have three daughters, Alison, Rachel, and Rebecca.

Shikari
in Galveston

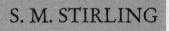

S. M. STIRLING

PROLOGUE: A FEASTING OF DEMONS

"I told you not to eat him!" the man in the black robe said. "Come out!"

He was alone, standing on a slight hillock amid the low marshy ground. The log canoe behind him held more—three Cossack riflemen, their weapons ready, a young woman lying bound at their feet, and a thick-muscled man with burn scars on his hands and arms. He whimpered and cowered and muttered *pajalsta*—please, please— over and over until he was cuffed into silence by one of the soldiers.

Beyond them the tall gloom of the cypresses turned the swamp into a pool of olive-green shadow, in which the Spanish moss hung in motionless curtains. There was little sound; a *plop* as a cottonmouth slipped off a rotting log and into the dark water, and muffled with distance the dull booming roar of a bull alligator proclaiming his territory to the world. The air was warm and rank, full of the smell of decay . . . and a harder odor, one of crusted filth and animal rot.

"Come out!" the one in black snapped again; he was a stocky man in his middle years, black-haired, with a pale high-cheekboned face and slanted gray eyes.

They did; first one, then a few more, then a score, then a hundred. The man laughed in delight at the sight of them: the thickset shambling forms, the scarred faces and filed teeth, the roiling stink. One with a bone through his broad nose and more in his clay-caked mop of hair came wriggling on his belly like a snake through the mud to press his forehead into the dirt at the man's feet.

"Master, master," the figure whined—in his language it was a slightly different form of the word for *killer*, and closely related to the verb *to eat*.

"He sickened," the savage gobbled apologetically. "We only ate him when he could not work."

The robed man drew back a foot and kicked him in the face; the prone figure groveled and whimpered.

"A likely story! But the Black God is good to His servants. I have brought you another blacksmith . . . and weapons."

He half turned and signaled. Most of the men in the canoes kept their rifles ready and pointed; a few dragged boxes of hatchets and knives out and bore them ashore. A moaning chorus came from the figures, and hands reached out eagerly. The man in black uncoiled a whip from his belt and lashed them back.

"Who do you serve?" he asked harshly.

"The Black God! The Black God!" they called.

"Good. See you remember it. Keep this man healthy! Set more of your young to learning the smelting and working of the iron! No one is to hunt or kill or eat such men, for they are valuable! It is more pleasing to the Black God when you eat His enemies than when you prey on each other—"

He let the moaning chorus of obedience go on for a moment while he lashed them with words, then signaled; the young woman was pushed forward. She was naked, a plump swarthy Kaijan girl trying to scream through the gag that covered her mouth. There would be a time for her to scream, but not quite yet.

"And the Black God has brought you food, tender and juicy!" the robed man called, laughing and grabbing her by the back of the neck in one iron-fingered hand. She squealed like a butchered rabbit through the cloth as the eyes of the watchers focused on her.

A moment's silence, and another cry went up, hot and eager: "*Eat! Eat!*"

"We shall eat, my children," he laughed. "But the killing must be as the God desires, eh? Prepare the altar!"

They scurried to obey. When the work was done, the man who commanded their service drew a long curved knife from his girdle; the rippling damascened shape was sharp enough to part a hair, unlike the crude blades of the savages.

"If you want the Black God to favor you, you must kill his enemies—kill them in fight, on the altar, by ambush and stealth. Kill them! Take their lands! Hunt them down!"

"*Kill! Kill all Tall Ones! Kill and eat!*" A vicious eagerness was in the words, and an ancient hate.

"And on that good day, I shall return to bring you His blessing! Now we shall make sacrifice, and feast."

He reached down and flicked off the gag, and the sacrifice gave the first of the cries prescribed in the rite, as he swept the blade of the khindjal from throat to pubis in an initial, very shallow cut. The man sighed with pleasure and swept his arms open and up, invoking the Peacock Angel.

"*Eat!*" the swamp-men screamed. "*Eat!*"

Technically, they should be chanting the Black God's name at this point in the ritual. But it was all the same, in the end. For would not Tchernobog eat all the world, in time? He cut again, again . . .

"*Eat! Eat!*"

I: THE BEAR IN HIS STRENGTH

Robre—Robre sunna Jowan, gift-named the Hunter, of the Bear Creek clan of the Cross Plains tribe—grunted as he strode southward past the peeled wands that marked the boundaries of the Dannulsford Fair. There were eleven new heads set on tall stakes in the scrubby pasture outside the stockade, fresh enough with the fall chill that the features could still be seen under the flies. One was of his own people, to judge from the yellow beard and long flaxen hair;

that color wasn't common even among the Seven Tribes and rare as hen's teeth among outlanders. He thought he recognized Smeyth One-Eye, an outcast from the Panthers who lived a little north and west of here.

Finally caught him lifting the wrong man's horses, he supposed with idle curiosity. One-Eye had needed shortening for some time, being a bully and a lazy, thieving one at that. *Or maybe it was lifting the wrong woman's skirts.*

The other heads were in a clump away from One-Eye's perch, and their features made him look more closely, past the raven damage—they weren't as fresh as the outlaw's. They were darker of skin than his folk, wiry-haired, massively scarred in zigzag ritual patterns that made them even more hideous in death than they had been in life, several with human finger-bones through the septums of their noses. The lips drawn back in the final rictus showed rotting teeth filed to points.

Man-eaters, Robre thought, and spat.

He waved greeting to the guards at the gate—Alligator clansmen, since Dannulsford was the seat of their Jefe. The Bear Creek families had no feud with the Alligators just at the moment, but he would have been safe within the wands in any case. A Fair was peace-holy; even outright foreigners could come here unmolested along the river or trade roads, when no great war was being waged.

Two of the Alligator warriors stood and leaned on their weapons, a spear and a Mehk musket, wearing hide helmets made from the head-skins of their totem and keeping an eye on the thronging traffic. They wouldn't interfere unless fights broke out or someone blocked the muddy path, in which case they could call for backup from half a dozen others who crouched and threw dice on a deerhide. Those warriors kept their weapons close to hand, of course, and one had an Imperial breech-loading rifle that the Bear Creek man eyed with raw but well-concealed envy. The Alligators were rich from trade with the coastlands, and inclined to be toplofty.

One of the gamblers looked up and smiled, gap-toothed. "Heya, Hunter Robre," he said in greeting.

"Heya, Jefe's-man Tomul," Robre said politely in return, stopping to chat. "A raid?" He jerked his thumb at the stakes with the ten heads. "Wild-men?"

The hunter stood aside from a string of pack mules that was followed by an oxcart heaped with pumpkins; axles squealed like dying pigs, and the shock-headed youth riding the vehicle popped his whip. The three horses that carried Robre's pelts were well trained and followed him, bending their heads to crop at weeds when their master stopped.

"*Yi-ah*, swamp-devils, right enough." The Alligator chieftain's guardsman nodded. "Burned a settler's cabin east of Muskrat Creek—old Stinking Pehte."

"Not Stinking Pehte the Friendless? Pehte sunna Dubal?"

"Him 'n' none other; made an ax-land claim there 'n' built a cabin two springs ago, him 'n' his wife 'n' younglings. Set to clearing land for corn. Jefe Carul saw the smoke 'n' called out the neighborhood men in posse. Caught 'em this side of the Black River. Even got a prisoner back alive—a girl."

Robre's eyebrows went up. "Surprised they didn't eat her," he said.

"They'd just started in to skin her. Ate her kin first. 'S how we caught 'em—stopped for their fun."

Stinking Pehte must have been an even bigger fool than everyone thought, to settle that far east, Robre thought, but it wouldn't do to say it aloud. Men had to resent an insult to one of their own clan and totem, even if they agreed with it in their hearts.

"Where's ol' Grippem 'n' Ayzbitah?" the guard asked, looking for the big hounds that usually followed the hunter.

Robre cleared his throat and spat into the mud of the road, turning his head to cover a sudden prickle in his eyes. "Got the dog-sickness, had to put 'em down," he said.

The guards made sympathetic noises at the hard news. "Good hunting?" Tomul went on, waving toward the rawhide-covered bundles on the Bear Creek man's pack saddles.

"Passable—just passable," Robre replied, with mournful untruth. He pushed back his broad-brimmed, low-crowned hat to scratch meditatively at his raven-black hair. "Mostly last winter's cure, the second-rate stuff I held back in spring. Hope to do better this year."

"Jefe Carul killed two cows for God-thanks at sunrise," Tomul said; it was two hours past dawn now. "Probably some of the beef left if you've a hunger."

Robre snorted and shook his head. Sacrificial beef was free to any man of the Seven Tribes, but also likely to be old and tough. Lord o' Sky didn't care about the quality of the cattle, just their number, it being the thought that counted. He wasn't *that* short of silver.

Tomul went on: "See you around, then; we'll drink a mug. Mind you don't break the Fair's peace-bans while you're here, or it's a whuppin' from the Jefe."

"I'm no brawler," Robre said defensively.

"Then give me these back," Tomul chuckled in answer, pulling down the corner of his mouth with a little finger to show two missing molars.

The other warriors around the deerskin howled laughter and Robre laughed back, taking up the lead rein of his forward pack horse and leading the beasts under the massive timber gateway, between hulking log blockhouses. The huge black-oak timbers that supported the gate on either side were carved and painted; Coyote on the left grinning with his tongue lolling over his fangs and a stogie in the corner of his mouth, the Corn Lady on the right holding a stalk of maize in one hand and a hoe in the other, and God the Father on the lintel above. Robre bowed his head for an instant as he passed beneath the stern bearded face of the Lord of Sky, murmuring a luck-word.

The pack horses followed him into the throng within, shying and snorting and rolling their eyes a bit. Robre sympathized; the crowds and stink were enough to gag a buzzard. Nearly a hundred people lived here year-round; Jefe Carul in his two-story fort-mansion of squared timbers, and his wives, his children; his household men and *their* wives and children in ordinary cabins of mud-chinked logs; a few slaves and landless, clanless laborers in shacks; plus craftsmen and tinkers and peddlers who found Dannulsford a convenient headquarters, and their dependents.

Now it swarmed with twenty times that number; the Dannulsford Fair got bigger every year, it seemed. This year's held more people than Robre had ever seen in one place before, until only narrow crowded lanes were left between booths and sheds and tents and more folk still spilled over into camps outside the oak logs of the stockade. The air was thick with wood smoke, smells of dung and frying food and fresh corn bread, man's sweat, and the smells of leather, horses, mules and oxen, and dogs. The Fair came after the corn and cotton were in but before hard frost and the prime pig-slaughtering season; a time for the Jefe to kill cattle for the Lord o' Sky and to preside over disputes brought for judgment, and for the assembled free men of the clan to make laws.

And, he thought with a grin, *to make marriages and chase girls and swap and dicker and guzzle popskull, boast, and tell tales.* Robre was a noted tale-teller himself, when the mood was on him. *Time to trade with outland men, too.*

Dannulsford was as far north on the Three Forks River as you could float anything bigger than a canoe; that meant the Fair of the Alligators was far larger than most. There were Kumanch come down over the Westwall escarpment with strings of horses and buffalo pelts; Cherokee from the north with fine tobacco, rock-oil to burn in lamps, and bars of wrought iron for smiths; Dytchers from the Hill Country with wine and applejack and dried fruits; and black-skinned men from the coast with sugar and rum, rice and cinnamon and nutmeg.

Some from even farther away. A Mehk trader rode by, wearing a broad sombrero and tight jacket and tooled-leather chaps over buttoned knee-breeches, his silver-studded saddle glistening. The great wagons behind him were escorted by a brace of leather-jacketed lancers, short stocky men with brown skins and smooth cheeks, bandannas on their heads beneath broad-brimmed hats, gold rings in their ears, machetes at their belts, sitting their horses as if they'd grown there.

Say what you like about Mehk, they can ride *for certain sure,* Robre thought: or at least their caballeros and fighters could. Among the Seven Tribes every free man was a warrior, but it was different beyond the Wadeyloop River.

The merchant the lancers served was crying up his wares as he went; fine drink distilled from the maguay cactus, silks and silver jewelry and bright painted pots, tools and sundries, dried hot peppers and gaudy feathers and cocoa and coffee in the bean. He had muskets and powder and round lead balls for sale, too; Robre's lip curled.

A smoothbore flintlock didn't have the range or accuracy of a good bow, and it was a lot slower to use—slower even than the crossbows some favored. A musket was useful for shooting duck with birdshot, or for a woman to keep around the cabin for self-defense, but he didn't think it was a man's weapon.

All the foreigners stood out, among his own folk of the Seven Tribes—the fearless free-striding maidens in shifts that showed their calves or even their knees, wives more decorous in long skirts and headscarves, men much like himself in thigh-length hunting shirts of linsey-woolsey or cotton, breechclouts and leggings of deer hide, soft boots cross-laced to the knee, their long hair confined by headbands and topped by broad-brimmed leather hats often decorated by a jaunty feather or two, their beards clipped close to the jaw.

Robre returned waves and calls with a polite *heya*, but stopped to talk with none, not even the children who followed him calling *Hunter! Robre the Hunter! Story, story, story!*

Partly that was a wordless shyness he would never confess at the sheer press of people; he was more at home in the woods or prairies, though he knew he cut a striking figure, and had a fitting pride in it, and in the fact that many men knew his deeds. He was tall even for his tall people, his shoulders and arms thick, chest deep, legs long and muscular, a burly blue-eyed, black-haired young man who kept his face shaved in an outland fashion just spreading among some of the younger set. His hunting shirt of homespun cotton was mottled in shades of earth brown and forest green; at his waist he bore a long knife and a short sword in beaded leather sheaths, with a smaller blade tucked into his right boot-top. Quiver and bow rode at his shoulder—he preferred the shorter, handier recurved horn-and-sinew Kumanch style to the more usual wooden longbow—and a tomahawk was thrust through a loop at the small of his back.

The man he sought should be down by the levee on the riverbank, where the flatboats and canoes clustered. And where . . .

Yes. That's it, and no other.

The boat from the coast was huge, for all its shallow draft, like a flat tray fifty feet long and twenty wide. At its rear was an odd contraption like a mill's wheel, and amidships was a tall thin funnel; a flag fluttered red and white and blue from a slender mast, a thing of diagonal crosses—the Empire's flag. Somehow a fire made the rear wheel go round to drive the boat upstream—

Robre made a covert sign with his fingers at the thought, and whistled a few bars of the Song Against Witches. The steamboat was an Imperial thing. Imperials were city folk, even more than the Mehk, and so to be despised as weaklings. Yet they were also the masters and makers of all things wonderful, of the best guns, of boats pushed by fire and of writing on paper, of fine steel and fine glassware and of cloth softer than a maiden's cheek. And they told tales wilder than any Robre had made around the fire of an evening, about lands beyond the eastern seas and a mighty queen who ruled half the world from a city with a thousand thousand dwellers and stone houses taller than old-growth pines.

Robre snorted and spat again. The Imperials also claimed their *Queen-Empress* ruled all the land *here*, which was not just a tall tale but a stupid, insulting one. The Seven Tribes knew that they and none other ruled their homes, and they would kill any man among them who dared call himself a king, as if free clansmen were no better than Mehk peons.

I figure the Imperials come from one of the islands in the eastern sea, Robre thought, nodding to himself. Everyone knew there were a mort of islands out there: England, Africa, the Isle of Three Witches. *Past Kuba or Baydos, even, maybe. They puff it up big to impress gullible folk down along the coast.*

The clansman pushed past an open-fronted smithy full of noise and clamor, where the blacksmith and his apprentices hammered and sweated, and on to a big shack of planks. The shutters on the front were opened wide, and he gave an inward sigh of relief. He'd have had to turn round and go home, if the little Imperial merchant hadn't been here; he usually stopped first at Dannulsford Fair on his yearly rounds, but not always.

"Heya, Banerjii," he said.

Banerjii looked up from the gloom inside the store, where he sat cross-legged on a cushion with a plank across his lap holding abacus and account book.

"*Namaste*, Hunter Robre, sunna Jowan," he said, and made an odd gesture, like a bow with hands pressed palm-to-palm before his face, which was his folk's way of saying *heya* and shaking hands.

"Come in, it being always wery good to see you," the trader went on, in good Seven Tribes speech but with an odd singsong accent that turned every *w* to a *v*.

Odd, Robre thought, as he sat and a few local boys hired by the trader saw to his baggage and beasts.

But then, the merchant was odd in all ways. He looked strange—brown as a Mehk, but fine boned and plump, sharp featured and clean shaven. His clothing was a jacket of lose white cotton, a fore-and-aft cap of the same, and an elaborately folded loincloth he called something like *dooty*. Even odder was his bodyguard, who was somehow an Imperial, too, for all that he looked nothing at all like his employer, being three shades lighter for starters; there were men of the Seven Tribes who were darker of skin. The guard was nearly as tall as Robre, and looked near as strong; and unlike his clean-shaved employer, he wore a neat spade-shaped beard. He also tucked his hair up under a wrapped cloth turban, wore pants and tunic and belt, and at that belt carried a single-edged blade as long as a clansman's short sword. He looked as if he knew exactly what to do with it, too, while Banerjii was soft enough to spread on a hunk of cornpone.

A young man who looked like a relative of the merchant brought food, a bowl of ham and beans, the luxury of a loaf of wheaten bread, and a big mug of corn beer. All were good of their kind; the cooked dish was full of spices that made his eyes water and mouth burn. He cleared it with a wad of bread and a draft of the cool lumpy beer, which tasted like that from Jefe Carul's own barrels. Banerjii nibbled politely from a separate tray; another of his oddities was that he'd eat no food that wasn't prepared by his own kin, and no meat at all. Some thought he feared poison.

They made polite conversation about weather and crops and gossip, until Robre wiped the inside of the bowl with the heel of the bread, belched, and downed the last of the beer. During the talk his eyes had kept flicking to the wall. Not to the shimmering cloth printed with peacock colors and beautiful alien patterns, though he longed to lay a bolt of it before his mother, or to the axes and swords and knives, or to the medicines and herbs, or to the tools. You could get cloth and cutlery and plowshares, needles and thread anywhere, if none so fine. It was the two rifles that drew his gaze, and the bandoliers of bright brass cartridges. No other folk on earth made *those*.

"So," Banerjii said. "Pelts are slow this year, but I might be able to take a few—for friendship's sake, you understand."

"Of course," Robre said. "I have six bearskins—one brown bear, seven feet 'n' not stretched."

The contents of the packs came out, all but one. They dickered happily, while the shadows grew longer on the rough pine planks of the walls; the prices weren't much different from the previous season. They never were, for all that Banerjii always complained prices were down, and for all that Robre kept talking of going to the coast and the marts of fabled Galveston on his own—that would be too much trouble and danger, and both men knew it. Robre smiled to himself as the Imperial's eyes darted once or twice to the last, the unopened, pack.

"Got some big-cat skins," he said at last.

Banerjii's sigh was heartfelt, and his big brown eyes were liquid with sincerity. "Alas, my good friend, cougar are a drug on the market." Sometimes his use of the language was a little strange; that made no sense in Seven Tribes talk. "If you have jaguar, I could move one or two for you. Possibly lion, if they are large and unmarked."

Robre nodded. Jaguar were still rare this far north, though more often seen than in his father's time. And there were few lion prides east of the Westwall escarpment. Wordlessly, he undid the pack and rolled it out with a sweeping gesture.

Banerjii said something softly in his own language, then schooled his face to calmness. Robre smiled as the small brown hands caressed the tiger-skins. *And not just tiger,* he thought happily. Both animals were some sort of sport, their skins a glossy black marked by narrow stripes of yellow gold. And they were huge, as well, each nine feet from the nose to the base of the tail.

"Got 'em far off in the east woods," he said. That was a prideful thing to say; those lands weren't safe, what with ague and swamp-devils. "You won't see the likes of *those* any time soon."

"No," Banerjii said. "And so, how am I to tell what their price should be?"

Robre kept his confident smile, but something sank within his gut. He would *never* get the price of what he craved. He was an only son, his father dead and his mother a cripple, with no close living kin—and his father had managed to quarrel with all the more distant ones. Most of what he gleaned went to buy his mother's care and food; oh, the clan would not let her starve even if Robre died, but the lot of a friendless widow was still bitter, doubly so if she could not do a woman's work. The price of the rifle was three times what he made in a year's trapping and trading . . . and if he borrowed the money from the merchant, he'd be the merchant's man for five years at least, probably forever. He'd need ammunition, too, not just for use but for practice, if the weapon was to do him any good.

The Imperial smiled. "But perhaps there is another thing you might do, and—" He dipped his head at the rifles. "I think, my good friend, you have put me in the way of something even more valuable than these pelts." He rubbed his hands. "Another of my countrymen has arrived. A *lord*—a Jefe—not a merchant like me, and a hunter of note. He will need a guide. . . ."

II: THE LORD IN HIS GLORY

"And I thought Galveston was bad," Lt. Eric King of the Peshawar Lancers said to his companion, laughing. "This—what do they call it, Dannulsford?—is worse."

Both were in the field dress of the Imperial cavalry: jacket and loose *pyjamy* trousers of tough khaki-colored cotton drill, calf-boots, leather sword-belts around their waists supported by a diagonal strap from right shoulder to left hip; their turbans were the same color, although the other man's was larger and more bulbous than his officer's, which was in the pugaree style with one end of the fabric hanging loose down his back.

"*Han, sahib,*" Ranjit Singh grunted in agreement as they stood at the railing of the primitive little steamboat. "It is so, lord. These *jangli-admis*"—jungle-dwellers—"live like goats."

The lands along the river had been pretty enough to his countryman's eye, in a savage fashion; swamp and forest on the banks, giving way to a patchwork of wood and tall-grass savannah to the west, with the occasional farm and stretch of plowed black soil. The settlements of the barbarians were few and scattered, crude log cabins roofed in mossy shingles, surrounded by kitchen gardens and orchards of peach and pecan, and farther out, patches of maize and cotton and sweet potatoes surrounded by zigzagging split-rail fences. Corrals were numerous, too, for they seemed to live more by their herds than their fields; the grasslands were full of long-horned, long-legged cattle and rough hairy horses, and the woods swarmed with sounders of half-wild pigs.

Woods stood thicker on the eastern bank, wilder and more rank. The air over the Three Forks River was full of birds, duck and geese on their southward journey, and types he didn't recognize. Some were amazing, like living jewels of jade and turquoise and ruby, darting and hovering from flower to flower with their wings an invisible blur. That sight alone had been worth stopping here, on his way back from the European outposts of the Empire to its heartland in India.

"Sahib," grumbled Ranjit Singh, "This wasteland makes England look like a cultivated garden—like our own land in Kashmir."

King nodded. England remained thinly peopled six generations after the Fall. Still, after long effort from missionaries and settlers you could say it was civilized again in a provincial sort of way; farms and manors, towns, and even a few small cities growing again in the shadow of the great ruin-mounds overgrown by wildwood. Four millions dwelt there now, enough to give a human presence over most of such a small island. The countryside here had the charm of true wilderness, if nothing else.

This little settlement called Dannulsford, on the other hand . . .

Squalid beyond words is too kind, he thought. The stink was as bad as the worst slum in Calcutta, which was saying a good deal; smoke, offal, sewage, hides tacked to cabin walls or steeping in tanning pits, sweat and packed bodies. The water smelled for a mile downstream, as well.

"Probably they're not as bad when they're not jammed in together like this," he said. "And we won't be here long. Off to the woods as soon as we can."

"Of woods we have seen enough, this past year and more, sahib," Ranjit Singh said, as he dutifully followed Eric down the gangplank. "Europe is full of them."

"And the woods there full of danger," Eric chaffed. He'd just spent six months as part of the escort for a party of archaeologists, exploring the ruins amid the lost cities of the Rhine Valley and points east. "We've earned a holiday."

"In more woods?" the Sikh said sourly.

"For shikari, not battle," Eric said. "Some good hunting, a few trophies, and then back home."

"After this, even Bombay will feel like home," the Sikh said. "When we leave the train in Kashmir, I shall kiss the dirt in thankfulness."

King shrugged, a wry turn to his smile. "Well, *daffadar*, you're free to spend your leave as you please."

Ranjit Singh snorted. "Speak no foolishness, *sahib*," he said. "If you wish to hunt, we hunt."

The Imperial officer shrugged in resignation. King's epaulettes bore the silver pips of a lieutenant; Ranjit's arm carried the three chevrons of a *daffadar*, a noncommissioned man. Besides being his military subordinate, Ranjit Singh was the son of a yeoman-tenant on the King estate, and his ancestors had been part of the Kings' fighting tail ever since the Exodus, martial-caste *jajmani*-clients who followed the sahib into the Peshawar Lancers as a matter of course. That mixture of the feudal and the regimental was typical of the Empire's military, and it made discipline a very personal thing. Ranjit Singh would obey without question, as long as the order didn't violate his sense of duty—by letting his sahib go off into the wilderness without him, for example.

They climbed log steps in the side of the natural levee and strolled up the rutted muddy street that led from the stretch of riverbank. The Imperial cavalrymen walked with their left hands on the hilts of their curved *tulwar*-sabers; besides those they carried long Khyber knives, and holstered six-shot revolvers, heavy man-killing Webley .455's. Otherwise they were alike in their confident straightbacked stride with a hint of a horseman's roll to it, and not much else.

Eric King was an inch over six feet, broad-shouldered and longlimbed, with a narrow high-cheeked, straight-nosed face, glossy dark-brown sideburns and mustache, and hazel eyes flecked with amber. Ranjit Singh was a bear to his lord's hunting cat, four inches shorter but thicker in the chest and shoulders, broad in the hips, as well, and showing promise of a kettle belly in later years. He was vastly bearded, since his faith forbade cutting the hair on head or face, and the black bush of it spilled from his cheekbones down to his barrel chest. His eyes were black, as well, moving swiftly despite the relaxed confidence of his stride, alert for any threat.

Mostly the mud is a threat to our boots, Eric thought. *Either sucking them off, or just* eating *them.*

Someone had laid small logs in an attempt to corduroy a sidewalk, but heels had pressed them into the blackish mud; passing horses and feet kicked up more, and a small mob of shouting children followed the two foreigners, pointing and laughing.

A wooden scraper stood at the door of their destination, the small building with BANERJII & SONS on the sign above, and they used it enthusiastically before pulling off their footwear and putting on slippers.

"*Namaste,* Lieutenant King sahib," the little Bengali merchant said. "I received your note. Anything I may do for the Queen-Empress's man . . ."

"*Namaste,* Mr. Banerjii," King replied, sinking easily cross-legged on the cushion and gratefully taking a cup of tea laced with cardamom, a taste of home. Sitting so felt almost strange, after so long among folk who used chairs all the time.

He handed over a letter. The merchant raised his brows as he scanned it. "From Elias and Sons of Delhi!" he murmured in his own language.

Bengali was close enough to King's native Hindi that he followed it easily enough for so simple a matter. "They're my family's Delhi men-of-business," he said modestly, keeping his wry smile in his mind.

Every trade has its hierarchy, he thought. *And in some circles, it's* we *who gain status from being linked to* them, *not vice versa.*

"I will be even more happy to assist an associate of so respectable a firm," Banerjii went on, in the Imperial dialect of English; that was King's other mother-tongue, of course. "As I understand it, you wish to see something of the country? And to hunt?"

King nodded. And to make a report to the military intelligence department in the Red Fort in the capital; likely nothing would come of it, but it couldn't hurt. North America *was* part of the British Empire in theory, even if Delhi's writ didn't run beyond a few enclaves on the coast in actual fact. Eventually it would have to be pacified, brought under law, opened up and developed; when that day came any information would be useful. That might be a century from now, but the Empire was endlessly patient, and the archives were always there.

"You will need a reliable native guide, servants, and bearers," Banerjii said.

"Are any available? The garrison commander in Galveston lent me a few men. Locally recruited there, but reliable."

And you should have asked for more, radiated from Ranjit Singh.

Banerjii shook his head. "Oh, most definitely you must hire locally," he said. "Coastal men would be of little use guiding and tracking here—" He gave a depreciatory smile. "—as useless as a Bengali in Kashmir. But the natives have some reliable people. They are savages, yes, indeed, but they are a clean people here, all the Seven Tribes and their clans. From the time of the Fall."

King nodded in turn; that was one of the fundamental distinctions in the modern world, between those whose ancestors had eaten men in the terrible years after the hammer from the skies struck, and those who hadn't. The only more fundamental one was between those who still did, and the rest of humanity.

"And they are surprisingly honest, I find, particularly to their oaths—oh, my, yes. But proud—very proud, for barbarians. There is one young man I have dealt with for some years, a hunter by trade, and—"

With a gesture, he unrolled the tiger-skins. King caught his breath in a gasp.

III: The Maiden in Her Wrath

Sonjuh dawtra Pehte thrust her way into the beer shop through the swinging board doors, halting for a second to let her eyes adjust to the bright earth-oil lamps and push back her broad-brimmed hat. The dim street outside was lit only by a few pine-knots here and there.

There were a few shocked gasps; a respectable girl didn't walk into a man's den like this unaccompanied. Some of the gasps were for her dress—she'd added buckskin leggings and boots, which made her maiden's shift look more like a man's hunting shirt, and so did the leather belt cinched about her waist, carrying a long bowie and short double-edged toothpicker dagger and tomahawk. A horseshoe-shaped blanket roll rode from left shoulder to right hip, in the manner of a hunter or traveler.

One man sitting on the wall-bench, not an Alligator clansman and the worse for corn-liquor, misinterpreted and made a grab for her backside. That brought the big dog walking beside her into action; her sharp command saved the oaf's hand, but Slasher still caught the forearm in his jaws hard enough to bring a yelp of pain. The stranger also started to reach for the short sword on his belt, until the jaws clamped tighter, tight enough to make him yell.

"You wouldn't have been trying to grab my ass uninvited, would you, stranger?" Sonjuh said sweetly. "'Cause if you were, after Slasher here takes your hand off, these clansmen of mine will just naturally have to take you to the Jefe for a whuppin'. 'Less they stomp you to death their own selves."

The man stopped the movement of right hand to hilt, looked around—a fair number of men *were* glaring at him now, distracted from their disapproval of Sonjuh—and decided to shake his head. A sensible man was very polite out of his own clan's territory. If he wasn't . . . well, that was how feuds started.

"No offense, missie," he wheezed.

"Loose him," Sonjuh commanded, and the dog did—reluctantly.

The man picked up his gear and made for the door; several of the others sitting on stools and rough half-log benches called witticisms or haw-hawed as he went; Sonjuh ignored the whole business and walked on.

The laughter or the raw whiskey he'd downed prompted the man to stick his head back around the timber doorframe and yell, "Suck my dick, you whore!"

Sonjuh felt something wash from face down to thighs, a feeling like hot rum toddy on an empty stomach, but nastier. She pivoted, drew, and her right hand moved in a chopping blur.

The tomahawk pinwheeled across the room to sink into the rough timber beside the door, a whirr of cloven air that ended in a solid *chunk* of steel in oak. The out-clan stranger gaped at his hand, still resting on the timber where the edge of the throwing-ax had taken a coin-size divot off the end of the middle finger, about halfway down through the fingernail. Then he leapt, howling and dancing from foot to foot and gripping the injured hand in the other as the mutilated digit spattered blood; after a moment he ran off down the street, still howling and shouting *bitch!* at the top of his lungs.

Most of the men in the beer shop laughed at that, some so loud they fell to the rush-strewn clay floor and lay kicking their legs in the air. She went and pulled the tomahawk out of the wood, wiped it on her sleeve, and reslung it; Slasher sniffed at something on the floor, then snapped it up. The roaring chorus of guffaws and he-haws was loud enough to bring curious bypassers to the door and windows, and send more hoots of mirth down the street as the tale spread; several men slapped her on the back, or offered drinks—offers she declined curtly. The older men were quiet, she noticed, and still frowning at her.

Instead she pushed through the long smoky room toward the back, where the man she sought was sitting. The air was thick with tobacco smoke—and the smell of the quids some men chewed and spat, plus sweat and cooking and sour spilled beer and piss from the alley out back. Still, she thought he'd probably seen all there was to see; those smoldering blue eyes didn't look as if they missed much.

"Heya," she said, and to her dog, "Down, Slasher."

"Heya, missie," he replied formally, as the big wolfish-looking beast went belly-to-earth.

"You Hunter Robre? Robre sunna Jowan?" The form of a question was there, but there was certainty in her voice.

"Him 'n' no other," the young man said. "You'd be Sonjuh dowtra Pehte, *naw?*"

His brows went up a little as she sat uninvited, pulling over a stool that was made from a section of split log, flat side sanded and the other set with four sticks. The rushes on the hard-packed clay floor rustled and crackled as she plunked it down and straddled it.

"*Yi-ah.*" She nodded, a little mollified that he hadn't used her father's gift-names. Nobody wanted to be called the daughter of the Stinker or the Friendless. "There's no feud between the Alligators 'n' the Bear Creek people, or quarrel between our kin."

"No feud, no quarrel," he acknowledged; both clans were of the Cross Plains folk, which meant they didn't have to assure each other that there was no tribal war going on either. It was more than a little unorthodox for a woman to go through the ritual, anyway.

"How'd you know who I was?" she added, curious, as she tore off some of the wheat-and-injun bread he had before him, dipped it in the salt and ate it; that satisfied courtesy, in a minimal sort of way.

He was supposed to be a sharp man, but as far as she knew they'd never met—her family had lived solitary. Robre was famous, after a fashion: Sonjuh dowtra Pehte had begun acquiring a little notoriety only in the last few weeks.

"Figured. Old Pehte had red hair like yours before he went bald, 'n' 'sides that, you favor him in your looks." He ate a piece of the bread himself, which meant he had at least to listen to her; then he went on: "He was a dab hand with a tomahawk, too; saw him win the pig 'n' turkey here at Dannulsford once when my father brought me, must be ten years ago now."

Sonjuh tossed her head, sending the long horse-tail of her hair swishing. Being unmarried—likely she would be anyway at nineteen, even were her father someone else—she wore her hair down and tied back with a snakeskin band, in a torrent the color of mahogany reaching to between her shoulder blades; a thick band of freckles ran across her cheeks and the bridge of her nose. Any man of the Seven Tribes would have accounted her comely, snub-nosed face and red lips and the long smooth curves of her figure as well, until he saw the wildness in those haunted leaf-green eyes.

"Nice throw, too, missie," Robre continued. "Pehte must've taught you well."

"I *missed*," she snapped. "Wanted to split his ugly face!"

Robre laughed, a quieter sound than most men's mirth, then stopped when he realized she wasn't even smiling.

"Welcome to a share," he said a little uneasily, indicating the pitcher of corn beer and clay jug of whiskey.

"Didn't come to drink," she said, after taking a token sip from the beer jug; refusing a man's liquor was a serious insult. "I came to talk business."

The young man's black brows went up farther. "Shouldn't your . . . oh."

Sonjuh nodded. "My father's dead." *Oh, merciful God, thank You he died first of all.* "So's my mother. So's my three sisters. I saw—"

Of itself, her hand shot out and grabbed Robre's glass. She tossed back the raw spirits and waited with her eyes clenched shut until the sudden heat in her stomach and a wrenching effort of will stopped the shaking of her hands and pushed away the pictures behind her eyelids. When she looked back up, Robre was frowning at her left forearm, where a bandage had slipped from a healing wound. A patch of skin had been removed—neatly, the way a skinning knife would do it in skilled hands.

She tugged the sleeve down over the rawness and went on: "Didn't come for sympathy, either. Like I said, I've got business to talk with you, Robre Hunter."

He took a pull at his mug of beer, wiped the back of one big callused hand across his mouth, and nodded. "I'm listening, missie."

That was more than she'd expected, if less than she'd hoped. "I didn't have brothers. My pa didn't hold with hiring help, either, so from my woman-time I've been doing a son's work for him. Hunting, too." She took a deep breath. "I know my pa wasn't well liked—"

Across the table, a polite lack of expression said as plainly as words: *He was about as disliked as a man can be and not be outlawed. Or just plain have his gizzard cut out.*

More than one had tried, too, but Stinking Pehte had been a good man of his hands, and it had always gone the other way. All fair fights and within the letter of the law, but killing within the clan didn't make you any better liked either. One or two was to be expected, in a hot-blooded man, but public opinion thought half a dozen excessive; the clan needed those hands and blades.

"—but he was a good farmer, 'n' no one ever called him lazy. We got our crop in before we were hit. Not much, but we sold most here in Dannulsford. Deer hides 'n' muskrat, too, 'n' ginseng, and potash from the fields we were clearing, 'n' soap 'n' homespun me 'n' my ma 'n' sisters made. The posse got back most of our cabin goods 'n' tools, 'n' our stock; then there's the land, that's worth something."

Not as a home-place; too ill-omened for that, and too exposed, as her family's fate proved. But someone would be glad to have the grazing, plus there was good oak-wood for swine fodder, and the Jefe would see that they paid her a fair share. That would probably amount to enough ham, bacon, and cow to put her meat on the table half the year.

"Glad to hear you're not left poor," Robre said.

"What it means is I can pay you," she said, plunging in. This time his eyes widened, as well.

"Pay me for what, missie Sonjuh?" he said.

She reached into the pouch that hung at her hip, supported by a thong over the shoulder; it was the sort a hunter wore, to carry tallow and spare bowstrings and a twist of salt, pipe or chaw of tobacco and a whetstone and suchlike oddments. What she pulled out of it was a scalp. The hair was loose black curls, coarser and more wiry than you were likely to find on a man of the Seven Tribes.

Robre whistled silently. Taking scalps was an old-timey, backwoods habit; Kumanch and Cherokee still did it, but few of their own folk except some of the very wildest. These days you were supposed to just kill evildoers or enemies, putting their heads up on a pole if they deserved it. And for a woman . . .

"I expect that's not some coast-man out of luck," he said.

"Swamp-devil," she said flatly. "Not no woman nor child, neither. That was a full-grown fighting man. Slasher 'n' I took him, bushwhacked him."

"Well . . . good," Robre said, with palpable uneasiness, blinking at the tattered bit of scalp-leather and hair. "One less swamp-devil is always good."

"That's what I want to hire you for," Sonjuh went on in a rush. "I can't . . . I swore 'fore God on my father's blood I'd get ten for my ma, 'n' ten for each of my sisters. I can't do it alone."

"Jeroo!" Robre exclaimed, and poured himself another whiskey. "Missie, that's unlucky, making that sort of promise 'fore the Lord o' Sky! Forty scalps!"

"Or that I'd die trying," she said grimly. "I need a good man to help. All the goods I've got is yours, if you'll help me. Jeroo! Everyone says you're the best."

"Missie . . ." There was an irritating gentleness in his tone. "A feud, that's a matter for a dead man's clansmen to take up. It wouldn't be right or fitting for me to interfere."

Her hand slammed the table, enough to make jug and bottle and cup rattle, despite the thick weight of wood. "The gutless *hijos* won't call for a war party! They say the ten heads they took were enough for honor! Well, they *aren't!* I can hear my folks' spirits callin' in the dark, every night, callin' for blood-wind to blow them to the After Place."

Some of those nearby exclaimed in horror at those words; many made signs, and two abruptly got up and left. You didn't talk openly of ghosts and night-haunts, not where the newly dead were concerned. Naming things called them. A ripple of whispers spread throughout the beer shop, and bearded faces turned their way.

"It's all because nobody liked my pa, 'n' because they're all *cowards!*" Her voice had risen to a shout, falling into the sudden silence.

"That's a matter for your Jefe, missie," Robre said. The soothing, humor-the-mad-girl tone made the blood pound in her ears. "'N' the gathering of your clan's menfolk."

"I came to offer you two Mehk silver coins each, if you'll come with me 'n' help me," she said, in a tone as businesslike as she could manage. "'N' you can show these gutless, clanless bastards that a girl 'n' an out-clan man can do what they can't."

"Sorry," he said; the calm finality shocked her more than anger would have. "Not interested."

"Then damn you to the freezing floor of hell!" she screamed, snatching up his mug and dashing the thick beer into his face. "Looks like I'm the *only* one in this room with any balls!"

That made him angry; he was up with a roar, cocking a fist—then freezing, caught between the insult and the impossibility of striking a freewoman of the Seven Tribes, and a maiden of another clan at that.

Shaking, Sonjuh turned on her heel, glad that the lanterns probably weren't bright enough to show the tears that filled her eyes. She stalked out through the shocked hush, head down and fists clenched, not conscious of the two weird foreigners who blocked the door until she was upon them. One twisted aside with a cat's gracefulness; the other stood and she bounced off him as she would off an old hickory post; then he stepped aside at the other's word.

Sonjuh plunged past them into the night and ran like a deer, weeping silently, with Slasher whining as he loped at her heel.

"I wonder what *that* was in aid of?" Eric King murmured to himself, raising a polite finger to his brow as the room stared at him and Ranjit Singh, then walking on as the crowded, primitive little tavern went back to its usual raucous buzz—although he suspected that whatever had just happened was the main subject of conversation.

Even in the barbarian hinterlands, he didn't think a girl that pretty dumped a pint of beer over a man's head and stalked out as if she were going to walk right over anyone in her way, not just every night. In a way, the sensation she'd caused was welcome; the two Imperial soldiers probably attracted less curiosity than they normally would. Eric waited courteously while the man he'd come to see mopped his face vigorously with a towel brought by a serving-girl, looking around as he did. This wasn't much worse than the dives he'd pulled soldiers overstaying their leave out of in many a garrison town; the log walls were hung with brightly colored wool rugs, and the kerosene lanterns were surprisingly sophisticated—obviously native-made, but as good as any Imperial factories turned out. He'd have expected tallow dips, or torches.

"Mr. Robre sunna Jowan?" he asked, when the man was presentable again. "I'm Lt. Eric King. This is my *daffadar* . . . Jefe's-man . . . Ranjit Singh."

"Robre Hunter, that's me," the native replied, rising and offering his hand. "Heya, King, Ranjeet."

The hand that met his was big, and callused as heavily as his own. They were within an inch or so of each other in height and of an age, but Eric judged the other man had about twenty or thirty pounds on him, none of it blubber. A slight smile creased a face that was handsome in a massive way, and the two young men silently squeezed until muscle stood out on their corded forearms. The native's blue eyes went a little wider as he felt the power in the Imperial's sword-hand, and they released each other with a wary nod of mutual respect, not to mention mutual shakings and flexings of their right hands. Eric read other subtle signs—the white lines of scars on hands and dark-tanned face, the way the local moved and held himself—and decided that native or not, this was a man you'd be careful of. And no fool, either; he was probably coming to the same conclusion.

"Dannul! Food for my guests from the Empire!" Robre bellowed. "And beer, and whiskey!"

King understood him well enough. The local tongue was derived from that of the Old Empire, and the Imperial cavalry officer had experience with the classical written tongue of the Pre-Fall period, with the speech of the Cape and Australian Viceroyalties, and some of the archaic dialects still spoken in remote parts of England, as well. With that, and close attention in weeks spent along the coast near Galveston, he could follow Robre's speech easily and make himself understood with a little patience. It was mostly a matter of remembering a few sound-changes and applying them consistently.

"No beef," he said. "Cow-meat," he added, when Robre looked doubtful. The vocabulary had changed a good deal, too. "It's . . . forbidden by our religion. Our Gods." He pointed skyward.

To oversimplify, he thought, as Robre nodded understanding.

"*Yi-ah*, like our totems," the Bear Creek clansman said. "I don't eat bear-meat, myself."

King smiled. *To* vastly *oversimplify*, he thought.

His grandfather had eaten beef now and then; so his father had, at formal banquets among the sahib-log, though rarely at home. His own generation mostly didn't touch it at all, although as Christians it wasn't against their religion in theory. *More a matter of not offending.* The idea made him a bit queasy, in fact. *Well, you don't expect a taboo to make rational sense. That doesn't make it any less real.*

Luckily, Ranjit Singh was a Sikh, and so—apart from cow's-flesh—had fewer problems with the ritual purity of his food than most Hindus. Nanak Guru, the founder of that faith, had made a point of having his followers eat from a common kitchen with con-verts of all castes, and even outcaste ex-Muslims; they were the Protestants of the Hindu world, more or less. It simplified traveling no end.

A stout middle-aged serving woman brought wooden platters of steaming-hot corn bread, butter, grilled pork-ribs slathered with some hot sauce, and bowls of boiled greens; the food was strange but good, in a hearty peasant-countryside sort of way. Local cour-tesy, according to Banerjii, meant that you had to eat with someone before getting down to serious business. And drink; the maize-beer was vile, but better than what the Seven Tribes called whiskey. The stuff they imported from the south, made from a cactus, was worse. The local wine was unspeakable even by those low standards.

"So," Robre said. "You two are from the Empire?"

"Yes," King said. *Technically, so are you, of course, my friend.* "We're here to hunt. Mr. Banerjii tells me that you're the man to see about such matters."

"Awful long way to come just to hunt," Robre said. "How'd you get the meat 'n' hides home?"

"Ah—" Eric frowned. Obviously, the concept of hunting for trophies wasn't part of the local scene. "We're on our way home from England to India, which is the . . . biggest part of the Empire. That's where I and my man here live. . . ."

Robre frowned. "*England* is part of your Empire? In the old songs, we spent a powerful amount of time fighting England." He threw back his head and half chanted

> *"Fired our guns 'n' the English stopped a-comin'*
> *Fired again, 'n' then they ran away—"*

"Ah . . . well, that was before the Fall, you see."

Local notions of geography were minimal; evidently these people had lost all literacy and most sense of the past during the Fall. Not surprising, since this area was on the southern fringe of the zone where total crop failure for three freezing-cold summers in a row had killed nearly everyone but a few cannibals who survived by eating their neighbors. These Seven Tribes might well be descended from no more than a handful of families. Small numbers meant fewer memories and skills passed down, and the older people who might remember most were most likely to die.

The lands farther south, what the old maps called Mexico, had preserved some remnants of civilization, with gunpowder and writing and a few small cities atop a peasant mass. India and the Cape and Australia had done much better, thanks be to Christ and Krishna and St. Disraeli. . . .

There was no sense in stretching poor Robre's idea of the world too far—and for that matter, King's own schooling hadn't covered the Pre-Fall history of the Americas in much detail. The Mughals and the East India Company had taken up a good deal more space, and so had the Romans. He did know that there had been a temporarily successful rebellion against the Old Empire here in North America by British colonists just about a century before the Fall, and that the New Empire had only started to make good its claim to the continent in the last couple of generations.

There's so much else to do, he thought wistfully.

The growing tension with Dai-Nippon, for example, or the chronic menace of the Czar in Samarkand, hanging over the North West Frontier, and the Caliphate of Damascus in the west. It was a shame that the Powers spent so much time hampering each other, when the world was so wide and vacant, but such seemed to be the nature of man, chained to the Wheel and prey to maya, illusion.

"I'm sorry if I, ah, interrupted," King went on, nodding back toward the door where the redhead had made her spectacular exit.

"*Naw,*" Robre said. "That was Sonjuh dawtra Pehte. Pretty girl, hey?"

"Indeed. Hope I wasn't queering your pitch," King said cautiously. He'd gotten the impression that the locals were more free-and-easy about such matters than most higher-caste Indians or other Imperials, but making assumptions about women was always the easiest way to get yourself into killing trouble in a strange land.

It required a little back-and-forth before his meaning was plain. Robre shook his head. "Coyote's dong, I'd sooner sport with a she-cougar. She's pretty, but mad as a mustang on loco-weed, or ghost-ridden, or both. Well, no wonder, seein' as she saw all her kin killed 'n' eaten by the swamp-devils, 'n' they held her captive for two, three days. 'S too bad. Not just pretty; she's got guts, too. Probably get herself killed some hard, bad way, mebbe some others with her."

King listened to the story with a frown: keeping the peace and putting down feud and raid was his hereditary caste duty, and such lawlessness irked him even in a place only theoretically under the Imperial Pax.

"Well, no wonder she's not looking for a man, then," he said.

That took another bout of struggling with the language, and then Robre shook his head. "Oh, swamp-devils don't force women. Kill 'em and eat 'em, yes; that, no."

"That's . . . extremely odd," King said, conscious of his eyebrows rising. *Unbelievably odd,* he thought. *Perhaps it's some sort of make-believe to protect the reputations of rescued women?*

Robre frowned, as if searching for some memory. "Near as I can recall, they questioned a swamp-devil 'bout it once, a whiles back. He wasn't quite dead when they caught him, 'n' he could talk—not all of 'em can. Anyways, story is he said our women didn't *smell* right." He shrugged. "Now, 'bout this hunt-outfit you want—"

Apparently there was a long-established etiquette for setting up a caravan, for trade or hunt. After an hour or two, they could talk well enough to exchange hunting stories. Robre enjoyed the one about the elephant in musth hugely, while obviously not believing a word of it—drawing the long bow was another local custom, in fact an art form, from what the merchant had said. . . . King found the story of the yellow-striped black tigers even more fascinating, and the circumstantial detail very convincing indeed. Killing *those* beasts, alone and on foot and with only bow and spear . . . that took a man. He'd already bought both pelts, for what he suspected was several times the sum Banerjii had paid—not that he'd queer the little Bengali's pitch by telling the natives, Imperials should stick together—but that wasn't the same thing at all as a trophy brought down on his own.

"My father will be dumbstruck, for once," he said, sobered by the thought of the fierce scarred face of the lord of Rexin. "He's always on about a lion he got in the Cape with a black mane big as a hayrick. It gets a little bigger every year, in fact."

Robre laughed and slapped the table. "My pa's dead, but I know that feeling from the old days, when I was young."

King kept his face straight; if the native wasn't within six months of his own twenty-two, he'd recite the Mahabaratha backwards. "It's a bargain, then," he said.

"A bargain," Robre agreed.

They shook hands again, not making it a trial of strength this time. "You can come collect the rifle tonight, if you want," King said.

He'd seen the naked desire in the blue eyes when they spoke of that payment; modern weapons were deliberately kept expensive by Imperial policy and taxation. Trade in guns over the frontier wasn't banned altogether, though, except in a few particular trouble spots: control over supplies of ammunition and spare parts was a powerful diplomatic tool, once buyers had become dependent on them. Robre surprised him by shaking his head.

"Put it with Banerjii," he said. "I wouldn't be good enough with one to be much use on this trip. Not enough time to practice— though I do expect some training with your weapons as part of the deal, you understand."

"*Koi bat naheen* . . . I mean, not a problem," King said, and yawned. The local whiskey tasted vile, but it did its business. "And now, adieu . . . I mean, see you tomorrow."

* * *

Sonjuh woke slowly, feeling stiff and sandy-eyed and with a dull throb in her head. Crying yourself to sleep did that, the more if you had been drinking; at least she hadn't woken herself up screaming again, though a heaviness behind her eyes told her that the dreams had been bad. She swallowed past a dry throat and scolded herself for the whiskey.

Jeroo, how much did I drink? It's too damn easy to crawl into a jug to forget, she told herself, rubbing her eyes fiercely. *You don't* want *to forget.*

She ignored the stiffness, as she ignored the small voice that said *oh, yes, you do*, and sat up, scratching and frowning as she cracked a flea. Slasher stirred and whined beside her as she rose from the straw of the loft. The beasts below were starting to stamp and blow in their stalls, and they'd be up in the farmhouse soon—her uncle wasn't what she considered a hard worker, and it wasn't the busy season, but a farmer got up with the sun, like it or not. She slipped down the ladder and watched the dog follow more cautiously—even now, the sight of Slasher on a ladder made her smile—and tossed hay into the feed troughs, took up pitchfork and wheelbarrow to muck out, rubbed them down. Two of the horses and a mule were hers, and the others all knew her, blowing affection at her and then feeding heartily.

Then she took down the bowie and tomahawk and worked the rest of the sand out of her joints by shadow-fighting, lunge and guard, stab and chop, her bare feet dancing across the packed dirt of the threshing floor outside the barn.

Move light and quick, she told herself, in an inner voice that sounded like her father's. *Light and quick. Anyone you fight'll have more heft, so you'd best move right quick.*

Pa had taught her; being sonless and indulgent with his eldest daughter, and living far enough offside that neighbors wouldn't be scandalized. Besides, a lone steading needed more than one fighter, and it was old law that a woman should fight when her home was attacked.

After a while sweat was running freely down her body, the sun was over the horizon, and her head felt clear. She worked the counterbalanced sweep to bring more water out of the well, drank as much as she could, then dashed more buckets over herself; at least her relative didn't grudge water, having three good wells and a creek. She was rubbing herself down with a coarse piece of cloth when she became aware of a disapproving glare from the cabin; her uncle Aydwah's wife, throwing cracked corn to the hens and taking in more wood for the hearth fire.

And she's no brighter a candle than those broody birds, Sonjuh thought. *Always there to have their heads chopped off just 'cause she throws them some corn of a morning. Still, no harm in being polite.*

She tied on a fresh breechclout, slipped on her leggings and laced them to her belt, cross-gartered the moccasin-boots up her calves, and then pulled on a clean shift of scratchy undyed cotton. By then the house was roused, adults and older children scratching and spitting as they spread out for their dawn chores, naked towhaired toddlers tumbling about, dogs keeping a wise distance from Slasher.

Aydwah had a big place, two shake-roofed log cabins linked by a covered dogtrot, several barns besides the one she slept in, loomhouse where the women of the family spun and wove, slatted corncrib of poles, toolsheds, smokehouse and more. Several poorer kin and hired workers lived with him, too, sleeping in attics and lofts, and a single Kumanch slave taken prisoner from a band raiding the westernmost of the Seven Tribes, beaten into meekness and sold east. It was a prosperous yeoman's spread, no wealthy Jefe's farm, but two steps up from her father's place.

Cooking smells came from the house, and Aydwah's wife came out to beat a long ladle against an iron triangle hanging by the cabin door. Sonjuh's belly rumbled as she sat with the others at the long trestle-table set out in the dogtrot, where everyone ate in good weather. Breakfast was samp-mush, with sorghum syrup and warm-fresh milk poured on, and she bent over her bowl with the wooden spoon busy.

Her uncle had the family hair, gray streaking bright fox red in his case, but he was heavier set than her father, slower of mind and words. His voice was a deep rumble as he spoke from the head of the table: "We've the last of the flax to plant today, 'n' the goobers to lift. Sonjuh, you'll—"

"I've got business of my own today, Uncle," she said, trying for respectful firmness and suspecting it came out as sullen. "I cleaned out the workstock barn."

Aydwah flushed; it showed easily, despite forty years' weathering of his fair freckled skin. "You'll do as you're told, girl, 'n' no back talk! I took you in—"

"'N' you're well paid for it," Sonjuh said. "This milk's from my folk's milch cow, isn't it? All that stock's mine, not yours—that's the law! You're getting more than I'd pay in Dannulsford for tavern-keep."

Her uncle's flush went deeper; that was the truth, and he knew it and that the Jefe would uphold her.

Her aunt-by-marriage was shriller: "'N' the stock 'n' gear might get you a husband, if you didn't gallivant around like some shameless hussy!"

Sonjuh restrained herself, not throwing the contents of her bowl in the older woman's face. Instead she set it down on the puncheon floor, where Slasher gave the huffing grunt that meant *don't mind if I do* in dog and went to it with lapping tongue and slurping sounds. He was used to yelling.

"I made an oath 'fore God, 'n' I can't make it good sitting in the loomhouse, or married off to some crofter you bribe to take spoiled goods with my kin's stock," she shouted back. "What's worse luck 'n oath-breaking to God?"

"Fighting is man's work, 'n' so are oaths 'fore the Lord o' Sky," her aunt screamed, shaking her fist at Sonjuh; several of the younger children around the table began to cry, and most of the adults were looking at their feet, or the rafters. "You're a hex-bearer, 'n' you'll bring His anger down on us all."

"Lord o' Sky saved us all in the Hungry Years, didn't he? Brought back the sun after Olsaytan ate it? Leastways, that's what the Jefe says come midsummer 'n' midwinter day when he kills cows for God; you telling me he's lying? Lord o' Sky hears an oath, don't matter who says the say."

Aydwah's head had been turning back and forth like a man watching a handball game. Now he rose to his feet and roared at her: "You speak to your aunt with respect, missie, or I'll take my belt to your backside—that's the law, too, me being your eldest male kin. Or have you forgot that part?"

"You could try!" Sonjuh yelled, all caution cast aside.

Her uncle's roar was wordless as he started a lunge for her. Sonjuh jumped backward from the bench, cat-lithe, looking around for something to grab and hit with—never hit a man with your bare hand unless you were naked and had your feet nailed to the floor, her father had told her. An ax handle someone had been whittling from a billet of hickory was close by, and she snatched it up and held it two-handed.

That wasn't needful; Aydwah froze as Slasher came up from beneath the table, paws on the bench and bristling until he looked twice his size—which was considerable, because the dog had more than a trace of plains wolf in his bloodlines, and outweighed his mistress's 115 pounds. His black lips curled back from long wet yellow-white teeth, and the expression made his tattered ears and the scars on his muzzle stand out. Slasher had been her father's hunting dog—fighting dog, too; the posse had found him clubbed senseless and left for dead at the ruins of her family's cabin, and he'd woken to track the war band that carried her off.

"Get me my bow," Aydwah said, slow and careful, not moving as others tumbled away from the table and backed to a safe distance. "Sami, get me my bow. That there dog is dangerous and has to be put down."

"You shoot at the dog saved my life, you die," Sonjuh said flatly. The words left her lips like pebbles, heavy dense things not to be called back. "I'm leaving. I'll send for my family's gear later; look after it real careful, or I'll call the Jefe to set the law on you."

She backed away toward the stable, her eyes wary and the ax handle ready, but none of the other grown folk tried to stop her; Aydwah wasn't quite angry enough to call on them to bind her, although his son Sami did bring his bow. By that time Slasher had followed her, walking stiff-legged and looking back over his shoulder frequently. Stunned silence fell, broken only by the idiot clucking of poultry and noises of stock and a few dogs barking at the fear and throttled anger they smelled. Sonjuh saddled one of her horses, stashed her traveling gear on the mule's pack saddle, slung the blanket-roll over her shoulder, and swung into the saddle; the morning's mush was a cold lump under her breastbone, but her face was a mask of pale, controlled fury. The last thing she did was to use the goatsfoot lever to cock her crossbow, setting one of the short, heavy steel-headed and leather-feathered bolts in the groove.

She held the reins in her left hand and the weapon in her right; the spare horse and mule were well-enough trained to follow without a leading rein. Aydwah waited by the laneway that led out across his land to the Dannulsford trace, between the tall posts carved with the figures of the Corn Lady and Lord o' Sky.

"I cast you out!" he called, as she came near. "You're no kin of ours! I put the elder's curse on you, Lord 'n' Lady hear my oath!"

There were gasps from the other folk of the farm; that was a terrible thing, to be without immediate family. Not as bad as being outlawed from your clan, but close. Sonjuh dropped the reins for an instant to flash the sign of the Horns at him, turning the curse.

There were more shocked exclamations at that, and someone burst out: "She's ghost-ridden!"

"Yes, I am—by my pa 'n' ma, 'n' my sisters, your blood you weren't man enough to get revenge for," Sonjuh said coldly. "I call their spirits down on you, Aydwah sunna Chorge, to haunt you sleeping 'n' waking, by bed 'n' field 'n' hearth, you 'n' all yours."

Aydwah raised his bow, a six-foot length of yellow-orange *bois-dawk* wood.

Sonjuh ignored the creak of the shaft being drawn and cast a jeering call over her shoulder: "Go ahead, Aydwah Kin-Killer—shoot your brother's girlchild in the back 'fore witnesses, 'n' put your head up on a pole!"

With that, she squeezed her mount with her thighs and left at a canter. The flat unmusical smack of the bowstring sounded behind her, but the shaft flashed off to one side to bury itself amid the stooked corn and pumpkins and cowpea vines; her uncle hadn't quite dared.

I wonder if this is how father felt, when he pushed a quarrel, she thought briefly; it was an intoxication, a release of frustration like a dam breaking. *Bet the hangover's worse than whiskey, though.*

IV: A GATHERING OF EAGLES

"Sah!"

The corporal in charge of the squad he'd borrowed from Galveston's garrison commander gave a crackling stamp-and-salute; Eric King returned the gesture. The noncom and his squad were natives, too, stalwart muscular men, dark brown of skin, with kinky hair and broad features. They'd been recruited from the farming and fishing tribes who were spread thinly over the central Texas coast, it being policy to raise local levies where possible, since they were always cheaper and often hardier than imported regulars.

But Imperial discipline puts down deep roots, King thought, as the man wheeled off to supervise his squad; they struck the tents and folded them for pack-saddle carriage with practiced efficiency.

An ox wagon had brought the gear this far from the steamboat; two tents, a large and a small—military issue—and a fair pile of boxed weapons, ammunition, equipment, and supplies—the latter including brandy from France-outre-mer, distilled in the hills near Algiers, and whiskey from New Zealand. Robre Hunter had raised his brows and smacked his lips over a small sample of each, and King made a mental note to advise Banerjii to keep some in stock. Being teetotal as well as a vegetarian, it probably hadn't occurred to the Bengali that booze came in different qualities and prices.

The native guide looked at the pile of equipment. "Lord o' Sky!" he said. "If you Empire men take this much on a hunting trip, what do you drag along on a war-party?"

"Considerably less," King said dryly, remembering fireless bivouacs in the Border hills, rolled in his cloak against blowing snow and gnawing a piece of stale chapatti while everyone listened for Pathan raiders creeping up on their bellies under cover of the storm.

"I'm hunting for pleasure and I'm not in a hurry. Why not be comfortable as possible? When we of the Angrezi Raj *fight*, all we care about is winning."

Robre nodded slowly. "Makes sense," he said. "Let's get on about it, then."

The Imperials had camped in the pasture of an outlying farm

owned by the Jefe of the Alligators, a few acres of tall grass drying toward autumn surrounded by oak and hickory and magnolias and trees he couldn't identify. It had a deep stillness, broken by the whicker of horses and the trilling of unfamiliar birds, and the smells were of sere grass and wet leaves and dew on dust. King smiled in sheer pleasure as he stood with hands on hips looking about him; an owl flew past him, out late or early, with a cry like *who-cooks-for-you*.

"What's that called?" he asked Robre.

The native guide blinked at him in astonishment. "You don't have 'em? That's a barred owl—come out in daylight more 'n most of their kind."

"That's the point of traveling," he said. "To see things you haven't got at home. Now, to business."

He sat in a folding canvas chair, Ranjit Singh on one side and Robre on the other. A table before him bore a register book, pen, ink bottle, and a pile of little leather bags cinched tight with thongs around their store of Imperial silver rupees. The natives here, he'd noticed, were fascinated and impressed by writing; very conveniently, they were also quite familiar with the concept of coined money as a store of value. Stamped silver came up in trade from the city-states farther south, although the Seven Tribes minted none themselves. He'd been in places where everything was pure barter, and the simplest transaction took forever.

"Step up," he said, in the local tongue, then sighed as they crowded around, yelling; the concept of standing quietly in line was *not* part of the local worldview.

About two dozen men had applied for the eight wrangler-muleteer-guard-roustabout positions; Robre knew some of them personally, and most by reputation. In fact, two slunk off immediately when they saw his face. Most were young, given leave by their fathers in this slack part of the farming year and eager for the rare chance to earn hard money.

Robre put them through their paces, checking their mules' and horses' backs for sores and their tack for cracked leather, watching them pack and unpack a load, follow a track, shoot at a mark, run and jump and wrestle.

King had Ranjit Singh handle the hand-to-hand testing. It was a good way to teach these wild natives a little respect, and none of them lasted more than a minute before finding themselves immobilized and slammed to the ground. The local style was catch-as-catch-can, the men strong and quick and active, quite oblivious of pain, but utterly unsophisticated. He wasn't surprised; it was often that way, with warrior groups like this. They put so much into their weapons that they neglected unarmed combat, and the style the Imperial military used drew on ancient Asian traditions.

The Sikh rose grinning from the wheezing, groaning body of the last, dusted his hands, beat dirt and bits of grass and weed off his trousers; sweat glistened on his thick hairy torso, where iron muscle rippled in bands and curves.

"Not bad," he said jovially. "For a man who knows nothing."

The Sikh said it in Hindi, which took the sting out, although the object of it could probably guess the meaning of the words as he sat up and rotated a wrenched shoulder; the other candidates laughed at his discomfort. He was older than most of them—in his thirties, a tall rawboned swarthy man.

"All right," the local said to the Sikh as he rose and rubbed his bruises. "You got some fancy wrasslin' there—'n' you're strong as a bear with a toothache 'n' twice as mean. Now, Jefe," he went on to King, "Who's going to be your trail-boss on this trip?"

"I'm in command," King said. "After me, my man Ranjit Singh here; after him, Robre sunna Jowan. Any problems with that—" He glanced down at the register. "—Haahld sunna Jubal?"

"You bet there is, by God. Robre is a good man of his hands 'n' a fine hunter, no dispute. But it's not fitting he should be trail-boss over older men, him so young 'n' not having wife nor child nor land of his own and all."

The rest stood silent; one or two seemed to agree. Robre flushed, but King put out a hand to restrain him. "In that case, you're free to go," he said cheerfully.

The face of the native standing before him turned darker. "That's a mighty high-top way to speak, stranger, considering you're far from home 'n' alone here. Who'd you think you are?"

King rose, still smiling slightly, but the other man took a step back. "I *know* I'm an officer of the Empire," he said calmly. "Which means that I'm an automatic majority wherever I go." He gestured to the moneybags. "If you take my silver, you take my orders. If you won't, get out."

His body stayed loose, but his hands were tinglingly aware of the position of saber and pistol and knife. He'd met men like these before, from peoples whose ways demanded that a man be prickly and quick to take offense and forever ready to fight. You had to begin as you meant to go on, and be ready to back it up, like the head wolf in a pack. The air crackled between them, and the native's eyes shifted slightly.

Just then the drumming sound of hooves turned heads. A ridden horse, a remount and a mule, all sweating a bit. And the rider . . .

Well, well, it's the little redhead, King thought. He'd gotten most of her story out of Robre, and felt a certain sympathy—it was a hard world, and harder still for an orphan. *Well, well, not so little, either.*

In sunlight and flushed with exertion she looked even better than the other night's tantalizing glimpse. She kicked a leg over the pommel of her saddle and slid to the ground, bosom heaving interestingly under the coarse cotton shift as she came toward him with her dog panting at her heel.

"Heya, Empire-Jefe King," she said bluntly.

"Hello, miss," he answered, amused. *I am* an *Imperial chieftain, I suppose.*

"Hear you're hiring," she said. "I want work." At a snicker from the crowd of clansmen, she turned around and glared. "And not as no bedwarmer, either!" Turning back to King, "I can carry my load, 'n' I know the eastern woods. Hunted east of the Three Forks since I was a girl, 'n' with my pa east of the Black River twice."

Beside King, Robre stirred, surprise on his face. *Evidently that's some claim; but she's not lying, I'd think. Intriguing!*

Haahld sunna Jubal snorted. "You got to be a fightin' man for this trip, missie, able to carry a man's load. Want me to test your wrasslin'?" The clansman roared with laughter.

Sonjuh's face flushed red, and her foot moved in a blur while Haahld sunna Jubal was still holding his sides and hooting. There was a meaty *thump* as the toe of the girl's boot slammed into the native's groin.

King's lips quirked upward; he thought he'd have been better prepared than the luckless Haahld, but then he'd stopped thinking of women as necessarily helpless when he was an ensign leading a patrol to break up a brawl in a military brothel in Peshawar Town. An Afghan tart crouching under a table had nearly cut his hamstrings with a straight-razor, and he'd never forgotten the raw terror of the moment.

The haw-hawing laughter turned into a strangled shriek of pain as the man doubled over and fell to the ground, clutching himself and turning brick red. *Ouch.* That hard a kick in the testicles was no joke—something might have been ruptured; the girl's long legs were slender, but muscled like a temple acrobat's from running and riding and tree-climbing. *Now*, there's *native talent*, he thought, grinning and wincing slightly.

She stood back in the sudden silence, then seemed to lose a little of her bristling aura as most of the company guffawed and slapped their thighs; even Robre, who seemed like a sobersided young man, grinned openly.

Haahld was puking helplessly now, and moaning. Someone threw a bucket of water over him, which seemed to give him a little strength, and he crawled away to haul himself upright along a tree trunk, still nursing his crotch with one hand. He got a good deal of witty medical advice about poultices from the crowd, although a few of the older and more respectable looked shocked and disapproving.

"Well, miss, generally if I want to kick a man in the groin, I handle it myself rather than hiring it done," King said, smiling. "Although I concede that was good work of its kind. What else can you do?"

"Ride. Rope. Run like a deer. Handle a pack mule. Track meatgame or big cat—or a man—through brush country; we lived aside in deep woods. I'm a pretty good shot, too."

She turned, unslung the crossbow from her saddle and fired it at the target eighty yards away. The snap of the string and the *thunk* of the bolt striking the magnolia came almost instantly, and the octagonal steel head sank deep into the midriff of the human figure chalked out on the bark. King raised a brow, impressed despite himself, and at the speed with which she reloaded. Then she slid the tomahawk from where it rested across the small of her back and threw; that went home in the center of the *X* they'd carved in a dead pine twenty paces away. Haahld winced away—he'd used that trunk to regain his feet—and fell again.

"Your man Robre there can look at my beasts," she said. "Sound backs 'n' feet, 'n' kept proper."

"Well and good," King said calmly, as Robre did just that, picking up hooves to check their shoeing and seeing that no bare gall-marks or sores hid beneath the tack.

King continued: "But why do you want to go on a dangerous expedition?"

"You're going into the east woods," she said. "Mebbe as far as the Black River, *naw?* I can't go that far by my own self; too dangerous."

King frowned; he'd heard of her obsession. "I'm not taking a . . . what's your term? War party? I'm going to hunt, not fight."

For the first time Sonjuh smiled, although it wasn't a particularly pleasant expression: "Mebbe not, but that won't be much of a never mind to the swamp-devils. If your trail-boss there—" She used her chin to indicate Robre. "—has told you it's unlikely, he's a mite too cheerful about the prospect, to my way of thinking."

"Well then, miss: can you cook?"

She flushed again, and opened her mouth, then closed it. When she spoke, it was with tight calm. "I'm not looking to hire on as kitchen help, Empire-Jefe."

"When I'm in the field, usually my man Ranjit does for both of us," King said. "But I need him for other work now. You can carry our provisions on your mule and do our cooking and Robre's; same daily rate for your work and your animals as the rest. Take it or leave it."

Their eyes locked, and after a long moment she nodded. *And you can control your temper* somewhat, *my red-haired forest nymph*, he thought, inclining his head slightly. He wasn't going to take a complete berserker along, no matter how attractive and exotic. *Stalking the wild Sonjuh will add a little spice to our expedition, eh, what?*

One of the pieces of advice his father had given him when he got his commission was that excitable women were wearing, but often worth the trouble.

A shout brought their heads around. Haahld had recovered enough to pull Sonjuh's tomahawk out of the dead pine. He'd also recovered enough to start shrieking again, a torrent of curses and threats. His first throw was erratic but vigorous; not only Sonjuh but also half a dozen others went flat as it pinwheeled by. The handle struck a mule on the rump, and the beast flung both heels back and plunged across the meadow braying indignantly, knocking Robre down and nearly stepping on him. Haahld wrenched at another throwing-ax stuck in the tree, froth in his beard; several men shouted, and Sonjuh did a rapid leopard-crawl toward her crossbow.

King wasted no time. His Khyber knife was slung at the back of his belt with its hilt to the right. He drew it, and threw with a hard whipping overarm motion; like many who'd served on the North West Frontier, he'd spent some time learning how to handle the versatile Pathan weapon.

His had a hilt fringed with tiny silver bells, but the business part was eighteen inches of pure murder, a thick-backed single-edged blade tapering to a vicious point, like an elongated meat-chopper from the kitchens of Hell. It turned four times, flashing in the bright morning sun, then pinned Haahld's arm to the stump like a nail, standing quivering with his blood running down the wood. The silver bells chimed. . . .

Another silence, and Haahld's eyes turned up in his head; his fall tore the *chora*-knife out of the wood, and the thump of his body on the ground was clearly audible.

"Somebody see to him," King said. "And to that mule."

Sonjuh was staring at him, in a way that made him stroke his mustache with the knuckle of his right hand in a quick sleek gesture; Robre was giving him a considering look, evidently reconsidering first impressions. Knife-throwing was more of a circus trick than a real fighting technique, but there were occasions when it was impressive, without a doubt.

"No trouble with your local laws?" King asked, sotto voce.

Robre shook his head. "*Naw.* Haahld fell on his own doings." A grin. "Couldn't hardly do anything right, after that she-fiend hoofed him in the jewels. He'd been beat by a woman—'n' beatin' her back would just make him look mean as well as weak."

"Well, their customs have the charm of the direct and simple," King muttered to himself, in Hindi.

Sonjuh had gone to investigate his supplies after she retrieved her tomahawk and beasts, unpacking her mule beside the boxes and sacks. She returned leading her riding horse.

"Four o' them *ru*pees," she said, holding out a hand. "The stuff you need, I can get it in Dannulsford 'n' be back in about an hour."

King blinked in mild surprise; he'd left purchasing trail supplies to Robre, who seemed unlikely to miss anything important. When he said so, Sonjuh snorted.

"You've got enough cornmeal 'n' taters 'n' bacon and such," she said contemptuously. "Plain to see a man laid it in. Men don't live like people on their ownesome; they live like bears with a cookfire. If I'm going to cook, I'm going to do it right—I have to eat it, too, don't I?"

King handed her the money and stood shaking his head bemusedly as she galloped off. Her dog sat near the pile of supplies she'd set him to guard, giving a warning growl if anyone approached them too closely.

"Hoo," Robre said, looking south down the pathway that led to the Alligator Jefe's steading. "Taking Sonjuh Head-on-Fire with us . . . ought to make the trip right interesting, Jefe King."

"My thought exactly," King said, and laughed.

"What's that?" King asked, waving a hand to indicate the loud *tock-tock-tock* sound that echoed through the open forest of oak and hickory.

Robre's brows rose; the Imperial was astonishingly ignorant of common things, for a man who was a better-than-good woodsman and tracker.

"That's a peckerwood, Jefe," he said. "A bird, sort of 'bout the size of a crow, with a red head 'n' white under the wings. Makes that sound by knocking holes in trees, looking for bugs to eat. The call's something like—"

The hard tocsin of the woodpecker's beak stopped and gave way to a sharp, raucous *keek-keek-keek*.

"—like that."

The fact that he'd fallen into the habit of calling the Imperial *Jefe*—technically the word for a clan chief, but often used informally for any important man—rather surprised him. Everyone else in the hunting party did, too, even Sonjuh, whose new gift-name of Head-on-Fire had stuck for good reason.

The men-at-arms from the coast obeyed like well-trained hunting dogs, of course, but they didn't count; although they'd fought hard in recent wars against his people and the Mehk, legend said they were descendants of those who'd been slaves to the Seven Tribes in the olden times.

No, it was something in the man himself that did it. Thinking back, Robre appreciated how shrewd it had been to let Ranjit Singh be the one who tested the hand-to-hand skills of the men. Singh had beaten them all easily—Robre suspected he would have lost himself, and had been picking up tips on his wrasslin' style since. That had let King's follower start out with the prestige of one who was a hard man for certain-sure. Then he'd shown himself to be fair, as well, good-humored, a dab hand at anything to do with horses, as ready to pitch in to help with a difficult job as he was to thump a man who back-talked him.

Which in turn made his unservile deference to King's leadership easy to copy.

Fact of the matter is, King's unnatural good at getting people to do what he wants, Robre mused.

Most of all, the Imperial officer simply *assumed* that he was a lord wherever he went, one of the lords of humankind. Not with blows and curses and arrogance, which would only have aroused furious—murderous—resentment among proud clansmen, but with a quietly unshakable certainty that went right down to the bone. It set Robre's teeth a little on edge, though he couldn't put his finger on anything specific.

King stopped and looked around, his double-barreled hunting rifle in the crook of his left arm; Robre had his bow in hand, and a short broad-bladed spear with a bar across the shaft below the head slung over his back.

"Pretty country," the Imperial said. "Not many farms these past two days, though. Not since that . . . what's your word for it?"

"Station," Robre said; that was the term for several families living close for defense, surrounded by a palisade. "No, not this far east. Too close to the Black River, 'n' the swamp-devils."

"Are there many of them?"

"Thicker 'n lice, down in the Big Thicket swamps. They hunt each other mostly, every little band against its neighbors, but every now 'n' then some try crossing the river for man's-flesh and plunder. More lately, what with more of our folk settling in the woods 'n' making ax-claims."

They'd been on the trail for a week and a half, counting from the morning they took the ferry across the Three Forks at Dannulsford, traveling without any particular hurry. Once past the bottomland swamps, too prone to flooding to have much permanent population, they'd traveled for two days through country where as much as a quarter of the land was cleared. Those new-won farms had petered out to an occasional outpost, then to land visited only for hunting and seasonal grazing, claimed by no clan. It rolled gently, rising now and then to something you might call a low hill, or sinking more and more often into swamp and marsh.

This particular stretch was dry and sandy, sun-dappled between tall wide-spaced trees, oak and hickory and tall sweet-scented pines; the lower ground was patched with a layer of sassafras—bright scarlet now—dogwood, and hophornbeam. The leaves of the oaks had turned a soft yellow brown where they weren't flaming red, and the hickories had a mellower golden tint; the leaf-litter was already heavy, rustling about their feet. To the east and south the woods grew denser, with water-loving types like tupelo and persimmon and live oak; that was laced together with wild grapevines and kudzu.

It was thick with birds now, as well, parakeets eating acorns off the trees, grouse and wild turkey on the ground, and squirrels rustling through the undergrowth after the nuts. And not only birds . . .

"Ah!" King exclaimed softly, going down on one knee.

A wetter patch of ground showed where he parted the spicebush. In it was the mark of a narrow cloven hoof, driven deep. The tips of each mark were too rounded and the impression too square overall for a deer. . . .

"Wild boar?" the Imperial asked softly.

"Don't know what a boar is," Robre said equally quietly; they often had to hunt for a word like that, though the Imperial had become fluent enough at the tongue of the clans, if thickly and weirdly accented. "Wild pig, right enough."

He cast forward, following the trail and gauging the weight and length of stride. "Big un, too. My weight 'n' half again. Might be a bull-pig with a sounder"—group of females and their young—"if one of the sows is in season." Wild pigs bred year-round in this mild climate.

"Let's go look, then," King said with a grin, wrapping a loop of his rifle's sling around his left elbow and pulling it taut; that gave him a firm three-point brace when the weapon was against his shoulder. "We could use some fresh pork."

Robre made a note of the trick with the sling; he'd been getting a thorough rundown on Imperial firearms and how to use them. He also noted that King wasn't the least bit bothered by the thought of going into thick bush after tricky, dangerous game. The clansman put an arrow to the knock of his recurved bow, a hunting broadhead with four razor-sharp blades to the pyramid-shaped iron head.

Damn, but I can't help but like this buckaroo, Robre thought. *Toplofty or no.* Aloud, he said, "You've hunted them before?"

"Boar? Yes. But in India we take them on horseback, with lances," King said casually, and Robre blinked at the thought.

"Well, mebbe yours are a might different. Ours here, they'll mostly run, 'less you get between a sow 'n' her young uns. Or a boar that's breeding, he'll charge you often as not 'cause he feels like killing something. Or sometimes they'll fight out of pure cussedness."

They followed the trail downhill, one to either side, walking at a slow steady pace with as little noise as possible; they kept trees between themselves and their goals as much as possible, and the wind was in their faces, giving no warning to any sensitive noses ahead.

Sonjuh was panting a little, trotting through an opening in the woods with the twenty-five-pound weight of the wild turkey on her back; she'd cleaned it and cut off the head—and removed her crossbow bolt—before throwing it over one shoulder and holding it by the feet as she headed back to camp, but it was a big cock-bird fat with feeding on fall nuts and acorns. It would make a pleasant change from dried provisions, now that the remaining venison from two days back was gone off, even if it would also be a chore to pluck it. But get the feathers off, rub a little chipotle on it, and roast it over a slow hickory fire with a few handfuls of mesquite pods thrown on the coals now and then—she'd bought a sack in Dannulsford—and stuffed with some corn bread, the pecans and mushrooms she'd gathered . . .

No better eating than a fat fall turkey cooked that way—

Her mouth watered. Then her gorge rose; sometimes just thinking of the word *eating* was enough to bring back the screams and the blood. . . . For a long moment she halted and pressed a hand to her eyes, fighting for control. Slasher's low warning growl brought her back to the light of day; he'd been trotting along, utterly content with the live-for-the-moment happiness of a dog out in the woods with his master, and wouldn't make that noise for anything but a present threat.

Now he crouched and bristled, his nose pointing like an arrow to some chest-high underbrush. The girl lowered the gutted bird to the rustling leaves and squatted in cover, bringing her crossbow around. A chill struck at her gut—could it be swamp-devils? This was farther west than her father's steading had been, but it was possible—

No. The bushes were moving, but in a random way; swamp-devils would be more cautious. Animals, then, but ones confident enough not to care if they were heard. That ruled out deer. Wild cattle or woods-bison would be visible, so—

Wind blew toward her, mild and cool. The dog's nostrils flared, and hers caught a familiar scent, gamy and rank.

Oh, jeroo, she thought, trying to make out numbers and directions. At least a dozen, counting yearlings; there were glimpses of black bristly hide through the shrubs, and the ground was too be-grown for a human to run fast or straight. A sounder of wild pig would go through it easy as snakes, and they were nearly as fast as a horse in a rush. She'd walked right into their midst in a brown study. *Stupid, stupid. This could be more lively than I'd like.* It all depended on which way they ran—it was a toss-up whether they'd flee or attack if they scented a human.

The ground rose to the south, and the underbrush opened out under tall hardwoods. She came to her feet and began to walk, placing her feet carefully and trying to look in all directions at once. If she was very lucky, none of them would be in her way.

Luck ran out. A low-slung form burst out of the reddish-yellow sassafras where it had been feeding on the seeds, squealing in panic; from its size, a four-month spring-born piglet. By pure reflex, Slasher spun in place and snapped, taking a nip out of the young pig's rump and lending a note of agony to its cries.

"Oh, *shee-yit on faahr*!"

Sonjuh was up and running when the piglet's squeals were joined by others, deeper and full of rage. She risked a look behind her and wished she hadn't; the young pig's momma was coming for her with legs churning in a blur of motion, big wicked head down, little eyes glinting and tusks wet and sharp—what woodsmen called a land-pike. It weighed more than she did, a long low-slung shape of bone and gristle tipped with knives, and well used to killing—wild pig ate anything they could catch from acorns and earthworms to deer and stray children, and even a cougar would hesitate to take on a full-grown adult. If this one caught her, they'd all feast this morning and crunch her bones for the marrow.

Slasher spun and charged the pig, mouth wide open and his growl ratcheting up into a roaring snarl-howl. Sonjuh spun, too, forced herself to steadiness, took stance, whipped the crossbow up to her shoulder. The fighting-dog was dancing around the wild pig, feinting, leaping back and rearing on his hind legs to dodge a slash that would have laid his belly open, then dashing in to snap at the hind-quarters. The sow kept those down, pivoting and whipping her short tusks in deadly arcs. The girl brought the business end of the weapon down, sighting over tailfeather and bolt-head, then squeezed the trigger.

Twunk!

The hickory thumped her shoulder through the shift. A blur

nearly too fast to see, the bolt hit the sow behind her shoulder, sinking almost to the stiff leather fletching. The animal screamed in pain, spinning again as it tried to reach the thing that hurt it, and the sound went out in a fine spray of blood from its muzzle. A lung-shot, fatal in minutes if not instantly.

Sonjuh didn't wait to see. She was running again instantly, slinging the weapon as she went, dodging and jinking through the underbrush, shouting: "Slasher! Follow!" over her shoulder.

More squeals followed her, and some of them—another glance over her shoulder showed what was coming. A boar, full-grown. No, *two* of them—they must have been getting ready to fight for the females, just when she came along. Coyote had sent her luck, his kind; or maybe Olsatyn: Lord o' Sky must be asleep, or out hunting, or sporting with his wives, because he certainly wasn't listening to her prayers.

Now both the boars were after her, with the instinct of their kind to mob a threat added to the mindless belligerence of rutting season. Both of them were huge, night-black except for the grizzled color of the bristles that thickened to manes on their skulls and the massive shoulders, better than twice a big man's weight, their short straight tails held up like banners. Long white tusks curled up and back on either side of their glistening snouts, sharp-pointed ivory daggers that could rip open a horse or bear, much less a human. They fanned out as they came, throwing up leaves and bits of bush in their speed, with all the grown females hot on their heels. Wet open mouths showed teeth and red gullets, let out hoarse rending screams of rage.

Breath burned dry in her throat, and her long legs flashed as she waited for the savage pain of a tusk knocking her down. There was a big oak ahead of her though, ten feet to the lowest branch—

—and two men coming out from behind hickories to either side.

"Run, you idjeets!" she screamed and went up the tree's root-bole at a full-tilt run without breaking stride, the bark blessedly rough under fingers and the soft flexible leather of her moccasin-boots' soles.

She leapt off that sideways, hands slapping down on the thick branch, her feet coming up as she hugged it like a lover with arms and legs both. A black missile flew through the air below her, and a bone dagger flashed inches below her back. With a convulsive effort she threw a knee over the limb and swung herself up and stood with an arm around the main trunk, panting and shuddering and on the edge of nausea as blood beat in her ears.

Eric King saw the red hair flying as Sonjuh Head-on-Fire cleared a bush with a raking stride and hit the ground in a blur of motion, head down and fists pumping as she ran—much like a deer, as she'd claimed, light on her feet and very quick.

"Run, you idjeets!" she screamed, as she went through the space between him and Hunter Robre, with her dog on her heels.

The boars were on her heels as well, far too close to shoot as they burst out of the undergrowth. King flung himself to one side with a yell, and heard Robre doing likewise. He landed on his back with a jarring thud, and the right barrel of the double rifle went off with a *crack* like thunder in his ear.

"Dammit," he wheezed as he came back up on one knee. Then he shouted *"Krishna!"*

Something shot out of the yellow-red underscrub at him like a cannonball, and he snapped the weapon up to his shoulder. Instinct and training brought the sights between a pair of furious red-glinting piggy eyes barely ten feet away, and the recoil punished his shoulder.

Crack!

It was a sow; less dangerous than the boars, but only in an academic fashion seeing as it was nearly on top of him. The heavy .477 slug blasted its way through the thick skull and the brain beneath it; the wild pig nosed into the leaf-mold and dropped at his feet, dead although its little sharp hooves were still kicking. King came back to his feet and broke open the action of the rifle, shaking out the spent brass and pulling two more long fat cartridges from the bandolier across his chest. As he snapped it shut, he saw a flickering montage: another sow dragging herself back into the bushes with her hind legs limp and one of Robre's arrows through her spine; a boar landing again after a leap that had nearly caught Sonjuh, landing with an agility unbelievable in so gross a beast; the girl's staring face in the tree; beyond that Slasher and the other boar whirling in a snapping, snarling, stabbing dance that cast up a fog of yellow leaves and acorns from the forest floor; Robre whipping out another arrow from his quiver and nocking it, drawing the shaft to his ear.

Then both men had more than enough to engage their attention, as the rest of the sounder boiled out of the brush and attacked with the reckless omnivore aggression that men and swine shared. It was a big group, in these man-empty woods so rich in their kinds of food, and not much afraid of humankind. King shot twice more before he had to use the empty double rifle to defend himself from a pig that seized it in her mouth, wrenching it away and then running off into the woods in panic flight. The rest of the sounder followed, less the dead.

Except for the boars.

King felt a profound wish for his rifle—loaded and in his hands, not lying uselessly a dozen paces off. Time seemed to slow like honey. Not far off a boar stood alone, the gouge of a bullet wound bleeding freely down one dusty-black flank, and an arrow standing out of a ham, making abortive stabs to either side with its tusks and panting like a steam engine in a Bihari coal mine. The other backed off from where Slasher held a natural fort behind a thick fallen log, turning just in time to take Robre's arrow in the armor-thick hide and bone around its shoulders rather than the vulnerable flank. It staggered and then charged, and Robre ripped free the spear slung across his back by the simple expedient of snapping the rawhide thongs that bound it by main strength. He brought it around, dropping to one knee and thrusting the blade of the spearhead out to receive the living missile that hurtled toward him, mud and leaves spraying out behind it.

King had his own boar, and nothing but the Khyber knife in his hand. Its charge was slowed a little—a very little—by the arrow wound, and it came silently save for the bellows-panting of near exhaustion. The Imperial tensed himself to leap aside and then in—not much of a chance, because he was weary, too, and the sidewise strike of the boar's head would be swifter than a hooded cobra.

"*Kuch dar nahin hai!*" he shouted, the ancient motto of his house. *There is no such thing as fear!*

A wolf-gray streak came from behind the boar, soaring over the litter of the forest floor, from shadow into light. Slasher's jaws clamped down like a mechanical grab edged with ripping fangs on the beast's hock just before it would have cannoned into the human. Snapping-swift it spun and tried to gash the dog, but the same motion flung Slasher around like a spinning top. King leapt as well, *onto* the boar. It was like landing on top of a living boulder, one that heaved beneath him with terrifying strength and ferocity, battering him about like a pea in a can. He reversed the *chora*-knife and slammed it into the thrashing mass beneath him, hanging on to the hilt like grim death with one hand and a handful of bristly mane with the other, working the blade back and forth between the boar's ribs. It was dying, blood spraying out of nose and mouth, but it could still kill him. He twisted his legs about it and put forth all the strength that was in him.

Hands came into his field of vision, long slender hands, well shaped but with dirt beneath the fingernails and ground into the knuckles, holding a crossbow. The string released, and the bolt blossomed from the base of the boar's skull. It shuddered, hammered the ground with its head, and died. King rose from the limp body.

Sonjuh was watching him, head tilted slightly to one side. "Why'd you jump in, when Slasher had him by the leg?" she said quietly. "You could've gone for your gun."

King shook his head, suddenly aware of how glorious the young morning sunlight was. "He'd have killed the dog," he said.

They were close. Suddenly the clan-girl was in his arms, and their lips met. The moment went on . . .

. . . until Robre cleared his throat. Sonjuh jumped back, two spots of red in her cheeks. King straightened, suddenly conscious that he'd lost his turban. The Bear Creek man was leaning on his spear beside the body of the other boar, scowling and brushing at a trickle of blood from his nostrils.

Eric King laughed, smoothing back his mustache with the knuckle of his right hand. "Looks like we're having pork tonight," he said gaily.

"I left a turkey just back there," Sonjuh blurted, and ran off after it,

'N' when the snow-winds lifted
Then summer came again;
Three summers of snow 'n' ice

Then the warmth once more;
Olsatyn, he cursed 'n' fled
No more he held the Sun enslaved
Black hammer that broke the Sun,
Broke on the sword of Lord o' Sky;
He called the tribes out!
Out from where they sheltered
Blessed them for staying clean
Not eating of man's-flesh,
When hunger was bitter;
Gave them His blessing
Gave seed corn 'n' stock
Set the bounds 'n' the bans
Named clan 'n' tribe 'n' law;
But those others who'd fallen
Who'd eaten of man's-flesh;
Them did God curse forever
Lord o' Sky gave us their lands;
With steel 'n' fire we drove them out
Drove the devils east into the swamps
Festering land of evildoers—

Eric King leaned back in his canvas chair and gnawed the last of the savory meat from a rib as he listened—one of the yearling piglets, to be precise, slathered with a fiery-hot tomato-based sauce full of garlic and peppers before grilling. Sonjuh dawtra Pehte had outdone herself, from the stuffed turkey to the pudding of corn-meal, molasses, and spices.

Hunter Robre sat on a log on the other side of the fire, his fingers moving on an instrument he called a *gittah*—surprisingly like the sitar in both form and name—as he half sang, half chanted his people's creation-myth. The flickering of the low fire showed a ring of rapt bearded faces. And one beardless one, her chin propped in a palm and the other scratching in the ruff of the great gray dog lying beside her, the firelight bringing out the ruddy color of her hair as she puffed meditatively on a corncob pipe.

A huge crimson oak stood over the campsite, and its leaves took fire as well from the yellow flames, shifting in a maze of scarlet and gold amid the rising column of sparks. The stars above were bright and many, if you let your eyes recover from the fire glow a little. The air had turned soft and a little cool, with wisps of mist drifting over the little stream to the south; it smelled pleasantly of cooking and hickory smoke and horses. Somewhere a beast squalled in the distance, and an owl hooted.

King tossed the bone into the coals as Robre finished. *Well, that's another,* he thought. *I've heard worse. I've definitely heard sillier ones.*

Every folk he knew of had some sort of legend attached to the Fall; even the Empire had Kipling's great Exodus Cantos, about St. Disraeli and the evacuation that had taken his own ancestors from England to India. He smiled wryly to himself. Kipling had made it all sound very heroic, but the Kings had a tradition of scholarship as well as Imperial service, and lived near refounded Oxford. From what he'd read in sources of the time, it had been more of a panic flight, teetering on the brink of chaos, with only the genius of Disraeli and Salisbury and the others to make it possible at all. A lucky few had made it out to India and the Cape and Australia before the final collapse; the other nine-tenths of the population had stayed perforce, and starved, and died.

Robre's version of his people's origins made the founders of the Seven Tribes a host of saintly warriors, when they'd probably been a handful of scruffy but successful bandits; the great battles against the "devils" were probably bloody little skirmishes with a few hundred, or perhaps a few score, on each side.

Still, the epic had a certain barbaric vigor; much like the people who had made it. They'd certainly done well over the past few generations, pushing their borders back on all sides . . . from what Banerjii and the garrison commander at Galveston had told him.

"Heya, Jefe," one of the clansmen said. "Tell us some more 'bout the Empire."

He did; a rousing tale of raid and counter-raid along the North West Frontier courtesy of the great Poet Laureate, and described the mountains in his own home province, Kashmir. They were even more eager for stories of the great cities and oceangoing steamships, locomotives and flying machines, but those they took as fables, more so than their own tales of haunts and witches and Old Man Coyote, evidently some sort of minor godlet-trickster. Their own bogies frightened them, but foreign marvels were merely entertainment.

Although I think Miss Head-on-Fire believes me somewhat, because she wants to, King thought, conscious of her shining eyes. *And you, as well, Robre Hunter, because you're no fool and can listen and add two and two.*

The clansman had noted the direction of Sonjuh's eyes, as well, and was half-scowling. *Jealous?* King thought. The big clansman hadn't shown much interest in the girl himself . . . but a man often didn't discover he wanted a woman until she turned to another, and that was as true among natives as among the sahib-log, as natural in a nighted forest about an open fire as in the blazing jeweled halls of the Palace of the Lion Throne in Delhi.

King smiled again, and had one of the kegs of New Zealand whiskey brought and set out on a stump near one of the other cooking fires. It was a bit of a waste, being finest Dunedin single-malt, but such gestures never hurt; and what was the point of being wealthy if you couldn't indulge yourself now and then? The local hirelings clustered about it eagerly; it was enough like their own raw corn-liquor to be familiar, and enough better that they recognized the difference. Robre brought three mugs over to where King sat and Sonjuh sprawled beside her villainous-looking guardian. He handed one to the girl—for a barbarian, his manners were almost courtly, in a rough-hewn way—and one to King.

"Sounds like a place worth seeing, your Empire," the clansman said.

"It's not a place, it's a world," King replied.

"Jeroo," Sonjuh said with a sigh. "Seems the world's a bigger place than we thought. Went to San Antwoin oncet with Pa, 'n' that was a wonder—stone walls, 'n' twice a hand of thousands within 'em. Sounds like that's no more than Dannulsford Fair next to your home, Empire-Jefe. But I'd like to see it."

King thought of her alone and bewildered and friendless on the docks of Bombay, or worse, Capetown, and winced slightly. Furthermore, she was just crazy enough to try getting passage on some tramp windjammer out of Galveston. She'd be a sensation at court if some wild chance took her that far, but that was no fate for a human being.

"That . . . that really wouldn't be a very good idea, my dear," he said. "A foreign land is more dangerous than these forests."

Robre nodded. "Bare is your back without clan to guard it," he said, with the air of someone quoting a proverb, which he probably was. "Cold is a heart among strangers."

The redhead pouted slightly, and he went on a little hastily: "They'll be a lot of sore heads tomorrow, if you were thinkin' of moving on, Jefe."

His nod took in the rowdy scene around the keg. Not everyone was there, of course; Ranjit Singh and the garrison troopers were standing picket tonight by turns. King might have trusted that duty to Robre, if none of the others, but the Sikh wouldn't hear of anyone not in the Queen-Empress's service doing guard duty.

"I was thinking of moving on," King said, taking a little more of the whiskey and sighing satisfaction. The transplanted Scots of the South Island's bleak Antarctic-facing shores had kept their ancestors' skills alive. "I want a crack at those tigers before I go. But we can't take the full caravan with us there."

"No, true enough," Robre said. "Not enough fodder for that many horses, either. And"—he flicked his eyes to Sonjuh—"that's mighty close to the Black River. Swamp-devils prowl there."

"Hmmm," King said, stroking his mustache. "How much of a problem are they likely to be?"

"Not so bad, if you're careful," Robre said. "Mostly they live farther south 'n' east, down in the Big Thicket country 'n' the Sabyn river swamps. You mostly won't see more 'n three, four of 'em together, grown bucks, that is, for all that there's a lot of them down there. Also they're short of real weapons, not hardly; they hate each other poison-bad, 'n' who'd trade with them?"

King nodded. That was the common way of things, with those who'd kept up the cannibal ways that brought their ancestors through the terrible years of hunger and death after the Fall. When men hunted each other to eat, there could be no trust, and trust was what let even the wildest men work together. Usually man-eaters had no groupings larger than an extended family, and often they barely retained the use of speech and fire. Human beings were not meant to live like that; only the hammer from the skies and the planetwide die-off could have warped so many of the survivors so bitterly.

Sonjuh stirred. "There was twenty in the gang that hit our place," she said. "Pa 'n' me 'n' the others, we killed four—they caught us by surprise. The posse got most of the rest, but a few escaped. 'N' they all had iron."

Of course, they can *change,* King thought. *A lot of the European savages are organized enough to be dangerous. Not to mention the Russians, who are* deadly *dangerous.*

Robre shook his head. "That was a freak, Head-on-Fire. There's not been a raid that size in . . . well, not since Fast-Foot Jowan 'n' his sons were killed, what, three years ago?"

"And the Kinnuh fam'ly, four before that. Before that, never, just bushwhacking by ones or twos. I tell you, they're learning, 'n' have been for years. If they ever learn to make big war parties—"

"Mebbe," Robre said dubiously. He turned his head back to King. "We needn't take more 'n four, five altogether," he said. "More 'n you're not likely to see the big cats. I went in alone, myself 'n' never saw sign of the swamp-devils 'tall."

"Four, then," King said. "Ranjit Singh I'll leave here to run the camp; he'll complain, but someone has to do it. You, of course, and me, and two of the garrison soldiers with their rifles just in case—"

"And me!" Sonjuh said, rising. Robre began to say something; King cut him off with a negligent gesture. The redhead went on: "I won't do anything hog-wild, I swear it by God. But you've seen I can take care of myself 'n' carry my load. 'N' if you do run into swamp-devils . . . this is what I came for!"

King thought for a long moment, tapping his fingers on the arm of his chair. "All right, then, true enough. I don't expect we'll be gone more than four or five days—I can't spend much more time than that anyway, my furlough is long but not indefinite. And you will *not* go haring off on your own. Understood?"

"I swear it, Empire-Jefe," she said.

Robre sighed. "You're the man payin' for this," he said unwill-ingly. "'N' she's right, Coyote nip her, she *is* as good a hunter as any-one on this trail but you 'n' me."

"Excellent," King said. "Well, time to—"

"I'm for a walk," Sonjuh said. She had relaxed from her cat-tense quiver, and smiled as she looked at him. "Care to walk along with me for a spell, Empire-Jefe?"

King smiled back; Robre gave a disapproving grunt and stalked away. Sonjuh tossed her head. "It's our law, an unwed girl can walk out with a man if she pleases," she said. "'N' if her Pa 'n' brothers don't object."

"What if her pa and brothers *do* object?" King asked, when they'd strolled far enough to be out of easy sight and hearing of the camp-fires.

Sonjuh looked up at him out of the corners of her eyes. "Why, they warn him off," she said slyly. "Then beat 'n' stomp him if he doesn't listen."

Good thing you're an orphan, King thought but carefully did not say aloud, as he slid an arm around her supple waist. The girl leaned toward him, her head on his shoulder, smelling pleasantly of wood smoke and feminine flesh.

Some time later, Sonjuh gave a moan and pushed herself up on her elbows, looking down to where he kneeled between her legs, a dazed expression on her face.

"*Jeroo!*" she panted. "Corn Lady be my witness, I didn't think there *was* so many ways of sporting!"

King grinned at her. "Benefits of a civilized education," he said.

He'd been given an illustrated copy of the *Kama Sutra* at twelve, and had never had much trouble finding someone to practice with; when you were young, handsome, well spoken, athletic, rich, and the eldest son of a zamindar, you didn't. From Sonjuh's surprise and artless enthusiasm, he gathered that the native men here went at things like a bull elephant in musth.

"But I've been having more fun than you," she said, and laughed. "And looks like you're ready for some."

His grin went wider, and he put a hand under each of her thighs, lifting them up and back.

She chuckled lazily: "Remember what I said about walkin' out?" He nodded, reaching for the pocket of his uniform jacket; the girl had tossed it when she ripped it off his back. "Well," she went on, "if the man gets her with child, then her Pa 'n' brothers—'n' the rest of the clan, too—see to it he takes her to wife. Just so you'd know, Empire-Jefe."

"Behold another wonder of civilization," he said, busy with fingers and teeth on one of the foil packets; being an optimist and no more modest than most young men, he'd slipped half a dozen into his pocket earlier that evening. "Vulcanized rubber."

Sonjuh stared for a moment, then burst into a peal of laughter. "Looks like it's wearin' a rain-cloak!"

King growled and seized a shin under each arm—

V: The People of the Black God

Hunter Robre spread his hands. "I can't make the cats come where they don't have a mind to," he said reasonably, then slapped at a late-season mosquito. Dawn had brought the last of them out, to feed before full sunlight.

The blind where they'd been waiting all night was woven of swamp-reeds, on a hillock of drier ground. The wild-cow yearling they'd staked out was beginning to smell pretty high, and all their night had gotten them was the sight of a couple of cougars sniffing around, and two red wolves who'd had to be shooed off. Forest stood at their back beyond the swamp, tupelo and live oak and cypress knotted into an impenetrable wall by brush and vines, the trees towering a hundred feet and more overhead. Even on a cool autumn morning the smell was heavy and rank, somehow less cleanly than the forests where he spent most of his time. Wisps of mist drifted over the surface of the Black River where it rolled sluggish before them; the other bank was higher than this, and thick with giant pine higher than ship's masts.

"No, you can't," Eric King said, infuriatingly reasonable. He sighed. "I don't expect that tigers of any sort are too numerous here, although it's perfect country for them."

"They aren't common," Robre agreed. "Weren't never seen until my pa's time, when he was my age." Then he puzzled at the way the Imperial had said it. "Why shouldn't there be more tigers here, if it's such good tiger-country? And how would you know?"

King pulled a pack of cigarettes from his breast pocket—that cloth coat had a hunting shirt beat all hollow, and Robre had decided to have a seamstress run him up one—and offered one to his guide. Robre accepted; they were tastier than a pipe, and a lot less messy than a chaw. For a moment they puffed in silence, blowing plumes of smoke at lingering mosquitoes: it didn't matter now if the scent warned off game.

"There weren't any tigers here before the Fall—before the time when Olsaytn stole the Sun, you'd say."

Robre's brows went up. *Odd*, he thought. When he thought of the Before Time, it was simply as *very long ago*, the time of the songs and the heroes; certainly before his grandsire's grandsire's time. The Imperial seemed to think of it more as a set date, as if it were something that had happened in his own lifetime. *Odd way to think. Mebbe it's all that writing they do.*

"Why not?" Robre said. "Plenty of beasts a tiger can tackle that a cougar or wolf can't. What were those fancy words you used last night . . . *ecological niche?*"

King shrugged. "I don't know. There just weren't, or so our *books* say. Why are there elephants in India, and not here? Nobody knows."

Robre grunted noncommittally; he wasn't quite sure if he believed in elephants yet.

King went on: "No lions either. When the fall came, they—the ancestors of the ones you've got now—probably escaped from *circuses*, or *zoos*."

They thrashed out the meaning of those words. Robre rubbed his chin, feeling stubble gone almost silky and reminding himself to shave soon. "Wouldn't folks have eaten them?" he said.

"They probably did eat the elephants in the menageries." King grinned. "But a few predators would have been turned lose before people realized how bad things were going to get. Then, in the chaos, when every man's hand was against every other's . . . well, hungry tigers used to being around people, they'd be good at picking off stragglers, wouldn't they? And most of the dying happened *fast;* by the third or fourth year, people were scarce again in these lands, very scarce. Other things—game and feral livestock that survived in out-of-the-way corners, or country farther south—bred back faster than humans, spreading over the empty lands as the vegetation recovered, and so gave the big cats plenty to hunt. They breed quickly themselves, so even a few pairs could produce a lot of offspring. Eventually they'll fill all the land humans haven't taken over again, but that will need another century or two."

Robre nodded. It made sense in a twisty sort of way, like most of what King said when he wasn't doing an obvious leg-pull. It still made his head itch on the inside. . . .

"And because they're descended from so few, they'll have a lot of mutants . . . freaks, that is, due to inbreeding. Like the black-with-yellow-stripes you shot . . . What's that, by the way?" King said casually, pointing with the hand that held the cigarette.

"What's what?"

Robre turned and looked upstream, across the Black River. Then his eyes grew very wide, and he whipped the cigarette out of his mouth, crushed it out, did the same with King's. The Imperial froze as Robre laid a hand across his mouth, and they crouched watching through the slits in their blind.

The light was growing now, and the mist on the river to the north was lifting. What had showed as mere hints of shape turned hard and definite. A canoe, a big cypress log hollowed out and pointed at both ends, big enough for ten men to kneel and drive their paddles into the mirror-calm surface of the morning river. Beside him King leveled his binoculars and swore, swore very softly in a language Robre didn't understand. He did understand the sentiment, especially since it was the first time the Imperial had seen the swamp-devils. Robre's own eyes went wide as a second canoe followed the first, then a third . . . more and more, until a full ten were in view, the foremost nearly level with them.

He put out a hand, and after a moment King passed him the

binoculars. He'd learned to use them well—another thing he'd save to buy from Banerjii, if he could—and his thumb brought the image sharp and clear.

It is *swamp-devils,* he thought helplessly. *But it* can't *be. Not that many together!*

There was no mistaking them, though. The sloping foreheads and absent chins, faces hideously scarred that grew only sparse bristly beards, huge broad noses, narrow little eyes beetling under heavy brows. The build was unmistakable, too, heavy shoulders and long thick arms, broad feet.

"I thought they were men," King whispered, shaken.

"They were, or leastways their fore-folks were, when we drove 'em into the east."

Swamp-devils right enough, but only a few carried the clubs of ashwood with rocks lashed into a split end that were the commonest tool-weapon of the cannibals. Nearly all the rest had spears with broad iron heads, black bows with quivers of arrows, knives and tomahawks at their belts. They couldn't have gotten all that in raids on his folk and the Kaijan settlements east beyond the Sabyn.

After an eternity, the last of the canoes passed—a full hundred swamp-devil bucks, in plain sight of each other and without a fight breaking out. They kept silence as well, paddling swiftly along the eastern bank, occasionally scanning the western shore. He could feel the weight of their stares, and froze into a rabbit's immobility until the last one pulled out of sight.

"Lord o' Sky!" he gasped. "Lord o' *Sky!*"

"Well," King said whimsically. "I gather that this means trying for tiger on the east bank of the river is definitely out."

Sonjuh dawtra Pehte hummed tunelessly to herself as she stirred the ham and disks of potato in the frying pan—small children had been known to cry when she sang, but *she* liked the sound, which was what mattered. The morning was bright, and cool by the standards she was used to; the smell of the frying food mingled pleasantly with the damp dawn forest. Birds were calling, in a chorus of clucks and cheeps and—

Jeroo, I'm actually happy, she thought. That brought a tang of guilt, but only slightly—the Lord o' Sky had heard her oath, and she intended to keep it or die trying. The Father-God wouldn't care whether or not she regretted the dying. *Of course, E'rc doesn't plan on staying.* That brought a stab, and he'd never hidden it, either. . . .

Running feet sounded through the woods. Slasher woke and pointed his nose in their direction. Sonjuh caught them a few seconds later; she'd already set the food aside and reached for her crossbow. The two coastlander men-at-arms in Imperial service dropped their camp chores—armfuls of wood in one case, fodder gathered for their single pack mule in the other—and went for their rifles. They moved quickly to kneel behind cover on either side of the camp, looking outward in either direction as they worked the actions of their weapons and loaded a cartridge. Even then, she had an instant to notice that. Her people had never had much use for the coastmen, but these were *very* smooth; evidently they'd learned a lot, in the twenty years or so since the Imperial ships arrived to build their fort on Galveston Island.

She relaxed a bit as it became clear that it was Robre and Eric King loping back to the little forward camp. Not much, because she could see their faces.

"Swamp-devils?" she said.

"More 'n I've ever seen in one place," Robre said grimly.

She turned and kicked moist dirt over the fire, stamping quickly to put it out before it could smoke much.

Robre nodded, and gave a concise description of the canoes they'd seen. "You were right, Head-on-Fire. Fore God the Father, there were a hundred of 'em if there were one. What's *happening?*"

"Whatever it is, it's not good," Sonjuh said, her voice stark. *Jeroo, there goes being happy, all of a sudden.* She didn't feel bad, though. Alert, the blood pumping in her ears, everything feeling ready to go. *Pa, Ma, sisters—soon you can rest easy, stop comin' to me in dreams.*

Eric had spread a map out on the ground; she craned forward to look at it. The written names were nothing to her or Robre, but the bird's-eye view of the land was easy enough to grasp, and they'd both learned how to use them.

"We're here," Eric said, tapping their location—not far from the west bank of the Black River. "As I understand it, the . . . swamp-devils . . . live mostly here." His finger moved down to a patch of stylized reeds and trees.

"The most of 'em," Robre confirmed. "But you'll find little bands all through—" His hand swept upward, north and east. "Then they sort of thin out, there's big patches of empty country, 'n' then Cherokee 'n' Zarki; I don't know much about them—nobody does. Then east beyond the Sabyn, you get the Kaijun; sort of backwards, from what I hear, but clean."

"Well, what we just saw was a large group of them moving from north to south, where most of them are. I'd say it was in the nature of a gathering, wouldn't you?"

The two natives looked at each other. "Jeroo," Sonjuh whispered, past a throat gone thick. "If the devils is gathering, then our folk have to know—raids, big raids."

"Raids with *hundreds* of 'em," Robre said. "Lord o' Sky, that's not a raid, that's a *war*, like with the Kumanch or even the Mehk—but they don't kill everyone 'n' eat the bodies."

"A pukka war," Eric said. When Sonjuh gave him a puzzled look, he went on: "A real war, a big war, a proper war."

Robre put up a hand. "Wait a heartbeat," he said. "What *are* we going to tell our folks?"

Sonjuh felt a flash of anger. "That the swamp-devils—"

"That the swamp-devils use canoes? That we saw a big bunch of 'em?" Robre shook his head. "What's Jefe Carul of your Alligators, or Jefe Bilbowb of us Bear Creek folk—never mind clans farther west or south—going to say?"

"Ahhh," Eric King said, and Sonjuh closed her mouth.

If they both thought that, there was probably something to it. She reached for her pipe—it always helped her to think—then made her hand rest on her tomahawk instead.

"We need to learn more," she said, shifting on her hams.

"We do that, 'n' nothing else," Robre said, giving her a respectful glance; Sonjuh warmed a little to him for that.

"So," King said. "Who goes, and who goes back to give a warning."

The girl furrowed her brows. "Well, no sense in *me* going back—Mad Sonjuh Head-on-Fire, dawtra Stinking, Friendless Pehte."

Robre had the grace to blush. "Everyone knows I've a wasp-nest betwixt my ears about the swamp-devils. Wouldn't listen."

"Nor to an outlander like myself," King said thoughtfully. "Robre would be the best, then; he has quite a reputation."

Robre flushed more darkly under his outdoorsman's tan, his blue eyes volcanic against it. "Run out on my friends? And I'm the best woodsman, meaning no offense. You'll need me."

The three looked at each other. They had less than sixty years between them, and when Sonjuh gave a savage grin the two men answered the expression with ones of their own, just as reckless.

"I'll send the two privates . . . the men-at-arms . . . back to Ranjit Singh at the main camp," King said. "And as for us, we'll go see what the hell is brewing."

"What hell indeed, Jefe," Robre said somberly, his smile dying. "Hell indeed."

The telescopic sight brought the canoe closer than Eric King would have wanted, on aesthetic grounds; and while there was no disputing their usefulness, he generally considered scope sights unsporting. *But this isn't a game,* he thought, as he kept the cross-hairs firmly on the lead man . . . or man-thing . . . in the vessel. The three swamp-devils were as hideous as the ones he'd seen before; even knowing what inbreeding, intense selection and genetic drift could do, it was hard to believe that their ancestors had been men.

More like a cross between a giant rat and a baboon, he thought.

They had their wits about them, though; they came down from the north three-quarters of the way toward the western shore, beyond easy bowshot from the east and where it would be simple to run the cypress-log dugout into a creek and disappear. All three kept their eyes moving, and they had bows and quivers or short iron-headed spears to hand. He closed his mind on a bubble of worry, and switched his viewpoint southward. A little hook of land stood fifty yards out in the Black River, covered in reeds and dense vine-begrown brush. At the water's edge lay a deer—a yearling buck, with a broken arrow behind its right shoulder, still stirring and trying to rise. He nodded approval; that had been a very good touch.

The westering sun was touching the tops of the trees behind them, throwing long shadow out over the water. It would dazzle eyes trying to look into the deep jungle-like growth along the riverbank proper, under the heavy foliage of the tupelos and sweet gums.

His lips curled in a satisfied snarl as the swamp-devils froze, their paddles poised and dripping water that looked almost red in the sunset-light. His finger touched delicately against the trigger, hearing the first *click* as it set, leaving only a feather-light pressure to fire. Still, that would be noisy.

The savages turned their canoe toward the mud, gobbling satisfaction at the sight of so much meat ready-caught; they'd assume the deer had run far with the shaft in it, losing whoever shot it. They drove the dugout ashore and the first two hopped out, grabbing the sides and pushing it farther into the soft reed-laced dirt.

Yes, shooting would be far too likely to attract unwelcome attention. He turned his head and nodded fractionally to Sonjuh. The girl let her breath out in a controlled hiss and squeezed the trigger of her own weapon. The deep *tunngg* of the crossbow's release still brought the first swamp-devil's head up; he was just opening his mouth to cry out when the quarrel took him below the breastbone, and he fell thrashing to the ground. At the same instant Slasher came out of the tall grass before them and charged baying, belly low to the ground as he tore forward. King and the native girl charged, as well, on the dog's heels, tulwar and Khyber knife in his hands, bowie and tomahawk in hers.

The second swamp-devil let out a horrified screech, turning back and snatching for his spear, almost turning in time for the point to be of use. Then Slasher was upon him, and he was rolling on the ground screaming and trying to keep those fangs from his face and throat. The third was quicker-witted, or perhaps had just a second longer. He lifted his bow, and was drawing on the ambushers when an eruption of water and mud behind the canoe distracted him. Snake-swift he threw the bow aside and pulled out his tomahawk, half rising to meet Robre's onslaught. The two struck, and fell into the mud at the edge of the water with a tremendous splash.

King accounted himself an excellent runner, but Sonjuh drew

ahead of him, her feet light on the soft ground that sucked at his boots. *I'm eighty pounds heavier, that's all*, he thought. Slasher's teeth were an inch from the screaming swamp-devil's face when she scooped up the spear he hadn't had time to use, thrust it under his ribs, then turned and threw it three paces into the back of the last. Robre wrenched himself free of the slackening grip and chopped twice with his tomahawk.

"I'd have had him in a second," he grumbled. "But thanks."

"Then he wouldn't have counted," Sonjuh said, flashing him a smile. She bent, grabbed a handful of the man's filthy, matted hair and cut a circle through the scalp before wrenching the bloody trophy free.

King swallowed. *Oh, well, she* is *a native*, he thought, and pulled the spear out of the swamp-devil's back instead of speaking. He washed it in the stream, then peered at the head. The light was uncertain, but he could see that the edge of the weapon was ragged, although wickedly sharp. *Uneven forging*, he thought. That happened if you didn't keep the temperature even enough. *An amateur did it*. Not at all like the work of the Seven Tribes, whose smiths were excellent in their primitive way. But the long-hafted hatchet still in the savage's belt was very well made, and the knife likewise. He frowned; according to what he'd been told, the eastern savages had no knowledge of ironworking themselves, but . . .

"Is there much iron ore in these woods?" he asked.

"Plenty," Robre said, wading back ashore after washing the mud and blood off in the river. "Bog-iron, grows in lumps in the swamps. That's one reason our Seven Tribes folks have been pushing across the Three Forks into the forest country—charcoal and ore. Iron from the Cherokee and Mehk costs."

"Well, I think someone has been teaching your swamp-devils how to smelt for themselves," King said grimly. "And how to work it."

Robre snorted. "Be a good trick, to keep 'em from eating their teachers."

Sonjuh shook her head. "No, it makes sense, Hunter-man. Like their gathering in big bands. They're *changing*, 'n' not for the better."

Well, technically, it is *for the better*, King thought. *They're starting to live a* little *more like human beings and a little less like mad beasts. The problem is that men are more dangerous than beasts. And they're still a lot closer to vicious mad beasts than to* real *human beings, like my friends here.*

"What's this?" Robre said. "Never seen anything quite like it."

He pulled something from the ear of the savage who'd been rear paddle—steersman—in the canoe. King took it, looked, and felt sweat break out on his brow; his stomach clenched, and a feeling of liquid coldness stole lower in his guts.

It was a piece of silver jewelry, shaped to the likeness of a peacock's tail. The two natives gaped at him; like any high-caste member of the sahib-log, he was not a man given to quick emotions, or to showing those he did have. The way his soul stood naked on his face for an instant astonished them.

"You seen that before?" Robre asked sharply.

"It's Russian," he said softly, after a moment to bring himself back to self-mastery. "It's the sign of initiation into the cult of Tchernobog—the Black God. The Peacock Angel is one of His other names. Yes, I've seen this before."

The Czar in Samarkand had always been among the Empire's worst enemies. Partly that was a rivalry that went back before the Fall—St. Disraeli had spent much of his earlier life frustrating Russian designs on the Old Empire's territories, or so the records said. Most of the rivalries were Post-Fall, though, after the Russian refugees in Central Asia had made contact with the descendants of the British Exodus in India. There had been some direct conflict, though not much: the Himalayas lay between, and the uninhabited wastelands of Tibet, and the all-too-inhabited hill country of Afghanistan and the Hindu Kush. Fighting through a hostile Afghanistan was like trying to bite an enemy when you had to chew your way through a wasp's nest first. The Afghans hated the *Angrezi Raj* only somewhat less than they loathed the *Russki*.

"They're enemies of ours," King said. "Man-eaters."

"Like the swamp-devils 'n' us?" Robre asked.

"Not very. During the Fall . . . It's a long story. They ate their subjects, not their own people, mostly; afterwards they kept it up as part of their new religion, making human sacrifices to their Black God, and then eating the bodies as a . . . rite that bound them together. Their nobles and rulers, at least. But they like to spread their cult, when they can. I can see how it would change your swamp-devils, too—it would give them a way to work together."

Robre made a disgusted sound, and Sonjuh swore softly before she said, "Like I said. We've *got* to get more scout-knowledge about this."

"So we do," Robre said grimly.

"So we do indeed," King added in the same tone. "For the Empire, as well."

His mind drew a map. The center of Russian power was in Central Asia, between Samarkand where the Czar had his seat, and Bokhara, the religious capital, where the High Priests of Tchernobog were centered. Theoretically the Czar claimed much of European Russia, but it was still mainly wasteland, thinly populated by tribes whom he tried to reclaim with missionaries and Cossack outposts.

Still, they could get out through the Baltic and the Black Sea, King thought. There were Imperial bases in the lands facing reclaimed and recivilized Britain, but they were little more than trading posts and bases for explorers and traders and missionaries of the Established Church. The interior . . . he'd just come from there, and parts of it were almost as bad as this.

Yes, they could slip small groups out—pretend to be something else, Brazilians or whatever—travel by ship . . . But why spend the energy to interfere in this barbarous wasteland? What difference could it make to the contending Powers?

Well, the area is theoretically part of the Empire, he thought, with the part of his mind trained at Sandhurst, the Imperial military academy in the Himalayan foothills. *It's naturally rich, has plenty of unexploited resources, and it could become populous. When we finally get around to developing it, we'll probably rely on the Seven Tribes—make them an autonomous federation, and give them backing.*

That was one of the standard methods, far cheaper and more productive than outright conquest, *if* you could find suitable natives.

If the Czar can weaken them and strengthen their enemies—and Krishna, we'll never give the swamp-devils anything but the receiving end of a punitive expedition—it'll make this region less of a source of strength to the Empire. Which means, he realized dismally, *that this ceases to be an adventure that I could back out of, and becomes a duty that has to be seen through to the end. Oh, well.*

"Let's go," he said aloud.

Robre Hunter hopped out of the canoe. Slasher disappeared into the blackness ahead, silent as a ghost; Sonjuh followed him, nearly as quiet. King and he pushed together, running the dugout into the soft mud under an overhang; the current had cut into a bluff, exposing the root-ball of a big live oak tree and making what was almost a cave. They arranged bushes and reeds to hide the vessel and waited until Sonjuh returned. It was very dark here, with the rustling leaf-canopy above cutting out most of the starlight, and the moon wouldn't be up for a while. The smell of silt-heavy water and decay was strong, but he found himself sniffing deeply to catch the unmistakable man-eater stink.

Now, don't get yourself worked up into a lather, he told himself sternly. *No more dangerous than those there wild pigs.*

Although there was something about the prospect of being eaten by things that walked on two legs and could talk that made his scrotum draw itself up the way no pack of wolves or wild dogs or stalking big cat could do. He was relieved when Sonjuh stuck her head over the tangle of roots and gave a slight *hiss.*

The Imperial made a stirrup of his hands to boost Robre up, and a flash of a grin with it; the unexpected resentment he had felt over her walking out with the Imperial faded a little more. There was a faint path on the natural levee above, more of a deer-track than anything else. Traveling on a beaten way was dangerous, but it saved time—and the noise you made in the underbrush was dangerous, too, in hostile country. He took the lead, with King in the middle and Sonjuh on rear guard; Slasher was weaving in and out ahead of them, dropping back for contact with his mistress every now and then.

Even then, he felt a tinge of envy toward Sonjuh for the well-trained beast. *Quite a girl in every damn way,* he thought, then, *Keep your mind on business, idjeet.*

Eyes were little good in dark this deep. He kept his ears working as he walked, nose, the feeling you got from air on your skin. Once he held up a clenched fist, and the others paused. Slasher had his nose pointed in the same direction, quivering. They went to their bellies in the trailside growth, eeling their way along, until the glimmer of firelight came through. More cautious still, moving with infinite care, he came closer and parted a final screen of tall grass with his fingers, making just enough space to see out.

Oh, shee-it on faahr, he thought.

There were the canoes they'd seen, and as many again, drawn up on the beach. A campfire burned higher, and something seethed in a big iron pot hung; knowing swamp-devils, his stomach twisted at what might be cooking, from the pork-smell of it. Every troop or family of them had one such pot, heirloom and symbol . . . A clump of them sat around the fire, at least half a dozen, reaching in to pull gobbets out or dip up hot broth in wooden ladle-spoons, talking in their gobbling, grunting tongue, snarling and snapping at each other occasionally. One sank his teeth into another's ear, hanging on until three or four of the others kicked him loose.

King came up beside him, whispered in his ear: "We could make our retreat a little safer, don't you think? I wouldn't like to come running back and meet those chappies." He went on for a few soft sentences.

"Good idea, Jefe," Robre said; it was a risk, but it would give them an added margin of safety on their return if it worked. If it didn't and the sentries were able to rouse their fellows deeper in the woods, the three of them could just high-tail it.

He drew an arrow from his quiver, stuck its point in the earth, drew more and set them ready to hand. Sonjuh settled in behind branches, down on belly and elbows—that was one advantage of a crossbow, you could shoot it lying down. When—if—he came back from this trip, he'd have an Imperial rifle that could do that and more besides. Still, the bow had some advantages. King turned to take rear guard, with the firepower of his rifle.

I'd have done the same in his place, Robre thought. *But I'd have argued about it.* The Imperial was a good man in a tight place, and not the least shy—no doubt about it. But he was disturbingly . . . cold-blooded, *that's the word.* Though not too cold-blooded to attract the attentions of a very attractive girl—

He thrust everything from his mind save the bow as he came

erect. It was a hundred long paces from here to the fire, a long shot in the night. The sinew and horn and wood of the Kumanch weapon creaked as he drew, a full 120 pounds of draw. Back to the angle of the jaw, sighting over the arrowhead and then up . . . he loosed, and the string snapped against the black buffalo-hide bracer on his left wrist.

One of the grisly figures around the fire looked up suddenly, perhaps alerted by the whisper of cloven air; half-animal they might be, but the savages were survivors of generation upon generation of survivors in a game where losers went into the stewpot. He began to spring erect, but that merely put the arrow through his gut rather than into his chest. With a muffled howl he dropped backwards into the flames and lay there, screeching and sprattling, the iron pot falling on him and its contents gushing out to three-quarters smother the fire. His second shot was on its way before the first hit, and the third three seconds after that, and then he was firing as steadily as a machine. Sonjuh fired her crossbow—and then had to take a third of a minute to reload it, bracing her foot in the stirrup at its head and hauling back on the jointed, curved lever that bent the heavy bow and forced the thick string into the catch.

By that time his quiver was about empty. The cannibals had churned about for a moment, eyes blinded by the fire they'd been grouped around, until more of them fell. Then they turned and ran howling at the woods from where the deadly shafts came; Robre answered, firing smooth and quick, oblivious of the shafts that were whickering around him from the swamp-devil's bows. One had a better idea; he turned and ran yelling up the trail that led away from the riverbank. Robre drew, drew until his arms and chest felt as if the muscle would rip loose from the bone. He loosed, watched— and four seconds later that last shaft dropped out of the night into the fleeing cannibal's back, sending him pitching forward limp at the edge of sight.

"Let's go," King said, his voice stark. He slapped Robre on the shoulder as he passed. "Well done, man. Well shot indeed."

Sonjuh touched his arm, as well. "Better 'n well. That shot was three hundred paces, in the night—it'll be told around the fires for a hundred year 'n' more."

"If anyone gets back to tell," he mumbled, embarrassed.

The men spent a few hectic minutes pushing the dugouts into the current, sending them on their long journey down to the Gulf— the Black River reached the sea to the northeast of Galveston Bay. The log canoes were heavy, but none of them so heavy two strong men couldn't shift them; they glided away silently into the darkness, turning slowly as they glided empty into the night. While they worked Sonjuh went from one body to the next with her tomahawk and knife in hand, recovering Robre's arrows and making sure the enemy dead were unlikely to twitch. King looked up and winced slightly; the clansman blinked in surprise. The only good swamp-devil was a dead one . . . and for that matter, even if they deserved a favor you weren't doing a man one leaving him with an arrow through the gut and burns over half his body.

"Let's leave one canoe," Robre gasped, as they finished their work. "We might be coming back faster than we go—rather not have to dog-leg a half a mile north, if that's so."

King nodded. "And now, let's see what's going on."

Ten, Sonjuh dawtra Pehte thought exultantly as she eeled forward on her belly. *Ten scalps! Ma, you can rest quiet. Mahlu, Mahjani, Bittilu, soon you can rest, my sisters.*

It was not quite so dark as it had been earlier, with the moon huge on the northeastern horizon, hanging over the swamp-forest ahead. The land sloped down here, away from the section of natural levee along the river behind them. It grew thicker and ranker, laced with impenetrable vine and thicket along the trail, then opened out into cypress-swamp, glowing ghostly as the lights of many fires on islets and mounds in the muddy shallow water filtered through the thick curtains of Spanish moss. They stopped there, at the border where the trail opened out, and stared.

"*Shiva Bhuteswara,*" King muttered, in the odd other language he sometimes fell into. "Shiva, Lord of Goblins."

They pullulated over the swamp, squatting in mud and on beaten-down reeds, swarming, erupting in screaming throat-rending fights that ended when others appointed to the task clubbed them down again. Hundreds, perhaps thousands. On the patches of higher ground crude altars of logs stood, with figures strapped across them—swamp-devils, and others that looked like normal men and women. Those were mostly hundreds of yards away, and she was thankful for it. What she *could* see brought memories back and the taste of vomit at the base of her throat. In the center stood an altar taller than the others, built on a platform of cypress logs. Standing upon it was a figure in black, silhouetted against a roaring fire. He raised his arms and silence fell, save for the screams—then a chanting, discordant at first, growing into unison.

"Tchernobog! Tchernobog! Tchernobog!"

Drums joined it, war-drums of human hide stretched over bone, thuttering to the beat of callused palms. The beat walked in her blood, shivered in her tight-clenched teeth.

"What does that mean?" Robre asked.

"Tchernobog," King whispered back. "Black God. Peacock Angel; the Eater of Worlds. That's the one who taught them." He hesitated, looked at both of them. "If I kill him, there's a chance they'll be demoralized and run. On the other hand, there's a chance they'll come straight for us. At the very least, they'll be short of leadership beyond the kill-and-eat level. Shall I?"

Robre nodded. Sonjuh did, as well. "He's the cause of our hurts," she said. "Kill him!"

King nodded in the gloom, the shadow of his turban making his outline monstrous. He unslung the heavy double rifle, lay behind a fallen log, waited a long second. A silence seemed to fall about him, drinking in sound. He could be more *still* than any man she'd ever met, and it was a bit disconcerting—like his habit of crossing his legs in an impossible-looking position and doing what he called *meditating*.

Now there was a slight, almost imperceptible hiss of exhaling breath, and his finger stroked the trigger.

Crack. The sound was thunder-loud, and she'd never seen the weapon fired at night. The great bottle-shaped blade of red-orange fire almost blinded her, and left her eyes smarting and watering. She looked away to get her night vision back, blinking rapidly. The foreigner who'd taught the wild men to act together—the *Russki*—was staggering in a circle. At six hundred paces, Eric's weapon had torn an arm off at the shoulder; the swamp-devils were throwing themselves flat in terror, their voices a chorus of shrieking like evil ghosts.

Crack. The distant figure fell.

"Dead as mutton," King said. "And now, let's *go*."

Scarred chinless faces were turning their way now, the huge goblin eyes staring. The moonlight would be enough for them; legend said that they saw better by night than true men did. Sonjuh came to her feet and ran, with Slasher trotting at her heel. Behind her the sound of the others' feet came, and behind them more of the squealing, shrieking horde. There must be hundreds of hundreds of them. . . .

The gun roared again, and again. Below it she could hear Robre's bow snapping; they must be discouraging the foremost pursuers. Sonjuh kept her head down and *ran*, the cool wet air of the river-bottom night was good for it. She blinked in surprise as the riverside came into sight, moonlight making a long rippling highway on it. There was no time to waste; she tossed her crossbow into the last of the big dugouts and dug her heels into the mud, putting her back to the wood and pushing.

Nothing happened, nothing save that stars and glimmers danced across her vision as she strained. It *did* give her a good look at what was going on behind. Eric came out first, panting so that she could hear him across fifty paces, turned, knelt, breaking open his weapon and reloading. Behind him Robre came, turned, drew, shot, drew, shot—incredibly graceful and swift for so large a man. Sonjuh abandoned her efforts at the canoe, scurried over the sand, grabbed the quivers of the dead swamp-devils, pitched them into the canoe, went back to shoving. Was that a slight movement, a sucking sound in the mud? Her feet churned through slickness.

"*Lord o' Sky* burn *you, you stupid log,* move!" she shrieked in frustration; her own sweat was stinging her chewed lips like fire.

Another *crack—crack* as Eric fired his rifle. Two cannibals almost to spearcast of Robre pitched backwards, one with most of the top of his head disappearing in a spray of blood that looked black in the moonlight. Robre came pelting back past the Imperial, threw his bow into the canoe, bent to put his shoulder beside hers.

A spray of swamp-devils came out of the trailhead into the open, howling like wolves with every step, their tomahawks and knives glittering like cold silver fire in moonlight and starlight. Eric had slung his rifle; now he drew the revolver from his side. He stood erect, shoulder turned to his enemies, his feet at right angles to each other and his left hand tucked into the small of his back, weapon extended. It seemed a curiously formal pose. . . .

Crack. Much lighter than the boom of the hunting rifle; more like a spiteful snap, with a dagger of red flame in the night. The foremost swamp-devil stopped as if he'd run into an invisible wall, arms flying out to right and left, weapons turning and glinting as they flew, then collapsed; the next tripped over him and never rose. The Imperial's long arm moved, leisurely and sure, and the pistol snapped. Again and again, six times, and there were six bodies lying still or writhing on the sandy mud. The seventh came leaping over the pile of them, screeching and swinging a mace of polished rock lashed to a handle with human tendons. Eric's sword flashed out, a clean burnished-steel blur in the moonlight, cut again backhand. The cannibal staggered, gaping at a forearm severed and spouting blood in pulsing-fountain spurts, then collapsed as his guts spilled out through his rent belly. An eighth lay silent as Slasher rose from his body, jaws wet. The Imperial turned and ran.

The canoe was moving, finally moving. King was nearly to them; Slasher soared by him, hit the ground and leapt again, flashing over the two clansfolks' heads like a gray arrow. Dark figures moved behind King's back, more of the swamp-devils come from their sabbat, loosing as they ran in a chorus of wolf-howls, pig-squeals, catamount screeches. Black arrows began to flicker past Sonjuh in a whispering hiss of cloven air, invisible until they were almost there; some of them went *thunk* into the canoe and stood quivering with a malignant hum like evil bees.

The heavy craft was in the water now, river up to her knees, then her thighs, soaking into her leggings and chill against flesh heated by running and the pounding of her heart. She rolled over the side; Robre was pushing hard, his greater height letting him wade out. Sonjuh stuck her head up enough to see over the upcurved stern-end of the dugout, and saw Eric splash into the water at speed, lunging forward to grasp the wood. She also saw more arrows heading toward her like streaming horizontal rain, and ducked down again. King landed atop her, driving the breath out of her with an *oof!* and grinding her back into the inch or two of water that swilled around in the middle of the hollowed-out cypress log.

The man gave a sharp cry and then spoke fast in that other, utterly unfamiliar language he had—she could tell the difference when he was speaking the one that sounded almost-but-not-quite like Seven Tribes talk. From the sound of it, he was swearing with venomous sincerity. Robre was in the hull now, digging his paddle into the water and looking back to find out why King wasn't.

Sonjuh had a good idea why, even if it was a little too dark to be sure. She wiggled out from under King and felt down along his legs.

"Arrow," she said—more were falling into the water about them. "Nearly through the calf slantwise—missed the bone—head's just under the skin here."

"Push it through and break it off," Eric King wheezed. At her hesitation— "*Do* it, there's no time!"

She drew her tomahawk, drew a deep breath, as well, and hammered the arrow through with the flat of the hatchet against the nock. The long body beside hers went rigid for an instant, with a snarling exhalation, his hands clamping on the wood. She used the sharp edge of the weapon to cut the shaft off to stubs on either side, moving his leg so that wood rested on wood for a quick strong flick of the hatchet-blade.

"Give me a hand," he said tightly; she helped him to a sitting position, and he seized a paddle and set to work.

So did she, in the more conventional kneeling manner; the canoe was long and heavy, made for ten or fifteen men. They managed to drive it out past midpoint, and the rain of arrows ceased. Glancing over her shoulder, Sonjuh gave a harsh chuckle at the screams of rage, as hundreds of the swamp-devils poured onto the riverbank and found their canoes gone.

"That—won't—hold—'em—long," Robre panted between strokes. "They'll—have—more—close by."

"Or swim, or use logs and rafts," Sonjuh said unhappily.

* * *

We are screwed up, she thought.

Oh, the wound wasn't all that serious—unless it mortified, which was always a danger and doubly so with something a swamp-devil had handled. It wasn't even bleeding seriously; arrow wounds often didn't, while the shaft was plugging them up. But with his leg injured, there was no way the Imperial could run, or fight beyond sitting and shooting. King reached for his rifle, fired again, reloaded and fired before he put it down and resumed paddling. "That'll keep them cautious for a bit," he said.

There was no energy to spare for a while after that; paddling went easier once they had reached the ebb-water on the other shore, driving northward to the little semi-islet they'd left. Robre hopped overboard and took a line over his shoulder, hauling them into a tongue of water, halting when the canoe touched bottom. Instead of trying to haul it out solo, he tied off a leather painter to a nearby dead cypress root. Meanwhile Sonjuh got their weapons in order and helped the wounded man out. He hobbled upward, supporting his weight on her shoulder; their supplies were undisturbed, and when she let him down next to them he immediately broke out a box of shells and refilled bandolier and pistol. Then he took out a notebook, made quick notes, tore out the sheet of paper and folded it. Robre squatted nearby, replacing scavenged enemy arrows with shafts from his own bundles.

"All right," King said, looking from one to the other. He closed the notebook; when he spoke, his voice had more of the hard, clipped tone than it had shown in a while. "What you've got to do is get this to Banerjii back at Donnulsford. He'll see that the garrison commander in Galveston gets it. And you have to warn your own people on the way—?"

"Wait just one damn minute," Sonjuh said hotly. "You expect me to *leave* you here?"

"Well, yes, of course," he said, peering at her in the moonlight. He smiled. "My dear, do think—"

She restrained herself from slapping him with a visible effort. "What're you thinking of me, that I'd take up with a man 'n' walk off from him when he's hurt, like some town trull?"

King winced, since he'd obviously been thinking something like that. He went on more gently: "Sonjuh, remember how *many* of them there were. The only thing that they could have gathered in numbers like that for was war. They're going to come swarming over the border and hit your people's frontier settlements like Indra's lightning—like Olsaytn's hammer. They might not even stop at the Three Forks River. Your people have to be warned."

Sonjuh opened her mouth, then closed it, then brightened. "Robre can do that. I'll stay to keep you safe—we can hide you—"

Robre shook his head. "Empire man, I swore to guide 'n' help you, not leave you for the swamp-devils to eat, 'n' that's a fact."

King's face went grimmer. "I might have expected more logic, even from a native," he said.

Sonjuh felt herself flushing with anger again—she'd guessed what *that* word meant—but Robre surprised her by laughing.

"No, Jefe, you're not going to argue me into leaving you, 'n' you're not going to anger me into it, either. I figure we'll stock the canoe, then try 'n' get you down past the swamp-devils. Your folk hold the coast, no?"

King gaped at him. Sonjuh unwillingly admitted to herself that there was some sense in that, cold-blooded though it was. Fighting their way for days downriver, through hordes of the cannibals, with only three warriors and one of them wounded, in a canoe too big and heavy for them to handle well—

"We hold *Galveston*, and we patrol the coast to either side . . . lightly and infrequently," King said. "Talk sense, man!"

"You do the talkin'," Robre said cheerfully; his face was grim. "I'll get busy on loading the canoe."

King was swearing again when Sonjuh put her hand across his mouth for silence. Slasher was on his feet again, bristling, fangs showing in a silent snarl, his nose pointed landward whence came the wind. The humans froze, peering about, and then Robre quietly put the box of supplies down and stepped backward to dry land to reach for where his bow leaned against another.

"Down!" she called.

They all flattened themselves. Arrows whipped by at chest-height above them, and a howling broke free from the woods to the eastward. More screeches answered it, out on the river; Sonjuh looked that way, and saw canoes boiling out from the bluff there, paddles stabbing into the water.

A rhythmic cry rose from the crews, near enough to her tongue that she could understand the words: *"Meat! Eat! Meat! Eat!"*

"Watch the land!" King shouted, rolling behind a couple of sacks of cornmeal and aiming his rifle riverward. *Crack . . . crack*, and a canoe went over as a rower sprang up in the final convulsion of death.

Howls came from landward. Sonjuh prepared her crossbow with hands that would have shaken, if she had permitted it. *They must have sent runners up the bank and then over,* she thought. *And had more canoes there . . . too smart, for swamp-devils. They've been* learning, *damn them!*

The cry from the woods turned into a chant: *"MEAT! EAT!"*

"I was never so glad to hear good old-fashioned Imperial volley-fire . . . *ai!*"

The last was a brief involuntary exclamation as Ranjit's thick-fingered right hand pulled the arrow-stub free with one long surging draw. His left poured the disinfectant, and King felt it through the wound and in streaks up the nerves of his leg, into his groin and belly. It was far from the worst pain he'd ever experienced, but it was certainly among the top five in an adventurous life. To deal with it as the Sikh's experienced fingers tied on the field dressing, he looked past Sonjuh's anxious face where she knelt holding his leg for the bandage and to the eastern shore where the sun rose over tall forest, across a river like molten metal wisped with mist. Were hating black eyes looking at him? *Probably,* he thought. *We only killed a dozen or two of them*—it was hard to tell how many bodies had gone into the water, especially since a patrol of alligators had gone by, picking up snacks—*and there were thousands over there. I'd be surprised if they aren't crossing north and south of here already. Dismally determined types.*

The clansmen and soldiers were grouped around the islet, less three dead and several wounded. The stink of the cannibals' corpses was strong, stronger than the newly dead usually were; flights of ravens and great-winged buzzards waited, on the wing or perched in trees nearby.

"How did you get here so fast, on foot?" King went on.

Ranjit Singh grinned whitely in his black beard. "I mounted us all on the pack animals, *huzoor*," he said. "By turns; each man on foot to hold onto a strap while he ran. So we made good time."

King nodded; that had been clever. The trick had been used before; sometimes cavalry brought infantry forward so during an attack, with a foot soldier clinging to a stirrup while the horse trotted.

"Did you hear?" he called over to Robre, who was sitting in a circle with his fellow tribesmen, amid fast speech and gestures.

"Yup," Robre said, turning to face the Imperial. "Figure you're planning on leaving us now?"

"To get help," he said, and at Robre's dubious look, "We have several vessels at Galveston, and this river is navigable to the coast. It'll take me some time to get there, with Ranjit and the garrison soldiers. Your people need to be warned."

"Am I comin' with you?" Sonjuh asked quietly.

"My dear—" Eric winced slightly at the hurt in her eyes. "My dear, we should each go to our own people now. Believe me, it's best."

She nodded quietly and picked up her pack, rising and turning away. He winced again, for himself, and then shrugged. *Well, I'll be over it by the time we make the coast. If we make the coast.* Six guns was not much to run that river of darkness.

"Let's go," he said briskly.

Robre Hunter rose up from behind the overturned oxcart and loosed once more. The fresh wound in his left arm weakened the draw, but the target was only thirty feet away—and the swamp-devil went down coughing out blood, with the arrowhead through the upper part of his right lung. The others wavered and fell back a little; they were the outer wave of the onrushing cannibal flood, a scouting party. The clansman looked behind him; the last of the settlers they'd warned were out of the road through the woods, and probably across the cornfield. He worked a dry mouth, hawked, spat, suddenly conscious.

"Let's go!" he called.

Slasher came out of the brush on the left side of the trail, licking wet jaws. Sonjuh came from the right, her bright hair hidden by an improvised bandage with a little blood leaking through it, almost like a wife's headscarf.

Robre looked back down the road; there were swamp-devil bodies scattered along it, and two of the men who'd come back from the Black River with them. It galled him to leave the dead men for the enemy to eat, but there was nothing that could be done—it was a miracle so many of the settlers had gotten away. Pillars of smoke smudged the horizon, from burning cabins and hayricks and barns, filling the air with the filthy smell of things that should not burn, but far fewer of his people were dead in them than might have been.

Sonjuh flashed him a brief smile. *Ten miles of grit and bottom that girl has and no mistake*, the hunter thought admiringly. Aloud, he went on: "Let's run."

They turned and trotted out of the woods. The fields beyond still had occasional oak and hickory stumps in them—this was ax-claim land—but mostly they were full of cornstalks, tall and dryly rustling. The rutted path through them showed the twelve-foot logs of the station stockade; it was littered with goods refugees had dropped . . . and the narrow gate was closed.

A howling broke out behind them, far closer than he liked; the swamp-devils had found the bodies of their scouting party.

"Made your tally of scalps yet?" he gasped to the girl running beside him, bow pumping in his hand as he bounded ahead. She kept pace easily, despite his longer stride.

"I have," she said. "Doesn't seem so important, no more."

Well, that's different, he thought.

The howls behind them grew louder; the two clansfolk gave each other a glance and stepped up the pace, almost sprinting. Normally a half-mile wouldn't be anything much, but they'd been running and fighting for near a week now, and even their iron fund of endurance was running low. Slasher panted, as well, tongue unreeled, his gray fur matted with blood; some of it was his, and he limped a little.

"No use telling them to open the gate," Robre grunted, as an arrow went *whissst-thunk!* into the red mud behind him. "We'll have to go over. You first."

"Won't hear me complaining," Sonjuh gasped.

Robre looked over his shoulder. The swamp-devils had hesitated a little; the sun was shining directly into their eyes as they pursued, and they weren't enthusiastic about coming into the open in daylight anyway. But they were coming on now, not graceful on their short powerful legs, but as enduring as one of the Imperials' steam engines. At the sight of two enemies on foot, their screeching ran up the scale to the blood-trill, and even now the hair along Robre's spine tried to stand up.

"Lord o' Sky with us!" he shouted, and made a final burst of speed.

More arrows were whickering past him now, on to thud into the dry oak timbers of the palisade; luckily the marksmanship wasn't good, with the sun in their eyes and shooting while they ran. Breath panted hard and dry through a parched throat, and his muscles were one huge ache. He threw his bow up over the palisade—it was lined with cheering spectators—and bent, making a stirrup of his hands. Sonjuh covered the last ten yards in her old bounding deer-run, then leapt high for the last; her foot came down into his hands, and he flung her upward with all the strength that was in him. She soared, clapped hands around the pointed end of a log, and eager hands dragged her over it. Slasher whined as Robre's hands clamped on his fur ruff and a handful at the base of his tail, and he made a halfhearted snap. The man ignored it, swung him around in two huge circles and flung him upward likewise; he *did* bite a couple of the people who pulled him over. Then a rope dangled down for the man. He jumped, caught it three feet above his head-height and swarmed up; the wound in his left arm betrayed him, and he would have fallen at the last if Sonjuh had not leaned far over and grabbed the back of his hunting shirt.

He gasped for a moment as he lay on the fighting platform inside the little log fort that made up the Station; three families lived here usually, but now it was crowded with refugees, their faces peering upward awestruck at him.

"Get those idjeets under cover!" he shouted; a few arrows were already arching over the walls to land in the mud-and-dung surface of the courtyard.

Winded, he still forced himself back erect, took his bow, looked to right and left. The swamp-men were pouring out of the woods, a black insect tide in the lurid light of the sunset. Some stopped to prance and flaunt bits of loot at the defenders—a woman's blood-stained dress, the hacked-off, gnawed arm of a child. Others were cutting pine trees, bringing them forward, trimming off branches to use them as scaling-ladders.

"What are you waiting for?" he bellowed, to the men—and a few women—who crowded the fighting platform. "We'll need torches up here, water, more arrows. Move!"

The horde poured forward. A sleetstorm of arrows, crossbow bolts, and buckshot met it; the howling figures pressed on, and a counterstream of black arrows hissed upward—

There had been fighting all along the Three Forks River, fierce fighting before the walls of Dannulsford. The tents and brush shelters of refugees clustered thickly all about it, and the eastern horizon was still hazy with the burning cornfields, and the air heavy with the smell of it. More tents sprawled to the west, where fresh war parties of wild young fighting-men from all the clans poured in each day—the war-arrow had been sent throughout the lands of the Seven Tribes, by relays of fast riders. Other aid poured in as well, wagons filled with shelled corn, hams, bacon, wheat, jerked beef, cloth, and whiskey. By the western gate the skulls of bear, bison, wild cow, cougar, plains-lion, and wolf stood high beside the alligator, the standards of many a clan Jefe. No heads on poles were there now, but many were being set up along the river—hanging in bunches rather than impaled singly, to save work. Canoes and ferries went back and forth without cease. Noise brawled surflike through the stink and crowding, voices, shouts, songs, war whoops, the neighing of horses and bellowing of oxen; the wind was out of the west, cool, dry, and dusty.

And in the middle of the stream floated a steamboat; not the little wooden stern-wheeler of a few weeks ago, but a steel-hulled gunboat, likewise shallow-draft but bristling with Gatling guns behind shields, an arc-powered searchlight, and a rocket launcher.

The Empire's flag floated over the bridge, and the bosun's pipes twittered as the chiefs left. Or most of them—one young war-chief, newly come to fame as a leader, stayed for a moment. Beside him stood a young woman in the garb of a male woods-runner; she clung to his hand with a half-defiant air, and her dog bristled when crewmen came too close. The captain of the craft and the colonel who commanded the Empire's garrison in Galveston had discreetly withdrawn, as well.

"*Yi-ah,*" Robre Devil-Killer said. "We heard how this—" He gestured about at the Imperial warcraft, which rather incongruously bore the tile *Queen-Empress Victoria II* in gilt on its black bows. "—turned 'em back when it steamed up the Black River. We might have lost all the east-bank settlements, without that. The ones who got across 'fore you came back weren't enough to do that, or cross the river and take Dannulsford."

"Glad the Empire could help," Eric King said sincerely.

He was in uniform again, his turban freshly wrapped, although he also carried a stick and limped heavily. He looked at their linked hands, smiled, and murmured, "Bless you, my children," in Hindi.

"What was that?"

"Just that I'm glad to have met you. Met you both," he said. "In India, it's customary to give gifts to friends on their wedding. I understand that's in order?"

He called, and Ranjit Singh came up with a long rosewood chest strapped with brass and opened it. A double-barreled hunting rifle lay within.

Robre nodded, grinning as he took the weapon and broke the action open with competent hands; he'd received the single-shot weapon as pay from Banerjii, but this new treasure was pure delight. Sonjuh smiled at last, as well.

"Well," King went on, "For the bride, I could have given a cradle . . . or a spinning wheel . . ." The smile on the girl's face was turning to a frown. "But since it looks like you'll be having other work to do first—"

Another case—this held a lighter weapon, the cavalry-carbine version of the Martini-Metford rifle. She mumbled thanks, blushing a little, then laughed out loud as King solemnly presented Slasher with a meaty ham-bone; the dog looked up at his mistress for permission, then graciously accepted it.

The Imperial and the clansman shook hands, hands equally callused by rein and rope, sword-hilt and tomahawk.

"Good-bye, and good luck in your war," King went on. "I hope you exterminate the brutes."

"So do I, Jefe," Robre said. "But I doubt it. They're a mighty lot of 'em, the swamps are big, 'n' they can fight. Fight even harder in their home-runs, I suppose."

"In the end, you'll beat them," King said. "You're more civilized, and the civilized always win in the end, barring something like the Fall."

Robre looked around at the gunboat, frowning slightly at a thought. "Could be you're right," he said. "Time will tell."

The slight frown was still on his face when he stood on the bank and watched the smooth passage of the *Queen-Empress Victoria II* downstream. Then he turned to the girl beside him and met her smile with his own.

WHY THEN, THERE

Alternate history has many uses. One of them is to revive literary worlds that time has rendered otherwise inaccessible to us. Writers like Edgar Rice Burroughs or A. A. Merritt could, with some small degree of initial plausibility, litter the remoter sections of the world with lost races and lost cities; their models, writing a generation earlier, had a broader canvas to work with, as exploration wasn't nearly so complete.

By the 1930s, Burroughs was taking his heroes to other planets and to a putative world within the hollow core of ours, and the last lost races were tribes in the interior of New Guinea. Even Mars and Venus were taken from us a little later, their six-armed green men, canals, and dinosaurs replaced with a boring snowball of rust and a sulphuric-acid hell ... although alternatives to *that* are another story, one which I hope to tell someday.

Likewise, the supply of exploits available to a dashing young cavalry officer became sadly limited after 1914. Being machine-gunned at the Somme just isn't up to the standards of the sort of exploit conveyed by Kipling, Henty, or (in nonfiction) the young Winston Churchill, who participated in one of the last quasi-successful charges by British lancers in 1898, against the Mahdists at Omdurman. Dervish fanatics tend to use plastique these days, rather than swords. Pirates are rather ho-hum Third World extortionists and sneak thieves, rather than characters like Henry Morgan—who was sent home in chains and ended up as governor of Jamaica, after a private audience with Charles II!

In short, by the second decade of the last century the gorgeous, multicolored, infinite-possibility world that opened up with the great voyages of discovery of the sixteenth century was coming to an end. So was the fictional penumbra that accompanied, mirrored, and even inspired it—for the Spanish conquistadors were themselves quite consciously emulating the feats of literary heroes, of the knights of the *Chanson du Roland* or the fantastic adventures of Amadis of Gaul.

From a literary point of view, this was a terrible misfortune. It's often forgotten in these degenerate times how close to the world of the pulp adventurers the real world could be in those days.

Allan Quatermain, of H. Rider Haggard's *She* and *King Solomon's Mines*, was based fairly closely (fantasy elements like immortal princesses aside) on the exploits of Frederick Selous, explorer and frontiersman.

What writer could come up unaided with a character like Richard Francis Burton, the devilish, swashbuckling swordsman-adventurer who fought wild Somalis saber-to-spear, once escaped certain death on an African safari when he ran six miles *with a spear through his face*, snuck into at least two "forbidden" cities (Mecca and Medina) in native disguise, and translated the *Thousand and One Nights* to boot, after writing a firsthand account of the red-light district of Karachi?

Or Mary Kingsley, who went singlehanded into the jungles of Gabon and did the first field enthnography among the cannibal Fang. In her books, she recommended from personal experience a nice thick set of petticoats, which was exactly what was needed when falling into a pit lined with pointed stakes, and noted that said skirts should contain a convenient pocket for a revolver, "which is rarely needed, but when needed is needed very badly."

Who could devise adventures more unlikely and fantastic than the real life of Harry Brooks in the 1830s, who sailed off to the East Indies in a leaky schooner with a few friends, fought pirates and headhunters, and made himself independent raja of Sarawak? And *he* was at the tail end of a tradition that began with Cortés and Pizzaro setting off on private-enterprise quests to overthrow empires at ten thousand-to-one odds.

That world is still available to us through historical fiction, of course, but that is sadly limiting in some respects; the "end" of the larger story is fixed and we know how it comes out. The Western Front and the Welfare State are waiting down at the end of the road.

Like many another, I imprinted on the literature of faraway places and strange-sounding names at an early age, and never lost the taste for it—or for the real-world history and archaeology to which it led. Fortunately, I also discovered *alternate* history, a genre within the larger field of speculative fiction, which allows a rigorous yet limitless ringing of changes.

Alternate history can give writer and reader a breath of fresher air, of unlimited possibility, of that world where horizons are infinite and nothing is fixed in stone; where beyond the last blue horizon waits the lost city, the people of marvels, the silver-belled caravan to Shamballah and the vacant throne. . . .

"Shikari in Galveston" springs from the backbone of my novel *The Peshawar Lancers*. The universe of *The Peshawar Lancers* stems from an alteration in the history of the nineteenth century: a catastrophic strike by a series of high-velocity heavenly bodies. We know that this sort of thing actually happens, and that a similar (though larger) impact ended the dinosaurian era 65 million years ago.

Being fictional, my impacts could be precisely controlled by authorial fiat, within the boundaries of the physically possible. What they did was to derail "progress" by taking out the most technologically advanced part of the world, and by drastically reducing the world's overall population.

And so the twentieth and twenty-first centuries see a world where the most advanced regions are only just surpassing the Victorian level of technology and social development, and much remains sparsely inhabited by a wild variety of cultures at a very low level of technology.

In other words, a world larger and better suited to the classic adventure story than ours.

The Peshawar Lancers took place mostly in India, the center of the British Empire and the most advanced state of its day; "Shikari in Galveston" is set on the Imperial frontiers, in the wilds of a re-barbarized Texas. Both put people in situations that suit the definition of "adventure": somebody else in very bad trouble, very far away.

I hope you enjoy reading this as much as I enjoyed writing it!

S. M. Stirling was born in Metz, France, in 1953; his father was an officer in the RCAF, from Newfoundland, and his English-born mother grew up in Lima, Peru. He has lived in Europe, North America, and East Africa, and traveled extensively elsewhere. After taking a history BA, he attended law school at Osgoode Hall, Toronto, but decided not to practice and had his dorsal fin surgically removed. After the usual period of poverty and odd jobs, his first book sold in 1984 (*Snowbrother*, from Signet), and he became a full-time writer in 1988. That was the same year he was married to Janet Cathryn Stirling (née Moore), also a writer, whom he met at a World Fantasy convention in the mid-1980s.

His works since then include the *Draka* alternate history trilogy (currently issued in a combined volume under the title *The Domination*), the *Nantucket* series (*Island in the Sea of Time*, *Against the Tide of Years*, and *On the Oceans of Eternity*), *The Peshawar Lancers*, and *Conquistador*.

He and Janet and the obligatory authorial cats currently live in Santa Fe, New Mexico. He's currently working on a new alternate history novel, *Dies the Fire*, which will be published by Roc.

Steve Stirling's hobbies include anthropology, archaeology, history in general, travel, cooking, and the martial arts.

THE LOGISTICS
OF CARTHAGE

MARY GENTLE

I have put this document together from the different sources included in the Ash papers, and have again translated the languages into modern English. Where necessary, I have substituted colloquial obscenities to give a flavour of the medieval original. Let the casual reader, expecting the Hollywood Middle Ages, abandon hope here.

PIERCE RATCLIFF, A.D. 2010

"MOST women follow their husbands to the wars. . . . *I* followed my son."

Yolande Vaudin's voice came with the grunt and exhalation of physical effort. Guillaume Arnisout looked at her down the length of the corpse they were carrying.

He grinned. "Your son? You ain't old enough to have a grown-up son!"

She appeared a wonderfully perverse mix of male and female, Guillaume thought. The clinging of her belted mail shirt, under her livery jacket, showed off the woman's broad hips. Her long legs seemed plump in hose, but were not: were just not male. Shapely and womanly . . . He got a kick out of seeing women's legs in hose: entirely covered, but the shape so clearly defined—and hers were worth defining.

She had her hair cut short, too, like a page or young squire, and it curled sleekly onto her shoulders, uncovered, the rich yellow of wet straw. *She* had been able to slip her helmet off before the sergeant noticed: it was buckled through her belt by the chin strap. That meant he could see all of her wise and wicked face.

She's willing to talk, at least. Can't let the opportunity go to waste.

He put his back against the Green Chapel's doors and eased them open without himself letting go of the corpse's ankles. Yolande held her end of the dead woman's body tightly under the arms, taking the weight as he backed through the door first. The blue-white flesh was chill against his palms.

Not looking down at what she held, Yolande went on. "I had Jean-Philippe when I was young. Fifteen. And then, when he was fifteen, he was called up in the levy, to be a soldier, and I followed."

The partly open door let in the brilliant sunlight from the barren land outside. It glittered back off the white walls of the monastery's other buildings. Guillaume twisted his head around to look inside the chapel, letting his eyes adjust, unsure of his footing in the dimness. "Didn't he mind you being there?"

Her own sight obviously free of the morning glare, Yolande pushed forward. The legs of the body were stiff with rigor, and they shoved against him. Bare feet jabbed his belly. There was black dirt under the toenails.

He backed in, trying to hold one door open with his foot while Yolande maneuvered the dead woman's shoulders and head through it.

"He would have minded, if he'd known. I went disguised; I thought I could watch over him from a distance. . . . He was too young. I'd been a widow five years. I had no money, with his wages gone. I joined the baggage train and dyed my hair and whored for a living, until that got old, and then I found I could put a crossbow bolt into the center of the butts nine times out of ten."

The chapel's chill began to cool the sting of sunburn on the back of his neck. His helmet still felt excruciatingly hot to wear. Guillaume blinked, his sight adjusting, and looked at her again. "You're *not* old enough."

Her chuckle came out of the dimness, along with the shape of the walls and tiled floor.

"One thing a woman can always look like is a younger man. There's her," Yolande said, with a jerk of her head downward at the rigid dead body between them. "When she said her name was Guido Rosso, you'd swear she was a beardless boy of nineteen. You take her out of doublet and hose and put her in a gown, and call her 'Margaret Hammond,' and you'd have known at once she was a woman of twenty-eight."

"Was she?" Guillaume grunted, shifting the load as they tottered toward the altar. He walked backward with difficulty, not wanting to stumble and look stupid in front of this woman. "I didn't know her."

"I met her when she joined us, after the fall." Yolande's fingers visibly tightened on the dead woman's flesh. There was no need to specify which fall. The collapse of Constantinople to the Turks had echoed through Christendom from East to West, four years ago.

"I took her under my wing." The woman's wide, lively mouth moved in an ironic smile. Her eyes went to the corpse's face, then his. "*You* wouldn't have noticed her. I know what you grunts in the line fight are like—'Archers? Oh, that's those foulmouthed buggers hanging around at the back, always saying "fuck" and taking the Lord their God's name in vain. . . .' I dunno: give you a billhook and you think you're the only soldier on the battlefield."

Guillaume liked her sardonic grin, and returned it.

So . . . is she flirting with me?

They staggered together across the empty interior of the Green Chapel. Their boots scraped on the black and white tiles. He could smell incense and old wood smoke from the morning's prayers. Another couple of steps . . .

"I used to help her back to the tents, drunk. She was never this heavy. There!" Yolande grunted.

Just in time, he copied her, letting the stiff ankles of the body slide down out of his dirty grip. The body thunked down onto the tiles at his feet. No one had cleaned it up. The bones of her face were beaten in, the mess the same color as heraldic murrey: purple red.

His skin retained the feel of hers. Stiff, chill, softening.

"*He Dieux!*" Guillaume rubbed at his back. "That's why they call it *dead* weight."

He saw the dead Rosso—Margaret—was still wearing her armor: a padded jack soaked with blood and fluids. Linen stuffing leaked out of the rips. Every other piece of kit from helmet to boots was gone. Either the jacket was too filthy and slashed up to be worth reclaiming, or else the charred and bloodstained cloth was all that was still holding the body's intestines inside it.

Yolande squatted down. Guillaume saw her try to pull the body's arms straight by its sides, but they were still too stiff. She settled for smoothing the sun-bleached, blood-matted hair back. She wiped her hands on her peacock blue hose as she stood.

"I saw her get taken down." The older woman spoke as if she was not sure what to do next, was talking to put off that moment of decision—even if the decision was, Guillaume thought, only the one to leave the corpse of her friend.

The light from the leaf-shaped ogee windows illuminated Yolande's clear, smooth skin. There were creases at her eyes, but she had most of the elasticity of youth still there.

"Killed on the galley?" he prompted, desperate to continue a conversation even if the subject was unpromising.

"Yeah. First we were on one of the cargo ships, sniping, part of the defense crew. The rag-heads turned Greek fire on us, and the deck was burning. I yelled at her to follow me off—when we got back on our galley, it had been boarded, and it took us and Tessier's guys ten minutes to clear the decks. Some Visigoth put a spear through her face, and I guess they must have hacked her up when she fell. They'd have been better worrying about the live ones."

"Nah . . ." Guillaume was reluctant to leave the Green Chapel, even if it was beginning to smell of decomposing flesh. He felt cool for the first time in hours, and besides, there was this woman, who might perhaps be an impressed audience for his combat knowledge. "You never want to leave one alive under your feet. Somebody on the ground sticks a sword or dagger up and hits your femoral artery or your bollocks— Ah, 'scuse me."

He stopped, flustered. She gave him a look.

Somewhere in his memory, if only in the muscle-memory of his hands and arms, is the ferocity with which you hack a man down, and follow it up without a second's hesitation—*bang-bang-bang-bang!*— your weapon's thin, sharp steel edges slamming into his face, throat, forearms, belly; whatever you can reach.

He looked away from the body at his feet, a woman to whom some soldier in the Carthaginian navy has done just that. Goose pimples momentarily shuddered over his skin.

"Christus Viridianus! I couldn't half do with a drink." He eased his visored sallet back on his head, feeling how the edge of the lining band had left a hot, sweaty indentation in his forehead. "Say, what *did* happen to your son? Is he with the company?"

Yolande's fingers brushed the Griffin-in-Gold patch sewn onto the front of her livery jacket, as if the insignia of their mercenary company stirred memories. She smiled in a way he could not interpret. "I was a better soldier than he was."

"He quit?"

"He died."

"Shit." *I can't say a thing right!* "Yolande, I'm sorry."

Her mouth quirked painfully. "Four months after he went to war. What was I thinking, that I could *protect* him? He was carrying shot in the first siege we were at, and a culverin inside the castle scored a direct hit on the powder wagon. When I found him he'd had both his hands blown off, and he'd bled to death—before his mother could get to him."

"Jeez . . ." I wish I hadn't asked.

She's *got* to be ten years older than me. But she doesn't look it.

He guessed Yolande had not, like "Guido Rosso," even temporarily tried to pass as a man.

Because she's a woman, not a girl.

"Why did you stay with the company?"

"My son was dead. I wanted to kill the whole world. I realized that if I had the patience to let them train me, the company would let me do just that."

In his stunned silence, Guillaume could hear goat bells jingling outside and some shuffling noises closer to hand. A warm breeze blew in through the Green Chapel door, which had lodged open on a pebble. The smell of death grew more present now, soaking into the air. Like the back of a butcher's shop in a heat wave.

"Shit." He wiped at his mouth. "It's going to get hot later in the morning. By evening . . . she's going to be really ripe by Vespers."

Yolande's expression turned harsh. "Good. Then they can't

ignore her. She's going to smell. *That* should get the bloody rag-heads moving. The captain's right. This is the only thing to do."

"But—"

"I don't care what the fucking priests say. *She's going to be buried here like the Christian soldier she is.*"

Guillaume shrugged. For himself, he would as cheerfully have chucked all the bodies overboard, to go with the Carthaginian Visigoths and feed the fish; evidently this wasn't the thing to say to Yolande right now. Especially not if you want to get into the cross-bow woman's knickers, he reminded himself.

"If the abbot can ignore the stink she's going to make . . ." He let his grin out, in its different context. "What do you bet me he'll send for the captain before Sext? Hey, tell you what . . . I bet you a flagon of wine she's buried by midday, and if I lose, I'll help you drink it tonight. What do you say?"

What she would have answered wasn't clear from her expression, and he didn't get to hear a reply.

The scuffling noise that had impinged on his consciousness earlier grew louder, and he spun around and had his bollock dagger out of its sheath at his belt and pointing at the altar a full second before a boy rolled out from under the altar cloth and sat staring down at the woman soldier's corpse.

"Aw—shit!" Guillaume swore, exasperated.

He saw the thin iron ring welded around the boy's throat. Some slave skiving off work. Or hiding from the big bad Frankish mercenaries—*not that I blame him for that.*

"Hey, *you*—fuck off out of here!"

The youth looked up, not at Guillaume, but at Yolande. There was a quiver about him that might have been fear or energy. He looked to be anywhere in his early or middle teens, a pale-skinned Carthaginian Visigoth with dark hair flopping into his eyes. Guillaume realized instantly, She's thinking he's fifteen.

"I wasn't listening!" He spoke the local patois, but it was plain from his ability to answer that he understood one Frankish language at least. "I was foreseeing."

Guillaume flinched, thought, Were we saying anything I don't want to hear back as gossip? No, I hadn't got round to asking her if she fucks younger men— And then, replaying the kid's remark in his head, he queried: "Foreseeing?"

Silently, the young man pointed.

Above the altar, on the shadowed masonry of the wall, there was no expected Briar Cross. Instead, he saw a carved face—a Man's face, with leaves sprouting from the creepers that thrust out of His open mouth.

The carving was large: perhaps as wide as Guillaume could have spanned with his outstretched hands, thumb to thumb. There is something intimidating about a face that big. Vir Viridianus: Christ as the Green Emperor, as the Arian Visigoths prefer, heretically, to worship Him. The wood gleamed, well polished, the pale silvery grain catching the light. Holm oak, maybe? The eyes had been left as hollows of darkness.

"I dream under the altar," the young man said, as hieratic as if he had been one of the monastery's own priests, and not barefoot and with only a dirty linen shirt to cover his arse.

Guillaume belatedly realized the scrabbling noise hadn't ceased with their stillness. The hilt of his bollock dagger was still smooth in his hand. He stepped back to give himself room as the altar cloth stirred again.

An odd, low, dark shape lifted up something pale.

Guillaume blinked, not processing the image, and then his mind made sense both of the shape and of the new smell that the odor of the corpse had been masking. A pale flat snout lifted upward. A dark hairy quadruped body paced forward, flop ears falling over bright eyes. . . .

The young man absently reached out and scratched the pig's lean back with grimy fingers.

A pig-boy asleep under the Green Man's altar? Guillaume thought. Sweet dead Jesus on the Tree!

"I had a seeing dream," the young man said, and turned his face toward the living woman in the chapel; toward Yolande. "I think it is for you."

Yolande glanced down at the dead body of Margaret Hammond. "Not in here! Outside . . . maybe."

She caught the billman's nod, beside her. He said, "Yeah, let's go. We don't want to be in here now. We got this place under lockdown, but there's going to be *plenty* of shit flying before long!"

The pig's sharp trotters clicked on the tiles, the beast following as the Visigoth swineherd walked to the left of the altar. The young man pushed aside a wall hanging embroidered with the She-wolf suckling the Christ-child to disclose a wooden door set deep into the masonry. He opened it and gestured.

Yolande stepped through.

She came out in the shade of the wall. The world beyond the shadow blazed with the North African sun's fierceness. A few yards ahead was a grove of the ever-present olive trees, and she walked to stand under them, loving their shade and smell—so little being green after the company's previous stopover in Alexandria.

She heard Guillaume stretch his arms out and groan, happily, in the sun behind her. "Time enough to go back to Europe in the summer. *Damn*, this is the place to have a winter campaign! Even if we're not where we're supposed to be . . ."

She didn't turn to look at him. From this high ridge of land she could see ten or fifteen miles inland. Anonymous bleak rock hills lifted up in the west. In that direction, the sun was weak. The blue sky defied focus, as if there were particles of blackness in it.

The edge of the Penitence. Well, I've been under the Darkness Perpetual before now . . . We *have* to be within fifty or sixty leagues of Carthage. Have to be.

Guillaume Arnisout sauntered up beside her. "Maybe Prophet Swineherd here can tell us we're going to wipe the floor with the enemy: that usually pays."

She caught the billman's sardonic expression focused on the pig-boy. Guillaume's much better looking when he's not trying so hard, she thought. All long legs and narrow hips and wide shoulders. Tanned face and hands. Weather-worn from much fighting. Fit.

But from where I am, he looks like a boy. Haven't I always preferred them older than me?

"If you're offering to prophesy," Yolande said to the swineherd, more baldly than she intended, "you've got the wrong woman. I'm too old to have a future. I haven't any money. If any of us in the company had money, we wouldn't be working for Hüseyin Bey and the goddamn Turks!"

"This isn't a scam!" The boy pushed the uncut hair out of his eyes. His people's generations in this land hadn't given him skin that would withstand the sun—where there was sun—and his flush might have been from the heat, or it might have been shame.

She squatted down, resting her back against one of the olive tree trunks. Guillaume Arnisout immediately stood to her left; the Frenchman incapable of failing to act as a lookout in any situation of potential danger—not even aware, perhaps, that he was doing it.

And how much do I do, now, that I don't even know about? Being a soldier, as I am . . .

"It's not a scam," the boy said, patiently now, "because I can show you."

"Now look—what's your name?"

"Ricimer." He'd evidently watched more than one Frank trying to get their tongues around Visigoth pronunciation and sighed before she could react. "Okay—Ric."

"Look, Ric, I don't know what you think you're going to show me. A handful of chicken bones, or rune stones, or bead-cords, or cards. Whatever it is, I don't have any money."

"Couldn't take it anyway. I'm the Lord-Father's slave."

"That's the abbot here?" She held her hand high above the ground for theoretical illustration, since she was still squatting. "Big man. Beard. Loud."

"No, that's Prior Athanagild. Abbot Muthari's not so old." The boy's eyes slitted, either against the sun off the white earth or in embarrassment: Yolande couldn't tell which.

She frowned suddenly. "What's a *priest* doing owning slaves?"

Guillaume put in, "They're a load of bloody heathens in this monastery: who knows what they do? For fuck's sake, who cares?"

Ric burst out, "He owns me because he saved me!" His voice skidded up the scale into a squeak, and his fair skin plainly showed his flush. "I could have been in a galley or down a mine! That's why he bought me!"

"Galleys are bad." Guillaume Arnisout spoke after a moment's silence, as if driven to the admission. "Mines are worse than galleys. Chuck 'em in and use 'em up, lucky if you live twenty months."

"Does Father Mu—" She struggled over the name. "—Muthari know you go around prophesying?"

The boy shook his head. The lean pig, which had been rootling around under the olive trees, paced delicately on high trotter toes up to his side. Sun glinted off the steel ring in its black snout. Yolande tensed, wary.

The vicious bite of the pig will shear off a man's hand. Besides that, there is the stink, and the shit.

The pig sat down on its rear end, for all the world like a knight's hound after a hunt, and leaned the weight of its shoulder against Ricimer's leg. Ric reached down and again scratched through the hair on its back, and she saw its long-lashed eyes slit in delight.

"Hey!" Guillaume announced, sounding diverted. "Could do with some roast pork! Maybe the rag-heads will sell us a couple of those. 'Lande, I'll go have a quick word, see what price they're asking. Won't be much; we got 'em shit-scared!"

He turned to go around the outside of the Green Chapel, calling back over his shoulder, "Kid, look us out a couple of fat weaners!"

The thought of hot, juicy, crunchy pork fat and meat dripping with sauce made Yolande's mouth run with water. The memory of the smell of cooked pork flooded her senses.

If you burn the meat, though, it smells exactly the same as the Greek fire casualties on the galley.

"Demoiselle!" Ricimer's eyes were black in a face that made Yolande stare: his skin gone some color between green and white. "Pigs are unclean! You can't eat them! The meat goes rotten in the heat! They have tapeworms. Tell him! Tell him! We don't eat—"

Yolande cut off his cracking adolescent voice by nodding at the long-nosed greyhound-pig. "What do you keep them for, then?"

"Garbage disposal," he said briefly. "Frankish demoiselle, *please*, tell that man not to ask the Lord-Father!"

So many things are so important when you're that age. A year or two and you won't care about your pet swine.

"Not up to me." She shrugged; thought about getting to her feet. "I guess the fortune-telling is off?"

"No." Still pale and sweaty, the young man shook his head. "I have to show you."

The determination of a foreign boy was irritating, given the presence of Margaret Hammond's dead body in the chapel behind her. Yolande nonetheless found herself resorting to a diplomatic rejection.

Young men need listening to, even when they're talking rubbish.

"If it's a true vision, God will send it to me anyway."

The boy reached out and tugged at her cuff with fingers dusty from the pig's coarse hair. "Yes! God will send it to you *now*. Let me show you. We'll need to sit with Vir Viridianus and pray in the chapel—"

The face of the woman came vividly into her mind, as it had been before the bones were bloodied and the flesh smashed. Margie— Guido—grinning as she bent to wind the windlass of her crossbow; mundane as a washerwoman wringing out sheets between her two hands.

"Not with Margie in there!"

"You need the Face of God!"

"The Face of God?" Yolande tugged at the leather laces that held the neck of her mail shirt closed. She fumbled down under the riveted metal rings, between her gambeson and linen shirt and her hot flesh, and pulled out a rosary. "This?"

Dark polished beads with a carved acorn for every tenth bead; and on the short trailing chain, carved simply with two oak leaves and wide eyes, the face of the Green Christ.

The boy stared. "Where'd you get that?"

"There's a few Arians in the company: didn't you know?" She laughed softly to herself. "They won't stay that way when the company goes north over the seas again, but for now, they'll keep in good with God as He is here. Doesn't stop them gambling, though. So: you want me to pray to this? And then I'll see this vision?"

He held his hand out. "Give it to me."

Reluctantly, Yolande passed the trickle of beads into his cupped

palms. She watched him sort through, hold it, lift the rosary so that
the carved Green Man face swung between them, alternately catching shafts of sunlight and the darkness of shade. Swinging. Slowing.
Stopping.

A pendant face, the carved surface of the wood softly returning
the light to her eyes.

Where I made my mistake, she thought later, was in listening to
a boy. I had one of my own. Why did I expect this one to be as smart
as a man?

At the time, she merely slid under the surface of the day, her vision blurring, her body still.

And saw.

Yolande saw dirt, and a brush. Dusty dirt, within an inch or two of
her face. And it was being swept back with a fine animal-hair brush,
to uncover—

Bones.

Yolande was conscious of sitting back up on her heels, although
she could not see the bits of one's body one usually sees out of pe-
ripheral vision. She looked across the trench, conscious that she was
in an area of digging—someone throwing up hasty earth-defenses,
maybe?—and not alone.

A woman kneeling on the other side of the gash in the dirt sat up
and put a falling swath of dark hair back behind her equally dark
ear. Her other hand held the small and puzzling brush.

"Yes," the woman said thoughtfully. "I suppose you would have
looked just like that."

Yolande blinked. Saw cords staked a few inches above the
ground. And saw that what also poked out of this trench, blackened
in places and in some cases broken, were teeth.

"A grave," Yolande said aloud, understanding. "Is it mine?"

"I don't know. How old are you?" The brown woman waved her
hand impatiently. "No, don't tell me; I'll get it. Let me see. . . . Mail
shirt: could be anywhere from the Carthaginian defeats of Rome
onward. But that looks like medieval work. Western work. So, not a
Turk." Her shaped thick eyebrows lowered. "That helmet's a give-
away. Archer's sallet. I'd put you in the fifteenth century some-

where. Mid-century . . . A European come over to North Africa to fight in the Visigoth-Turkish wars, after the fall of Constantinople. You're around five and a half centuries old. Am I right?"

Yolande had stopped listening at *helmet*. Reaching up, startled, she touched the rim of her sallet. She fumbled for the buckle at her jaw.

Why do I see myself dressed for war? This is a divine vision: it's not as though I can be hurt.

The helmet was gone. Immediately, all the sounds of the area rushed in on her. Crickets, birds; a dull rumbling too close to be thunder. And a clear sky, but air that stank and made her eyes tear up. She ruffled her fingers through her hair, still feeling the impress of the helmet lining on her head. The cool wind made her realize it was morning. Early morning, somewhere in North Africa . . . in the future that exists in God's mind?

"Is that my grave?"

The woman was staring at her, Yolande realized.

"I said, is that my—"

"Don't know." The words bit down sharply, overriding her own. The dark eyes fixed on her face in concentration, evidently seeing more of it now the sallet was off.

Yolande drew composure around her as she did before a fight, feeling the same churning bowel cramps. *I thought it would be like a dream. I wouldn't be aware I was having a vision. This is terrifying.*

"I won't know," the woman said, more measuredly, "until I get to the pelvis."

That was curious. Yolande frowned. *Some of this I will only discover the meaning of by prayer afterward. Pelvis? Let me see: what do I remember of doctors—is that what she is, this woman, grubbing in the dirt? Odd kind of medic . . .*

"I have borne a child," Yolande said. "You don't need to find my bones: I can tell you that myself."

"Now that would be something." The woman shook her head. "That would be really something."

The woman wore very loose hose, and ankle boots, and a thin doublet with the arms evidently unpointed and removed. Her Turkish-coffee skin would take the sunlight better, Yolande thought. But I would still cover up long before Nones, if it were me.

The woman sounded sardonic. "Finding a female soldier who was a mother—what kind of an icon would that be?"

Yolande felt a familiar despair wash through her. Why is it always the women who don't believe me?

"Yes, I've been a whore; no, I'm not a whore now." Yolande repeated her catechism with practiced slickness. "Yes, I use a crossbow; *yes*, I have the strength to wind the windlass; *yes*, I am strong enough to shoot it; *yes*, I can kill people. Why is it so hard to believe? I see tradeswomen in butcher's yards every day, jointing carcasses. Why is it so difficult to think of women in a similar trade? That's all this is."

Yolande made a brief gesture at what she could feel now: her mail shirt and the dagger and falchion hanging from her belt.

"It's just butchery. That's all. The only difference is that the animals fight back."

She has been making the last remark long enough to know that it usually serves only to show up any ex-soldiers in a group. They will be the ones who laugh, with a large degree of irony.

The dark-haired woman didn't laugh. She looked pained and disgusted. "Do you know what I was before I was an archaeologist?"

Yolande politely said, "No," thinking, A *what?*

"I was a refugee. I lived in the camps." Another shake of the other woman's head, less in negation than rejection. "I don't want to think there has been five, six hundred years of butchery *and nothing's changed*."

The wind swept across the diggings. Which evidently were not defenses, since they made no military sense. They more resembled a town, Yolande thought, as one might see it from a bluff or cliff overlooking it from a height. Nothing left but the stumps of walls.

"Every common man gets forgotten," Yolande said. "Is that what this is showing me? I— Is this her grave, not mine? Margie's? I know that few of us outlive our children's memories. But I—I need to know *now* that she's recognized for what she is. That she's buried with honor."

Margaret would have died fighting beside any man in the company, as they would have died at *her* shoulder. This is what needs recognition, this willingness to trust one another with their lives.

Recognition—and remembrance. *Honor* is the only word she would think of that acknowledged it.

The woman reached down and brushed delicately at the hinge of a jawbone. "Honor . . . yes. Well. Funerals are for the living."

"Funerals are for God!" Yolande blurted, startled.

"If you believe, yes, I suppose they are. But I find funerals are for the people left behind. So it's not just one more body thrown into a pit because cholera went through the tents, and it was too danger-ous to leave the bodies out, and there was no more wood for pyres. So they've got a grave marker you can remember, even if you can't visit it. So they're not just—one more image on a screen."

Screen? A little sardonically Yolande reflected, We are not the class of people who are put into tapestries, you and I. The best I'll get is to be one of a mass of helmets in the background. You might get to be a fieldworker, while the nuns spend all their skills embroidering the lord's bridle and all his other tack.

"If you believe?" Yolande repeated it as a question.

"If there was a God, would He let children die in thousands just because of dirty water?"

If the specifics evaded Yolande, the woman's emotion was clear. Yolande protested, "Yes, I've doubted, too. But I see the evidence of Him every day. The priests' miracles—"

"Oh, well. I can't argue with fundamentalism." The woman's mouth tugged up at the side. "Which medieval Christianity cer-tainly is."

A voice interrupted, calling unintelligibly from somewhere off in the destroyed village settlement.

"I'm coming!" the woman shouted. "Hold on, will you!"

The settlement's layout was not familiar, Yolande realized with relief. It was not the monastery.

So if I am fated to die on this damned coast, it isn't yet.

The woman turned her head back. There was an odd greediness about the way she studied Yolande's face.

"They'll put it into the books as 'village militia.' Any skeleton with a female pelvis who's in a mail shirt must have picked up armor and weapons as an act of desperation, defending her town."

There was desperation in her tone, also. And self-loathing; Yolande could hear it.

And this mad woman is not even a soldier. What can it matter to *her*, digging in the dirt for bodies, whether Margie and I are remembered as what we were?

The woman pointed at her. Yolande realized it was the mail shirt she was indicating. "Why did you do this! War? Fighting?"

"It . . . wasn't what I intended to do. I found out that I was good at it."

"But it's wrong." The woman's expression blazed, intense. "It's sick."

"Yes, but . . ." Yolande paused. "I enjoy it. Except maybe the actual fighting."

She gave the woman a quick grin.

"All the swanning around Christendom, and gambling, and eating yourself silly, and fornicating, and *not working*—that's all great. I mean, can you see me in a nunnery, or as a respectable widow in Paris? Oh, and the getting rich, if you're lucky enough to loot somewhere. That's good, too. It's worth risking getting killed every so often, because, hey, *somebody* has to survive the field of battle; why not me?"

"But killing other people?"

Yolande's smile faded. "I can do that. I can do all of it. Except . . . the guns. I just choke up, when there's gunfire. Cry. And they always think it's because I'm a woman. So I try not to let anyone see me, now."

The dark-skinned woman rested her brush down on the earth.

"More *sensitive*." The last word had scorn in it. She added, without the ironic tone, "More sensible. As a woman. You know the killing is irrational."

Yolande found herself self-mockingly smiling. "No. I'm not sensible about hackbuts or cannon—the devil's noise doesn't frighten me. It makes me cry, because I remember so many dead people. I lost more than forty people I knew, at the fall."

The other woman's aquiline face showed a conflicted sadness, difficult to interpret.

Yolande shrugged. "If you want *scary* war, try the line fight. Close combat with edged weapons. That's why I use a crossbow."

The woman's dignified features took on something between sympathy and contempt.

"No women in close-quarters fighting, then?"

"Oh, yeah." Yolande paused. "But they're idiots."

Guillaume's face came into her mind.

"*Everybody* with a polearm is an idiot. . . . But I guess it's easier for a woman to swing a poleax than pull a two-hundred-pound longbow."

The other woman sat back on her heels, eyes widening. "A poleax? *Easier?*"

"Ever chop wood?" And off the woman's realization, Yolande gave her a *there you are* look. "It's just a felling ax on a long stick . . . a thinner blade, even. Margie said the ax and hammer were easier. But in the end she came in with the crossbows, because I was there."

And look how much good *that* did her.

"Not everybody can master the skills of crossbows or arquebuses. . . ." This was an argument Yolande had had before, way too often. "Why does everybody think it's the *weapons* that are the difficult thing for a woman fighting? It's the guys on your own side. Not the killing."

The fragments of bone and teeth in the earth had each their own individual shadow, caused by the sun lifting higher over the horizon.

"The truth is important." Yolande found the other woman watching her with wistfulness as she looked up. Yolande emphasized, "That's the *truth*: she was a soldier. She shouldn't have to be something else just so they can bury her."

"I know. I want proof of women soldiers. And . . . I want no soldiers, women *or* men." The woman recovered her errant lock of hair and pushed it back again. Yolande saw the delicate gold of an earring in the whorl there: studded barbarically through the flesh of the ear's rim.

"Of course," the woman said measuredly, getting to her feet, "we have no idea, really. We guess, from what we dig up. We have illuminations, dreams. I visualize you. But it's all stories."

She stared down at Yolande.

"What matters is who tells the stories, and what stories never get told. Because people *act* on what the histories are. People live their lives based on nothing better than a skull, a fragment of a mail ring, and a misremembered battle site. People *die* for that 'truth'!"

Moved by the woman's distress, Yolande stood up. She rubbed her hands together, brushing off the dust, preparatory to walking forward to help the woman. And it was the oddest sensation possible: she rubbed her hands together and felt nothing. No skin, no warm palms, no calluses. Nothing.

"Yolande! *Yolande!*"

She opened her eyes—and that was the most strange thing, since she had not had them shut.

Guillaume Arnisout squatted in front of her, his lean brown fingers holding her wrists in a painful grip. He was holding her hands apart. The skin of her palms stung. She looked, and saw they were red. As if she had repetitively rubbed the thin, spiky dust of the courtyard between them.

A cool, hard, flexible snout poked into her ribs, compressing the links of her mail shirt. Yolande flinched; turned her head. The sow met her gaze. The animal's eyes were blue-green, surrounded by whites: unnervingly human.

What have I been shown? *Why?*

A yard away, Ricimer lay on his side. White foam dried in the corners of his mouth. Crescents of white showed under his eyelids.

Yolande turned her wrists to break Guillaume's grip on her forearms. The sow nosed importunately at her. *It will bite me!* She knelt up, away from it; leaned across, and felt the boy's face and neck. Warm, sweaty. Breathing.

"Kid had a fit." Guillaume was curt. "'Lande, I met your sergeant: the Boss wants us. The report on Rosso. I had to say you were praying. You okay? We got to go!"

Yolande scrambled up onto her feet. It was cowardice more than anything else. There was no assurance that the boy would live. She turned her back on him and began to walk away, past the chapel.

Visions! Truly. Visions from God—to *me*—!

"No. I'm not okay. But we have to go anyway."

"What did you see? Did you see anything? 'Lande! Yolande!"

* * *

The captain's wiry brass-colored beard jerked as he bellowed at the assembled monks.

"She will have a soldier's burial!" His voice banged back flatly from the walls of the monastery's large refectory. "A Christian burial! Or she stays where she is until she rots, and you have to bury her with a *bucket*!"

Johann Christoph Spessart, the captain of the company of the Griffin-in-Gold, was the usual kind of charismatic man. Guillaume would not have been in his company if he had not been. He was no more than five feet tall, but he reminded Guillaume of a pet bantam that Guillaume's mother had kept—a very small, very bright-feathered cock that intimidated everything in the yard, chicken or not, and gave the guard mastiffs pause for thought.

He was a lot more magnificent back in France, Guillaume reflected, when he wore his complete, if slightly battered, Milanese harness. But even highly polished plate armor doesn't lend itself to the hot sun of the North African coast.

Now, like half his men, Spessart was in mail and adopted a white Visigoth head cloth and loose trousers tucked into tough antelope-hide boots.

Still looks like a typical Frankish mercenary hard case. No wonder they're shitting themselves.

"You. Vaudin." The Griffin captain pointed to Yolande. The woman's head came up. Guillaume's gut twisted at her blank, bewildered stare.

Dear God, let the captain take it for piety and think she's been praying for her dead friend! What *happened* back there?

"Yes, sir?" Her voice, too, was easily recognizable as female. The monks scowled.

Spessart demanded, "Is Margaret Rosso's body laid out before the altar of God?"

Guillaume saw Yolande's mouth move, but she did not correct the captain's mangling of the dead woman's name. After a second, voice shaking, she said, "Yes, sir."

It could have been taken for grief: Guillaume recognized shock.

"Good. Organize a guard roster: I want a lance on duty at the chapel permanently from now on, beginning with yours."

Yolande nodded. Guillaume watched her walk back toward the main door. *I need to talk to her!*

He found himself uncomfortably on the verge of arousal.

"Arnisout?"

"Yes, Captain." Guillaume looked down and met the German soldier's gaze.

"What does the Church say about Christian burial, Arnisout?"

Guillaume blinked, but let the sunlight coming off the refectory's whitewashed walls be the excuse for that. "Corpses to be buried the same day as they die, sir."

"Even a foot soldier knows it!" The Griffin captain whirled around. "Even a billman knows! Now, I don't go so far as some commanders—I don't make my soldiers carry their own shrouds in their packs—but I keep to the Christian rites. Burial the same day. She died *yesterday*."

"I appreciate your point of view, *qa'id*." The abbot of the monastery hid his hands in his flowing green robes. Guillaume suspected the man's hands were shaking, and that was what he desired to hide. "I hesitate to call anyone damned for heresy. Christ knows who worships Him truly, no matter what rite is used. But we *cannot* bury a scandalous woman who dressed as a man and fought—killed."

Guillaume found himself admiring the small spark of wrong headed courage. The abbot spoke painfully, from a bruised and swollen mouth.

"*Qa'id*, the answer is still no."

And now he calls Spessart *qa'id*, general!

Guillaume grinned at the plump abbot: a man in his early middle age. *Not surprising, given what happened yesterday . . .*

Guillaume had been up on the ramparts, squinting across the acres of sun-scalded rock to see what progress the hand chain was making. From up here, the men had looked tiny. A long line of figures: crates and barrels being passed or rolled from one man to the next, all the way up the chine from the desolate beach. Food. And—

One of the men ducked out of line, arms over his head, a sergeant beating him; shouting loudly enough that Guillaume could hear it. A water barrel had splintered and spilled. *Okay, that's down to nine hundred-odd . . .*

Guillaume, squinting, could just see part of the hull of the beached galley. The round-bellied cargo ships were anchored a few hundred yards offshore, in deeper water; the side boats ferrying the stores ashore as fast as they could be rowed. White heat haze hung over the blue sea and islands to the north.

A shadow fell on Guillaume's shoulder. *The corporal, of course: he has to catch me the one minute I'm not doing anything.*

"If we're really lucky, there could be any number of Visigoth galleys out there, not just the two that bushwhacked us . . ." Lance Corporal Honoré Marchès came to stand beside Guillaume, gazing satirically out to sea. "Not like we're up the Turkish end of the Med now, with their navy riding shotgun on us."

"We could do with the Turkish shipwrights." At Marchès' look, Guillaume added, "Carpenters say they were right, sir. Patching up the galley is going to need skilled work. They can't do it. We're stuck here."

"Oh, Boss is going to love that! How's the unloading coming along, Arnisout?"

"Good, sir." Guillaume turned around, away from the coast. It was obvious to a military eye: the monastery here had taken over an ancient Punic fort. One from the days when it had been a forested land, and any number of armies could march up and down this coast road. Now the fort was covered with monastic outbuildings as a log is covered with moss, but the central keep would be still defensible in a pinch.

"I've got the lances storing the cargo down in the deep cellars, sir."

A large enough cargo of food that it could feed an army—or at least a Turkish division coming up from Tarābulus, somewhere to the east now, which is what it's intended for. And *water*. On this coast, water. The days when you could bring an army up the coast road from Alexandria to Carthage without resupplying by sea are gone with the Classical age.

"Yeah, that should do it." Marchès turned, signaling with a nod, and led the way down the flight of stone steps from the parapet to the ground. Over his shoulder, he remarked, "Fucking lot of work, but the Boss is right: we can't leave it on board. Not with no galley cover. Okay, Arnisout, get your team and come along with me; Boss is going to have a little talk with the abbot here."

Guillaume nodded obedience and bellowed across to Bressac and the others who shared the ten-man tent that made them a team. Bressac waved a casual hand in acknowledgment.

Marchès snapped, "Now, Arnisout! Or do you want to tell the Boss why we kept him waiting!"

"No, sir! Bressac!"

There was some advantage in having one's officer be part of the captain's command group, Guillaume thought as he yelled at his men, pulling them out of the chain of sweating mercenaries swearing with all apparent honesty that physical labor was for serfs and varlets, not honest soldiers.

One is never short of news to sell, or rumors to barter. On the other hand—we get to be there when Spessart proves *why* he's a mercenary captain.

Guillaume had arrived sweating in the big central hall the monks used as their refectory, and not just because of the heat. A barked order got his men into escort positions around the captain—a round dozen European mercenaries in jacks and hose, most with billhooks resting back across their shoulders in a gleam of silver gray, much-sharpened metal.

"Nothing until the Boss says so," Marchès warned.

The familiar tingle of tension and the piercing feeling in the pit of his belly began to build into excitement. Guillaume halted as Spessart did. A great gaggle of entirely unarmed men flooded into the hall from the door at the far end, wearing the green robes of the heretic Christianity practiced here. All uncertain, from their expressions, whether these Franks considered them proper clerks and so a bad idea to kill.

The hall smelled of cooking. Guillaume's gut growled as he stood at Marchès' shoulder. The older man kept his gaze on the hefty oak doors by which they had entered, in case someone should try to interrupt the captain during his deliberations. A wind blew in from the arid land outside, smelling of goats and male sweat and the sea.

Guillaume was conscious of the stiff weight of the jack buckled around his chest and the heat of plate leg harness, articulations sliding with oiled precision—and of how *safe* one feels, ribs and groin and knees protected. A delusional safety, often enough; but the feeling obstinately remains.

"I understand there's trouble with the burials," Spessart rasped. His eyes swept over the African priests as a group, not bothering, evidently, to concern himself with who exactly might be their Father-in-Christ. "What's the problem? Bury the bodies! We're not working for your masters, but common Christian charity demands it. Even if you are the wrong sort of Christians."

Ah, that's our tactful captain. Guillaume bit his lip to keep his smile from showing.

A tall man with a black-and-white badger beard stepped forward, waving his arms. "She isn't a man! She is an abomination! We will not have her soil the rocks of the graveyard here!"

"Ah. It's about Rosso. Now look, Father Abbot—"

A shorter, plumper man, perhaps five and thirty years old, stepped past the bearded man to the front of the group. He interrupted.

"I am abbot here. Prior Athanagild speaks for us all, I am afraid. We will bury no heathen whores pretending to be soldiers."

"Ah, *you're* the abbot. Tessier! I ordered you to find this man for me before now."

"Sir." The knight who was the officer of Guillaume's lance glared at Corporal Marchès.

Before there could be recriminations, which was entirely possible with Tessier—the Burgundian knight was not a man to keep his mouth shut when it was necessary—Spessart turned back to the plump abbot.

"You, what's your name?"

"Muthari," the monk supplied. Guillaume saw a flash of annoyance from the man's eyes. "Abbot Lord-Father Muthari, if we are being formal, Captain."

"Formal be fucked." Spessart took one step forward, reversing the grip he had on his war hammer. He slammed the end of the shaft into the abbot's body between ribs and belly.

The monk sighed out a breathless exclamation, robbed of air by sheer pain, and dropped down on his knees.

"How many messengers have you sent out?" Spessart said. He

stared down, evidently judging distance, drew back his boot, and kicked the gasping man. It would have been in the gut, but the abbot reared back and the boot caught him under his upper lip. Guillaume bit his own lip again to keep from laughing as the captain nearly overbalanced.

"How many of your rats have you sent off to Carthage?"

Blood leaked out of the abbot's mouth. "I— None!"

"Lying shitbag," Spessart announced reflectively. He shifted his grip expertly on the war hammer, grasping the leather binding at the end of the wooden shaft, and lightly stroked the kneeling man's scalp with the beaked iron head. A streak of blood ran down from Muthari's tonsure.

"None, none, I haven't sent anybody!"

"All right." Guillaume saw the captain sigh. "When you're dead, we'll see if your prior's any more cooperative."

Spessart spoke in a businesslike tone. Guillaume tried to judge if that made it more frightening for the abbot, or if the chubby man was decoyed into thinking the captain didn't mean what he said. Guillaume's pulse beat harder. Every sense keyed up, he gripped the wooden shaft of the bill he carried, ready to swing it down into guard position. Constantly scanning the monks, the hall, his own men . . .

"Tessier." Spessart spoke without looking over his shoulder at the down-at-heels knight. "Make my point for me. Kill one of these priests."

Guillaume's gut cramped. Tessier already had his left hand bracing his scabbard, his thumb breaking the friction seal between that and the blade within. His other hand went across to the hilt of the bastard sword. He drew it in one smooth movement, whipping it over and down, aiming at a tall skinny novice at the front of the group.

The skinny novice, not over twenty and with a badly cropped tonsure, froze.

A tall monk with wreathes of gray white curls flowing down to his shoulders and the face of an ex-*nazir*, a Visigoth corporal, straight-armed the skinny guy out of the way.

The novice stumbled back from the outstretched arm—

Tessier's blade hit with a chopping, butcher's counter sound. Guillaume winced. The *nazir*'s arm fell to the floor. Cut off just below the elbow. Arterial blood sprayed the six or seven men closest. They jolted back, exclaiming in disgust and fear.

The ex-*nazir* monk grunted, his mouth half open, appalled.

"*He Dieux!*" Tessier swore in irritation. He ignored the white-haired man, stepped forward, and slammed the yard-long steel blade toward the side of the skinny novice's head.

Guillaume saw the boy try to back up, and not make it.

The sword's edge bit. He dropped too fast and too heavily, like a falling chunk of masonry, smacking facedown into the flagstones. A swath of red and gray shot up the whitewashed wall, then dripped untidily down. The young man sprawled on the stone floor under it, in widening rivulets of blood.

There is no mistaking that smell.

Tessier, who had brought two hands to the hilt on his stroke, bent and picked up a fold of the dead man's robe to clean his sword. He took no notice of the staring eyes a few inches away from his hand, or of the shouting, screaming crowd of monks.

Two of them had the white-haired man supported, one whipping his belt around the stump, the other talking in a high-pitched voice over the screaming; both of them all but dragging the man out— toward the infirmary, Guillaume guessed.

In the silence, one man retched, then vomited. Another made a tight, stifled sound. Guillaume heard a spatter of liquid on the flagstones. Someone involuntarily pissing from under their robes.

The tall, ancient prior whispered, his voice anguished and cracking. "Huneric! *Syros* . . ."

It looked as if he could not take his eyes off the young novice's sliced, bashed skull and the tanned, freckled forearm and hand of the older man.

The limb lay with the body on the stone floor, in wet blood, no one willing to touch it. Guillaume stifled a nauseous desire to laugh.

He saw Tessier glance back at the captain, face red. Anger and shame. *Messy. Not a clean kill.* The knight sheathed his sword and folded his arms, glaring at the remaining monks.

Guillaume understood the silence that filled the refectory. He had been on the other side of it. Men holding their breaths, thinking, Not me, oh Lord God! Don't let me be next! One of the slaves back at the kitchen door sniveled, crying wetly. His own chest felt tight. The captain of the Griffin-in-Gold has long held to the principle that it's easier to kill one or two men at the beginning to save hassle later on.

Guillaume wiped his mouth, not daring to spit in front of the captain. *He's right. Of course. Usually.*

"Now." Spessart turned back briskly toward Abbot Muthari, signing to Tessier with his hand.

"*Wait!*" The Lord-Father sprawled back untidily on the floor, his bare legs spread and visible under his robe. "Yes! I sent a novice!"

"Only one?"

The man's eyes were dazed. Muthari looked as though he could not understand how he came to be on the floor in front of his juniors, undignified, hurt, bleeding.

If he had any sense, he'd be grateful. Could be *him* dead or maimed. The captain is only keeping him alive because his men are used to him as their leader.

"No! Two! I sent Gauda, but Hierbas insisted he would go after."

"That's better. Which way did you send them?"

"Due west," the abbot choked out. Not with pain or fear, Guillaume saw, but shame. *He's betraying them in front of his congregation.* "I told them to stay off the main road from here, from Zarsis—"

Ah, is that where we are? And is it anywhere near where we *should* have dropped the supply cache?

Close enough to Tarābulus for the Turks to get here in time? Guillaume kept his face impassive.

"They will be aiming for the garrison at Gabès. But traveling slowly. Because it is so far." The Lord-Father Muthari sat motionless, terror on his face, watching Spessart.

"There. I knew we could come to a mutual agreement."

The German soldier bent down, which did not necessitate him bending far, and held out his hand.

Too afraid not to, the fatter and taller man reached up and gripped it. Guillaume saw Spessart's face tense. He hauled the monk up onto his feet with one pull and a suppressed grunt of effort.

"This place will do as well as any for us to wait for our employers. Tessier, take your men out and find and capture the novices."

"Sir."

Tessier beckoned Marchès. Guillaume glanced back and got his team together and ready with only eye contact.

"You cannot behave like this!" he heard Athanagild protesting; and Muthari's voice drowning the bearded man out: "Captain, you will not harm any more of us; we are men of God—"

Three or four hours' searching in the later part of the afternoon had brought them up with the fleeing novices. To Guillaume's surprise, Tessier kept them alive. Guillaume, mouth filled with dirt by far too much scrambling up rocky slopes and striding down dusty gullies, was only too happy to prod them home with blows from the iron-ferruled butt end of his billhook.

He had seen the fugitives as he marched back into the refectory today. One, his gaze full of hatred, had whispered loudly enough to be heard. "I'll see you in Hell!"

Guillaume had grinned. "Save me a seat by the fire . . ."

Whether or not it was deliberate, today the German captain halted on the spot where the skinny, tall novice had been killed eighteen hours earlier.

The flagstones were clean now, but the whitewashed wall held a stain. The scrubbed, pale outlines of elongated splashes.

"I have no more patience!" Spessart snapped.

"Captain . . . *qa'id* . . ." Muthari blinked soft brown eyes as if in more than just physical pain. "Syros is dead. Huneric has now died. There must be no more killing—over a *woman*."

At the mention of the ex-*nazir* monk Huneric, Guillaume saw Tessier assume an air of quiet satisfaction. Vindication, perhaps.

"I don't want to kill a monastery full of priests," the captain remarked, his brilliant gaze turned up to Muthari. "It's bad luck, for one thing. We're stuck here until the Turkish navy turns up with expert carpenters, or the Turkish army turns up as reinforcements. Meantime, I'd rather keep you priests under lockdown than kill you. I *will* kill you, if you put me in a situation where I have to."

The abbot frowned. "Who knows who will come first? Your Turkish masters—or a legion from Carthage?"

"Oh, there is that. It's true we won't be popular if some *Legio* turns up on the doorstep here and finds an atrocity committed."

Johann Spessart smiled for the first time. Guillaume, as ever, could see why he didn't do it that often. His teeth were yellow and black, where they were not broken.

"Then again, if Hüseyin Bey and his division come up that road . . . they'll want to know why we didn't crucify every last one of you on the olive trees."

Prior Athanagild looked appalled. "You would kill true Christians for a Turkish bey?"

"We'll kill anybody," Spessart said dryly. "Turk, Jew, heathen; Christian of whatever variety. I understand that's what they pay us for."

Abbot Muthari stiffened.

The fat priest is getting his balls back, Guillaume thought. Bad idea, Abbot.

Abbot Muthari said, "We *are* priests. We *are* gifted with the grace of God. You cannot force us to perform the small miracles of the day here. *You* may not need them. Can you know that all your men feel the same way?"

"No." Spessart's voice dropped to a harsh rasp. "I don't care. They're my men. They'll do what I tell them."

The captain raised his head to gaze up at the monks. It might almost have been comic. Guillaume would have bet Johann Christoph Spessart couldn't even be seen from the back of the crowd: he would be hidden below other men's shoulders. *But that isn't the point.*

Guillaume felt his chest tighten with disgust. Ashamed, he thought, On the field of battle, yes. But killing in cold blood turns my gut. Always has.

Spessart raised his voice to be heard all across the refectory. The voice of the commander of the Griffin-in-Gold was used to carrying through shrieks, trumpets, gunfire, steel weapons ripping into each other, the screams of the dying. Now it eradicated whispers, murmurs, protests.

Spessart said, "Understand me. I know very well, the sea is only a half mile from here. There are caves under this fort. Plenty of places to dispose of an embarrassing corpse. *Don't do it.*"

Spessart paused. An absolute silence fell. Guillaume could hear his own heart beat in his ears.

The mercenary captain said, "If her corpse is moved, if you even attempt the sacrilege of touching her body except to inter it, *I will kill every human being over the age of thirteen in this place.*"

Yolande's lance handed over to Guillaume's at the Green Chapel without any opportunity for him to speak to her.

He fretted away three hours on guard, while Muthari and his fellow monks celebrated the offices of Sext and Nones, the abbot with his nose screwed up but singing the prayers all the same, carefully walking around the blackening, softening body of Guido Rosso/ Margaret Hammond, as if she could not be deemed to share in the previous day's prayers for their own dead.

Guillaume and the squad occupied the back of the chapel, restless, in a clatter of boots, butt ends of billhooks, and sword pommels rubbing against armor.

"Spessart'll do it," the gruff northern *rosbif*, Wainwright, muttered. "Done it before. But they're *monks*."

"Wrong sort of monks!" Bressac got in.

Wainwright scowled. "They're Christian, not heathen. I don't want to go to Hell just because I screwed some monks."

The Frenchman chuckled. "How if it were nuns, though?"

"Oh, be damned and happy, then!"

It was, to give them credit, ironically said. *And I have a taste for gallows humor myself.* Guillaume allowed himself a glance down the chapel at the celebrants: all white-faced, many of them counting out prayers on their acorn rosaries. "He's left us no choice, now."

There were murmurs of agreement. No man as reluctant as one might hope; long campaigning numbed the mind to such things.

All of the priests sang as if they were perfectly determined to go on this way through Terce, Sext, Nones, Vespers . . . all through the long day until sunset, and beyond. Compline, Matins, Prime. Every three hours upon the ringing of the carved hardwood bell.

I could pray, too, Guillaume reflected grimly, *but only that they'll have given in before my next shift on guard. This place is getting high.*

When Nones was sung—with some difficulty, down by the altar, because of the clustering flies—the Lord-Father Abbot paced his way back up the chapel, and stopped in front of Guillaume.

Before the Visigoth clerk could speak, Guillaume said grimly, "Bury Margaret Hammond, master. All you have to do is say a few words over her and put her under the rocks."

The boneyard was just visible through the open chapel doors—distant, away on the southern hill slopes. Cairns, to keep jackals and kites off. Red and ocher paint put on the rocks, in some weird Arian ceremony. But nonetheless a sort-of-Christian burial.

"Tell me, *faris*," the abbot said. "If we were to offer the heretic woman's heart in a lead casket, to be sealed and sent home to her family and buried there, would that content your captain?"

Guillaume felt an instant's hope. The Crusaders practiced this. But . . .

"No. He's put his balls on the line for a burial here. The guys want it. *Do* it."

"I would lose my monastery—the monks, that is."

Guillaume had an insight, staring at Muthari perspiring in his robes: Power always appears to lie with the leaders. But it doesn't. Under the surface, they're all trying to find out what the men need, what the men will leave for if they don't have it. . . .

Guillaume shrugged.

The abbot pulled out a Green Emperor rosary, kissed it, and returned to the altar.

When Guillaume's shift ended and he came out into the blazing afternoon sun, he thought: Where the hell is Yolande!

His mind presented him with the sheer line of her body from her calf and knee to her shapely thigh. The lacing of her doublet, stretched taut over the curves of her breasts. He felt the stir and fidget of his penis under his shirt, inside his cod-flap.

"Good God, Arnisout," the lanky blond billman, Cassell, said, walking beside him toward the tents. "We know what *you're* thinking! She's old enough to be your grandmother."

"Yours, maybe," Guillaume said dryly, and was pleased with himself when Cassell blushed, now solely concerned with his own pride. Cassell was a billman very touchy about being seventeen.

"Catch you guys around." Guillaume increased his pace, walking off toward the area where the camp adjoined the old fort.

Yolande Vaudin—oh, that damn woman! Is she all right? Did she really have a *vision?*

He searched the clusters of tents inside the monastery walls, the crowded cook wagon, the speech-inhibiting clamor of the armorers' tent, and (with some reluctance) the ablutions shed. He climbed up one flight of the stone steps that lined the inner wall of the keep, with only open air and a drop on his right hand, and stared searchingly down from the parapet.

Fuck. He narrowed his eyes against the sun that stung them. *Where is she?*

Yolande walked down the shadow of the western wall, in the impossible afternoon heat. She pulled at the strings of her coif, loosening it, allowing the faint hot breeze to move her hair. Off duty, no armor, and wearing nothing but hose, a thin doublet without sleeves, and a fine linen shirt, she still sweated enough to darken the cloth.

The rings in their snouts had not been sufficient to prevent the pigs rootling up the earth here. Fragments, hard as rock, caught between her bare toes. She paused as she came to the corner of the fort wall, reaching out one arm to steady herself and brushing her hand roughly across the sole of her foot.

As she bent, she glimpsed people ahead under a cloth awning. Ricimer. The abbot Muthari. Standing among a crowd of sleeping hogs. She froze. They did not see her.

The priest swiftly put out a hand.

What Yolande assumed would be a cuff, hitting a slave in the face, turned out to be a ruffle of Ric's dark hair.

With a smile and some unintelligible comment, the Lord-Father Muthari turned away, picking his way surefootedly between the mounds that were sleeping boars.

Yolande waited until he had gone. She straightened up. Ricimer turned his head.

"Is that guy Guillaume with you? Is he going to kill my pigs?"

"Not right now. Probably later. Yes." She looked at him. "There isn't anything I can do."

He was white to the thighs with dust. Yolande gazed at the lean lumps of bodies sprawled around him in the shade cast by linen awnings on poles. Perhaps two dozen adult swine.

"You have to do something! You owe me!"

"Nobody owes a slave!" Yolande regretted her spite instantly. "No—I'm sorry. I came here to say I'm sorry."

Ric narrowed his eyes. His lips pressed together. It was an adult expression: full of hatred, determination, panic. She jerked her head away, avoiding his eyes.

Who would have thought? So this is what he looks like when he isn't devout and visionary. When he isn't meek.

The young man's voice was insistent. "I gave you God's vision. You left me. You owe me!"

Yolande shook her head more at herself than him as she walked forward. "I shouldn't have left you sick. But I can't do anything about your pigs. We won't pass up fresh pork."

One of the swine lifted a snout and blinked black eyes at her. Yolande halted.

"I want to talk to you, Ric," she said grimly. "About the vision. Come out of there. Or get rid of the beasts."

The boy pushed the flopping hair back out of his face. The light through the unbleached linen softened everything under the awning. She saw him glance at her, at the pigs—and sit himself down on the earth, legs folded, in the middle of the herd.

"You want to talk to me," he repeated.

Yolande, taken aback, shot a glance around—awnings, then nothing but low brick sheds all along the south wall, driftwood used for their flat roofs. Pig sheds. Stone troughs stood at intervals, the earth even more broken up where they were. *A dirty, dangerous animal.*

"Okay." She could not help her expression. "Okay."

She stepped forward, ducking under the awning, her bare feet coming down within inches of the round-bellied and lean-spined beasts.

The boar is the most ferocious of the wild animals: that is why so many knights have it as their heraldry. And what is a pig but a tame boar?

And they're huge. Yolande found herself treading up on her toes, being quiet enough that she heard their breathy snorts and snores. What had seemed no more than dog-sized, walking with Ricimer, was visibly five or six feet long laying down on its side. And their heads, so much larger than human heads. It's not right for a *face* to be so big.

"Now—you can tell me about the vision." Yolande kept her conciliatory tone with an effort. "And I mean *tell* me about it. No more putting visions in my head! I don't know what I'm meant to make of that. What God wants me to do. But I do know it scared me."

The young man ignored her.

"I'm getting a farrowing shed ready." Ric nodded across to the huts against the wall.

Yolande saw one with the wooden door standing open, and bracken and thin straw piled inside on sand used for litter.

So those strip fields do yield a grain or two—I thought we were never going to eat anything else but tunny.

"Screw your goddamned farrowing shed! I want to know—"

"So I ought to be working," he interrupted, glancing around, as slaves do. "*I* want to speak to *you*."

"What about?"

Another nod of his head, this time taking in the sprawled and noon-dozing swine. "These. They *have* to be safe!"

"Ric, they're . . . *pigs*." Yolande took her courage in both her hands and squatted down. This close, there was a scent to the pigs—more spicy and vegetable than those back home. Particularly the boars'. And they were not dirty. A little dusty only.

Mud—that's what I'm missing. I expected them to be covered in mud and shit. . . . Maybe they have dust baths here, like chickens.

She felt the shaded earth cooler under her hands, and sat down nervously, shifting her gaze from one to the other of the large animals. "Your church is different; Leviticus, I suppose. 'Unclean flesh.' We just . . . eat them."

"*No, not these!*"

His vehemence startled the animals. One of the younger swine got up from a heap of gilts, with much thrashing and rolling, and stood with its head hanging down, peering directly at Yolande. It began to move toward her, agile now it was on its feet.

About to jump back, she felt Ric's large hand grip her upper arm. If she had not been so disturbed, he would not have come that close. She restrained herself only an instant from smashing her elbow into his nose.

"You can stroke her."

Held, Yolande was motionless on the ground for just long enough that the pig ambled up to her, wrinkled its slightly damp snout forward and back, scenting her.

The boy's hand pushed her arm forward. Her fingers touched the sow's warm flank. She expected it to snap; tensed to snatch back her hand.

It slowly moved, easing itself down toward the earth—and fell over sideways.

"*What?*" Yolande said.

The boy's hand released her. "Her name is Misrātah—like the salt marshes? Scratch her chest. She likes that."

Misrātah had her eyes closed. Yolande sat, more terrified by the animal's proximity than by the fight on the deck of the galley. It shifted its snout closer to her thigh and—eyes still closed—gave a firm and slightly painful nudge.

"Hell!" she yelped.

Ricimer's strained face took on a grin. "You don't want her to rootle you hard! Scratch her!"

Yolande reached out again to the slumped, breathing body of the pig. She encountered a warm, soft pelt. She dug her fingers into the coarse hair over the pig's ribs. The body rolled—leaning over, disclosing the teat-studded belly. A grunt made the flesh vibrate under Yolande's fingers. The dense, solid body shifted. She startled.

"You just got to be careful. They're big and heavy." The young man spoke with a quiet professionalism, as if they were not in the middle of a quarrel. "She would only hurt you without meaning it."

"Oh, that's a comfort!"

The sow's long body rolled over even further onto its side, with a resonant short grunt. Misrātah stretched out all four long legs simultaneously, as a dog stretches, and then relaxed.

"It's solid." Yolande pushed the pads of her bare fingers against meat-covered ribs. "Hard."

"It's all muscle. That's how come they move so fast? *Bang!*" His illustration, palms slammed together, made a couple of the larger boars lift their heads, giving their swineherd a so-human stare.

"One minute they're standing, next second they're in your lap. All muscle. Three hundred pounds. You can't force them out of the way. If they want something, they'll push their way to it." Ric gave her a mock malicious grin of warning. "Whatever you do, don't stop scratching. . . ."

There was something not entirely unpleasant about sitting on the dry ground, surrounded by breathing clean animals, with her fingers calling out a response of satisfaction from Misrātah.

"Oh . . . I get it." Yolande ran tickling fingers down the hairless skin. The pig in front of her let its head fall back in total abandon, four legs splayed, smooth belly exposed. It grumpled. "They're like hounds."

He pounced. "So how can you *eat* them!"

"Yeah, well, you know what they say about hounds—eight years old, they're not fit to do more than lick ladles in the kitchen. Nine years old, they're saddle leather."

"*Shit.*" Ric put his hand over his mouth.

"No one's going to listen to me, frankly," Yolande said. "If I go to Spessart . . . He's over in the command tent right now, thinking, 'Rosso's giving me trouble even when she's *dead.*' What's he going to say if another woman comes in and asks him to please not slaughter the local swine? I'll tell you what he'll say: 'Get the fuck—'"

"All right!"

Her thoughts completed it: Get the fuck out of here and back to the baggage train; quit using the crossbow, because you're plain crazy.

Prostitution again, at my age?

Ric glared at her, rigid and angry. His fury and disappointment stung her in a raw way she had thought could no longer happen.

"Ask Guillaume Arnisout." The words were out of her mouth before she thought about them. *But it isn't that stupid an idea.* "Guillaume's a man. He might get listened to. If you can get him to speak for you. Wouldn't the abbot try to speak for you? He's your master?"

"My master—"

He broke off. A different pig heaved herself up, walked forward, dipped her snout to Ric's knee where he sat, and with slow deliberation let herself fall down with her spine snug up against his leg.

"Lully . . ." The boy slid his fingers down behind her ear, into the soft places. Yolande thought, Dear God, I recognize a *pig*. This is the one he had at the chapel.

"I've been here since I was eight." Ric's girl-long lashes blinked down. "I don't remember much before. A banking house. The men used to travel a lot. I used to hold the horses' reins for them."

Yolande could picture him as a page, small and slender and dark-haired. He would have been attractive, which was never an advantage for a slave.

I wonder how much the fat Lord-Abbot paid for the boy? And how much he would ask for him now?

She caught herself. No. Don't be a fool. The most you can afford is a few derniers for someone from the baggage train to help armor you up. You can't pay the price needed to get a full-time page or varlet.

Maybe I could borrow the money. . . .

"And then," Ric said. "And—then. The Lord-Father came. Abbot Muthari. I have to know!"

Her expression must be blank, she realized.

"My *master*. Your *qa'id*'s going to kill him, isn't he?"

"If he doesn't bury Margaret."

"He won't do that." Ricimer wiped at his face, leaving it white with dust, his eyes showing up dark and puffy. "He won't. I know he won't."

"Look, you'll be all right; you can pass for under thirteen, if you try—"

"That's not it!" His anger flashed out at her. "The Lord-Father— he mustn't be killed! You're not *going* to kill him. Please!"

"Muthari?" Yolande found herself bewildered. "You want *Muthari*'s life, too? Your master?"

"Yes!"

He spoke vehemently, where he sat, but with a restraint unlike such a young man. Certainly her son Jean-Philippe was never prone to it.

He doesn't want to startle his animals.

"I'll tell." His eyes fixed on her. "I'll tell my abbot and your *qa'id*. You had a vision. You did sorcery."

Yolande stared. *A threat?* "You said it was from God! That's what I came here to ask—what it means—what I'm supposed to do with— *Sorcery?*"

"It was from God. But I'll say it wasn't."

Slaves have to be shrewd. She had seen slaves in Constantinople who maneuvered the paths of politics with far more skill than their masters. Being able to be killed with no more thought than men give to the slaughter of a farmyard animal will do that to you. Slaves listen. Notice. Notice what Spessart says to Muthari, and how the Lord-Father reacts, and what the mercenary captain needs right now . . . because knowledge, information, that's all a slave has.

Ric said, "I counted. There's a hundred of you. There are seventy monks here. Your *qa'id* needs the place kept quiet. If he hears about a woman having visions from God . . . that's trouble. He can't have trouble."

Well, damn. *Listen* to the boy.

Yes, the company's no larger than a *centenier* right now. And, yes, he can threaten to tell Spessart. The captain's always been half and half about women soldiers: wants us when we're good, doesn't want any of the trouble that might come with us.

"I'll tell them you made me do it," he added. "The sorcery. They'll believe it."

"They will, too." Yolande gazed down at him. *Because I'm old enough to be your mother.* "They probably would burn me. Even Spessart wouldn't tolerate a witch," she said quietly. "But Spessart doesn't have any patience. He solves most problems by killing them. Including heretic priests who have heretic visionaries in their monastery."

Ric stared, his face appalled.

Yolande put her hands in the small of her back, stretching away a sudden tension. "The Griffin-in-Gold is a hard company. I joined to kill soldiers, not noncombatants. But there's enough guys here who just don't care who they kill."

A crescent of light ran all along both underlids of the boy's eyes.

A gathering of water. She watched him swallow, shake his head, and suppress all signs of tears.

"I *won't* have the Lord-Father die. I won't have my pigs *eaten*."

"You may not be able to stop it." Yolande tried to speak gently.

"I had another dream."

For a second she did not understand what he had said.

His voice squeaked: adolescent. "I don't understand it. I didn't *understand* the *first* one."

Yolande's breath hitched in her throat. No. He's lying. Obviously!

"Another dream for me?"

Another vision?

This is some kind of threat to strong-arm me into protecting his pigs and Muthari's arse. . . . *Muthari*. His master. His pigs.

He's just trying to look after his own.

Without preamble, not stopping for cowardice, she demanded, "Give me this second vision, then!"

The wind blew the scent of rock-honey, and pigs, and she was close enough to the young man to smell his male sweat. Ric's dark eyes met hers, and she saw for the first time that he was fractionally taller than she.

He said, "I *have* to! It's God's. If I could hold it back any longer, until you promise to help . . . I *can't*. We have to go to the Green Chapel!"

There's no time. I'm on duty again in an hour. And how can I sneak him in there to have a vision—*if* I do—with the captain's guard on the place?

The next thought followed hard on that one, and she nodded to herself.

"Meet me outside the chapel. Two hours. Vespers. We'll see if you're lying or not."

A young voice emerged from the depths of the dimly lit Green Chapel. "Christ up a Tree, it stinks in here!"

Guillaume grinned as he entered from checking the sentries. "Cassell, I think that's the idea. . . ."

Ukridge and Bressac snickered; Guillaume decided he could afford not to hear them. *The more bitching they do about this duty, the less likely they are to slide off to the baggage-train trollops and make me put them up for punishment detail in the morning.*

Bressac got up and paced around on the cold tiles, evidently hoping to gain warmth by the movement. He did not look as though he were succeeding. Now that it was past Vespers, it was cold. Guillaume pulled his heavy lined wool cloak more securely around him. The other Frenchman walked over to the woman's body, where it lay swollen and chill in front of the altar, under a lamp and the face of Vir Viridianus.

"You'd think she wouldn't smell so much in this cold."

"This is nothing. You want *real* smell, you wait until tomorrow." Guillaume, feeling the tip of his nose numb with cold, found it difficult to remember the blazing heat of the day. He kept it in his memory by a rational effort.

Bressac paced back to the group. "I went to an autopsy once. Up in Padua? Mind, that corpse was fresh; smelled better than this. . . . They were doing it in a church. Poor bitch had her entrails spilled out in front of two hundred Dominican monks. And she was some shop owner's wife: doubt she even showed an ankle in public before."

"Some of those Italians . . ." Ukridge gave a shrill whistle at odds with his beef-and-bread English bulk. "Over in Venice, they wear their tits out on top of their gowns. I mean, shit, nipples and everything . . ."

"So that's how you know the Italian for 'get your tits out for the lads'?" Cassell's chuckle spluttered off into laughs and yelps as the big man got him in a headlock and ruffled his coarse brown hair.

A voice over by the door exclaimed, "Viridianus! I prefer the company of *real* pigs to you guys."

Yolande! Guillaume saw Bressac look up and chuckle with an air of familiarity as Lee and Wainwright, outside, passed the crossbow woman in. *She certainly picks her moment.*

Bressac called, "Come on in, 'Lande. Bring a bit of class to the occasion."

Guillaume managed to stop himself from bristling at the other Frenchman's informality. It was no more than the usual way of treating her: somewhere between a whore and a friend and a mother. For a moment he felt shame about his desire for the older woman.

A shorter figure emerged from the dark shadows behind the crossbow woman. Ric's still alive, then, Guillaume thought sourly.

Not that much shorter, he abruptly realized. Is she really no taller than a youth?

"You ought to be pious," the boy said, with an apparent calm that Guillaume found himself admiring. It took courage to face down heavily armed Frankish mercenaries. "If she's your friend, this dead woman, you don't want to disgrace her."

"Little nun!" Ukridge jeered, but it was sotto voce.

Guillaume judged it time to speak. "The boy's right. Rosso's still one of the company. This is a dead-watch, no matter why the Boss put her here. Let's have a little respect."

There was muttering, but it seemed to be in general agreement, with no more than the normal soldiers' dislike for being told to do something.

"She's still working for the company," Guillaume added. "Or she will be, when the sun comes up."

Bressac snickered approvingly.

Guillaume nodded to Yolande, feeling awkwardly formal in his command role—*even if it is only five grunts and the metaphorical dog . . . hardly company commander.* He studied her as well as he could in the light of two pierced-iron lanterns. Even with the door of one lantern unlatched—he leaned over and unhooked the catch—it was difficult to read her expression by a tallow candle's smoky, reeking light.

Yolande's mouth seemed tightly shut, the ends of her lips clamped down in white, strained determination. Her eyes were dark, and they met his with such directness that he almost flinched away, thinking she could read his lust.

But she doesn't seem to mind that.

She's afraid, I think.

"I might need you to bring me back, Guillaume."

Ignoring the puzzled remarks of the other men, Guillaume exploded. "You've come here for that? You're not letting that damn pig-boy practice sorcery on you again!"

She flinched at the word. "It isn't sorcery. He has grace. It's prayer."

"It's dangerous." Guillaume blinked a sudden rolling drop of sweat out of one eye. The moisture was stingingly cold. "You were somewhere else, 'Lande. Your spirit was. What happens if you don't come back? What happens if he has another fit! What if you do? What if God's too much for you?"

The holm-oak carving over the altar was only a collection of faint highlights off polished wood, not distinguishable as a face.

With a shudder he would have derided in another man, Guillaume said, "I believe in God. I've seen as many miracles as the next man. I just don't believe in a *loving* God."

"It's all right." Her smile suggested that she was aware of his reasons for being overprotective. He searched for signs that she was angry. He saw none.

"I'm going to pray now." She walked to the altar. Guillaume saw her reach for the lantern there. She bent down, holding it close to the corpse.

"*Shit* . . ." The stench made Yolande clamp her hand over her mouth.

By the lantern's light, Guillaume saw that Margaret Hammond's bare hands and feet were white on top, purple underneath, flesh shrinking back to the bone. On duty here, you could watch her flesh shrink, swell, bubble. The front of her head, where her face had been, was black, lumpy, wriggling with mites. Her slim belly had blown out, and contained by the jack she wore, it made her corpse look ludicrously pregnant.

Yolande's voice sounded low, angry. "She should have been buried before we saw her like this!"

She knelt down clumsily on the cold stone tiles by Margaret Hammond's reeking body. The knees of her hose became stained with the body fluids of her friend. She closed her eyes, and Guillaume saw her place her hands across her face—across her nose, likely—and then bring them down to her breast, where she still wore the mail shirt over her gambeson and doublet.

Layers of wool, for the cold nights . . . under which would be her breasts, warm and soft.

Breasts pulled with the suckling of one boy who would be older now than Cassell, if he had lived. *I need to forget that. It's—confusing.*

"What's she doing?" Cassell asked in a subdued voice.

"The boy gets visions. *Gives* visions," Guillaume corrected himself.

A mixture of respect and fear was in the air. God has His ways of sending visions, dreams, and prophecies to men. Usually through His priests, but not always. It is not unusual for someone born a peasant, say, in a small village near Domremy, to rise to be a military prophet by God's grace.

Guillaume shivered. And if Ricimer is that, too? The Pucelle put the king of France back on his throne. The last thing we need is a male Pucelle out of Carthage, knocking the Turks arse over tit. Not while we're signed up with the Bloody Crescent.

The young man brushed past Guillaume, toward Yolande, catching his gawky elbow against the heavy wool cloak. Guillaume watched Ric's back as he walked up behind her. His voice was gruff, with the cracks of young manhood apparent in it.

"I still have your rosary."

"Yes. Yes, of course." Yolande put her hand to her neck. She let it fall down onto her thighs, where she knelt. "Show me more."

"But—these men—"

"Show me more."

It's nothing but the repetition of the words in a different tone. Guillaume doubted she even knew she was doing it. But her voice carried the authority of her years. And the authority that comes with being shot, shelled, and generally shat on, on the field of battle. *The pig-boy doesn't stand a chance.*

"I need to pray first." Ric's thinner frame was silhouetted against the altar, where the second lantern stood. He knelt down beside the crossbow woman. Out of the corner of his eye, Guillaume saw that Bressac and Cassell had both linked their hands across their breasts and closed their eyes. Sentimental idiots.

Ukridge put his water container to his lips, drank, wiped his face with the back of his hand, and suppressed a loud belch to a muffled squeak.

The pig-boy sat back on his heels and held up the woman's rosary. The dark wood was barely visible against the surrounding dimness of the chapel.

"Look at the light." Ric's voice sounded more assured. "Keep looking at the light. God will send you what is good for you to know. Vir Viridianus, born of the Leaf-Empress, bound to the Tree and broken . . ."

The words of the prayer were not different enough. They skidded off the surface of Guillaume's attention. He found himself far from pious, watching the woman and the boy with acute fear.

Yolande stood up.

She said, very clearly, "*Shit.*"

She fell backward.

She fell back utterly bonelessly. Guillaume threw himself forward. He got his sheepskin-mittened hands there just in time to catch her skull before it thumped down on the tiles. He yelled with the pain of the heavy weight crushing his fingers between floor and scalp-padded bone. Bressac and Cassell leaped forward, startled, drawing their daggers in the same instant.

Guillaume stared at the pig-boy across Yolande's body. Yolande Vaudin, laid out beside Margaret Hammond's corpse, in precisely the same position.

"*Get her back!*"

Sand had sifted into the gaps between the small flat paving stones so no grass or mold could grow between them. Dry sand. No green grass.

One of the old Punic roads, Yolande thought. Like the Via Aemilia, down through the Warring States, but this doesn't look like Italy. . . .

The oddest thing about the vision, she thought, was that she was herself in it. A middle-aged and tired soldier. A woman currently worrying that hot flushes and night sweats mean she's past bearing another child. A woman who curses the memory of her only, her dead, son because, God's teeth, even stupid *civilians* have enough sense to stay alive—even a goddamned *swineherd* has enough sense to stay alive, in a war—and he didn't. He died like just another idiot boy.

"Yeah, but they do," a stranger's voice said, and added in a considering manner: "*We* do. If shit happens."

The stranger was a woman, possibly, and Yolande smiled to see it was another woman disguised as a man.

This one had the wide face and moon-pale hair of the far north, and a band of glass across her eyes so that Yolande could not see her expression. Her clothes were not very different from those that Yolande was familiar with: the hose much looser, and tucked into low, heavy boots. A doublet of the same drab color. And a strange piece of headgear, a very round sky-colored cap with no brim. But Yolande has long ago discovered in her trailing around with the Griffin-in-Gold that all headgear is ridiculous. Between different countries, different peoples, nothing is so ridiculous as hats.

"This is Carthage," Yolande said suddenly. "I didn't recognize it in the light."

Or, to be accurate, it is not far outside the city walls, on the desert side. A slope hides the main city from her. Here there are streets of low, square, white-painted houses, with blank frontages infested with wires. And crowds of people in robes, as well as more people in drab doublets and loose hose.

And the sky is brilliant blue. As brilliant as it is over Italy, where she has also fought. As bright and sun-infested as it is in Egypt, where the stinging power of it made her eyes water, and made her wear the strips of dark cloth across her eyes that filter out something of the light's power.

Carthage should be Under the Penitence. Should have nothing but blackness in its warm, daytime skies.

This is a vision of the world much removed from me, if the Penitence is absolved, or atoned for.

"What have you got to tell me?"

"Let's walk." The other woman smiled and briefly took off the glass that shielded her eyes. She had brilliant blue cornflower eyes that were very merry.

Yolande shrugged and fell in beside her. The woman's walk was alert, careful. She expects to be ambushed, here? Yolande glanced ahead. There were six or seven men in the same drab clothing. Skirmishers? Aforeriders? Moving as a unit, and this woman last in the team. They walked down the worn paving of the narrow road. People drifted back from them.

This is a road I once walked, a few years back, under the Darkness that covered Carthage.

And that, too, is reasonable: it's very rare for visions to show you something you haven't seen for yourself previously. This is the road to the temple where she sacrificed, once, for her son Jean-Philippe's soul in the Woods beyond the living world.

A stiff, brisk breeze smelled of salt. She couldn't see the sea, but it must be close. Other people passed their chevauchée, chattering, with curious glances—at the woman in the loose drab hose, Yolande noted, not at herself. The woman carried something under her arm that might have been a very slender, very well-made arquebus, if such things existed in God's world. It must be a weapon, by the way that the passing men were reacting to it.

Topping the rise, Yolande saw no walls of Carthage. There was a mass of low buildings, but no towering cliffs. And no harbors full of the ships from halfway around the world and more.

No harbors at Carthage!

Of the temple on this hill, nothing at all remained but two white marble pillars broken off before their crowns.

A dozen boys were kicking a slick black-and-white ball around on the dusty earth, and one measured a shot and sent the ball squarely between the pillars as she watched.

That's English football! Margie described it to me once. . . .

Yolande watched, walking past, trailing behind the team. Children playing football in the remains of Elissa's chapel. Elissa, called the Wanderer, the *Dido*; who founded this city from Phoenician Tyre, eons before the Visigoths sailed across from Spain and conquered it. Elissa, who was never a mother, unless to a civilization, so maybe not a good place for a mother's prayer.

Nothing left of Elissa's temple now, under this unfamiliar light.

"Is that what I'm here to see?" she asked, not turning to look at the woman's face as they walked. "Do you think I need telling that everything dies? That everything gets forgotten? That none of us are going to be remembered?"

"Is that what you need?"

The strange woman's voice was measured, with authority in it, but it was not a spiritual authority; Yolande recognized it.

"Is *that* it? That you're a soldier?" Yolande smiled with something between cynicism and relief. "Is that what I'm being shown? That we will be recognized, one day? You're still disguised as a man."

The woman looked down at herself, seemingly startled, and then grinned. "Of course. That's what it would look like, to you. And you'd think my dress blues were indecent, I should think. Skirts at knee-level."

Yolande, ignoring what the woman was saying in favor of the tone in which it was said, frowned at what she picked up. "You . . . don't think I'm here, do you?"

The other woman shook her head. "This is just a head game. Something I do every time we check out the ruins."

The woman's strange accent became more pronounced.

"We're not over here to fight. We're here to stop people fighting. Or, that's what it should be. But . . ."

A shrug, that says—Yolande fears it says—that things are still the same as they ever were. Yolande thought of the "archaeologist," her hands muddy with digging, her face impassioned with revulsion at the prior behavior of what she unearthed.

"Why *are* we doing this?" she said.

"You mean: it's such a shit job, and we don't even get the recognition?" The woman nodded agreement. "Yeah. Good question. And you can never trust the media."

A grinding clatter of carts going past sounded on the road at the foot of the hill. No, not carts, Yolande realized abruptly. Iron war wagons, with culverin pointed out of the front, like the Hussites use in battle. No draft beasts drawing them, but then, this is a vision.

"Judges, chapter one, verse nineteen!" Yolande exclaimed, made cheerful. Father Augustine used to read the Holy Word through and through, at his classes with the prostitutes in the baggage train. She remembered some parts word for word. "'And the Lord was with Judah; and he drave out the inhabitants of the mountain; but could not drive out the inhabitants of the valley, because they had chariots of iron'!"

"K78s." The other woman grinned back. "Counter-grav tanks. They're *crap*. The K81's much better."

Yolande peered down toward the road. Dust drifted up so that she could no longer see the pale-painted chariots of iron. "So why not use the—K81—instead?"

The other woman's tone took on a familiar and comfortable sound. Soldiers' bitching.

"Oh . . . because all the tank transporters are built to take the K78. And all the workshops are set up for it, and the technicians trained to repair it. And the aircraft transport bay pods are made to the width of the K78's tracks. And the manufacturers make the shells and the parts for the K78, and the crew are trained to *use* the K78, and . . ."

She grinned at Yolande, teeth white below her strip of dark glass. "Logistics, as always. You'd have to change everything. So we end up with something that's substandard because that's what we can support. If we had the K81s, we'd be stuffed the first time one of them stripped its gears. . . ."

Yolande blinked in the amazing Carthaginian sunlight. "To change one thing . . . you have to change everything?"

The other woman stepped back from the edge of the bluff, automatically scanning the positions of the men in her team. "Yeah. But, be fair: the K78 was state-of-the-art in its day. It just takes decades to get the next version up and running and into the field—"

A black hole appeared on the woman's shoulder, far to the right, just below the collarbone.

In a split second, Yolande saw the woman's white face turn whiter and her hand go to her doublet. Saw her scream, her hand pressing a box fixed to her breast. Saw the neat wound flow out and darken all the cloth around it. And heard, in the dry morning, the very muffled crack that was too quiet, but otherwise resembled gunfire.

Soldiers shouted, orders erupting. The woman took three long, comically staggering steps and ended rolling into the shade and cover of one of Elissa's pillars. There were no children. The slick-surfaced ball remained, perfectly still on the sun-hardened earth.

"Doesn't anything change?" Yolande demanded. She stood still, not diving for cover. "Why *are* we doing this?"

The woman shouted at the small box as if it could help her.

Not a serious wound, unless things have gravely changed—and yet they may have: obviously have, if an arquebus ball is no longer heavy enough to shatter the bones of a shoulder joint.

Yolande saw puffs of dust and stone chippings kick up out of the old Punic road toward her. The hidden man with the arquebus is walking his shots onto target, like a gun crew with a culverin. Sniping, as she does with her crossbow. But the reload time is amazing: *crack-crack-crack!*, all in the space of a few rapid heartbeats.

I can't be hurt in a vision.

The world went dark with a wrench that was too great for pain, but pain would come afterward, in a split second—

No pain.

Dark . . .

It's dark because this is the chapel, she realized.

The dark of a church, at night, lit only by a couple of lanterns.

She was lying on the glazed tiles, she discovered. Or at least was in a half-sitting position, her torso supported against the knees and chest of Guillaume Arnisout. He was shivering, in the stone's chill. His wool cloak was wrapped around her body.

She thought she ought to be warm, with his body heat pressed so close against her, but she was freezing. All cold—all except what had been hot liquid between her legs, and was now tepid and clammy linen under her woolen hose.

Embarrassed, she froze. Bad enough to be female, but these guys can just about cope with thinking of her as a beautiful hard case: a woman warrior. If they have to see me as a fat, middle-aged woman, cold white buttocks damp with her own pee . . . No romance in *that*.

Ah—the cloak—they can't see—

"You had foam coming out of your mouth." The youngest man, Cassell, spoke. She could hear how scared he was.

"You had a fit." Guillaume Arnisout sounded determined about it. "I warned you, you stupid woman!"

Ukridge peered out of the dark by the door. "It isn't Godly! It's a devil, in't it!"

Yolande snickered at his expression: a big man wary as a harvest mouse. She extricated her arm from the cloak and wiped her nose.

"It's grace," she said. "It's just the same as Father Augustine when he prays—prayed—over the wounded. Calling on God's grace for a small miracle. A vision's the same."

Guillaume's voice vibrated through her body. "Is it? 'Lande, you have to stop this!"

She thought Guillaume sounded the least scared so far. And way too concerned. She moved, unseen in the near dark, wrapping the cloak's folds around her now-chilled thighs.

I hope they can't read him as easily as I can. He'll be ribbed unmercifully. And he's . . . well. He doesn't deserve that.

She looked around. "Where's Ric?"

"Ric is the swineherd?" Bressac enquired, looming up into the candlelight from the darkness by the far door. "We threw him out. No need to be afraid of him, Yolande. We can keep him away from you."

"But—did he have a fit? Was he hurt?"

Guillaume shrugged, his chest and shoulder moving against her back, unexpectedly intimate.

She realized she was smelling the stink of meat gone off.

Lord God! That's still Margie, there. Tell me how this vision helps *her*.

"I don't understand," she whispered, frustrated.

Guillaume Arnisout grinned, mock consoling. "'Salright, girl. Me neither!"

Yolande reached her hand up and touched the rough stubble on his jaw.

She would pray, she would sleep, she would question the boy again, and maybe one of the Arian priests, too: she knew that. For this moment, all she wanted to do was rest back against the man who held her, his straggling black hair touching her cheek, and his arms shuddering with cold because he had covered her.

But it's never that easy.

She got to her feet, fastening the cloak around her neck, and walked to the altar. She reached up and took the carved Face down from the wall.

She heard one of the men curse behind her. It came down easily. Someone had fixed the Face there with a couple of nails and a length of twisted wire, and under it, covered but not expunged, was painted a woman's face.

Her nose was flat, and her eyes strangely shaped in a way that Yolande couldn't define. The worn paint on the stone made her skin look brownish-yellow. There were leaves and berries and ferns in her hair, so many that you could barely see her hair was black. Her eyes, also, were painted black—black as tar.

There was no more of her than the face, surrounded by painted flames. Elissa, who died on a pyre? Astarte the child-eater goddess?

"Elissa," the young man Cassell said, prompt on her thoughts. Still holding the Face in her hands, she turned to look at him.

He blushed and said, "She founded New City, *Qart-hadasht*, before the Lord Emperor Christ was born. She set up the big temple of Astarte. The one the Arians took over, with the dome? She took a Turkish priest off Cyprus, on her way from Tyre—a priest of Astarte. That's why they think Carthage is their Holy City. The Turks, I mean. Like Rome, for us. Even though there's no priests of Astarte there anymore."

Yolande lifted the carved oak Face and replaced it, with a fumble or two, against the bitter chill stone wall.

"They'll be pleased when they get here," Guillaume's gruff voice said behind her. "The Beys. She looks one tough bitch, too."

"They used to burn their firstborn sons as sacrifices to her," the Frenchman, Bressac, added. "*What?* What did I say?"

"I'm going back to my tent," Yolande said. "Guillaume, if you don't mind, I'll give you the cloak back in the morning."

Guillaume Arnisout slipped out in the early morning for his ablutions.

If I move *fast*, I can call on Yolande before rollcall. . . .

It was just after dawn. The air was still cool. He picked his way among the thousands of guy ropes spider-webbing between squad tents. A few early risers sat, shoulders hunched, persuading camp fires to light. Moisture kept the dust underfoot from rising as his boots hit the dirt. He scratched in the roots of his hair as he walked down past the side of the monks' compound to the lavatory.

It was a knock-together affair—whatever the Arian monks were, they weren't carpenters. A long shack was built down the far side of the compound on the top of a low ridge, so that the night soil could fall down into the ditch behind, where it could be collected to put on the strip fields later.

Best of luck with mine, Guillaume thought sardonically. Usually, with the wine in these parts, I could do it through the eye of a cobbler's needle. Now? You could load it into a swivel gun and shoot it clear through a castle wall. . . .

The lavatories were arranged on the old Punic model: a row of holes cut into wooden planks, and a sponge in a vinegar bowl. With a sigh, Guillaume pulled the lacing of his Italian doublet undone. He slid doublet and hose down in one piece, to save untying the points at his waist that joined them together. Slipping his braies down, he sat. The morning air was pleasant, cool with just his shirt covering his torso.

So—am I going to make my approach to Yolande? Because I think the door is unbarred. I *think* so . . .

He sat peacefully undisturbed for a number of minutes, having the place to himself. He listened to the clatter of pans from the monks' kitchen, and heard a rustling of rats here and there across the courtyard and below him in the ditch. There was more movement now the sun was up, but this yard remained deserted.

Abbot Muthari and his monks rang for service every hour through the night. They *can't* keep that up; they're bound to quit today and plant her . . . she's starting to leak over the floor.

If it was me, I wouldn't worry about a dead archer, no matter how smelly she's getting. I'd worry about the live archer. *Two* visions! You can't tell me she didn't have another one, in the chapel. I need to get 'Lande away from that damned kid. . . .

"Ah, *Dieux*!" Guillaume folded his arms across his belly and bent forward a little to alleviate his sudden cramp. A spasm eased him. He sighed with happiness, feeling his body begin another.

A cold, hard object suddenly shoved up against his dilated anus.

It hit with surprising force, lifting him an inch off the plank. Before he could react in any way, something warm and wet wiped itself almost instantaneously from his scrotum down the crack of his arse, and finished at his anus again.

He was not conscious that he screamed, or that his flesh puckered up and shut in a fraction of a second. The next thing he knew, he

was hopping out into the courtyard, his hose trapped around his ankles, hobbling him, and the rest of his clothes pulling behind him
through the dust.

"It's a demon!" he shrieked. "It's a demon! *I felt teeth!*"

Two monks came running up at the same time as Bressac and one
of the company's artillerymen.

"What?" Bressac yelled. "Gil!"

His shirt was caught under his armpits and the wind blew chill
across his bare arse.

I *knew* we shouldn't have left an unblessed corpse in a chapel, I
knew it, *I knew it!*

"It's a demon!"

"Where?" The foremost monk grabbed Guillaume by the arm. It
was the abbot, Muthari, his liquid eyes alert. "*Where* is this demon?"

"Down the goddamned shit-hole!"

The abbot goggled. "Where?"

"Fucking thing tried to climb up my arse!" Guillaume bellowed,
hauling hopelessly at his tangled hose. He gave up, grabbed the abbot by the arm, and hobbled back across the courtyard toward the
long shed. "You're a fucking *monastery*! You didn't ought to have
demons in the *lavatory*!"

Once under the tiled roof, the abbot pulled his arm out of Guillaume's grip. Guillaume glared, breathless. The abbot leaned a hand
against the wooden pillar that supported the lavatory's roof, and
peered down the hole. His shoulders convulsed under his robe. For
a split second Guillaume thought the monk was becoming possessed.

Bressac shoved past, pushed the abbot aside, and stared down
the hole. A cluster of monks and soldiers was growing out in the
yard. Guillaume stood with his clothes still around his ankles. He
yanked the tail of his shirt down, gripping it in a fist with white
knuckles. The feeling of cold, unnatural hardness prodding at his
most vulnerable area was still imprinted in his skin. That, and the
warm, wet sensation that followed. He felt he would never lose the
belly-chilling fear of it.

"God damn it, let *me* see!" Guillaume heaved his way bodily between Bressac and the Visigoth.

The hole in the plank opened into emptiness.

Beneath the plank was a shallow gully full of rocks and the remnants of night soil. And something else. A recent-looking landspill from the far side had raised the level of the gully here, until it was only a yard or so under the wooden supports.

As he watched, a quadruped shape turned back from waddling away down the slope and lifted its head toward him.

He gazed down through the hole at a brown-snouted pig.

It gazed back hopefully at him, long-lashed eyes slitted against the bright light.

"Jesus Christ!" Guillaume screamed. "It was *eating* it. *It was eating my fucking turd while I was shitting it!*"

Bressac lost it. The abbot appeared to control himself. His eyes were nonetheless very bright as he waved other approaching monks back from the shed.

"We feed the pigs our night soil." Muthari raised his voice over Bressac's helpless and uncontrolled howling. "It appears that one of them was anxious to, ah, get it fresh from the source."

The faintest stutter betrayed him. Guillaume stared, affronted. The Lord-Father Abbot Muthari went off into yelps and breathless gasps of laughter.

"*It's not funny!*" Guillaume snarled.

He bent down, this time managing to untangle his dusty hose and his doublet and pull them up. He dipped his arms into his sleeves, yanking his doublet on, careless that he was rucking his shirt up under it. He shuddered at the vivid remembrance of a hot, overlarge tongue. A *pig's* tongue.

Taken by surprise by a realization, Guillaume muttered, "Oh, *shit*—!", and Bressac, who had got himself upright, sat down on the plank and wept into his two hands.

"*Shit,*" Guillaume repeated, deliberately. He ignored all the noise and riot and running men around him. Ignored the mockery that was beginning as the story was retold. He stared down the shit-hole again at the thoughtfully chewing pig.

"Shit . . . we were going to *eat* one of those."

* * *

There was no more talk of pork. But there was endless discussion of the incident, and Guillaume glimpsed even Spessart smile when one of the archers yelled "Stinker Arnisout!" after him.

"Animal lovers are never appreciated," Bressac said gravely, strolling beside him. "St. Francis himself was exiled, remember?"

"Ah, *fuck* you!"

Bressac whooped again. "Only—trying—to help!"

Guillaume passed the day in anger and hunched humiliation, going through his duties in a haze. He registered another row between Spessart and the monks—the captain swearing quietly afterward that it would be better to kill every man of the Visigoths here, and that he would do it, too, if the company's only priest had not been killed on the galleys. Guillaume thought ironically that it was not just he who missed Father Augustine.

He stood escort for the captain again after the hot part of the day, when tempers flared in another confrontation at the chapel door, and Spessart knocked down Prior Athanagild, breaking the elderly man's arm. That would have been the signal for a general massacre, if Gabès had not been uncomfortably close to the west, and men difficult to control when they are panicking and dying. Both parties, monks and soldiers, parted with imprecations and oaths, respectively.

Off duty, Guillaume hung about the fringes of the camp as the evening meal was served, and afterward found himself wandering among the ordered rows of tents that led out from the fort's main courtyard to the sand that ran unobstructed toward Carthage. Tent pegs had been driven hard into the ocher earth. The outer ring of the camp should have been wagons, if this were a normal war, but arriving by sea meant no wagons to place. They had settled for stabling the few knights' horses at that end, knowing that any strange scent would have them bugling a challenge.

Guillaume found Yolande sitting between two tents, in a circle of men, playing at cards round the fire pit. She smiled absently as he sat down beside her. He put his arm around her shoulder, heart thudding. She didn't object. She was playing hard, and for trivial amounts of money, and losing, he saw.

Toward what short twilight there was in these parts, the woman ran her purse dry and threw her cards down.

"Nothing to spend it on here, anyhow," Guillaume said, trying to be comforting.

She gave him a sharp look.

"So . . . ah . . . you want to walk?" he asked.

A slow smile spread on her face. His belly turned over to see it. He knew, instantly, that she had heard the nickname being bandied about the camp. That she was about to say *Walk with you, Stinker? The idea's a* joke.

"I don't mind," she said. "Sure. Let's do it."

There was no privacy in the tents, and none in the cells of the fort; none, either, down among the packed cargo-cog stores—far too well guarded—and the desert itself would be chilly, snake-ridden, and dangerous.

The woman said, "I know somewhere we could go."

Guillaume tried to read her expression by starlight. She seemed calm. He was shaking. He tried to conceal this, rubbing his fingers together. "Where?"

"Down this way."

He followed her back past the keep, stumbling and swearing, and quietening only when she threatened to leave him and go back to the tents. She led him to the back of the fort, and a familiar scent, and he was about to turn and go when she grabbed his arm and pulled him down, and they tumbled on top of each other through a low doorway.

"A *pig* shed?" Guillaume swatted twigs out of his hair—no, not twigs. A familiar scent of his boyhood came back to him. Bracken. Dried bracken.

"It's been cleaned out." Too innocent, the woman's voice, and there was humor in her face when his eyes adjusted to the dimness. "The occupant doesn't need it yet. It's not going to be in use tonight."

"Oh, I wouldn't say that. . . ." Steeling himself to courage—*I have known women to back out at* this *stage*—Guillaume reached out his arm for her.

"Now you just wait."

"*What?*"

"No, wait. We should sort something out first. What are we going to do, here?"

Despairing, he spluttered. "What are we going to *do*? What do you think we're going to do, you dumb woman!"

He intended it as an insult, but it came out comic, fuelled by his frustration. He was not surprised to hear her snort with laughter. Guillaume groped around in the dark until a white glimmer of starlight on skin allowed him to grab her hand. Her flesh was warm, almost hot.

He pushed her hand into his crotch.

"That's what you're doing to me! And you ask me what we're going to do?"

His voice squeaked with the incredulity that flooded him. She laughed again, although it was soundless. He only knew about it by the vibration of her hand.

"That isn't helping. . . ."

"No." Fondness sounded in her voice, and amusement, and something breathless. Her face was invisible. Her voice came out of the dark. "I find it helps to sort out these things in advance."

Guillaume almost made a catastrophic error. *You mean you're arranging a price?* He bit his tongue at the last minute. She used to be a whore—but this isn't whoring.

His understanding of how much hurt the question could inflict on her drained his impatience of its violence.

"Am I going to suck *this*," her voice continued, out of the darkness, "and then you lick me? And that would be it? I'm past the age of having a child, but you never know. Or are we going to fuck?"

Guillaume heaved in a harsh breath, dizzy. Her fingers were kneading his crotch, and he could not speak for a moment. He clamped his hand down on top of hers. The throbbing of his penis was all-encompassing, as far as his mind went. His fingers and hers around his cod: oh dear Lord, he prayed, completely unself-consciously, don't let me spill my seed before I have her!

"I want you," he said.

He felt his other hand taken, and pressed, and after a second realized that it was pushed up between linen shirt and hot flesh, cupping the swell of a heavy breast. His fingers touched a rock-hard nipple.

"I want you," Yolande said, out of the dark. "But is it that easy?"

The sounds of the monastery were muffled: the bells for Compline from the Green Chapel, the groaning chorus of hungry pigs, the rattle of boots outside as men went past to the refectory.

"You can have sex whenever you want," she said, long-eroded anger in her voice. "And it doesn't change anything. If I have sex, it changes everything. If I 'belong' to a man. Or to many. Whether I'm safe to rape. Whether I'm going to be trusted when we're fighting . . ."

All true, but . . . Guillaume grunted in frustration. In comic despair, he muttered, "And on the *good* side?"

A chuckle came out of the darkness.

She likes me. She actually likes me.

He felt her rest her arm down in the warm, dry bracken, close to his arm. A sudden shine of silver—moonrise—let him distinguish her face as his eyes adjusted.

"On the good side . . ." she finished, "you're not in my lance. You're not another archer. And you maybe won't commit the cardinal sin if we get into combat . . ."

Guillaume kept himself still with an effort. "Which is?"

"Trying to protect me."

He stopped with one hand on her shoulder, the other still inside her shirt. Actually stopped. After a second, he nodded. "Yeah. I get it. You're right. I won't."

Some expression went across her face, so close now to his, that he couldn't properly make it out. Amusement? Lust? Liking? Respect?

Her nipple hardened under his palm. An immense feeling went through him, which he realized after a moment was relief.

She can't deny she wants me, too.

She wants *me*.

A little too straight-faced, Guillaume said, "But it's not a problem if you can't have sex often, is it? *Men* want it all the time, but women don't really like sex. . . ."

Her anger was only half mockery. "So it doesn't matter if I have to go without?"

Deadpan, he said, "Of course it doesn't—"

She threw her arms around his chest. He abandoned caution, tried to kiss her, but she rolled them both over in the bracken. He ended on his back: felt her straddling him.

"'Lande!"

Her voice came out of the darkness, full of joy. "You should have listened to the monks—women are *insatiable*!"

"Good!" he grunted, reaching up.

One of her hands clamped down on his groin. The other grabbed his long black hair, holding his head still. She brought her mouth down on his.

Guillaume cradled her against him when she fell asleep in his arms, in the rising moon's light; her clothing half pulled up around her, bracken shrouding her bare shoulders. He was dazzled and aroused again by the glimpse of her rounded belly, striated silver here and there; and her surprisingly large and dark-nippled breasts.

He tightened his embrace and looked down at Yolande's sleeping face. All the lines were wiped out of her face by relaxation. She appeared a decade younger. It was a phenomenon he was familiar with: it happens when people sleep, and when they're dead.

"I *did* know him!" Guillaume exclaimed aloud.

Yolande's eyes opened. She had evidently picked up the soldiers' trick of coming awake almost instantly. She blinked at him. "Know who?"

"Your Margie Hammond. *Guido Rosso!* Bright kid. All boy!"

The moon's light, slanting into the pen, let him catch a wry smile from Yolande. Too late to explain his definition. *Impulsive, dashing, daring.*

"You know what I mean! I just didn't—" Guillaume shook his head, automatically pulling her close and feeling the sweaty warmth of her body against his. "I guess there was no way I was going to recognize the face."

"When we put her in the chapel, she didn't *have* a face."

Guillaume nodded soberly.

He remembered Rosso now, a young man prone to singing in a husky boy's voice, always cheerful, even in the worst weather; who would sit out any dancing on the excuse of his very minor damage to one hip and thighbone, and use the time to chat up the women. *I prefer to dance with the enemy*, he'd say, priming the girls to regard him as a wounded hero—the limp, of course, was very small; enough to give him a romantic, dashing air, but not enough to keep him out of the line fight. He had gone to the archers anyway, and Guillaume had not, at the time, known why.

"We used to call him Crip," Guillaume said. "He limped. And *he* was a girl? That girl—that woman—we carried into the chapel . . . ? *That's* Crip Rosso, and he was female?"

"She wouldn't marry the man her parents picked out for her. Her mother locked her in her room and beat her with a stick until she couldn't stand. That's where she got the limp." Yolande stared past him, into the darkness of the pig shed, apparently seeing pictures in her mind. "She limped to the altar on her bridal day. When she'd had a couple of children that lived, her husband said he'd let her go to a nunnery, because she was a bad influence on them. She ran away before she got there."

Guillaume whistled quietly.

"He—she—always seemed so cheerful."

"Yes. Well." Out of the silver shadows, Yolande's voice was dry. That was not so disconcerting as the feeling of withdrawal in all the flesh she pressed against him: skin and muscle tensing away from his body. "Wouldn't she be? Misery gets no company."

"Uh—yeah." He reached over to touch her cheek and got her mouth instead. Wet saliva, the sharpness of a tooth. She grunted in discomfort. He blushed, the color hidden by the dark, but the heat of it probably perfectly apparent to her.

Does she think *I'm* a boy? he wondered. Or is she—I don't know— Is this it: over and done with? Do I care, if it is?

"'Lande . . ."

"What?"

"Doesn't matter."

"I'm awake now." She rummaged about in the dark, and he felt her haul at something. She pulled the woolen cloak that covered them up around her own shoulders, uncovering Guillaume's feet to the cold. He said nothing.

The moon rose on up the sky. The strip of white light shining in between the hut's walls and roof now barely let him see the shine of her naked flesh in the darkness. He put his hand on her, stroking the skin from thigh, buttock, belly, up to her ribs. Warm. Soft. And hard, under the soft surface.

"So Crip joined the company because no man would have her?" He hesitated. "Oh . . . *shit.* That was meant to come out as a joke."

He couldn't distinguish her expression. He didn't know if Yolande heard his rueful truthfulness and credited it.

After a second, she spoke again. "Margie told me she ran away on the journey to the nuns. I don't know how she got as far south as Constantinople, but she was already dressing as a man. That's why she got raped, before she joined the company. Revenge thing, you know?"

Guillaume froze, his fingers pressing against her warm skin. He heard her voice falter.

"They had the fucking nerve to tell her she was *ugly*, while they were doing it. 'Crip.'"

The bracken moved under him and crackled. There was a grunt from the next shed over. One of the sows rising, with a thrash of her trotters, and then settling again.

Guillaume winced. "Nothing I could say would be right. So I'll say nothing."

There was the merest nod of her head visible in the dim light. Yolande's muscles became tense. "The name stuck, after she signed on with the company."

"Stuck?" He felt as if his pause went on for a whole minute. His heart thumped. Incredulous, he said, "It was one of *us* who raped her?"

"More than one." She kept her voice deliberately bland. Still she shook, held within his arms.

Guillaume felt cold. "Do I know the guys that did it?"

"I don't know their names. She wouldn't tell me."

"Do you *think* you know?"

"How could I tell?"

He almost burst out, *Of course you can tell the difference between one of us and a rapist!* But recalling what she would have seen at sacks of towns, he thought, Perhaps she has cause to doubt.

"We wouldn't have treated her like that," he said. "Not when she was one of us."

Not out of morality—lives depend on loyalty. Men-at-arms and archers together, each protecting the other, and the bows bringing down cavalry before it could ever reach the foot soldiers. And the billmen keeping the archers safe from being ridden down. *Safe*.

Yolande's voice came quietly as her body leaned back against him. "I guess she didn't think about the rape much, later. We could all die any time, the next skirmish, field of battle, whatever. What's the point of remembering old hurts if you don't have to?"

An obscure guilt filled him. Guillaume felt angry. Why must women always *talk* at moments like this? And then, on the heels of that, he felt an immense sadness.

"Tell that to your Ric," he said. "When his master's dead."

She was silent momentarily. He was fairly sure she thought he had not been listening to her recounting the day's happenings. She confirmed it, a note of surprise in her voice.

"I didn't think you were paying attention."

"Ah, well. Full of surprises."

A small, spluttered chuckle; her relief apparent. "Evidently. You're—not quite what I expected you to be."

He didn't stop to work out what that might mean. Guillaume hitched his freezing feet up under his cloak. "His pigs are safe. But . . . Spessart might not kill Ric, but I'd take a bet with you that Muthari won't make it—or I would, if I had any money."

She gave him a look he couldn't interpret at *money*.

"Yeah. At least the pigs won't die." She sounded surprised by her own thought. "These pigs, I mean . . . more like dogs than pigs."

"All pigs are." Guillaume could just see surprise on her face. He shrugged. "We had pigs. My dad always got in a hell of a black mood when it came to slaughtering day. Loved his pigs, he did. Hated his sons but loved his pigs . . ."

"So what happened to you and Père Arnisout and the pigs?"

"What always happens in a war. Soldiers killed my father, raped my mother, and took me away to be their servant. They burned the house down. I would guess they ate the pigs and oxen; it was a bad winter. . . ."

Her arms came around him. Not to comfort him, he realized after a second of distaste. To share closeness.

She said dispassionately, "And now you're on this side of the fence."

He put his hand up past his head, where his sword lay in the bracken, and touched the cross-hilt. "Aren't we all. . . ."

"I'll have to see Ric again." The moonlight was gone now, her face invisible; but her voice was sharp and determined.

"About Muthari?"

"About the visions." Her hands sought his arms, closing over his muscles. "Two of them, Gil. And I don't understand either. Maybe things would be clearer if I had another." Her tone changed. He felt her laugh. "Third time lucky, right? Maybe God believes things come in threes, too."

"Well, fuck, ask him, then—the pig-boy," Guillaume clarified. "Maybe he *can* tell you when the enemy's going to drop on us from a great height. I'd also give money to know who'll turn up first, Hüseyin Bey or the Carthaginian navy. If I had any money." He grinned. "Poverty doesn't encourage oracles, I find."

She sounded amused in the dark. "*And* he might know why God bothers to send visions to some mercenary soldier. . . ."

"Or not."

"Or not . . ."

He depended on sensation—the softness of her waist under his hand, the heat of her skin against him. The smooth, cool wool that sheltered them from the night's cold. The scent of her body, that had been all day in the open air.

He felt his way carefully, as if speech could be tactile. "What we were saying—about Crip Rosso?"

"Yes." No hint of emotion in her voice.

"I was going to ask . . . were you ever raped?" Guillaume was suddenly full of raw hatred that he could not express. "I—hope not. Just the thought's made my prick wilt, and talking about that *isn't* the way to bring it up again. Not in my case. Though I've soldiered with men who would come to attention instantly at the thought."

His eyes adjusted to starlight. It illuminated shapes—the precise curlicues of bracken, and the crumpled linen mass of his doublet under them, colorless now; and her own hand, where it rested on his chest.

Guillaume whispered, "I'd take all your hurts away if I could," and bent his head to nip at her heavy breasts.

"Yes . . ." Yolande smiled.

He felt her body loosen.

Her voice became half-teasing. "But that's because you're one of the good guys. I think."

"Only think?" he gasped, mouth wet from trailing kisses across her body, under her pulled-up shirt. He reached down and put her hand on him, to encourage his prick upright again. "I'm good. What do you want, letters of recommendation?"

She spluttered into a giggling laugh.

"You see? In the dark, you could be sixteen." He put her remaining hand to his face, and let her fingers trace his grin. "I knew I could make you happy again."

With Prime and Vespers always at six A.M. and six P.M. here, it made the hours of the day and the night the same length, which Guillaume found odd.

On the cusp of dawn, he began a dream. Forests where it was hot. Holm-oak woods. Dwarf elephants, no bigger than horses. Men and women in red paint, who burned their children alive—sacrifices to deforestation, so that cities could survive. A scream that was all pain, all desolation, all loss. Then he was lost in the African forests again. And again.

He woke with a start, the nightmare wrenching him awake. Cold drafts blew across the pen, counteracting the bracken's retained heat. Cool blue air showed beyond the half door.

Morning.

"*Green Christ!* What *time* is it? 'Lande." He untangled himself gracelessly, shaking her awake. His breath showed pale in the cold air. "'Lande! It's past roll call! We're meant to be on duty—oh, shit."

Running feet thumped past outside. Lots of running feet. Men shouting. Hauling his clothes on, wrenching at knotted points, clawing under the bracken for a missing boot, he gasped, "It's an attack! Listen to them out there!"

Loud voices blared across the morning. He cursed again, rolling over, trying to pull on his still-laced-up boot.

Damn! Hüseyin Bey's division ought to be a fortnight behind us at most. At *most*. We can stand a siege—if there hasn't already been a battle to the east of us. If Hüseyin's Janissaries aren't all dead.

"Don't hear the call to arms!" Yolande pulled her shirt down and her hose up. She finished tying off her points at her waist, and knelt up in the bracken like a pointing hound.

"What? What, 'Lande?"

"That's at the chapel!"

"Bloody hell."

He struggled out of the pig shed behind her, shaking off bracken, not worrying now if anyone saw them together. It was a bright crisp morning, sometime past Prime by the strength of the dawn. So the rag-head monks would be there, to celebrate mass, and this racket must mean—

"Rosso! Margie!" he grunted out, having to run to keep up with Yolande.

"Yes!" Impatient, she elbowed ahead of him, forging into the crowd of mercenary soldiers already running toward the chapel doors.

He tried to catch a hackbutter's arm, ask him what was the matter, but the other man didn't stop. Guillaume heard the captain's voice way ahead, piercing loud above the noise, but couldn't make out all the words. Only one came through, clean and clear:

"—sacrilege!"

Yolande barged through the black wooden doors into a rioting mess of men and—*pigs?*

She reared back from the smell. It hit her as soon as she was through the doors. Hot, thick, rich. Rotten blood, fluids, spoiled flesh. Dung. And the eye-watering stink of concentrated pig urine. Yolande gasped.

In front of her, an archer bent down, trying to stop a sow. The small, heavy animal barged into him and knocked him away without any effort. Yolande caught at his arm, keeping him upright.

"What the hell is this?" she shrieked over the noise of men bawling, pigs shrieking and grunting, metal clattering and scraping against stone.

"The fucking pigs et her!" the archer bawled back. His badge was unfamiliar, a tall man from another lance, his face twisted up in rage or anguish, it was impossible to guess which.

"Ate her?" Yolande let go of him and put one mud-grimed hand over her mouth, muffling a giggle. "You mean—ate her body?"

The archer swore. "Broken bones of Christ! Yes!"

Another pig charged past, jaws gaping. Yolande jumped back against the Green Chapel's wall as the gelded boar, mouth wide open to bite, chased a green-robed monk toward the open doors.

"Grab it!" the monk yelled, holding the Host in its holm-oak box high over his head. "Grab that animal! Help!"

Yolande's hand pressed tight against her mouth, stifling another appalled snicker.

Ten or twelve or fifteen large pigs ran around between her and the altar, screaming and honking and groaning. And two dozen soldiers, easily. And the monks who had come in to celebrate Prime. A sharp smell of pig dung filled the air. There were yellow puddles on the tiles where pigs had urinated in fear or anger.

"Who . . ." she stuttered. "Who let them in here?"

The nearest man, a broad-shouldered elderly sergeant, bellowed, "Clear the fucking House of God! Get these swine out of here!"

Yolande shoved forward, then slowed. Men moved forward past her. The lean-bodied pigs were not large. But heavy. All that muscle.

A knight had his legs and arms wide, trying to herd a young black sow away from the altar. The animal shoulder-charged past him, bowling him over in a tangle of boots and armor. Yolande realized, on the verge of hysteria, that she recognized the beast—Ric's favored sow, Lully.

The black-haired pig scrabbled past her as Yolande dodged aside. The tiled floor was covered in dark dust. Boot prints, the marks of pigs' trotters, the prints of bare feet. Dust damp with the early morning's dew.

And something white, kicked and trodden underfoot.

Yolande bent down. She kept close to the wall and out of the way of the struggle ahead—men flapping their arms, clapping, shouting, doing everything to harry the pigs away from their focus, a few yards in front of the altar. She squatted, reached out, and snared the object.

It had a rounded, shiny end. The back of it had a bleached stump, and blackened meat clinging to it. She recognized it all in a split second, although it took moments for the realization to plod through her mind. It's a bone. A thigh joint. The thigh bone's been sheared off it—

By the jaws of pigs.

That guy was right. They ate her.

She thrust her way between the men, ignoring the skid of her heels in pig dung on the floor. She got to the altar. What was in front of her now were pig backs, lower down than anything else. Hairy sharp rumps. Pigs with their snouts snuffling along the tiles, wrenching and snatching things between them. Heads lifting and jaws jerking as they swallowed.

Bones.

Meat.

There was not enough left to know that it had been a human skeleton.

The pigs had had her for a long time before they were caught, Yolande could see. Almost all of the flesh was gone. *He did say his pigs ate carrion . . . 'garbage disposal.'* Most of the bone fragments had been separated from each other. There was nothing left of Margie's skull or face. Only a fragment of bottom jaw. Pigs can cut anything with their shearing teeth.

"Margie," she whispered under her breath, not moving her fingers away from her mouth. Her breath didn't warm her stone-cold flesh.

Now there is nothing to bury. Problem solved.

She felt wrenching nausea, head swimming, mouth filling with spit.

I didn't always *like* her. Sometimes I hated her guts. There was no reason we should have anything in common, just because we were two women. . . .

The body of Margaret Hammond, Guido Rosso, such as it was now, was a number of joints and bones and fleshy scraps, on the floor and in the jaws of pigs. She saw the captain, Spessart, reach down to grab one end of a femur. He yelled, cursed, took his hand back and shook it. Yolande saw red blood spatter, and then the brass-bearded man was sucking at the wound and swearing at one of the monks while it was bound up.

"You knew this would happen!" Spessart bawled.

The round face of Abbot Lord-Father Muthari emerged into Yolande's notice. She saw he stood back from the fracas. One white hand held his robe's hem up from the mess of rotten flesh and dung on the tiles.

"I did *not* know," Muthari said clearly.

"You knew! I swear—execute—*every one of you over thirteen*—"

"This is an accident! Obviously the slave in charge of the animals failed in his duty. I don't know why. He was a good slave. I can only hope he hasn't had some accident. Has anyone seen him?"

Yolande stood perfectly still. Memory came back to her. She could hear it. The shrill complaints and groans of hungry pigs. The stock know when their feeding time is. And if they're not fed . . .

We *heard* them. They weren't fed last night. That's why they're so hungry now. That's why they've—eaten everything in here.

Her hands dropped to her sides. She made fists, pressing her nails into her palms, trying to cause enough pain to herself that she would not shout hysterically at the abbot.

Ric would have fed them last night.

And these animals have been locked in here, she thought, dazed, staring back at the door where the crowd was parting. Or they'd be off at the cook tent, or foraging . . .

Someone stabbed a boar, sending it squealing; others, flailing back from the heavy panicking animal, began to use the hafts of their bills to push the swine back and away.

A European mercenary in dusty Visigoth mail pushed through the gap in the men-at-arms, grabbing at Spessart's shoulder, shouting in the captain's ear.

Yolande could hear neither question nor answer, but something was evidently being confirmed.

Spessart swung round, staring at Abbot Lord-Father Muthari.

"You're damned lucky!" the captain of the Griffin-in-Gold snarled. "What's coming down the road now is the Legio XIV Utica, from Gabès. If the Turkish advance scouts were coming up the road, I'd give them this monastery with every one of you scum crucified to the doors!"

Yolande began to move. She walked quite calmly. She saw Muthari's face, white in the shadows away from the ogee windows, blank with shock.

"So consider yourself fortunate." The captain's rasp became more harsh as he looked at the fluid pooled before the altar. "We have a contract now with the king-caliph in Carthage. You and I, Muthari, we're—allies."

He's going to pull that one once too often one day. Yolande numbly pushed her way between taller men, heading for the small door beside the altar, under the embroidered hanging. Mercenary companies who change sides in the middle of wars get a bad rep.

But then . . . six thousand enemies a few miles away, no support for us: time to say 'Hey, we have supplies, *and* we can tell you where there are food caches farther down the coast . . .'

The handle of the door was rough in her palm. A ring of cold black iron. She turned it, and the heavy bar of the latch lifted. Yolande stepped through.

The air outside hit her. A smell of dry dust, honey, and olive trees. The sun was well up. Did I just spend so long in there?

She walked calmly and with no unnecessary speed down past the olives, past the broken walls of this end of the monastery, and down to where the pig shelters stood.

Here, in the shadow of the southern wall, there were still patches of frost on the earth.

She walked up past the first low hut. The boy was lying at the foot of the flight of stone steps that came down the fort's wall. His back was toward her. She stopped, reached down, felt him quite cold and dead.

Dead for many hours.

She maneuvered his stiff, chill body around to face her. He was almost too heavy. Frost-covered mud crackled underfoot.

It was not the first time she had felt how someone's head moved when their neck was broken. Snapped, with the neck held, the jaw clamped into someone's hand and jerked sideways—

No one will prove it. It looks perfect: He had a fit, and fell.

Spessart will accept it as an accident. It solves all his problems.

No woman's body to bury; no living man to blame.

She heard the voices of men coming after her.

Yolande turned her head away and stared up at the flight of steps, leaving her fingers on Ric's smooth, bitter-cold flesh. How easy to take hold of a young man by the iron ring around his neck. Just get close, inside his guard.

He took this from someone he trusted to get close. He was a slave. He didn't trust many people.

Yolande's thoughts felt as cold as the boy's dead body.

I hope Muthari broke his neck from behind.

I hope he let Ric die without ever knowing he had been killed by someone he loved.

Guillaume Arnisout leaned his hip against the rail on the galley's prow. He braced the burden that he carried.

The thing that had been part of him for so long—his polearm, the hook-bladed bill—was no longer propped beside him, or lying at his feet, or packed in among the squad tents. *Because they won't put me into a line fight now. Not with a broken knee. And I can't say I blame them.*

The warm wood under his hand and the salt air whipping his hair stiff were part of him now, so long had the *Saint Tanitta* been on its way to Italy. The brilliant sun on the waves was still new—the ship having been Under the Penitence as far as Palermo, on the coast of Sicily.

He looked back down the galley, finding Yolande Vaudin. *But nothing fills the gap, after Zarsis monastery—not for her. Nothing.*

Archers sprawled on the deck, their kit spread out around them. Every plank was covered with some mercenary, or some mercenary's gear. Men arguing, drinking, laughing, fighting. Yolande was squatting down with her hand in the crotch of a blond Flanders bowman.

Guillaume could not hear what she said to the big man at this distance. By now, he didn't need to. It was always the same—and one of the reasons for keeping a distance in the first place.

She tries everything. . . .

Yolande hauled the man up by his arm. He laughed. Guillaume watch them lurch as far as the butt end of the ship. Yolande touched the man's chest. The two of them vanished behind a great heap of sailcloth and coiled ropes. As much privacy as might be found on shipboard, when all of a mercenary company is crowded into one galley.

He turned back to the rail, shifting his leg under him.

Threads of pain shot through his knee and the bone beneath it.

Better than two months ago in Carthage: at least I can stand up without it giving way.

Guillaume shifted the burden he carried against his chest, moved his shattered and mending knee again, and swore.

Bressac came and leaned on the ship's rail beside him. He had lost a lot of weight. The other Frenchman made pretense of looking out across the milky blue sea toward Salerno. He sniggered very quietly. "Got left holding the baby again?"

Guillaume looked down at his burden—the child in its tight swaddling bands, resting against his chest.

The lengths of linen bands bound it to a flat board. He had had the carpenter drill a couple of holes in the wood, and now he had loops of rope over his shoulders to hold the swaddling board against his body. It left the child facing him. All that could be seen of her were her bright eyes that followed his movements everywhere.

"I don't mind. She's all right, for a Visigoth." Guillaume spoke carelessly, edging one linen band down and giving her a finger to suck. "Have to find the wet nurse soon. Right hungry little piglet, she is. Ain't you, Mucky-pup?"

"Daah," the baby said.

Bressac snickered again.

The red tile roofs of Salerno became distinct, floating above the fine blue haze. Birds screamed.

Bressac said, not laughing now, "She ought at least to come and *look* at the damn brat, after we went to so much trouble to get it."

Guillaume took his finger back from the hard gums, and the baby gave him a focused look of dislike. He said, "First time in the entire bloody voyage this little cow hasn't been crying, or puking up all over me. Looks cute enough to get her interested in it again."

At Bressac's look, Guillaume admitted, "Well, maybe not *that* . . ."

"She's drinking too much to have the infant. Drop it overboard, probably." Bressac glanced over his shoulder and then, sentimental as soldiers anywhere, said, "Give it here."

Guillaume slid the ropes of the swaddling board off his shoulders and handed the baby over to rest her nose against Bressac's old and smelly arming-doublet. To his surprise, she neither cried nor puked. *Can't win, can I?*

"Yolande's drinking too much," he said. "And angry too much."

Bressac joggled the baby. "She keeps going on about that pig-boy—'Oh, the abbot killed him; oh, it was murder.' I mean, it's been half a year, we've had an entire damned campaign with the Carthaginian legions; you'd think she'd get o—" His voice cut off abruptly. "Damn! Kid just threw up all over me!"

"Must be your tasteful conversation." Guillaume took the baby back as she began to wail, and wiped her face roughly clean with his kerchief. The wail changed from one of discomfort to one of anger.

Bressac, swiping at himself, muttered, "Green Christ! It's just some slave's brat!", and wiped his hands on the ship's rail.

Above him, the company silk pennant cracked, unrolling on the wind: azure field merging with azure sky, so it seemed the gold griffin veritably flew.

Bressac said, "'Lande was *drunk*, remember? Kept saying she wanted a baby and she was too old to have one. She *insisted* we haul this one out of goddamn Carthage harbor. Now she's bored with it. Green Christ, can't a bloody slave commit infanticide in peace?"

"You think it was a slave?"

"Hell, yes. If the mother had been freeborn, she could have *sold* it."

"Maybe we should find a dealer in Salerno, for the Turkish harems." Guillaume was aware he was only half joking.

If she's got bored with the kid . . . so have I.

Merely being honest about moral failings is not an excuse.

It's not boredom. Not for Yolande. It's just that the kid isn't Ric —or Jean-Philippe. Saving this kid . . . isn't the same. And that's not the baby's fault.

"This *isn't* a place for a baby." Guillaume looked guiltily around at the company. "Kid deserves better than old sins hanging round her neck as a start in life. What can she ever hope for? Like 'Lande keeps on saying, to change anything—"

The words are in his mind, Yolande repeating the words with the care of the terrifyingly drunk:

"To change anything . . . we'd have to change everything. And I don't have the time left that that would take."

Blue sea and white foam streaked away in a curve from this side of the galley's prow. He went as far as unknotting the ropes from the swaddling board and sliding them free.

Splash and gone. So easy. A lifetime of slogging uphill gone. When we meet under the Tree, she'll probably thank me.

Bressac's voice broke the hypnotic drag of the prow wave. "So. You going to talk it over with the master gunner? Ortega will have you for one of the gun crews; they're shorthanded now. Not much running about, there . . ."

There was a look in Bressac's eyes that made Guillaume certain his mind and proposed action had been read. Not necessarily disapproved of.

A seabird wheeled away, screaming, searching their wake for food. The perpetual noise of sliding chains from the belly of the ship, where the rowers stood and stretched to the oars, quickly drowned out the bird's noise.

"Sure," Guillaume said. "A gunner: sure. That'd suit a crip, wouldn't it?"

The baby began to wail, hungry again. Guillaume looped the board back on one shoulder and slid a finger under the linen band. He tucked the baby's still white-blonde birth hair carefully back underneath.

"Maybe I could do with a vision," he said wryly. "Not that they helped 'Lande. Or the kid. What's the point of seeing things centuries on? He needed to see what that son of a bitch Muthari was like now."

"One of us would have to have done it," Bressac observed, his long horse face unusually serious. "You know that? If there wasn't going to be a massacre?"

Guillaume heard sudden voices raised.

Farther down toward the slim belly of the galley, Yolande Vaudin was standing now, shouting—spitting with the force of it—into the face of the company's new priest.

The priest evidently attempted to calm her, and Guillaume saw Yolande slap his hand away, as a woman might—and then punch him in the face, with the strength of a woman who winds up a cross-bow for cocking.

"'*Ey!*" The sergeant of the archers strode over, knocked Yolande Vaudin down, and stood over her, yelling.

Guillaume felt himself tense his muscles to hand the baby to Bressac and run down the deck. *And . . . run?* The sergeant abruptly finished, with a final yell and a gesture of dismissal. Guillaume felt frustration like a fever.

Yolande got to her feet and walked unevenly up toward them at the prow. One hand shielded the side of her face.

She halted when she got to them. "Stupid fucking priest."

Bressac reached out to move her hand aside. Guillaume saw him stop, frozen in place by the look she shot him.

"Want to take the baby?" he offered.

"I do *not*." Yolande moved her hands behind her back.

A bruise was already coming up on her cheek. Red and blue, nothing that arnica wouldn't cure. Guillaume didn't stand. He lifted the baby toward her.

Her gaze fixed on its face. "Damn priest said I was asking him to do fortune-telling. It isn't fortune-telling! I wanted to know if what I saw was *real*. And he won't tell me."

"Maybe he doesn't know."

"Maybe." Yolande echoed the word with scorn. "He said . . . *he* said none of it was a half millennium in the future. He said the hea-then boy had been telling *my* future—that *I'd* never be recognized.

That *I'd* die a mercenary soldier, shot by some hackbutter. And that foretelling my future was witchcraft, and so it was right the abbot should kill such a boy—that's when I hit him."

Guillaume found himself nodding. The sensation of that possible future being truncated—of it being a translated form of this woman's desires and terrors—eased some fear he had not been aware he still had. Although it had given him nightmares in the infirmary, after his wound.

I don't like to think about five, six hundred years in the future. It makes me dizzy. But then . . .

"Priest might be frightened it *is* true foresight," Guillaume said quietly. "Either way . . . as a future, are you so in love with it?"

The old Yolande looked at him for a moment, her expression open and miserable. "You know? I can't think of anything better. Recognition. Acceptance. And a better death than disease. I wanted it for so long. . . . Now I know I ought to be able to think of something *better* than this. And . . . I can't."

Guillaume rested the baby back against him. He didn't say anything about families, farms, retirement into city trades.

What's the point? Neither of us are going to stop doing what we do. No matter what. This is what we are now.

No wonder she drinks. I wonder that I don't.

"Been doing it too long." The other Frenchman's voice was gently ironic. Bressac nodded down the deck toward the sergeant of archers, who was standing with his fists on his hips, talking to one of the corporals, glaring after Yolande Vaudin. "All the same . . . That isn't the way to behave to a sergeant."

"Oh, so, what am I supposed to be afraid of?" Scorn flashed out in her tone. "A black mark against my name on the rolls? It's not like they're ever going to make *me* an officer, is it? A woman giving orders to men!"

So easily caught by those old desires, Guillaume thought. If I could go back into the line fight, as the team's boss . . . How long would I hesitate? A heartbeat? Two?

Bressac grinned. "You want to do leadership the way Guillaume here does it—he finds out what we're going to do, then he tells us to do it!"

There was enough truth in that that Guillaume couldn't help smiling. Bressac's face clouded.

"As Guillaume here *used* to do it," Guillaume commented.

The wind smelled suddenly of fish and blood as it veered—the stink of the fish-shambles, in Salerno. A brown-haired woman, the wet nurse, approached from the direction of the other rail. Guillaume noticed she ignored Yolande pointedly.

In a stilted French, she said, "Master, I'll take the baby; she needs changing now."

"Oh—sure, Joanie." Guillaume shifted, grunting with his knee's pain, and handed over the infant. Whatever was passing between the two women was not accessible to him, although he could see there was unspoken communication. Condemnation. On both sides?

He watched the wet nurse kneel down, untie the swaddling bands from the board and then from the child, and coil up the soiled wrappings and set them aside. The smell of baby shit and milk was way too familiar for a billman-turning-gunner.

"Joanie will keep it with her," Yolande announced, over the other woman's bent head. "I don't want anything more to do with this."

"'Lande—"

"It was a *mistake*. She isn't . . . I'm sorry for the child, but . . . Joan, I'll bring you money, out of my pay; you'll continue to feed it, and keep it by you—yes?"

The brown-haired woman nodded without looking up. "As long as I'm paid."

She fumbled down her bodice for clean linen bands. The baby, laid facedown on the warm wooden deck, hitched with elbows and knees and made a slight wriggling progression. Evidently she had not been used to swaddling bands before she fell into the hands of a Frankish nurse.

Guillaume bent down, picked the baby up from under so many feet, and tucked it under his arm. The infant made vague, froglike motions.

"How long will that last?" he demanded.

Joanie got up, dusting her hands on her skirt. "I have forgot the new bands. Look after it now, master, while I fetch them." She walked away toward the head of the gangway.

Yolande shrugged.

She turned and leaned her forearms on the rail, beside Guillaume. She had something in her hands—the Arian rosary, he saw. She trickled it from one hand into the other, while the wind and spray whipped her short hair into her eyes.

"Some people have the grace of God," she said, just audibly. "Some people can look down the chain of our choices and tell us what might happen in future years." She held the use-polished Christus Imperator up in front of her face. "I'm not one of them. Never will be. Ric was. And he . . ."

She opened her hand. The carved holm-oak rosary fell and disappeared, lost in spray and the Gulf of Salerno.

Yolande cast an eye up at Bressac. "Shall we walk?"

It was an invitation, although not as whorish a one as Joanie had been giving earlier in the day, Guillaume noted. The other Frenchman began to smile.

"See you," Yolande said neutrally, looking down at Guillaume. She was more than mostly drunk, Guillaume could see, if he looked at her without illusion.

Too many months' practice in hiding it, that's all. And now she's brawling with priests, and fucking who she pleases, and out of control. She'll cause fights, and bad discipline, and she *wants* to.

Someone has to pay for Ricimer—and if it's not going to be Muthari, I guess she's decided it's going to be her. . . .

Yolande walked away across the deck. Bressac gave Guillaume a look compounded both of apology and of disbelief in his own good luck, and followed her.

The woman wore a pleated velvet doublet against the wind's chill, and the sunlight illuminated how it nipped in at her waist, and the skirt of it ended just short of her lower hip, so that the curve of her lower buttocks could be seen as she walked away. And all the long length of her shapely legs. A woman in doublet and hose: the cast lead Griffin badge pinned to her upper arm and even the sunlight showing the worn patches in the velvet could not spoil her attraction.

She'd still fuck, if I asked.

I think she knows I won't ask.

That's not what I ended up wanting from her.

Guillaume sat back on the oak chest, his spine against the rail, the infant firmly in the crook of his elbow. He felt her warm, solid, squirming. If I put her down now, she'd be across this deck in a heartbeat, no matter how few months she has to her. It's in her. It's in all of us, surely.

He looked at the carved black walking stick beside him, and with his free hand eased at the muscles above his knee.

"Well, now."

With some awkwardness, he shifted the baby out from under his arm, and plumped her astride his other knee. She kicked her heels against his old, patched hose. The sun, even through this fog, would scald her, and he looked up for Joanie's return—and saw no sign of the wet nurse—and then back at the baby.

Knowing my luck, it's about to piss down my leg. . . .

The master gunner, Ortega, appeared out of the port gangway, two or three of his officers with him, and stood talking energetically, gesturing.

"Well, why not?" Guillaume said aloud. "The pay's as good, as a gunner. What do you think?"

The baby, supported under her armpits by his hands, blinked at him with her human eyes. She weighed less than a weaner piglet, although she was weeks older.

"Maybe I'll put a few shillings in, with Yolande," he said quietly, his eyes scanning the deck. "A few a month. Joanie'll probably soak me dry, telling me you've got croup, or whatever infants have." His mouth twisted into a grin he could feel. "At least until I'm killed in a skirmish, or the Italian diseases get me . . ."

The salt wind blew tangles in his hair. He wiped his wrist across his mouth, rasping at stubble. Joanie, coming back, was accosted by Ortega. Guillaume heard her laugh.

"Fortuna," Guillaume said, prodding the baby's naked round belly. The infant laughed. "The chain of choices? It's not a chain, I think. Choices are free. I believe."

The baby yawned, eyes and nose screwing up in the sunshine.

Feeling self-conscious, Guillaume brought the infant to his chest and held her against his doublet, with both his arms around her.

The weight of her increased—becoming boneless, now, with sleep, and trust. She began a small, breathy snore.

"It's not all sitting around in the gunners, you know," Guillaume lectured in a whisper, watching Italy appear from the mist. "I'll be busy. But I'll keep an eye on you. Okay? I'll keep a bit of a watch. As long as I can."

1477 AND ALL THAT

Sellars and Yeatman's wonderful book *1066 and All That* says that History is all you can remember from your schooldays. *Ash: A Secret History*, of which "The Logistics of Carthage" is a piece of flotsam, says that History is all you can remember . . . *and it's wrong.*

The links between alternate history and secret history fiction run deep. With *Ash*, I wanted not only to consider a moment at which history as we think we know it might have turned out differently, but to think about the nature of history itself. History as narratives that we make up—aided, of course, by things we take to be evidence—to tell ourselves, for one or another reason. "History" as distinct from "the past," that is.

The past happened. It's just that we can't recover it. History is what we can recover, and it's a collection of fallible memories, inconvenient documents, disconcerting new facts, and solemn cultural bedtime stories.

I went a stage further with *Ash*—the past didn't happen, either, not as we're told it did, and the scholar Pierce Ratcliff uses history to work that out. Well, history plus those inconvenient things upon which history is based: memoirs, archaeological artifacts, fakes, scholarship tussles, and quantum mechanics. It's different for a writer, thinking of an alternate history point of departure in these terms. History is not a road on which we can take a different turning. The road itself is made of mist and moonbeams.

And then there's A.D. 1477. And A.D. 416. And between the two of them is A.D. 1453, which is where "The Logistics of Carthage" got its genesis, even though the story itself takes place four years later in A.D. 1457.

In A.D. 1477, Burgundy vanished.

This is straightforward textbook history. The country that had been Burgundy—a principality of France, according to France; an independent country, according to the princely dukes of Burgundy—vanishes out of history in January of 1477—1476 in the pre-Gregorian calendar. Duke Charles the Bold (or "Rash," as 20:20 hindsight has it) lost a battle to the Swiss, was inconveniently found dead without leaving a male heir, and, to cut a short story shorter, France swallowed Burgundy with one gulp.

And rich and splendid and *powerful* Burgundy vanishes instantly from the history books. You would never know that for large periods of medieval history, Western Europe was not solely divided between the power blocs of Germany, Spain, and France. I'm not the only writer to be fascinated by this phenomenon. M. John Harrison's splendid and non-alternate-universe novel *The Course of the Heart*, for example, revolves around it in an entirely different way. Tropes of history and the past and memory are endlessly valid. But it was my starting point for *Ash: A Secret History*, which is, of course, the *real* story of why Burgundy vanished out of history in A.D. 1477, and what took its place.

Of course it's the real story: would I lie to you?

I am shocked—shocked!—that you think I would. . . .

And then there's A.D. 429. In history as we know it, this is the start of Gothic North Africa. A Vandal fleet sails over from mainland Europe under Gaiseric, who kicks the ass of the Roman inhabitants, and—becoming pretty much Roman himself in the process—establishes the rich and powerful kingdom of Vandal North Africa, with its capital established in Carthage by A.D. 439. In A.D. 455, Gaiseric sails east and sacks great Rome itself.

For *Ash*, I thought it would be neat if it hadn't been the Vandals who invaded North Africa.

I preferred the Visigoths—a rather different Gothic people who had ended up conquering the Iberians and running Spain, and whose elective-monarchy system by the early medieval period is, as one of the characters in *Ash* says, "election by assassination." I decided I'd have a Visigoth North Africa instead.

Then, while wandering through a book on post-Roman North Africa, I discovered there had indeed been a vast Visigoth invasion fleet that set off toward North Africa. Thirteen years before the Vandals.

It was sunk by a storm.

So I had A.D. 416, a concrete and inarguable point of departure for an alternate universe that I would have been perfectly happy to set up as a hypothetical what-if. History plays these wonderful tricks, always. I love it.

And then we come to A.D. 711, when in our timeline the Muslims decided, quite reasonably as they thought, to invade Visigoth Spain. This resulted in a long occupation of chunks of Spanish kingdoms, a number of *taifa* buffer states that were part-Christian and part-Muslim, and a self-defined "entirely beleaguered and all-Christian" north. It's a story that doesn't end until A.D. 1492, when the last of the Moors leave Granada, and one of the most fascinating mixed cultures of Western Europe goes belly-up.

However, for *Ash*, having had my earlier point of departure set up as a non-Arabic North Africa, I ended up with a Visigoth Arian Christian invasion of a Spain that was part of the Church of the Green Christ. That rumbled along nicely from A.D. 711 until the 1470s, with the North African Visigoths largely taking the place of the Byzantines in our history. It may say in the KJV that nations have bowels of brass, but we know that history is endlessly mutable. . . .

And then there's "The Logistics of Carthage." Which I had not intended to write, after *Ash*. No way! When a 500,000-word epic is over and done, trust me, you do not want to see any more of it. Two walk-on characters tugging at one's elbow and remarking that they, too, have their story that they would like to tell, is something guaranteed to have the writer running off gibbering.

So I gibbered, and I decided I wouldn't write it, because the story of *Ash* is over. *Over* over, not here-is-a-sequel over. Not nearly over, but really sincerely over.

Ah yes, they said to me: but this isn't a sequel. For one thing, it's set twenty years before the main action of the book. For another, one of the people whose story it is was a minor character, and the other appears solely for a half sentence in one place in the book. And it's set somewhere we didn't get to in *Ash*. And, and . . .

And there's the Fall of Constantinople, you see.

A.D. 1453, and one of the defining points of Western European history. The great capital of the Byzantine empire, Constantinople, falls to the Turks and becomes Istanbul. Among the things that come out of the city with the flood of refugees are all the Hermetic writings of Pico and Ficino, who themselves have what amounts to an alternate-universe history of what the world is *really* like. The fall of Constantinople (in some theories) turbo-charges the Italian Renaissance, which kicks off the Renaissance in the rest of Europe, and leads to the Scientific Revolution, the Industrial Revolution, and hello modern world.

But "The Logistics of Carthage" isn't about that.

It's about the war *after* A.D. 1453, when the Turks move on the next obvious enemy in the *Ash* history: the Gothic capital of Carthage, under the Visigoth king-caliphs. A war taking place on the coast of North Africa, where a troop of European mercenaries heading toward Carthage in the pay of the Turks find themselves with a corpse they cannot bury because of a religious dispute, and we start to get a look at a love story—and pigs—and the mechanisms of atrocity.

Carthage, you will note, is another entity that vanishes out of history. Frequently. There isn't anything particularly mysterious about it. The Punic city of Carthage gets flattened by the Romans in 146 B.C., in a very marked manner, and sown with salt. Roman Carthage gets sacked, in turn; Gothic Carthage is taken by the Arabs in A.D. 698. Tunis grows up in the same area, and has its own troubles. History has a way of happening to cities.

But, mystery or not, Carthage has fascinated me for rather the same reasons as Burgundy does: here is something completely gone, its people do not remain, and how do we *know* that the history we hear is anything like what really happened?

In "The Logistics of Carthage," one of the soldiers has what she takes to be dream visions, sent by God. It wasn't possible to bring on stage, in a novella, the reasons why they're not dreams—they are glimpses of the real future, five hundred years ahead from where she is—but the rationale is present in *Ash*, and for the purposes of these people, it doesn't matter whether what Yolande sees is scientific or theological. What she *feels* about it is real.

And I get to push the history that runs from these points of departure on a stage further, which I naturally couldn't do in *Ash*, and am therefore glad to have the chance. Yolande sees future-Carthage, future–North Africa, and they are not our twenty-first-century Carthage and North Africa, just the up-to-date version of what the history would become, if it was to become our time.

But the alternate-universe story isn't always about "Cool, a POD!" Stories of people's experience are only rarely about seeing history turn. This story, which wouldn't let me go until I wrote it, is about a woman who followed her son to the wars, and how it feels to her then to be working for the worshipers of the child-eater goddess Astarte (which is where, in this history, the Turks get their red Crescent Moon flag). Military history gives short shrift to mothers—but then, Guillaume, finding himself with a reluctant appreciation of a woman's usual role in history, is as much a mother as Yolande.

And pigs. Never forget the pigs.

They don't know a damn thing about history, pigs.

They just become its victims—as people without power tend to.

And for those readers who have read *Ash* . . . yes, you do recognize a few names. And, yes, this is the early life of those particular people. I didn't know it either, until I came to write the story.

Oh, and the baby is precisely who you think she is. But she isn't important to this narrative. For these people, it could have been any nameless baby at all.

For most of us, after all, names are the first thing lost by history.

Mary Gentle was born in 1956, in England; one of her mothers was a house-wife and local cinema employee, the other is a professional astrologer. She left school at sixteen, but has since returned three times; the first time for a BA in politics and English, the second for an MA in seventeenth-century studies, and the third for an MA in war studies.

Her first book, *A Hawk in Silver*, was written when she was eighteen. After an initial period in the workforce, she has been a full-time professional writer since 1979, and considers it very well said that the self-employed person has an idiot for a boss. However, since this beats having any *other* idiot for a boss, she plans to stay self-employed as long as she can get away with it.

After her books having been regularly on the short list of more awards than she cares to think about, she is extremely pleased that *Ash: A Secret History* won the British Science Fiction Award and the Sidewise Award for Alternate History. *Ash* was also one of the *Locus* listed fantasy books for 2000. She is immensely cheered by having science fiction, fantasy, and alternate history accolades for the same book.

THE LAST RIDE
OF GERMAN FREDDIE

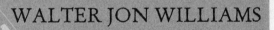

WALTER JON WILLIAMS

"*ECCE homo*," said German Freddie with a smile. "That is your man, I believe."

"That's him," Brocius agreed. "That's Virgil Earp, the lawman."

"What do you suppose he wants?" asked Freddie

"He's got a warrant for someone," said Brocius, "or he wouldn't be here."

Freddie gazed without enthusiasm at the lawman walking along the opposite side of Allen Street. His spurred boots clumped on the wooden sidewalk. He looked as if he had somewhere to go.

"Entities should not be multiplied beyond what is necessary," said Freddie, "or so Occam is understood to have said. If he is here for one of us, then so much the worse for him. If not, what does it matter to us?"

Curly Bill Brocius looked thoughtful. "I don't know about this Occam fellow, but as my mamma would say, those fellers don't chew their own tobacco. Kansas lawmen come at you in packs."

"So do we," said Freddie. "And this is not Kansas."

"No," said Brocius. "It's Tombstone." He gave Freddie a warning look from his lazy eyes. "Remember that, my friend," he said, "and watch your back."

Brocius drifted up Allen Street in the direction of Hafford's

Saloon while Freddie contemplated Deputy U.S. Marshal Earp. The man was dressed like the parson of a particularly gloomy Protestant sect, with a black flat-crowned hat, black frock coat, black trousers, and immaculate white linen.

German Freddie decided he might as well meet this paradigm.

He walked across the dusty Tombstone street, stepped onto the sidewalk, and raised his gray sombrero.

"Pardon me," he said. "But are you Virgil Earp?"

The man looked at him, light eyes over fair mustache. "No," he said. "I'm his brother."

"Wyatt?" Freddie asked. He knew that the deputy had a lawman brother.

"No," the man said. "I'm their brother, Morgan."

A grin tugged at Freddie's lips. "Ah," he said. "I perceive that en-tities *are* multiplied beyond that which is necessary."

Morgan Earp gave him a puzzled look. Freddie raised his hat again. "I beg your pardon," he said. "I won't detain you."

It is like a uniform, Freddie wrote in his notebook that night. Black coats, black hats, black boots. Blond mustaches and long guns in the scabbards, riding in line abreast as they led their posse out of town. As a picture of purposeful terror they stand like the *Schwarzrei-ter* of three centuries ago, horsemen whom all Europe held in fear. They entirely outclassed that Lieutenant Hurst, who was in a *real* uniform and who was employing them in the matter of those stolen army mules.

What fear must dwell in the hearts of these Earps to present themselves thus! They must dress and walk and think alike; they must enforce the rigid letter of the dead, dusty law to the last comma; they must cling to every rule and range and feature of medi-ocrity. . . . It is fear that drives men to herd together, to don uni-forms, to impose upon others a needless conformity. But what enemy is it they fear? What enemy is so dreadful as to compel them to wear uniforms and arm themselves so heavily and cling to their beliefs with such ferocity?

It is their own nature! The weak, who have no power even over themselves, fear always the power that lies in a *free* nature—a nature fantastic, wild, astonishing, arbitrary—they must enslave this spirit first in themselves before they can enslave it in others.

It is therefore our duty—the duty of those who are free, who are natural, valorous, and unafraid, those who scorn what is sickly, cowardly, and slavish—we must *resist these Earps!*

And already we have won a victory—won it without raising a finger, without lifting a gun. The posse of that terrible figure of justice, that Mr. Virgil Earp, found the mules they were searching for in Frank McLaury's corral at Baba Comari—but then the complainant Lieutenant Hurst took counsel of his own fears and refused to press charges.

It is wonderful! Deputy Marshal Earp, the sole voice of the law in this part of Arizona, has been made ridiculous on his first employment! How his pride must have withered at the joke that fortune played on him! How he must have cursed the foolish lieutenant and his fate!

He has left town, I understand, returned to Prescott. His brothers remain, however, stalking the streets in their dread black uniforms, infecting the town with their stolid presence. It is like an invasion of Luthers.

We must not cease to laugh at them! We must be gay! Laughter has driven Virgil from our midst, and it will drive the others, too. Our laughter will lodge, burning in their hearts like bullets of flaming lead. There is nothing that will drive them from our midst as surely as our own joy at their shortcomings.

They are afraid. And we will *know* they are afraid. And this knowledge will turn our laughter into a weapon.

Ike Clanton was passed out on the table. The game went on regardless, as Ike had already lost his money. It was late evening in the Occidental Saloon, and the game might well go on till dawn.

"It's getting to be hard being a Cowboy," said John Ringo. "What with having to pay *taxes* now." He removed cards from his hand, tossed them onto the table. "Two cards," he said.

Brocius gave him his cards. "If we pay taxes," he said, "we can vote. And if we vote, we can have our own sheriff. And if we have our own sheriff, we'll make back those taxes and then some. Dealer folds." He tossed his cards onto the table.

· Freddie adjusted his spectacles and looked at his hand, jacks and treys. He tossed his odd nine onto the table. "One card," he said. "I believe it was a mistake."

Brocius gave Freddie a lazy-lidded glance as he dealt Freddie another trey. "You think John Behan won't behave once we elect him?"

"I think it is unwise to give someone power over you."

"Hell, yes, it was unwise," agreed Ringo. "Behan's promised Wyatt Earp the chief deputy's job. Fifty dollars." Silver clanged on the tabletop. Ike Clanton, drowsing, gave an uncertain snort.

"That's just to get the votes of the Earps and their friends," Brocius said. He winked at Freddie. "You don't think he's going to keep his promises, do you?"

"What makes you think he will keep his promises to *you*?" Freddie asked. He raised another fifty.

"It will pay him to cooperate with us," Brocius said.

Ringo bared his yellow fangs in a grin. "Have you seen Behan's girl? Sadie?"

"Are you going to call or fold?" Freddie asked.

"I'm thinking." Staring at his cards.

"I thought Behan's girl was called Josie," said Brocius.

"She seems to go by a number of names," Ringo said. "But you can see her for yourself, tonight at Shieffelin Hall. She's Helen of Troy in *Doctor Faustus*."

"Are you going to call or fold?" Freddie asked.

"Helen, whose beauty summoned Greece to arms," Ringo quoted, "and drew a thousand ships to Tenedos."

"I would rather be a king," Freddie said, "and ride in triumph through Persepolis. Are you going to fold or call?"

"I'm going to bump," Ringo said, and threw out a hundred-dollar bill, just as Freddie knew he would if Freddie only kept on nagging.

"Raise another hundred," Freddie said. Ringo cursed and called. Freddie showed his hand and raked the money toward him.

"Fortune's a right whore," Ringo said, from somewhere else out of his eccentric education.

"You should not have compromised with the authorities," Freddie said as he stacked his coin. "Once you were the free rulers of this land. Now you are taxpayers and politicians. Why do you bring this upon yourselves?"

Curly Bill Brocius scowled. "I'm on top of things, Freddie. Behan will do what he's told."

Freddie looked at him. "But will the Earps?"

"We got two hundred riders, Freddie," Brocius said. "I ain't afraid of no Earps."

"We were driven out of Texas," Freddie reminded. "This is our last stand."

"Last stand in Tombstone," Ringo said. "That doesn't have a comforting sound."

"I'm on top of it," Brocius insisted.

He and his crowd defiantly called themselves Cowboys. It was a name synonymous with *rustler*, and hardly respectable—legitimate ranchers called themselves stockmen. The Cowboys ranged both sides of the American-Mexican border, acquiring cattle on one side, moving them across the border through Guadalupe and Skeleton Canyons, and selling them. Most of the local ranchers—even the honest ones—did not mind owning cattle that did not come with a notarized bill of sale, and the Cowboys' business was profitable.

In the face of this threat to law from the two hundred outlaws, the United States government had sent to Tombstone exactly one man, Deputy Marshal Virgil Earp, who had been sent right out again. The Mexicans, unfortunately, were more industrious—they had been fortifying the border, and making the Cowboys' raids more difficult. The Clantons' father, who had been the Cowboys' chief, had been killed in an ambush by Mexican *rurales*.

Brocius now led the Cowboys, assuming anyone did. Since illegitimate plunder was growing more difficult, Brocius proposed to plunder legitimately, through a political machine and a compliant sheriff. His theory was that the government would let them alone if he lined up enough votes to buy their tolerance.

German Freddie mistrusted the means—he did not trust politicians or their machines or their sheriffs—but then his opinion did not rank near Brocius's, as he wasn't, strictly speaking, a Cowboy, just one of their friends. He was a gambler, and had never rustled stock in his life—he just won the money from those who had.

"Everybody ante," said Brocius. Freddie threw a half-eagle into the pot.

"May I sit in?" asked a cultured voice. *Ay*, Freddie thought as he looked up, *the plot thickens very much upon us*.

"Well," Freddie said, "if you are here, now we know that Tombstone is on the map." He rose and gestured the newcomer to a chair. "Gentlemen," he said to the others, "may I introduce John Henry Holliday, D.D."

"We've met," said Ringo. He rose and shook Holliday's hand. Freddie introduced Brocius and pointed out Ike Clanton, still asleep on the table.

Holliday put money on the table and sat. To call him thin as a rail was to do an injustice to the rail—Holliday was pale and consumptive and light as a scarecrow. He looked as if the merest breath of wind might blow him right down Skeleton Canyon into Mexico. Only the weight of his boots held him down—that and the weight of his gun.

German Freddie had met Doc Holliday in Texas, and knew that Holliday was dangerous when sober and absurd when drunk. Freddie and Holliday had both killed people in Texas, and for much the same reasons.

"Is Kate with you?" Freddie asked. If Holliday's Hungarian girl was in town, then he was here to stay. If she wasn't, he might drift on.

"We have rooms at Fly's," Holliday said.

Freddie looked at Holliday over the rim of his cards. If Kate was here, then Doc would remain till either his pockets or the mines ran dry of silver.

The calculations were growing complex.

"Twenty dollars," Freddie said.

"Bump you another twenty," said Holliday, and tossed a pair of double eagles onto the table.

Ike Clanton sat up with a sudden snort. "I'll kill him!" he blurted.

"Here's my forty," Ringo said. He looked at Ike. "Kill who, Ike?"

Ike's eyes stared off into nowhere, pupils tiny as peppercorns. "I'm gonna kill him!" he said.

Ringo was patient. "Who are you planning to kill?"

"Gonna kill him!" Ike's chair tumbled to the floor as he rose to his feet. He took a staggering step backwards, regained his balance, then began to lurch for the saloon door.

"Dealer folds," said Brocius, and threw in his cards.

Holliday watched Ike's exit with cold precision. "Shouldn't one of you go after your friend? He seems to want to shoot somebody."

"Ike's harmless," Freddie said. "Besides, his gun is at his hotel, and in his current state Ike won't remember where he left it."

"What if someone takes Ike seriously enough to shoot *him*?" Holliday asked.

"No one will do that for fear of Ike's brother Billy," said Freddie. "He's the dangerous one."

Holliday nodded and returned his hollow eyes to his cards. "Are you going to call, Freddie?" he asked.

"I call," Freddie said.

It was a mistake. Holliday cleaned them all out by midnight. "Thank you, gentlemen," he said politely as he headed toward the door with his winnings jingling in his pockets. "I'm sure we'll meet again."

John Ringo looked at the others. "Silver and gold have I none," he quoted, "but such as I have I'll share with thee." He pulled out bits of pasteboard from his pockets. "Tickets to *Doctor Faustus*, good for the midnight performance. Wilt come with me to hell, gentlemen?"

Brocius was just drunk enough to say yes. Ringo looked at Freddie. Freddie shrugged. "Might as well," he said. "That was the back end of bad luck."

"Luck?" Ringo handed him a ticket. "It looked to me like you couldn't resist whenever Doc raised the stakes."

"I was waiting for him to get drunk. Then he'd start losing."

"What was in your mind, raising on a pair of jacks?"

"I thought he was bluffing."

Ringo shook his head. "And you the only one of us sober."

"I don't see that you did any better."

"No," Ringo said sadly, "I didn't."

They made their way out of the Occidental, then turned down Allen Street in the direction of Shieffelin Hall. The packed dust of the street was hard as rock. The night was full of people—most nights Tombstone didn't close down till dawn.

Brocius struck a match on his thumb as he walked, and lit a cigar. "I plan to go shooting tomorrow," he said. "I've changed my gun—filed down the sear so I can fan it."

"Oh, Lord," Ringo sighed. "Why'd you go and ruin a good gun?"

"Fanning is for fools," Freddie said. "You should just take *aim*—"

"I ain't such a good shot as you two," Brocius said. He puffed his cigar. "My talents are more *organizational* and *political*. I figure if I got to jerk my gun, I'll just fan it and make up for aim with *volume*."

"You'd better hope you never have to shoot it," Freddie said.

"If we win the election," Brocius said cheerfully. "I probably won't."

Even the drinking water must be carried to us on wagons, Freddie wrote in his notebook a few hours later. The alkali desert is unforgiving and unsuitable for anything but the lizards and vultures who were here before us. Even the Indians avoided this country. The ranchers cannot keep enough cattle on this wretched land to make a profit—thus they are dependent on the rustlers and smugglers for their livelihood. The population came because of greed or ambition, and if the silver ever runs out, Tombstone will fly away with the dust.

So why, when I perceive these Cowboys in their huge sombreros, their gaudy kerchiefs and doeskin trousers, do I see instead the old Romans in their ringing bronze?

From such as these did Romulus spring! For who was Romulus? A tyrant, a bandit, a man who harbored runaways and stole the cattle—and the daughters—of his neighbors. Yet he was noble, yet a hero, yet he spawned a great Empire. History trembles before his memory.

And now the Romans have come again! Riding into Tombstone with their rifles in the scabbards!

All the old Roman virtues I see among them. They are frank, truthful, loyal, and above all *healthy*. They hold the lives of men—their own included—in contempt. Nothing is more refreshing and wholesome than this lack of pity, this disdain for the so-called civilized virtues. They are from the American South, of course, that defeated country now sunk in ruin and oppression. They are too young to have fought in the Civil War, but not so young they did not see its horrors. This exposure to life's cruelties, when they were still at a tender age, must have hardened them against pieties and hypocrisies of the world. Not for them the mad egotism of the ascetic, the persistent morbidity—the *sickness*—of the civilized man. These heroes abandoned their defeated country and came West—West, where the new Rome will be born!

If only they can be brought to treasure their virtues as I do. But they treat themselves as carelessly as they treat everything. They possess all virtues but one: the will to power. They have it in themselves to dominate, to rule—not through these petty maneuverings at the polls with which Brocius is so unwisely intoxicated, but through themselves, their desires, their guns. . . . They can create an empire here, and must, if their virtues are to survive. It is not enough to avoid the law, avoid civilization—they must wish to *destroy* the inverted virtues that oppose them.

Who shall win? Tottering, hypnotized, sunken Civilization, or this new Rome? Ridiculous, when we consider numbers, when we consider mere guns and iron. Yet what was Romulus? A bandit, crouched on his Palatine Hill. Yet nothing could stand in his way. His will was greater than that of the whole rotten world.

And—as these classical allusions now seem irresistible—what are we to make of the appearance of Helen of Troy? Who better to signal the end of an empire? Familiar with Goethe's superior work, I forgot that Helen does not speak in Marlowe's *Faustus*. She simply parades along and inspires poetry. But when she looked at our good German metaphysician, that eye of hers spoke mischief that had nothing to do with verse—and the actor knew it, for he stammered. Such a sexual being as this Helen was not envisioned by the good British Marlowe, whom we are led to believe did not with women.

I do not see such a girl cleaving to Behan for long—his blood is too thin for the likes of her.

And when she tires of him—beware, Behan! Beware, Faustus! Beware, Troy!

Freddie met Sheriff Behan's girl at the victory party following the election. Brocius's election strategy had borne fruit, of a sort—but

Johnny Behan was rotten fruit, Freddie thought, and would fall to the ground ere long.

The Occidental Saloon was filled with celebration and a hundred drunken Cowboys. Even Wyatt Earp turned up, glooming in his black coat and drooping mustaches, still secure in the illusion that Behan would hire him as a deputy; but at the sight of the company his face wrinkled as if he'd just bit on a lemon, and he did not stay long.

Amid all this roistering inebriation, Freddie saw Behan's girl perched on the long bar, surrounded by a crowd of men and kicking her heels in the air in a white froth of petticoats. Freddie was surprised—he had rarely in his life met a woman who would enter a saloon, let alone behave so freely in one, and among a crowd of rowdy drunks. Behan—a natty Irishman in a derby—stood nearby and accepted congratulations and bumper after bumper of the finest French champagne.

Freddie offered Behan his perfunctory congratulations, then shouldered his way to the bar where he saw John Ringo crouched protectively around a half-empty bottle of whiskey. "I have drunk deep of the Pierian," Ringo said, "and drunk disgustingly. Will you join me?"

"No," said Freddie, and ordered soda water. The noise of the room battered at his nerves. He would not stay long—he would go to another saloon, perhaps, and find a game of cards.

Ringo's melancholy eyes roamed the room. "Freddie, you do not look overjoyed," he said.

Freddie looked at his drink. "Men selling their freedom to become *citizens*," he snarled. "And they call it a victory." He looked toward Behan, felt his lips curl. "Victory makes stupid," he said. "I learned that in Germany, in 1870."

"Why so gloomy, boys?" cried a woman's voice in a surprising New York accent. "Don't you know it's a party?" Behan's girl leaned toward them, half-lying across the polished mahogany bar. She was younger than Freddie had expected—not yet twenty, he thought.

Ringo brightened a little—he liked the ladies. "Have you met German Freddie, Josie?" he said. "Freddie here doesn't like elections."

Josie laughed and waved her glass of champagne. "I don't know that we had a *real election*, Freddie," she called. "Think of it as being more like a *great big felony*."

Cowboy voices roared with laughter. Freddie found himself smiling behind his bushy mustache. Ringo, suddenly merry, grabbed Freddie's arm and hauled him toward Josie.

"Freddie here used to be a Professor of Philosophy back in Germany," Ringo said. "He was told to come West for his health." Ringo looked at Freddie in a kind of amazement. "Can you picture that?"

Freddie—who had come West to die—said merely, "Philology. Switzerland," and sipped his soda water.

"You should have him tell you about how we're all Supermen," Ringo said.

Freddie stiffened. "You are *not* Supermen," he said.

"*You're* the Superman, then," Ringo said, swaying. The drunken raillery smoothed the sad lines of his eyes.

"I am the Superman's prophet," Freddie said with careful dignity. "And the Superman will be among your children, I think—he will come from America."

"I suppose I'd better get busy and have some children, then," Ringo said.

Josie watched this byplay with interest. Her hair was raven black, Freddie saw, and worn long, streaming down her shoulders. Her nose was proudly arched. Her eyes were large and brown and heavy-lidded—the heavy lids gave her a sultry look. She leaned toward Freddie.

"Tell me some philology," she said.

He looked up at her. "You are the first American I have met who knows the word."

"I know a lot of words." With a laugh she pressed his wrist—it was all Freddie could do not to jump a foot at the unexpected touch. Instead he looked at her sternly.

"Do you know the Latin word *bonus*?" he demanded.

She shook her head. "It doesn't mean something extra?"

"In English, yes. In Latin, *bonus* means 'good.' Good as opposed to bad. But my question—the important question to a philologist—"

He gave a nervous shrug of his shoulders. "The question is what the Romans meant by 'good,' you see? Because *bonus* is derived from *duonus*, or *duen-lum*, and from *duen-lum* is also derived *duellum*, thence *bellum*. Which means 'war.'"

Josie followed this with interest. "So war was good, to a Roman?"

Freddie shook his head. "Not quite. It was the *warlike man*, the bringer of strife, that was good, as we also see from *bellus*, which is clearly derived from *bellum* and means 'handsome'—another way of saying *good*. You understand?"

He could see thoughts working their way across her face. She was drunk, of course, and that slowed things down. "So the Romans— the Roman warriors—thought of themselves as good? By definition, good?"

Freddie nodded. "All the aristocrats did—*all* aristocrats, all conquerors. The aristocratic political party in ancient Rome called themselves the *boni*—the good. They *assumed* their own values were universal virtues, that all goodness was embedded in themselves— and that the values which were not theirs were debased. Look at the words they use to describe the opposite of their *bonus*—*plebeian*, 'common,' 'base.' Even in English—*debased* means 'made common.'" He warmed to the subject, English words spilling out past his thick German tongue. "And in Greece the rulers of Megara used *esthlos* to describe themselves—'the true,' the real, as opposed to the ordinary, which for them did not have a real existence." He laughed. "To believe that you *are the only real thing*. That is an ego speaking! That is a *ruler*—very much like the Brahmins, who believe their egos are immortal but that all other reality is illusion . . ."

He paused, words frozen in his mouth, as he saw the identical, quizzical expression in the faces of both Ringo and Josie. *They must think I'm crazy*, he thought. He took a sip of soda water to relieve his nervousness. "Well," he said, "that is some philological thought for you."

"Don't stop," said Josie. "This is the most interesting thing I've heard all night."

Freddie only shook his head.

And suddenly there was gunfire, Freddie's nerves leaping with each thunderclap as he ducked beneath the level of the bar, his hand reaching for the pistol that, of course, he had left in his little room.

Ceiling lathes came spilling down, and there was a burst of coarse laughter. Freddie saw Curly Bill Brocius standing amid a gray cloud of gunsmoke. Unlike Freddie, Brocius had disregarded the town ordinance forbidding firearms in saloons or other public places, and in an excess of bonhomie had fanned his modified revolver at the ceiling.

Freddie slowly rose to his feet. His heart lurched in his chest, and a kind of sickness rose in his throat. He had to hold on to the bar for support.

Josie sat perfectly erect on the mahogany surface, face flushed, eyes wide and glittering, lips parted in frozen surprise. Then she shook her head and slipped to the floor amid a silken waterfall of skirts. She looked up at Freddie, then gave a sudden gay laugh. "These *men of strife*, these *boni*," she said, "are getting a little too *good* for my taste. Will you take me home, sir?"

"I—" Freddie felt heat rise beneath his collar. Gunsmoke stung his nostrils. "But Mr. Behan—?"

She cast a look over her shoulder at the new sheriff. "He won't want to leave his friends," she said. "And besides, I'd prefer an escort who's sober."

Freddie looked at Ringo for help, but Ringo was too drunk to walk ten feet without falling, and Freddie knew his abstemious habits had him trapped.

"Yes, miss," he said. "We shall walk, then."

He led Josie from the roistering crowd and walked with her down dusty Allen Street. Her arm in his felt very strange, like a half-forgotten memory. He wondered how long it had been since he had a woman on his arm—seven or eight years, probably, and the woman his sister.

In the darkness he sensed her looking up at him. "What's your last name, Freddie?" she asked.

"Nietzsche."

"Gesundheit!" she cried.

Freddie smiled in silence. She was not the first American to have made that joke.

"Don't you drink, Freddie?" Josie asked. "Is it against your principles?"

"It makes me ill," Freddie said. "I have to watch my diet, also."

"Johnny said you came West for your health."

It was phrased like a statement, but Freddie knew it was a question. He did not mind the intrusion: he had no secrets. "I volunteered for the war," he said, and at her look, clarified, "the war with France. I caught diphtheria and some kind of dysentery—typhus or cholera. I did not make a good recovery, and I could not work." He did not mention the other problems, the nervous complaints, the sudden attacks of migraine, the cold, sick dread of dying as his father had died, mad and screaming.

"We turn here," Josie said. They turned left on Fifth Street. On the far side of the street was the Oriental Saloon, where Wyatt Earp earned his living dealing faro. Freddie glanced at the windows, saw Earp himself bathed in yellow light, standing, smoking a cigar and engaged in conversation with Holliday. To judge by his look, the topic was a grim one.

"Look!" Freddie said in sudden scorn. "In that black coat of his, Earp looks like the Angel of Death come to claim his consumptive friend."

The light of the saloon gleamed on Josie's smile. "Wyatt Earp's a handsome man, don't you think?"

"I think he is too gloomy."

She turned to him. "*You're* the gloomy one."

He nodded as they paced along. "Yes," he admitted. "That is just."

"You are a sneeze," she said. "He is a belch."

Freddie smiled to himself as they crossed Fremont Street. "I will tell him this, when I see him next."

"Tell me about the Superman."

Freddie shook his head. "Not now."

"But you will tell me some other time?"

"If you wish." Politely, doubting he would speak a word to her after this night.

"Here's our house." It was a small place that she shared with Behan, its frame unpainted, and like the rest of the town, thrown up overnight.

"I will bid you good night then," he said formally.

She turned to face him, lifted her face toward his. "You can come in, if you like," she said. "Johnny won't be back for hours."

He looked into her eyes and saw Troy there, on fire in the night.

"Good night, miss," he said, and touching his hat he turned away.

She is a Jewess! Freddie wrote in his journal. Run away from her family of good German bourgeois Jews—no doubt of the most insufferable type—to become, here in Tombstone, a goddess among the barbarians.

Or so Brocius tells us. He says her name is Josephine Marcus, sometimes called Sadie.

I believe I understand this Helen now. She has sprung from the strangest people in all history, they who have endured a thousand persecutions, and so become wise—cunning. The world has tried with great energy to make the Jews base, by confining them to occupations that the world despises, and by depriving them of any hope of honor. Yet they themselves have never ceased to believe in their own high calling; and they are honored by the dignity with which they face their tormentors.

And how should we think them base? From the Jews sprang the most powerful book in history, the most effective moral law, Spinoza the most sublime philosopher, and Christ the last Christian. When Europe was sunk in barbarism, it was the Jewish philosophers who preserved for us the genius of the ancients.

Yet all people must have their self-respect, and self-respect demands that one repay both good and bad. Without the ability to occasionally revenge themselves upon their despisers, they could scarcely have held up their heads. The usury of which the Jews are accused is the least of it; it was the subtle, twisted, deceitful Jewish revolution in morals that truly destroyed the ancients—that took the natural, healthy joy of freedom, life, and power, that twisted and inverted that joy, that planted this fatal sickness among their enemies. Thus was the Jewish vengeance upon Rome.

And this is the tradition that our Helen has inherited. Her very existence here is a vengeance upon all that have tormented her people from the beginning of time. She is beautiful, she is gay . . . and what does she care if Troy burns? Or Rome? Or Tombstone?

When next Freddie encountered Josie, he was vomiting in the dust of Toughnut Street.

He had felt the migraine coming on earlier, but he was playing against a table of drunken stockmen who were celebrating the sale of their beeves and who were losing their money almost as fast as they could shove it across the table. Freddie was determined to fight on as long as the cards fell his way.

By the time he left the Occidental he was nearly blind with pain. The clink of the winnings in his pocket sounded in his ears like bronze bells. The Arizona sun flamed on his skull. He staggered two blocks—people turned their eyes from him, as if he were drunk— and then collapsed as the cramp seized his stomach. People hurried away from him as he emptied the contents of his stomach into the dust. The spasms racked him long after he had nothing left to vomit.

Freddie heard footsteps, then felt the firm touch of a hand on his arm. "Freddie? Shall I get a doctor?"

Humiliation burned in his face. He had no wish that his helplessness should even be acknowledged—he could face those people who hurried away; there could be a pretense that they had seen nothing, but he couldn't bear that another person should see him in his weakness.

"It is normal," he gasped. "Migraine. I have medicine in my room."

"Can you get up? I'll help you."

He wiped his face with his handkerchief, and then her hand steadied him as he groped his way to his feet. His spectacles were hanging from one ear, and he adjusted them. It didn't help—his vision had narrowed to the point where it seemed he was looking at the world through the wrong end of a telescope. He shuffled down Toughnut toward his room—he rented the back room of a house belonging to a mining engineer and his family, and paid the wife extra for meals that would not torment his digestion. He groped for the door, pushed it open, and stumbled toward the bed. He swiped off the pyramid of books that lay on the blanket and threw himself onto the mattress. A whirlwind spun through his head.

"Thank you," he muttered. "Please go now."

"Where is your medicine?"

He gestured vaguely to the wooden box by his washbasin. "There. Just bring me the box."

He heard her boot heels booming like pistol shots on the wooden floor, and fought down another attack of nausea. He heard her open the velvet-padded box and scrutinize the contents. "Chloral hydrate!" she said. "Veronal! Do you take this all the time?"

"Only when I am ill," he said. "Please—bring it."

She gasped in surprise as he drank the chloral right from the bottle, knowing from experience the amount necessary to cause unconsciousness. "Thank you," he said. "I will be all right now. You can go."

"Let me help you with your boots."

Freddie gave a weary laugh. "Oh, yes, by all means. I should not die with my boots on."

The drug was already shimmering through his veins. Josie drew off his boots. His head was ringing like a great bell. Then the sound of the bell grew less and less, as if the clapper were being progressively swathed in wool, until it thudded no louder than a heartbeat.

Freddie woke after dark to discover that Josie had not left. He wiped away the gum that glued his eyelids shut and saw her curled in his only chair with her skirts tucked under her, reading by the light of his lamp.

"My God," he said. "What hour is it?"

She brushed away an insect that circled the lamp. "I don't know," she said. "Past midnight, anyway."

"What are you doing here? Shouldn't you be with Sheriff Behan?"

"He doesn't own me." Spoken tartly enough, though Freddie suspected that Behan might disagree.

"And besides," Josie said, "I wanted to make sure you didn't die of that medicine of yours."

Freddie raised a hand to his forehead. The migraine was gone, but the drug still enfolded his nerves in its smothering arms. He felt stupid, and stupidly ridiculous. "Well, I did not die," he said. "And I thank you—I will walk you home if you like."

She glanced at the book in her hands. "I would like to finish the chapter."

He could not see the title clearly in the dim light. "What are you reading?"

"*The Adventures of Tom Sawyer.*"

Freddie gave a little laugh. "I borrowed that book from John Ringo. I think Twain is your finest American writer."

"Ringo reads?" Josie looked surprised. "I thought you were the only person in the whole Territory who ever cracked a book, *Herr Professor.*"

"You would be surprised—there are many educated men here. John Holliday is of course a college graduate. John Ringo is a true autodidact—born poor but completely self-educated, a lover of books."

"And a lover of other men's cattle."

Freddie smiled. "That is a small flaw in this country, miss. His virtues surely outweigh it."

The drug had left his mouth dry. He rose from the bed and poured a glass of water from his pitcher. There was a strange singing in his head, the beginnings of the wild euphoria that often took him after a migraine. Usually he would write in his journals for hours during these fits, write until his hand was clawed with cramp.

He drank another glass of water and turned to Josie. "May I take you home?"

She regarded him, oval face gold in the glow of the lamp. "Johnny won't be home for hours yet," she said. "Are you often ill?"

"That depends on what you mean by *often.*" He shuffled in his stocking feet to his bed—it was the only other place to sit. He saw his winnings gleaming on the blanket—little rivers of silver had spilled from his pockets. He bent to pick them up, stack them on his shelf.

"How often is often?" Patiently.

"Once or twice a month. It used to be worse, much worse."

"Before you came West."

"Yes. Before I—before I 'lit out for the Territory,' as Mr. Mark Twain would say. And I was very ill the first years in America."

"Were you different then?" she asked. "Johnny tells me you have this wild reputation—but here you've never been in trouble, and—" Looking at the room stacked high with books and papers. "—you live like a monk."

"When I came to America, I was in very bad health," he said. "I thought I would die." He turned to Josie. "I believed that I would die at the age of thirty-five."

She looked at him curiously. "Why that number?"

"My father died at that age. They called it 'softening of the brain.' He died mad." He turned, sat on the bed, touched his temples with his fingers. "Sometimes I could feel the madness there, pressing upon my mind. Waiting for the right moment to strike. I thought that anything was better than dying as my father had died." He laughed as memories swam through the euphoria that was flooding his brain. "So I lived a mad life!" he said. "A wild life, in hopes that it would kill me before the madness did! And then one day, I awoke—" He looked up at Josie, his face a mirror of the remembered surprise. "And I realized that I was no longer thirty-five, and that I was still alive."

"That must have been a kind of liberation."

"Oh, yes! But in any case that life was at an end. The Texas Rangers came to drive the wild men from the state, and—to my great shame—we allowed ourselves to be driven. And now we are here—" He looked at her. "Wiser, I hope."

"You write to a lady," she said.

Freddie looked at her in surprise. "I beg your pardon?" he said.

"I'm sorry. You were working on a letter—I saw it when I sat down. Perhaps I shouldn't have looked, but—"

Mirth burst from Freddie. "My sister!" he laughed. "My sister Elisabeth!"

She seemed a little surprised. "You addressed her in such passionate terms—I thought she was perhaps—" She hesitated.

"A lover? No. I will rewrite the letter later, perhaps, to make it less strident." He laughed again. "I thought Elisabeth might understand my ideas, but she is too limited, she has not risen above the

patronizing attitudes of that little small town where we grew up—"
Anger began to build in his heart, rising to a red, scalding fury. "She
rewrote my work. I sent her some of my notebooks to publish, and she
changed my words, she added anti-Semitic nonsense to the manu-
script. She has fallen under the influence of those who hate the
Jews, and she is being courted by one, a professional anti-Semite
named Förster, a man who *distributes wretched tracts at meetings*." He
waved a fist in the air. "She said she was *making my thoughts clearer*."
He realized his voice had risen to a shout, and he tried to calm himself, suddenly falling into a mumble. "As if she herself has ever had
any clear thoughts!" he said. "God help me if she remains my only
conduit to the publishers."

Josie listened to this in silence, eyes glimmering in the light of
the lantern. "You aren't an anti-Semite, then?" she said. "Your Superman isn't a—what is the word they use, those people?—Aryan?"

Freddie shook his head. "Neither he nor I am as simple as that."

"I'm Jewish," she said.

He ran his fingers through his hair. "I know," he said. "Someone
told me."

Bells began to sing in his head—not the bells of pain, those clang-
ing racking peals of his migraine, but bells of wild joy, a carillon that
pealed out in celebration of some pagan triumph.

Josie looked up, and he followed her glance upward to the pistol
belt above his head, to his Colt, his Zarathustra, the blue steel that
gleamed in the darkness.

"You've killed men," she said.

"Not so many as rumors would have it."

"But you have killed."

"Yes."

"Did they deserve it?"

"It is not the killing that matters," Freddie said. "It is not the de-
serving." A laugh burbled out, the strange rapture rising. "Any fool
can kill," he said, "and any animal—but it takes a Caesar, or a
Napoleon, to kill *as a human being*, as a moment of self-becoming. To
rise above that—" He began to stammer in his enthusiasm. "—that
merely human act—that foolishness—to overcome—to become—"

"The Superman?" she queried.

"Ha-ha!" He laughed in sudden giddy triumph. "Yes! Exactly!"

She rose from the chair, stepped to the head of the bed in a swirl of skirts. She reached a hand toward the gun, hesitated, then looked down at him.

"*Nicht nur fort sollst du dich pflanzen sondern hinauf,*" she said.

Her German was fluent, accented slightly by Yiddish. Freddie stared at her in astonishment.

"You read my journals!" he said.

A smile drifted across her face. "I wasn't very successful—your handwriting is difficult, and I speak German easier than I read it."

"My God." Wonder rang in his head. "No one has *ever* read my journals."

That is her Jewish aspect, he thought, *the people of the Book.* Reverence for thought, from the only people in the world who held literacy as a test of manhood.

Josie glanced down at him. "Tell me what that means—that we should propagate not only downward, but upward."

Weird elation sang through his head. "I meant that we need not be animals when—" He recalled the decencies only at the last second. "—when we marry," he finished. "We need not bring only more apes into the world. We can *create*. We can be together not because we are lonely or inadequate, but because we are whole, because we wish to triumph!"

Josie gave a low, languorous laugh, and with an easy motion slid into his lap. Strangely enough he was not surprised. He put his arms around her, wild hope throbbing in his veins.

"Shall we triumph, Freddie?" she asked. Troy burned in her eyes.

"Yes!" he said in sudden delirium. "By God, yes!"

She bent forward, touched her lips to his. A rising, glorious astonishment whirled in Freddie's body and soul.

"You taste like a narcotic," she said softly, and—laughing low—kissed him again.

It was an hour or so later that the shots began echoing down Tombstone's streets, banging out with frantic speed, sounds startling in the surrounding stillness. Freddie sat up. "My God, what is that?" he said.

"Some of your friends, probably," Josie said. She reached out her hands, drew him down to the mattress again. "Whoever is shooting, they don't need you there."

Is that Behan's motto? Freddie wondered. But at the touch of her hands he felt flame burn in his veins, and he paid no attention to the shooting, not even when more guns began to speak, and the firing went on for some time.

In the morning he learned that it had been Curly Bill Brocius who was shooting, drunkenly fanning his revolver into the heavens; and that when the town marshal, Fred White, had tried to disarm him, Brocius's finger had slipped on the hammer and let it fall. White was dead, killed by Brocius's modified gun that would not hold the hammer at safety. A small battle had developed between Brocius's friends and various citizens, and Brocius had been slapped on the head by Wyatt Earp's long-barreled Colt and arrested for murder.

The next bit of news was that Marshal White's replacement had been chosen, and that Deputy U.S. Marshal Virgil Earp was now in charge of enforcing the law in the town of Tombstone.

It is like Texas again! Freddie wrote in his journal. It is not so much the killing, but the mad aimlessness of it all. Would that Brocius had been more discriminating with those bullets of his! Would that he had shot another lawman altogether!

The good citizens of Tombstone are overstimulated, and to avoid the possibility of a lynching the trial will be held at Tucson. I believe that law in Tucson is no less amenable to reason than was the law in Texas, and I have no fear that Brocius will meet a noose.

But while Brocius enjoys his parole, Tombstone must endure the Earps, in their black uniforms, marching about the streets like so many carrion crows. It is their slave souls they hide beneath those frock coats!

But I stay above them. I look down at them from my new rooms in the Grand Hotel. My landlady on Toughnut Street did not approve of what she called my "immortality." Though she was willing to accept as rent the gambling winnings of a known killer, she will not tolerate love in her back room. The manager of the Grand Hotel is more flexible in regard to morals—he gives me a front room, and he tips his hat when Josie walks past.

But I must train his cook, or indigestion will kill me.

How long has it been since a woman held me in her arms? Three years? Four? And she was not a desirable woman, and did not desire anything from me other than the silver in my pocket.

Ach! It was a mad time. Life was cheap, but the price of love was two dollars in advance. I shot three men, and killed two, and the killing caused far less inconvenience than a few short minutes with a dance-hall girl.

Nor is Helen of Troy a dance-hall girl. She cares nothing for money and everything for power. The sexual impulse and conquest are one, and both are aspects perhaps of Jewish revenge. It is power that she seeks. But most atypically, her will to power is not based on an attempt to weaken others—she does not seek to castrate her men. She challenges them, rather, to match her power with their own. Those who cannot—like Behan—will suffer.

Those who act wisely, perhaps, will live. But I cannot be persuaded that this, ultimately, will matter to her.

"I don't understand," Freddie said, "how it is that Virgil Earp can be Town Marshal and Deputy U.S. Marshal at the same time. Shouldn't he be compelled to resign one post or another?"

"Marshal Dake in Prescott don't mind if his deputy has a job on the side," said John Holliday.

"I should complain. I should write a letter to the newspaper. Or perhaps to the appropriate cabinet secretary."

"If you think it would do any good. But I think the U.S. government likes Virge right where he is."

Holliday sat with Freddie in the plush drawing room of the Grand Hotel, where Holliday had come for a visit. Their wing chairs were pulled up to the broad front window. Freddie turned his gaze from the bright October sunshine to look at Holliday. "I do not understand you," he said. "I do not understand why you are friends with these Earps."

"They're good men," Holliday said simply.

"But *you* are not, John," Freddie said.

A smile crinkled the corners of Holliday's gaunt eyes. "True," he said.

"You are a Southerner, and a gentleman, and a Democrat," Freddie said. "The Earps are Yankees, not gentle, and Republicans. I fail to understand your sympathy for them."

Holliday shrugged, reached into his pocket for a cigar. "I saved Wyatt from a mob of Texans once, in Dodge City," he said. "Since then I've taken an interest in him."

"But why?" Freddie asked. "Why did you save his life?"

Holliday struck a match and puffed his cigar into life, then drew the smoke into his ravaged lungs. He coughed once, sharply, then said, "It seemed a life worth saving."

Freddie gave a snort of derision.

"What I don't understand," said Holliday, "is why you dislike him. He's an extraordinary man. And your two greatest friends admire him."

"You and who else?"

"Your Sadie," John Holliday said. "She is with Wyatt Earp this moment, across the street in the Cosmopolitan Hotel."

Freddie stared at him, and then his gaze jerked involuntarily to the window again, to the bare façade of the Cosmopolitan, built swiftly and of naked lumber, devoid of paint. "But," he said, "but—Earp is married—" He was aware of how ridiculous he sounded even as he stammered out the words.

"Oh," Holliday said casually, "I don't believe Wyatt and Mattie ever officially tied the knot—not that it signifies." He looked at Freddie and rolled the cigar in his fingers. "I thought you should hear it from me," he said, "rather than through the grapevine telegraph."

Freddie stared across the street and felt flaming madness beating at his brain. He considered storming across the street, kicking down the door, firing his Zarathustra, his pistol, again and again until it clicked on an empty chamber, until the walls were spattered with crimson and the room was filled with the stinging, purifying incense of powder smoke.

But no. He was not an animal, to act in blind fury. He would take revenge—if revenge were to be taken—as a human being. Coldly. With foresight. And with due regard for the consequences.

And for Freddie to fight for a woman. Was that not the most stu-

pid piece of melodrama in the world? Would not any decent drama-
tist in the world reject this plot as hackneyed?

He looked at Holliday, let a grin break across his face. "For a moment I was almost jealous!" he laughed.

"You're not?"

"Jealousy—pfah!" Freddie laughed again. "Sadie—Josie—she
is free."

Holliday nodded. "That's one word for it."

"She is trying to get your Mr. Earp murdered. Or myself. Or the
whole world."

"Gonna kill him!" said a voice. Freddie turned to see Ike Clanton, red-eyed and swaying with drink, dragging his spurs across the
parlor carpet. Ike was in town on business and staying at the hotel.
"Come join me, Freddie!" he said. "We'll kill him together!"

"Kill who, Ike?" Freddie asked.

"I'm gonna kill Doc Holliday!" Ike said.

"Here is Doc Holliday, right here," said Freddie.

Ike turned, swayed back on his boot heels, and saw Holliday sitting in the wing chair and unconcernedly smoking his cigar. Ike
grinned, touched the brim of his sombrero. "Hiya, Doc!" he said
cheerfully.

Holliday nodded politely. "Hello, Ike."

Ike grinned for a moment more, then remembered his errand and
turned to Freddie. "So will you help me kill Doc Holliday, Freddie?"

"Doc's my friend, Ike," Freddie said.

Ike took a moment to process this declaration. "I forgot," he said,
and then he reached out to clumsily pat Freddie's shoulder. "That's
all right, then," he said with evident concern. "I regret I must kill
your friend. Adios." He turned and swayed from the room.

Holliday watched Ike's exit without concern. "Why is Ike trying
to kick a fight with me?" he said.

"God alone knows."

Holliday dismissed Ike Clanton with a contemptuous curl of his
lip. He turned to Freddie. "Shall we find a game of cards?"

Freddie rose. "Why not? Let me get my hat."

Holliday took him to Earp country, to the Oriental Saloon. Freddie could not concentrate on the game—Wyatt Earp's faro table was in plain sight, Earp's empty chair all too visible; and visions of Josie and Earp kept burning in his mind, a writhing of white limbs in a hotel bed, scenes from his own private inferno—and Holliday calmly and professionally took Freddie's every penny, leaving him with nothing but his coat, his hat, and his gun.

"You don't own me." Freddie wrote in his notebook. She almost spat the words at me. It is her *cri d'esprit*, her defiance to the world, her great maxim.

"I own nothing," I replied calmly. "Nothing at all." Close enough to the truth. I must find someone to lend me a stake so that I can win money and pay the week's lodging.

I argued my points with great precision, and she answered with fury. Her anger left me untouched—she accused me of jealousy, of all ridiculous things! It is easy to remain calm in the face of arrows that fly so wide of the mark. I asked her only to choose a man worthy of her. Behan is nothing, and Earp an earnest fool. Worthy in his own way, no doubt, but not of such as she.

Ah, well. Let her go. She is qualified to ruin her life in her own way, no doubt. I will keep my room at the Grand—unless poverty drives me into the street—and she will return when she understands her mistake.

I must remember my pocketbook, and earn some money. And I must certainly stay clear of John Holliday, at least at the card table.

I think I sense a migraine about to begin.

"Freddie?" It was Sheriff Behan who stood in the door of the Grand Hotel's parlor, his derby hat in his hand and a worried look on his face. "Freddie, can you come with me and talk to your friends?"

Freddie felt fragile after his migraine. Drugs still slithered their cold way through his veins. He looked at Behan and scowled. "What is it, Johnny?" he said. "Go away. I am not well."

"There's going to be a fight between the Earps and the Clantons and McLaurys. Your friends are going to get killed unless we do something."

"You're the sheriff," Freddie said, unable to resist digging in the spur. "Put the Clantons in jail."

"My God, Freddie!" Behan almost shouted. "I can't arrest the *Clantons*!"

"Not as long as they're letting you have this nice salary, I suppose." Freddie shook his head, then rose from his wing chair. "Very well. Tell me what is going on."

Ike Clanton had been very busy since Freddie had seen him last. He had wandered over Tombstone for two days, uttering threats against Doc Holliday to anyone who would listen. When he appeared in public with a pistol and rifle, Virgil Earp slapped him over the head with a revolver, confiscated his weapons, and tossed him in jail. Ike paid the twenty-five-dollar fine and returned to the streets, where he went boasting of his deadly intentions, now including the Earps in his threats. After Ike's brief trial, Wyatt Earp had encountered Ike's friend Tom McLaury on the street and pistol-whipped him. Now Tom was bent on vengeance, as well. They had been seen in Spangenburg's gun shop, and had gathered a number of their friends. The Earps and Holliday were armed and ready. Vigilantes were arming all over Tombstone, ready for blood. Behan had promised to stave off disaster by disarming the Cowboys, and he wanted help.

"This is absurd," Freddie muttered. The clear October light sent daggers into his brain. "They are behaving like fools."

"They're down at the corral," Behan said. "It's legal for them to carry arms there, but if they step outside I'll—" He blanched. "I'll have to do something."

The first tendrils of the euphoria that followed his migraines began to enfold Freddie's brain. "Very well," he said. "I'll come."

The lethargy of the drugs warred within Freddie's mind with growing elation as Behan led Freddie down Allen Street, then through the front entrance of the O.K. Corral, a narrow livery stable that ran like an alley between Allen and Fremont Streets. The Clantons were not in the corral, and Behan was almost frantic as he led Freddie out the back entrance onto Fremont, where Freddie saw the Cowboys standing in the vacant lot between Camillus Fly's boarding house, where Holliday lodged with his Kate, and another house owned by a man named Harwood.

There were five of them, Freddie saw. Ike and his brother Billy, Tom and Frank McLaury, and their young friend Billy Claiborne, who like almost every young Billy in the West was known as "Billy the Kid," after another, more famous outlaw who was dead and could not dispute the title. Tom McLaury led a horse by the reins. The group stood in the vacant lot in the midst of a disagreement. When he saw Freddie walking toward him, Billy Claiborne looked relieved.

"Freddie!" he said. "Thank God! You help me talk some sense into these men!"

Ike looked at Freddie with a broad grin. "We're going to kill Doc Holliday!" he said cheerfully. "We're going to wait for him to come home, then blow his head off!"

Freddie glanced up at Fly's boarding house, with its little photographic studio out back, then returned his gaze to Ike. He tried to concentrate against the chorus of euphoric angels that sang in his mind. "Doc won't be coming back till late," he said. "You might as well go home."

Ike shook his head vigorously. "No," he said. "I'm gonna kill Doc Holliday!"

"Ike," Freddie pointed out, "you don't even have a gun."

Ike turned red. "It's only because that son of a bitch Spangenburg wouldn't sell me one!"

"You can't kill Holliday without a gun," Freddie said. "You might as well come back to the hotel with me." He reached out to take Ike's arm.

"Now wait a minute, Freddie," said Ike's brother Billy. "*I've* got a gun." He pulled back his coat to show his revolver. "And I think killing Holliday is a sound enough idea. It'll hurt the Earps. And no one 'round here likes Doc—nobody's going to care if he gets killed."

"Holiday and half the town know you're standing here ready to kill him," Freddie said. "He's heeled and so are the Earps. Your ambush is going to fail."

"That's what I've been trying to tell them!" Billy Claiborne added, and then moaned, "Oh, Lord, they'll make a blue fist of it!"

"Hell," said Tom McLaury. The side of his head was swollen where Wyatt Earp had clouted him. "We've got to fight the Earps sooner or later. Might as well do it now."

"I agree you should fight," Freddie said. "But this is not the time or the place."

"This place is good as any other!" Tom said. "That bastard Earp hit me for no reason, and I'm going to put a bullet in him."

"I'm with my brother on this," said Frank McLaury.

"Nobody can stand up to us!" Ike said. "With us five and Freddie here, the Earps had better start praying."

Exasperation overwhelmed the exaltation that sang in Freddie's skull. With the ferocious clarity that was an aspect of his euphoria, he could see exactly what would happen. The Earps were professional lawmen—they did not chew their own tobacco, as Brocius would say—and when they came they would be ready. They might come with a crowd of vigilantes. The Cowboys, half unarmed, would stand wondering what to do, would have no leader, would wait too long to reach a decision, and then they would be cut down.

"I have no gun!" Freddie told Ike. "*You* have no gun. And the Kid here has no gun. Three of you cannot fight a whole town, I think. You should go home and wait for a better time. Wait till Bill Brocius's trial is over, and get John Ringo to join you."

"You only say that 'cause you're a coward!" Ike said. "You're a kraut-eating yellowbelly! You won't stand by your friends!"

Murder sang a song of fury in Freddie's blood. His hand clawed as if it held a gun—and the fact that there was no gun did not matter; the claw could as easily seize Ike's throat. Ike took a step backwards at the savage glint in Freddie's eyes. Then Freddie shook his head, and said, "This is folly. I wash my hands of it." He turned and began to walk away.

"Freddie!" Behan yelped. He sprang in front of Freddie, bouncing on his neat polished brown boots. "You can't leave! You've got to help me with this!"

Freddie drew himself up, glared savagely at Behan. Righteous angels sang in his mind. "You are the sheriff, I collect," he said. "Dealing with it is your job!"

Behan froze, his mouth half-open. Freddie stepped around him and marched away, down Fremont to the back entrance to the O.K. Corral, then through the corral to Allen Street. Exaltation thrilled in his blood like wine. He crossed the street to the shadier south side—the sun was still hammering his head—and began the walk to the Grand Hotel. At Fourth Street he looked south and saw a mob—forty or fifty armed citizens, mostly hard-bitten miners—marching toward him up the street.

If this crowd found the Clantons, the Cowboys were dead. Surely Freddie's friends could now be convinced that they must fight another day.

Freddie turned and hastened along Allen Street toward the O.K. Corral, but then gunfire cracked out, the sudden bright sounds jolting his nerves, and he felt his heart sink even as he broke into a run. A shotgun boomed, and windows rattled in nearby buildings. He dashed through the long corral, then jumped over the fence, ran past the photography studio, and into the back door of Camillus Fly's boarding house.

John Behan crouched beneath a window with his blue-steel revolver in his hand. The window had been shattered by bullets, and its yellow organdy curtain fluttered in the breeze, but there was no scent of smoke or other indication that Behan had ever fired his pistol. Shrieks rang in the air, cries of mortal agony. Freddie ran beside the window and peered out. His heart hammered, and he panted for breath after his run.

The narrow vacant lot was hazy with gunsmoke. Lying at the far end were the bodies of two men, Tom McLaury and Billy Clanton. Just four or five paces in front of them were the three Earps and John Holliday. Morgan was down with a wound. Virgil knelt on the dry ground, leg bleeding, and he supported himself with a cane. Holliday's back was to Freddie—he had a short Wells Fargo shotgun broken open over one arm—and there were bright splashes of blood on Holliday's coat and trousers.

In Fremont Street, behind the Earps, Frank McLaury lay screaming in the dust. He was covered with blood. Apparently he had run right through the Earps and collapsed. His agonized shrieks raised the hair on the back of Freddie's neck.

Of Billy Claiborne and Ike Clanton, Freddie saw no sign. Apparently the unarmed men had run away.

Wyatt Earp stood over his brother Morgan, unwounded, a long-barreled Colt in his hand. Savage hatred burned in Freddie's heart. He glared down at Behan.

"What have you done?" he hissed. "Why didn't you stop it?"

"I tried!" Behan said. "You saw that I tried. Oh, this is horrible!"

"You fool. Why do you bother to carry this?" Freddie reached down and snatched the revolver from Behan's hand. He looked out the window again and saw Wyatt Earp standing like a bronze statue over his wounded brother. Angels sang a song of glory in Freddie's blood.

Make something of it, he thought. Make something of this other than a catastrophe. Make it mean something.

He cocked Behan's gun. Earp heard the sound and raised his head, suddenly alert. And then German Freddie put six shots into Earp's breast from a distance of less than a dozen feet.

"My God!" Behan bleated. "What are you doing?"

Freddie looked at him, a savage grin taut on his face. He dropped the revolver at Behan's feet as return fire began to sing through the window. He ran into the back of the studio, out the back door, and was sprinting down Third Street when he heard Behan's voice ringing over the sound of barking gunfire. "It wasn't me! I swear to Mary!" Mad laughter burbled from Freddie's lips as he heard the crash of a door being kicked down. Behan screamed something else, something that might have been "German Freddie!"—but whatever he was trying to say was cut short by a storm of fire.

A steam whistle shattered the air as Freddie ran south. Someone was blowing the alarm at the Uzina Mine. And when Freddie reached the corner, he saw the vigilante mob pouring up Allen Street, heading for the front gate of the O.K. Corral. He waited a few seconds for the leaders to swarm through the gate, and then he quietly crossed the street at a normal walking pace. Despite the way he panted for breath, Freddie had a hard time not breaking into a run.

He had never felt such joy, not even in Josie's arms.

By roundabout means he walked to the Grand Hotel. Once he had Zarathustra in his hand he began to breathe more easily. Still, he concluded, it was time to leave town. There were any number of people who could place him near the site of that streetfight, and possibly some of the vigilantes had seen him stroll away.

And then a thought struck him—he had no horse! He was a bad rider and had come to Tombstone on the Wells Fargo stage. The only way he could get a horse would be to stroll back to the O.K. Corral and hire one, with the lynch mob looking on.

He laughed and put Zarathustra in his coat pocket. He was trapped in a town filled with Earps and armed vigilantes.

"It is time to be bold," he said aloud. "It is time to be cunning."

He washed his hands, to remove the reek of gunpowder, and changed his shirt.

It occurred to him that there existed a place where he might hide.

He put his journal in another pocket, and made his way out of the hotel.

Oh, she is magnificent! Freddie wrote in his journal a few hours later. She hid me in Behan's house while Behan lay painted in his coffin in the front window of the undertakers—Ritter and Reams are making the most of this opportunity to advertise their art! I rested on Behan's bed while she received callers in the front room. And then, at nightfall, she had Behan's horse saddled and brought to the back door.

"Will I see you again?" she asked.

"Oh, yes," I said. "Destiny will not permit us to part for long."

"Do you have money?"

I confessed that I did not. She went into the house and came back with an envelope of bills which she put in my pocket. Later I counted them and found they amounted to five thousand dollars. The office of sheriff pays surprisingly well!

I took her hand. "Troy is afire, my Helen. Do you have what you desire?"

"I did not want this," she said. Her fingers clutched at mine.

"Of course you did," I said. "What else did you expect?"

I rode to Charleston with her kiss burning on my lips. Charleston is a town ruled by the Cowboys, and so I knew I could find shelter there, but it is also the first place a posse will come.

It will be a war now—my bullets have decreed it. I welcome that war, I welcome the trumpet that will awaken the new Romulus. Battles there shall be, and victories. And both those who die and those who live shall be awarded a Tombstone—what an irony!

I am curiously satisfied with the day's business. It is a man's life that I'm leading. Were I to live these same events a thousand times, I would find no reason to alter the outcome.

"There are more Earps than before," John Ringo observed from over the rim of his beer glass. "James and Warren have come to town. You're creatin' more Earps than you're killin', Freddie."

"Two hundred rifles," Freddie urged. "Raise them! Make Tombstone yours!"

Curly Bill Brocius shook his head. "No more shootings. The town's riled enough as it is. I don't want my parole revoked, and besides, I've got to make certain that our man gets in as sheriff."

"Let us purge this choler without letting blood," Ringo said, and wiped foam from his mustache.

"Still these politics!" Freddie scorned. "Who is our man this time?"

"Fellehy."

"The laundryman? What kind of sheriff will he make?"

Brocius gave his easy grin. "No kind," he said. "Which is *our* kind."

"He will be worse than Behan. And it was Behan's bungling that killed three of our friends."

Brocius's grin faded. "I don't reckon," he said.

Freddie had made good his escape and met Ringo and Brocius in the Golden Saloon in Tucson. He was not quite far enough from Tombstone—Freddie kept his back to a wall and his eye on the door, just in case a crowd of men in frock coats barged in.

"So when may we start killing Earps?" Freddie asked.

"We're going to do it legal-like," Brocius said. "Ike Clanton's going to file in court against the Earps and Holliday for murder. They'll hang, and we won't have to pull a trigger."

Disgust filled Freddie's heart. "You are making yourself ridiculous," he said. "These men have killed your friends!"

"No more shooting," said Brocius. "We'll use the law's own weapons against the law, and we'll be back in charge quick as a dog can lick a dish."

Freddie looked at Brocius in fury, and then he laughed. "Very well, then," he said. "We shall see what joys the law brings us!"

You could play the law game any number of ways, Freddie thought. And he thought he knew how he wanted to bid his hand.

"Ike Clanton said he was going to kill Doc Holliday," Freddie testified. "His brother supported him, and so did the McLaurys. Claiborne and I were trying to talk sense into their stupid heads, but Ike was abusive, so I left in disgust."

There was stunned silence in the courtroom. Freddie was a witness for the prosecution, but was handing the defense its case on a plate.

The prosecution witnesses had agreed on a story ahead of time, how the Cowboys had been unarmed, and the Earps the aggressors. Now Freddie was blowing the case to smithereens.

Price, the district attorney, was so stunned by Freddie's testimony that he blurted out what had to be absolutely the wrong question. "You say that Ike was *intending* to kill Mr. Holliday?"

Freddie looked at Ike from his witness chair. The man stared back at him, disbelief plain on his face, and out of the slant of his eye he saw Holliday look at him thoughtfully.

"Oh, yes," Freddie said. "But Ike is too much the drunken coward to actually carry out his threats. He ran away from the streetfight and left his brother to die in the dust."

Bullets or nothing, Freddie thought. *We shall honor valor or honor shall lie dishonored.*

"You son of a bitch," Ike Clanton said in the Grand Hotel's parlor, after the trial had adjourned for the day. "What did you say those things for?"

"Because they're true," Freddie said. "Do you think I would lie to protect a worthless dog like you?"

Ike turned red. "You skin that back, you bastard! Skin that back, or I'll settle with you!"

Freddie wiped Ike's spittle from his chin with his handkerchief. "It's Doc Holliday you hate, is it not?" he said. "Why don't you settle with him first?"

"I'm gonna get him! And you, too!"

"Do it now," Freddie advised, "while you're almost sober. You know where Holliday lives. Perhaps if you work up all your courage you can shoot him in the back." Freddie reached into his pocket, took hold of Zarathustra, and thumbed back the hammer. Ike's eyes widened at the sound. He made a little whining noise in his throat.

"Don't shoot me!" he blurted.

"You can kill Holliday now," Freddie said, "or I will shoot you like a dog where you stand. And who will take *me* to court for such a thing?"

"I'll do it!" Ike said quickly. "I'll kill him! See if I don't!"

"I believe you checked your gun with the desk clerk," Freddie reminded him.

Freddie followed him to the front desk and kept his hand on the pistol. Ike cast him frantic glances over his shoulder as he was given his gun belt. He made certain his hand was nowhere near the butt of the weapon as he strapped it on—he did not want to give a man with Freddie's murderous reputation a chance to shoot.

Freddie followed Ike out into the street and glared at him when it looked as if he would step into a saloon for some liquid courage. Ike saw the glare, then began to walk faster down the street. Freddie pursued, boots thumping on the wooden walk. At the end of the long walk, when Fly's boarding house came into sight, Ike was almost running.

Freddie paused then, and began a leisurely stroll to the hotel. Gunfire erupted behind him, but he didn't break stride. He knew Ike Clanton, and he knew John Holliday, and he knew which of the two now lay dead.

* * *

"The legal case will collapse without a plaintiff," Freddie said that evening. "The district attorney may file a criminal case, but why would he? He knows the defense would call me as a witness." He laughed. "And now, after this second killing, Holliday will have to leave town. That is another problem solved."

Josie stretched luxuriously in Behan's bed. She was wearing a little transparent silken thing that Behan had bought her from out of a French catalogue, and Freddie, lying next to her, let his eyes feast gratefully on the ripeness of her body. She seemed well pleased with his eyes' amorous intentions, and rolled a little in the bed, to and fro, to show herself from different angles.

"You seem very pleased with yourself," she said.

"I have nothing against Holliday. I like the man. I'm glad he will be out of it."

"You're the only man alive who likes him. Now that Johnny's killed Wyatt." A silence hung for a moment in the air, and then Josie rolled over and put her chin on her crossed arms. Her dark eyes regarded him solemnly.

"Yes?" Freddie said, knowing the question that would come.

"There are people who say it was you who shot Wyatt," she said.

Freddie looked at her. "One of your lovers shot him," he said. "Does it matter which?"

"Did you kill for me, Freddie?" There was a strange thrill in her voice. "Did you kill Wyatt?"

"If I killed Wyatt," Freddie said coldly, "it was not for you. I did not do it to make you the heroine of a melodrama."

She made as if to say something, but she turned her head away, laying her cheek on her hand. Freddie reached out to caress her rich dark hair. "Troy burns for you, my Helen," he said. "Is it not your triumph?"

"I don't understand you," she said.

"I am in love with Fate," Freddie said. "I regret nothing, and neither should you. Everything you do, let it be as if you would—as if you *must*—do it again ten thousand times."

She was silent. He reached beneath her masses of hair, took her chin in his fingers, raised her face to his. "Come, my queen," he said. "Give me ten thousand kisses. And let us not regret a one of them."

* * *

Ten thousand kisses! Freddie wrote in his journal. She does not yet understand her power—that she can change the universe, and all the universes yet to be born.

How many times have I killed Earp, in worlds long dead? And how many times must I kill him again? The thought is joy to me. I crave nothing more. Ten thousand bullets, ten thousand kisses. Forever.

Amor fati. Love is all.

"Sir." Holliday bowed. Not yet healed, he stood stiffly, and supported his wounded hip with a cane. "The district attorney is of the opinion that Arizona and I must part. I thought I would take my adieu."

Freddie rose from his wing-backed chair and offered his hand. "I'm sure we'll meet again," he said.

"Maybe so." He shook the hand, then stood, a frown on his gaunt face. "Freddie—," he began.

"Yes?"

"Get out of this," Holliday said. "Take Josie away. Go to California, Nevada, anywhere."

Freddie laughed. "There's still silver in Tombstone, John."

"Yes." He seemed saddened. He hesitated again. "I wanted to thank you, for your words at the trial."

Freddie made a dismissive gesture. "Ike Clanton wasn't worth the bullets it took to kill him," he said.

Holliday looked at Freddie gravely. "People might say that of the two of us," he said.

"I'm sure they would."

There was another hesitation, another silence. "Freddie," Holliday said.

"John." Smiling.

"There is a story that it was you who killed my friend."

Freddie laughed, though there was a part of his soul that writhed beneath Holliday's gaze. "If I believed all the stories about *you*—," he began.

"I do not know what to believe," Holliday said. "And whatever the truth, I am glad I killed that cur Behan. But it is your own friends—your Cowboys—who are spreading this story. They are boasting of it. And if I ever come to believe it is true—or if anything happens to Wyatt's brothers—then God help you." The words, forced from the consumptive lungs, were surprisingly forceful. "God help all you people."

Sudden fury flashed through Freddie's veins. "Why do you all place such a value on this *Earp*! I do not understand you!"

Cold steel glinted in Holliday's eyes. His pale face flushed. "He was worth fifty of you!" he cried. "And a hundred of me!"

"But *why?*" Freddie demanded.

Holliday began to speak, but something caught in his throat—he shook his head, bowed again, and hastened from the room as blood erupted from his ruined lungs.

Why was I so upset? Freddie wrote in his journal. It is not as if I do not understand how the world works. Homer wrote of Achilles and Hector battling over Troy, not about philosophers dueling with epigrams. It is people like the Earps whom the storytellers love, and whom they make immortal.

It is only philosophers who love other philosophers—unless of course they hate them.

If I wish to be remembered, I must do as the Earps do. I must be brave, and unimaginative, and die in a foolish way, over nothing.

"Why do I smell a dead cat on the line?" Brocius asked. "Freddie, why do I see you at the bottom of all my troubles?"

"Be joyful, Bill," Freddie said. "You've been found innocent of murder and you have your bond money back—at least for the next hour or two." He dealt a card faceup to Ringo. "Possible straight," he observed.

John Ringo contemplated this eventuality without joy. "These words hereafter thy tormentors be," he said, and poured himself another shot of whiskey from the bottle by his elbow.

"I have been solving your problems, not adding to them," Freddie told Brocius. "I have solved your Wyatt Earp problem. And thanks to me, Doc Holliday has left town."

Brocius looked at him sharply. "What did you have to do with *that*?"

"That's between me and Holliday. Pair of queens bets."

Looking suspiciously at Freddie, Brocius pushed a gold double eagle onto the table. Freddie promptly raised by another double eagle. Ringo folded. Brocius sighed, lazy eyelids drooping.

"What's the *next* problem you're going to solve?" Brocius asked.

"Other than this hand? It's up to you. After this last killing, your Mr. Fellehy the Laundryman will never be appointed sheriff in Behan's place. They'll want a tough lawman who will work with Virgil Earp to clean up Cochise County. Are you going to call, Bill?"

"I'm thinking."

"The solution to your problem—*this* problem—is to remove Virgil Earp from all calculations."

Ringo gave a laugh. "You'll just get two more Earps in his place!" he said. "That's what happened last time."

Brocius frowned. "Entities are not multiplied beyond what is necessary."

Freddie was impressed. "Very good, Bill. I am teaching you, I see."

Brocius narrowed his eyes and looked at Freddie. "Are you going to solve this problem for me, Freddie?"

"Yes. I think you should fold."

Brocius pushed out a double eagle. "Call. I meant the *other* problem."

Freddie dealt the next round of cards. "I think I have solved enough problems for you," he said slowly. "I am becoming far too prominent a member of your company for my health. I think you should arrange the solution on your own, and I will make a point of being in another place, in front of twenty unimpeachable witnesses."

Brocius looked at the table and scratched his chin. "You just dealt yourself an ace."

"And that makes a pair. And the pair of aces bets fifty." Freddie pushed the money out to the middle of the table.

Brocius looked at his hole card, then threw it down.

"I reckon I fold," he said.

*　*　*

"Oh, they have bungled it!" Freddie stormed. "They have shot the wrong Earp!"

He paced madly in Behan's parlor, while Josie watched from her chair. "The assassin was to shoot Virgil!" Freddie said. "He mistook his man and shot Morgan instead—and he didn't even kill him!"

"Who did the shooting?" Josie said.

"I don't know. Some fool." Freddie paused in his pacing to furiously polish his spectacles. "And I will be blamed. This was supposed to occur when I was in the saloon, playing cards in front of witnesses. Instead it occurred when I was in bed with you."

She looked at him in surprise. "Ain't I a witness, Freddie?" she said in her mocking New York voice.

Freddie laughed bitterly. "They might calculate that you are prejudiced in my favor."

"They would be right." She rose, took Freddie's hands. "Perhaps you should leave Tombstone."

"And go where?" He put his arms around her. The scent of her French perfume drifted delicately through his senses.

"There are plenty of mining towns in the West," she said. "Plenty of places to play poker. And almost all have theaters, and will need someone to play the ingenue."

He looked at her. "My friends are here, Josie. And it is here that you are queen."

"*Amor fati,*" she murmured. He felt her shoulders fall slightly in acknowledgment of the defeat, and then she straightened. "I had better learn to shoot, then," she said. "Will you teach me?"

"I will. But I'm not a very good shot—my eyesight, you know."

"But you're a—" She hesitated.

"A killer? A gunman?" He smiled. "Certainly. But all my fights took place at a range of less than five meters—one was in a small room, three meters square. But still—yes—why not? It can do us no harm to be seen practicing."

"What is the best way to become a gunman?" Josie said.

"Not to care if you die," Freddie said promptly. "You must not fear death. I was deadly because I knew I was dying. John Holliday is dangerous for the same reason—he knows he must in any case die soon, so why not now? And John Ringo—he does not value his own life, clearly."

She tilted her head, looked at him carefully. "But you weren't dying at all. You may live as long as any of us. Does that make a fight more dangerous for you?"

Freddie considered this notion in some surprise. He wondered if he now truly had reasons to live, and whether the chief one was now in his arms.

"I am at least experienced in a fight," he said. "I'll keep my head, and kill or die as a man. It is important, in any case, to die at the right time."

Small comfort: he felt her tremble. *Treasure this while you may,* he thought; *and know that you have treasured it before, and will again.*

In the event it was not Freddie who died first. Three days after James Earp was appointed sheriff, Curly Bill Brocius was found dead on the road between Tombstone and Charleston. Two friends lay with him, all riddled with bullets. The only Earp not a suspect was Morgan, with a near-mortal wound in his spine, who had been carried into the county jail, where he was guarded by a half-dozen of the Earps' newly deputized supporters.

The other three Earp brothers, and a number of their friends, were not to be found in town. For several days the sound of volleys boomed off the blue Dragoon Mountains, echoed over the dry hills. Apparently they were not all fired in anger: most were signals from the Earps to their friends, who were bringing them supplies. But still three Cowboys were found dead, shot near their homes; and the Clanton spread was burned. A day later John Ringo rode into town on a lathered horse, claiming he'd been chased by a half-dozen gunmen.

"And Holliday's with them," Ringo said. "I saw the bastard, big as life."

Freddie's heart sank. "I was afraid of that."

"His hip's still bothering him, and Virgil's leg. Otherwise they would have caught me." He blew dust from his mustache and looked at Freddie. "We need a posse of our own, friend."

"So we do."

They called out their friends, but a surprising number had made themselves scarce. Freddie and Ringo assembled a dozen riders, all that remained of Brocius's mighty outlaw army, and hoped to pick up more as they rode.

Josie surprised everyone by showing up in riding clothes at the O.K. Corral, her new pistol hanging from her belt. "I will go, of course," she said.

Freddie's heart sang in praise of her bravery, but he touched his hat and said, "I believe that Helen should remain on Ilium's topless towers, where it is safe."

She looked at him, and he saw the jaw muscles tauten. "Those towers burned," she said. "And I don't want to survive another lover."

Freddie's heart flooded over. He kissed her, and knew he would kiss her thus time and again, for infinity.

"Come then!" he said. "We shall meet our fate together!"

"Let slip the dogs of war," Ringo commented wryly, and they rode out of town into a chill dawn.

They followed a pillar of smoke, a mining claim that belonged to one of the Cowboys. No one had been killed because no one was home, but the diggings had been thoroughly burned. From the mine they followed the trail north. After two days of riding they were disappointed to discover that the trail led to the Sierra Bonita, the largest ranch in the district. Ringo and his friends had been running off Sierra Bonita's cattle for years. The place was built like a fort against Apache raids, and if the Earps and their friends were inside, then they were as safe as if they were holed in Gibraltar.

"*Hic funis nihil attraxit,*" Ringo muttered. This line has taken no fish. Freddie hoped he didn't smell Brocius's dead cat on the line.

The posse retreated from the Sierra Bonita to consider their options, but these narrowed considerably when they saw a cloud of dust on the northern horizon, a cloud that grew ever closer.

"Looks like we've been outposse'd," Ringo said. "Their horses are fresh—we can't outrun them."

"What do we do?" Freddie gasped. Two days in the saddle, even riding moderately, had exhausted him—unlike Josie, who seemed to thrive once cast in the role of Bandit Queen.

Ringo seemed almost gay. "They have tied us to the stake, we cannot fly." Freddie could have wished Ringo had not chosen *Macbeth*. "I think we'd better find a place to fort up," Ringo said.

Their Dunsinane was a rocky hill barren of life but for cactus and scrub. They hid the horses behind rocks and dug themselves in. Within an hour the larger outfit had found them: the Earps had been reinforced by two dozen riders from the Sierra Bonita, and it looked like a small army that posted itself about the hill and sealed off every exit. The pursuers did not attempt to come within gunshot: they knew all they had to do was wait for the Cowboys' water to run out.

Ringo's crew had a smaller store of water than their enemies probably suspected, and one night on the hill would surely exhaust it. "We shall have to fight," Freddie said.

"Yes."

"Few of those people have any experience in a combat. Holliday and Virgil Earp are the only two I know of. The rest will get too excited and throw away their fire, and that will give us our chance."

Ringo smiled. "I think we should charge. Come down off the hill first light screaming like Apaches and pitch into the nearest pack of them. If we run them off, we can take their horses and make a dash for it."

"Agreed. I will have to follow you—otherwise I can't see well enough to know where I'm going."

"I'll lead you into the hornet's nest, don't you worry."

Freddie sought out Josie, lying in the shade of some rocks, and took her hand. The sun had burned her cheeks; her lips were starting to crack with thirst. "We will fight in the morning," he said. "I want you to stay here."

She shook her head, mouthed the word *no*.

"You are the only one of us they will not harm," Freddie said. "The rest of us will charge out of the circle, and you can join us later."

The words drove her into a fury. She was in a state of high excitement, and wanted to put her pistol practice to use.

"It is not as you think," Freddie said. "This will not be a great battle, it will be something small and squalid. And—" He took her hands. She flailed to throw off his touch, but he held her. "Josie!" he cried. "I need someone to publish my work, if I should not survive. No one else will care. It must be you."

She was of the People of the Book; Freddie calculated she could not refuse. At his words her look softened. "All right, then," she said. He kissed her, but she turned her sunburned lips away. She would not speak for a while, and so Freddie wrote for an hour in his journal with a stub of pencil.

They spent a rough night together, lying cold under blankets, shivering together while Cowboys snored around them. As the eastern sky began to lighten, all rose, and the horses were saddled and led out. The last of the water was shared, and then the riders mounted.

Ringo seemed in good cheer. Freddie half expected him to give the Crispin's Day speech from *Henry V,* but Ringo contented himself with nodding, clicking to his horse, and leading the beast between the tall rocks, down the hill toward the dying fires of the Earps' camp. Freddie pulled his bandanna over his nose, less to conceal his identity than to avoid eating Ringo's dust, then followed Ringo's horse down into the gloom.

The horsemen cleared the rocks, then broke into a canter. They covered half the distance to the Earp outfit's camp before the first shot rang out; then Ringo gave a whoop and the Cowboys answered, the high-pitched yells ringing over the dusty ground.

Freddie was too busy staying atop his horse to add to the clamor. His teeth rattled with every hoofbeat. He wanted a calm place to stand.

Other, better horsemen, half-seen in the predawn light, passed him as he rode. A flurry of shots crackled out. Freddie clutched Zarathustra tighter. Startled men on foot dodged out of his way.

Abruptly the horse stumbled—Freddie tried to check it but somehow made things worse—and then there was a staggering blow to his shoulder as he was flung to the ground. He rolled, and in great surprise at his own agility rose with his pistol still in his hand. A figure loomed up—with dust coating his spectacles Freddie could not make it out—but he shot it anyway, twice, and it groaned and fell.

The yells of the Cowboys were receding southward amid a great boil of dust. Freddie ran after. Bullets made whirring noises about his head.

Then out of the dust came a horse. Freddie half raised his pistol, but recognized Ringo before he pulled trigger. "Take my hand, Freddie," Ringo said with a great grin, "and we're free." But then one of the whizzing bullets came to a stop with a horrible smack, and Ringo toppled from the horse. Freddie stared in sudden shock at his friend's brains laid out at his feet—Ringo was beyond all noble gestures now, that was clear, there was nothing to be done for him—Freddie reached for the saddle horn. The beast was frightened and began to run before Freddie could mount; Freddie ran alongside, trying to get a foot in the stirrup, and then the horse put on a burst of terrified speed and left Freddie behind.

Rage and frustration boomed in his heart. He swiped at his spectacles to get a better view, then ran back toward the sound of shooting. A man ran across his field of vision and Zarathustra boomed. The man kept running.

Freddie neared a bush and ducked behind it, polished his spectacles quickly on his bandanna, and stuck them back on his face. The added clarity was not great. The Earps' camp was in a great turmoil in the dust and the half-light, and people were shouting and shooting and running about without any apparent purpose.

Fools! Freddie wanted to shriek. *You do not even know how to live, let alone how to die!*

He approached the nearest man at a walk, put Zarathustra to the stranger's breast, and pulled the trigger. When the man fell, Freddie took the other's gun in his left hand, then stalked on. He fired a shot at a startled stranger, who ran.

"Stop, Freddie!" came a shout. "Throw up your hands!"

It was Holliday's voice. Freddie froze in his tracks, panting for breath in the cold morning air. Holliday was somewhere to his right—a shift of stance and Freddie could fire—but Holliday would kill him before that, he knew.

Troy is burning, he thought. *You have killed as a human being. Now die as one. Freely, and at the right moment.*

"Throw up your hands!" Holliday called again, and then from the effort of the shout gave a little cough.

Wild exhilaration flooded through Freddie's veins—Holliday's cough had surely spoiled his aim. Freddie swung right as he thumbed the hammer back on each of the two revolvers. And, for the last time, Zarathustra spoke.

The Earp posse caught up with Josie a few hours later as she rode her solitary way to Tombstone. John Holliday shivered atop his horse, trembling as if the morning chill had not yet left his bones. He touched his hat to her, but she ignored him, just kept her plug walking south.

"This was Freddie's, ma'am," Holliday said in his polite Southern way, and held out a book bound between cardboard covers, Freddie's journal. "You figure in his thoughts," Holliday said. "You may wish to have it."

Coldly, without a word, she took the worn volume from his hand. Holliday kicked his horse and the posse rode on, moving swiftly past her into the bright morning.

Josie tried not to look at the bodies that tossed and dangled over the saddles.

What have I found to cherish in this detestable land? Josie read when she returned to Tombstone. Comrades, and valor, and the woman of my heart. Who came to me *because she was free*! And for whom—*because she is free*—Troy will burn, and men will spill their lives into the dust. Every free woman may kill a world.

She will not chain herself; she despises the slavery that is modern life. This is freedom indeed, the freedom to topple towers and destroy without regard. Not from petulance or fear, but from greatness of heart! She does not *seek* power, she simply wields it, as a part of her nature.

Can I be less brave than she? For a gunman, or a philosopher, to live or die or scribble on paper is nothing. For a girl to overturn the order of the world—to stand over the bodies of her lovers and desire only to arm herself—for such a girl to become Fate itself—!

This Fate will I meet with joy. It is clear enough what the morning will bring, and the thought brings no terror. Let my end bring no sadness to my darling Fate, my joy—I have died a million times ere now, and will awake a million more to the love of my—of my Josie—

* * *

The words whirled in her mind. Her head ached, and her heart. The words were not easy to understand. Josie knew there were many more notebooks stacked in Freddie's room at the hotel, volume after volume packed with dense script, most in a frantic scrawled German that seemed to have been written in a kind of frenzy, the words mashed onto and over one another in a colossal road-accident of crashing ideas.

There was no longer any reason to stay in Tombstone: her lovers were dead, and those who hated her lived. She would take Freddie's journals away, read them, try to make sense of them. Perhaps something could even be published. In any case she would not give any of the notebooks to that sister Elisabeth, who would twist Freddie's words into a weapon against the Jews.

She had been Freddie's fate, or so he claimed. Now the notebooks—Freddie's words, Freddie's thoughts—were her own destiny.

She would embrace her fate as Freddie had embraced his, and carry it like a newborn infant from this desolation, this desert. This Tombstone.

AFTERWORD TO "THE LAST RIDE OF GERMAN FREDDIE"

It is appropriate that Friedrich Nietzsche be the subject of an alternate-worlds story, as his theory of Eternal Recurrence posited an infinity of universes, though these worlds were not, strictly speaking, *alternate:* instead the theory insisted on all the universes being alike, with the same people repeating the same actions again and again. It is not within my competence to judge whether Nietzsche actually believed this, or whether he used the theory as a metaphor to make the larger point that we should do nothing that we would regret doing over and over again, unto infinity.

"The Last Ride of German Freddie" sprang fully armed from my head in a discussion on the online forum Duelling Modems, in which I suggested that it might be fun if someone wrote an alternate history story in which Nietzsche went West and tested his theories of destruction at the O.K. Corral. No sooner had I suggested this than I realized that I should be the one to attempt the story.

All the characters actually existed, from German Freddie and Josie to Fellehy the Laundryman. Aside from introducing Freddie as a witness and eliminating some characters (like Bat Masterson and Texas John Slaughter) who had no effect on the action, I have followed history very precisely up till the moment of Freddie's intervention in the O.K. Corral gunfight.

In creating this story, I found that the chief obstacle was not in overcoming history but in overcoming the cinema. Most people gain their knowledge of the Old West from the movies, and the movies are romances, not history. Gunfights are presented at the climax of films, but the O.K. Corral fight was in reality the beginning of a war, not the end. Even the name "The Gunfight at the O.K. Corral" is the title of a film: until the film's release, the battle was known more simply as "the streetfight in Tombstone."

Another conception given us by the movies is that "gunfighter" was a job description: in reality, no one was ever paid for being a gunfighter. John Holliday was a gambler; Billy the Kid a ranch hand; Wyatt Earp a lawman; John Ringo an outlaw; Bat Masterson a sports writer and entrepreneur. I have chosen to make German Freddie a gambler, on the theory that a teetotaler with a good mind could earn a good living playing poker in saloons with drunks.

The story does not solve the central mystery of Wyatt Earp: why he is remembered and revered when others, equally well known in their day, are forgotten. Bill Tilghman was a more successful lawman; Clay Allison a deadlier shot; and Dirty Dave Rudabaugh more colorful. But only Wyatt Earp rides forever in the movies. Everyone who knew Wyatt Earp seems to have agreed that he was an extraordinary man, but none of them bothered to record why.

I have no answers to the question of Earp's fame, and so I have transferred my own lack of understanding to Freddie, making it a part of Freddie's character and an element in what motivates him.

For anyone whose knowledge of the events in Tombstone is limited to the movies, I include a brief summary of the lives of the principal characters.

Friedrich Nietzsche left the University of Basel in 1879 as a result of ill health, and devoted himself to writing, producing most of the works for which he is famous, including *Thus Spake Zarathustra, The Anti-Christian, The Genealogy of Morals*, and *Ecce Homo*. He suffered a breakdown in Turin in 1889, probably as a result of an old syphilitic infection, and remained insane until his death in 1900. His unpublished works fell into the hands of his sister, the notorious anti-

Semite Elisabeth Förster-Nietzsche, who edited and altered his works and who controlled access to his manuscripts. As a result of Elisabeth's tampering, Nietzsche's works gained a reputation that made him the intellectual darling of Imperial Germany and Hitler's Third Reich.

Josephine "Sadie" Marcus left Tombstone in the aftermath of the Earp-Clanton feud and lived briefly with her family until she again encountered Wyatt Earp. Though there is no record that they ever married, Josie lived with Wyatt until his death. She died in 1944.

Virgil Earp was ambushed after the O.K. Corral fight by the Cowboy faction, as a result of which his arm was paralyzed. Despite the handicap he lived a full, adventurous life, and died in 1905.

Morgan Earp was ambushed in a Tombstone pool hall by the Cowboy faction, and died within hours. It is possible that his killers thought they were shooting Wyatt. His death prompted the Vengeance Ride by the Earp faction, in which their posse killed or drove the principal Cowboy leaders from Tombstone.

Curly Bill Brocius remained the leader of the Cowboy faction until he and his gang attempted to ambush Wyatt Earp and a group of his friends at Iron Springs, near Tombstone. Wyatt Earp killed him with a shotgun.

John Ringo may have been the last victim of the Earp-Clanton feud. "The Hamlet among Outlaws," as Walter Noble Burns called him, was found dead near Tombstone with a pistol in his hand and a bullet in his brain. The wound may have been self-inflicted— there is evidence Ringo was a depressive. Wyatt Earp, however, claimed to have killed him, though Wyatt may have been in Colorado at the time. Ringo left behind a small library of classic works, including some in Latin, giving him a posthumous reputation as a frontier intellectual. It is unlikely that he ever attended university, and he seems to have been self-educated.

Ike Clanton fled Tombstone in the aftermath of the war he had done so much to start, but did not alter his belligerent, drunken ways, and was killed by detective J. V. Brighton in 1887.

John Behan, unable or unwilling to stop the violence in Tombstone, failed to win reelection as sheriff. Thanks to his political contacts he became warden of the Yuma prison, though there were those who claimed he should have been on the other side of the bars.

John Holliday continued to roam the West, usually with his Hungarian companion "Big Nose Kate" Elder, until his death from tuberculosis in 1887. Despite his long illness and hazardous life, he outlived all the men who wanted him dead.

Wyatt Earp never acted as a lawman after his spell in Tombstone, and instead became a gambler and entrepreneur. Traveling from one Western boom town to the next, he made and lost many fortunes, and in his later years became the friend of Jack London, William S. Hart, Tom Mix, Charlie Chaplin, and the film director John Ford. He lived happily with Josie Marcus until his death in 1929, and was buried in a Jewish cemetary near San Francisco.

Walter Jon Williams is an author, traveler, kenpo fiend, and scuba maven. He lives with his wife, Kathleen Hedges, on an old Spanish land grant in the high desert of New Mexico, and is the author of nineteen novels and two collections of shorter works. After an early career as a historical novelist, he switched to science fiction. His first novel to attract serious public attention was *Hardwired* (1986), described by Roger Zelazny as "a tough, sleek juggernaut of a story, punctuated by strobe-light movements, coursing to the wail of jets and the twang of steel guitars." In 2001 he won a Nebula Award for his novelette "Daddy's World."

Walter's subject matter has an unusually wide range, and includes the glittering surfaces of *Hardwired,* the opulent tapestries of *Aristoi,* the bleak science-tinged *roman policier Days of Atonement,* and the pensive young Mary Shelley of the novella "Wall, Stone, Craft," which was nominated for a Hugo, a Nebula, *and* a World Fantasy Award.

The fantasy *Metropolitan,* which was nominated for a Nebula Award, begins a sequence continued in a Nebula- and Hugo-nominated second novel, *City on Fire.*

Walter has written numerous works of alternate history, featuring Edgar Allan Poe ("No Spot of Ground"), Mary Shelley ("Wall, Stone, Craft"), Elvis Presley ("Red Elvis"), and the Empress Dowager of China ("Foreign Devils"). He has also contributed to the alternate history science fantasy series *Wild Cards.*

Walter has found time to earn a fourth-degree black belt in kenpo. When he's not at his desk, he is to be found in various exotic parts of the world, often underwater.

Walter's web page may be found at www.walterjonwilliams.net.

The Lufthansa airliner taxied toward the terminal at Heathrow Airport. First in German and then in English, the chief steward said, "Baggage claim and customs are to your left as you leave the aircraft. You must have your baggage with you when you clear customs. All bags are subject to search. Obey all commands from customs officials. Have a pleasant stay in London."

Obey all commands. Have a pleasant stay. Susanna Weiss snorted. The steward saw no irony there. Neither did the hack who'd written his script. And neither did the hack's bosses, who'd told him what to write.

"Purpose of your visit to the United Kingdom?" a British customs man asked in accented German.

"I am here for the meeting of the Medieval English Association," Susanna replied in English. She was more fluent in his tongue than he was in hers.

Maybe she was *too* fluent, fluent enough to get taken for a fellow national despite her German passport. Whatever the reason, the customs man went through her baggage with painstaking care while other passengers headed out to the cab stand. She fumed quietly. Arguing with a petty functionary while he did his job was likely to make him more thorough, to cost more time. At last, finding nothing more incriminating than copies of *Anglo-Saxon Prose* and *One Hundred Middle English Lyrics*, the customs man stamped her passport and said, "Pass on"—still in German.

"Thank you so much," Susanna said—still in English. The sarcasm rolled off him like water off oilcoth.

She let out a sigh of relief when she saw black British taxis still waiting at the cab stand. A cabby touched the brim of his cap. "Where to, ma'am?"

"To the Silver Eagle Hotel, please," Susanna answered.

"Right y'are," he said cheerfully, and tossed her bags into what the British called the boot. He held the door open for her, closed it after her, and got behind the wheel. The cab pulled away from the curb. Susanna had a momentary qualm, as she did whenever she came to Britain. Then she remembered they *did* drive on the left here, and the cabby wasn't drunk or insane—or, if he was, she couldn't prove it by that.

London's sprawl was even more vast than Berlin's. The British capital also had a far more modern look than the centerpiece of the Germanic Empire. After the fight Churchill's backers had put up trying to hold the *Wehrmacht* out of London, not much from the old days was left standing. Susanna had seen pictures of the old Parliament building, Big Ben, and St. Paul's cathedral. Pictures were all that remained. And after the war, London had taken a generation to start rebuilding, and still hadn't finished the job. German urban planners often came here to see how their British counterparts were doing what they needed to do. Whizzing past one newish block of flats or industrial park after another, Susanna wondered why. The British had worked here with a clean slate, which no one ever would with a German city.

A graffito, gone before she could read it. Then she saw another one, painted in big blue letters on the side of a wall. LET US CHOOSE! it said. A moment later, the same message appeared again.

"What's that all about?" she asked the taxi driver.

"What's what, ma'am?"

"Let us choose."'

"Oh." He drove on for a few seconds, then asked, "You're . . . not a Brit?"

She'd fooled him into thinking she was a native speaker. This time, unlike going through customs, that pleased her enormously. What praise could be higher for someone who'd learned a foreign language? But she had to answer: "No, I just got here from Berlin."

"Oh," he said again, more portentously this time. "There's . . . well, there's some talk of 'ow to run the British Union of Fascists." He nodded to himself. "Yes, that's what it is, all right."

That might have been some of what it was, but not all. Having lived so much of her life hiding things from others, Susanna recognized when somebody wasn't saying everything he might have. She didn't push the cabby. If she had, he would have decided she worked for the *Gestapo* or some other German security outfit, and would have clammed up altogether.

Even now, almost the Biblical threescore and ten after the conquest, people on the streets here were thinner and shabbier than their German counterparts. Their gaze had a certain furtive quality to it. It wouldn't rest on any one thing for long, but flicked now here, now there. Seldom did anyone meet anyone else's eye. In Germany, people were careful about the Security Police, but most of them knew they were unlikely to draw suspicion unless they stepped out of line. Here, security agencies assumed anybody could be the enemy, and everybody knew it.

"'Ere you are, ma'am," the cabby said, pulling up in front of a glass-and-steel pile decorated, if that was the word, with an enormous eagle of polished aluminum. It wasn't quite the Germanic eagle that so often bore a swastika in its talons, but it certainly made anyone who saw it think of that eagle at first glance. " 'Ope you 'ave a pleasant stay at the Silver Eagle. Your fare's four and tuppence."

Susanna handed him a crown. He pocket the big aluminum coin stamped with the image of Henry IX on one side and the lightning bolts of the British Union of Fascists on the other. "I don't need any change," she said, "but I would like a receipt."

"Right you are. I thank you very much." He wrote one for the five shillings she'd given him, then got her bags out of the boot and set them on the sidewalk.

He was about to drive off when she pointed across the street to the even bigger and more garish hotel there. A lot of the people—almost all of them men—going in and out of that hotel were in uniforms of one sort or another. "Is that where the British Union of Fascists is holding its meeting?"

"Yes, ma'am," the taximan said. "They always gather at the Crown, they do." A crown of aluminum anodized in gold outdid even the silver eagle on Suzanne's hotel for gaudiness. Before she could find any more questions, he put the cab in gear and whizzed away.

WELCOME, MEDIEVAL ENGLISH ASSOCIATION! The banner in the lobby of the Silver Eagle greeted newcomers in English, German, and French. Not all the people queuing up in front of the registration desk were tweedy professorial types, though. Close to half were hard-faced men in those not-quite-military uniforms. *Overflow from the Crown*, Susanna realized. This might prove a very . . . interesting meeting. She remembered the convention in Düsseldorf a few years before, when the medievalists had shared the hotel with a group of mushroom fanciers. She'd had the best omelette she'd ever eaten, but several of her colleagues and even more of the mushroom lovers had come down sick at a feast she'd missed. Luckily, no one had died, but she knew two or three professors who'd sworn off mushrooms for good.

Two British fascists in front of her talked as if they were alone in the hotel lobby. One said, "Nationalism and autonomy aren't just catchphrases to trot out on the wireless whenever morale needs a bit of pumping up."

"They'd bloody well better not be," his friend agreed. "We can run our own show here, by God. We don't need someone from the Continent to tell us how to handle the job."

The first man nodded so vehemently, his cap almost flew off his head. "That's right. Sir Oswald started banging heads almost as soon as Adolf did. If the Germans let *us* choose, we'll do fine. If they don't . . ."

Susanna didn't find out what he thought would happen then, because the pair of uniformed men reached the head of the queue and advanced on the desk clerk. A moment later, another clerk waved to Susanna.

To her relief, the hotel hadn't lost her reservation. She'd feared the fascist contingent might have had enough clout to oust the medievalists, but evidently not. "You are a German national?" the clerk asked.

"Yes, that is correct," Susanna answered. To the outside world, it was. How a Jew could feel like a German national after everything the Third *Reich* had done was a different question, but one each survivor wrestled with silently and alone, not in front of a registration clerk.

"Your passport, please," the man said. He was years younger than Susanna, but had shiny white teeth of perfect evenness and alarmingly pink gums: dentures. A lot of Englishmen and -women needed false teeth. Even before it was conquered, Britain hadn't been able to raise all the food it needed, and the people often pre-

ferred things like sweets and potato crisps to more nourishing food. They paid the price in dentistry.

"Here." Susanna handed him the document. He opened the red leatherette cover with the swastika-carrying eagle embossed in gold, compared her photograph to her face, and wrote the passport number in the registration book. Then he gave the passport back to her. She put it in her purse. Things were looser here than they were in France—looser here than they were for foreigners in Germany, too, for that matter. She didn't have to surrender the passport to the clerk for the duration of her stay.

He turned the registration book toward her and held out a pen. "Your signature, please. This also acknowledges your responsibility for payment. You will be in room 1065. The bank of lifts is around the corner to your left. Here is the key." He handed it to her. "Enjoy your stay."

"Thank you," she said. As if by magic, a bellman appeared with a wheeled cart to take charge of her bags. He was a scrawny little man with—almost inevitably—bad teeth and a servile smile that put them on display. She gave him a Reichsmark when they got up to the room. The swastika-bedizened banknote brought out another smile, this one broad, genuine, and greedy. A Reichsmark wasn't much to her, but it was worth more than a pound here; ever since the war, Germany had pegged the exchange rate artificially high. The bellman did everything but tug his forelock before bowing his way out of the room.

After unpacking, Susanna took the lift back downstairs to the lobby. She shared the little car with a professor from the Sorbonne whom she knew, and with two hulking, uniformed British fascists. Professor Drumont read, wrote, and understood modern English perfectly well, but did not speak it fluently. Susanna enjoyed the chance to practice her own rusty French.

The fascists' disapproval stuck out like spines. "Bloody foreigners," one of them growled.

He was at least thirty centimeters taller than Susanna. Since she couldn't look down her nose at him, she looked up it instead. *"Was sagen Sie?"* she inquired with icy hauteur.

Hearing her speak German as opposed to French—a losers' language—took the wind from his sails, as she'd thought it might. "Ah . . . nothing," he said. "I didn't mean anything by it."

She switched languages again, this time to English: "Let me see your identity card."

He didn't ask what right she had to see it. He just handed it over. She acted as if she had the right. As far as he was concerned, that put her above doubt. She studied the card, nodded coldly, pulled a notebook and pen from her handbag, and wrote something down (actually, it was "Whan that Aprill with his shoures soote," but the fascist would never know—and surely wouldn't have been able to read her scrawl anyhow). Only then did she return the identity document. Trembling, the Englishman put it back in his wallet.

"*Vous avez cran,*" Professor Drumont remarked as both fascists dashed from the lift and hurried away.

"Guts? Me? Give me leave to doubt." Susanna shook her head. "What I have is a-—how would you say it in French?—a low tolerance for being pushed around. I think that would be it."

Drumont shrugged a very Gallic shrug. "It amounts to the same thing in the end. Now, where do we register for the meeting?"

To Susanna's annoyance, they had to walk up a flight of stairs to find registration. "If I had known that, we could have got out sooner," she grumbled. "We would not have had to spend so much time in the car with those *salauds.*"

"It could be that you were too hard on them," Professor Drumont said gently. "You are, after all, a German. You may not always understand the . . . the strains upon other folk in the Germanic Empire."

That was a brave thing for him to say, or possibly a foolish one. Somebody from one security organization or another was bound to be keeping an eye on the Medieval English Association. Susanna could have been that person, or one of those people, as easily as not. The Frenchman's words were also funny, in an agonizing way. *I don't know about the strains on other folk in the Germanic Empire, eh?* She doubted that. Oh, yes. She doubted it very much indeed.

And yet . . . Her gaze flicked over to Professor Drumont. What did he look like? A gray-haired Frenchman, nothing else. But suppose he were a Jew. How could she tell? He would no more dare reveal himself to a near-stranger than would she. Sudden tears stung her eyes. She blinked angrily, there as she waited to get her name badge. *We might be ships passing in the night. We might be, but neither of us would ever know. And not knowing is the worst thing of all.*